The Real 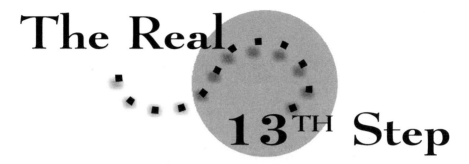 13TH Step

Revised Edition

Discovering Confidence,
Self-Reliance, and
Independence
Beyond the Twelve-Step Programs

By

TINA B. TESSINA, PH.D.

NEW PAGE BOOKS
A division of The Career Press, Inc.
Franklin Lakes, NJ

THE REAL 13TH STEP REVISED EDITION
Cover design by DesignConcept
Edited by Stacey A. Farkas
Typeset by Eileen M. Munson
Printed in the U.S.A. by Book-mart Press

To order this title, please call toll-free 1-800-CAREER-1 (NJ and Canada: 201-848-0310) to order using VISA or MasterCard, or for further information on books from Career Press.

The Career Press, Inc., 3 Tice Road, PO Box 687,
Franklin Lakes, NJ 07417

www.careerpress.com
www.newpagebooks.com

Library of Congress Cataloging-in-Publication Data

Tessina, Tina B.
   The real 13th step : discovering confidence, self reliance, and inde
pendence beyond the 12-step programs / by Tina Tessina.
     p. cm.
   Includes bibliographical references and index.
   ISBN 1-56414-548-4 (hardcover)
     1. Compulsive behavior—Treatment. 2. Twelve-step programs—
Psychological aspects. 3. Alcoholism—Psychological aspects. 4.
Autonomy (Psychology) 5. Self-reliance. I. Title: Real thirteenth step.
II. Title.

   RC533 .T47 2001
   362.29'18—dc21

                                     00-068120

To my father,

who made his share
of mistakes,
but who challenged
and encouraged
me to think for myself,
and who loved me first.

He has been gone for more
than 30 years,
but his influence remains.

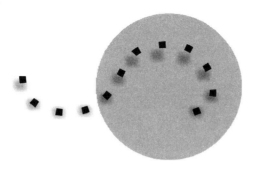

Acknowledgments

No one but a writer's spouse knows what patience and tolerance a writer must have to hang in there. My husband, Richard Sharrard, has all that and more. His unflagging love and support are a miracle in my life. He knows how to be a loveable child and a passionate adult, and when to be which. My love, thanks for so many moments, words, thoughts, and gestures in the last 19 years.

To my agent, Laurie Harper, who is a dynamo and an amazing support. I can't offer enough thanks for all you've done for my spirits, my motivation, and my career.

Joyful thanks to the cosmic support team, in (more or less) alphabetical order: Isadora Alman, Maggie and Ed Bialack, Victoria Bryan and Carrie Williams, Ron Creager, Sylvia and Glen Mc Williams, Bill and Joan Mueller, and Riley Smith who listened with interest, encouraged me with "I love you" phone calls, and even got me away from it all. You guys are my soul support, and life would be a lot less fun without you. Also to Beverly Terfloth, who has comforted me with tea and sympathy at the Vintage Tea Leaf, and Cindy Cyr and the staff at The Coffee Cup, my other writer's hangout.

To those who supported me in the first edition:

Denton Roberts, mentor and teacher, whose wisdom appears throughout the book. Richard FX O'Connor, colleague, friend, and editor, who read the original manuscript and added bits of wisdom. Jean Stine, the original editor, who carefully guided this book through its original creation. Jeremy Tarcher, and Al Saunders, the publishers who first took an interest in me and thought I could do it.

To the Career Press/New Page Books support team for this new edition:

Ron Fry, Publisher; Kirsten Beucler, Marketing Coordinator, Stacey A. Farkas, Editorial Director, and other members of the staff. Thanks for giving me the opportunity to revise and renew this book.

Contents

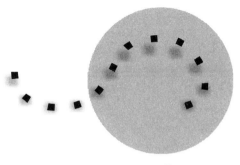

Preface

A number of things have changed in the 10 years since *The Real 13th Step* was originally published. In that time I've worked with many more clients who are recovering with the aid of twelve-step programs. In that time, sponsors have referred program members to me, and I have referred clients to the programs and to sponsors. The programs continue to be powerfully helpful to clients with addiction problems.

Research in addiction has progressed, recognizing new stages in the recovery process. Experts now say that people in second- and third-stage recovery can benefit from changing their relationship to Alcoholics Anonymous (AA) or other twelve-step programs. Clients, sponsors, and experts all agree today that psychotherapy is an important adjunct to the program, helping people in recovery with the aspects of recovery that are not covered by the Twelve Steps and Twelve Traditions.

In spite of changes in the recovery movement, my clients continue to need the information in *The Real 13th Step* as an adjunct to their recovery. Sponsors and group members now acknowledge that psychotherapy is not only helpful, but probably essential to recovery. Treatment centers report their best success rates when they use a combination of twelve-step and group psychotherapy techniques. In-patient treatment is usually brief because of insurance constraints, so most centers recommend that patients continue therapy after treatment along with their twelve-step attendance. "Drug courts," new court programs designed to reduce jail time for non-violent drug convictions and instead focus on treatment and recovery, also acknowledge the need for therapy along with twelve-step attendance.

This book contains—in exercises, information, and guidelines—the tools a person in recovery needs in order to complete the process. I have updated it to include new ideas and techniques. This is the work my clients do in therapy, and by following the program set forth in these pages, you can complete the same work. I have made it as rich and effective as possible.

Contrary to what some people have said, *The Real 13th Step* is *not* critical of AA or any other twelve-step programs. What I do here is to show how people with judgment problems can *misinterpret* their program in damaging ways, and how to correct those problems. You'll find it totally supportive of your involvement and progress in your program, and also encouraging in your discovery process beyond the twelve-step programs.

You can use this information by yourself, with your sponsor, with a peer group of others who have similar goals, or with a licensed therapist. In fact, in the years since the first edition was published, I have heard from many therapists who use this book with their clients, sponsors who use it with the members they sponsor, and treatment programs and alcohol counseling degree programs that make it part of their curriculum. If you decide to embark on this journey, it may take considerable time to effectively do all the exercises, but you'll find the process worthwhile and the results better than you dreamed.

Nothing is more gratifying for a counselor than watching a client who has struggled through the growth and recovery process then succeed in building a new life. I have laughed and cried with my clients, and supported and congratulated them as they graduated from therapy into fulfilling and satisfying lives. Clients have reported back to me, years later, that their relationships are working better than they ever imagined, and that they are happy and content as they never thought they'd be. This book is designed to help those people I cannot see in person to achieve the same results.

I wish you the best of luck, and a life after recovery that is full of satisfaction and happiness.

Tina B. Tessina,Ph.D., Long Beach, CA 2001

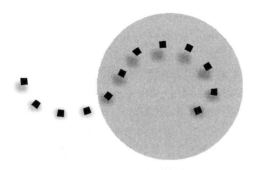

Introduction

Support groups are the answer for 15 million Americans...
500,000...will be attended...this week...Support groups work.
                                                      —*Newsweek,* July 9, 1990

In my work as a consultant, I have observed clients becoming
addicted to the twelve-step program and unable to transcend it.
—Drug Counselor Bob Holder, *New Age Magazine,* 1989

Since the founding of Alcoholics Anonymous (AA) in 1935, twelve-step-based recovery programs have proved very effective in helping victims of addictive, obsessive, and compulsive behavior put a stop to that behavior and the damage it has created in their lives. Up to now, these programs provided almost the sole support, hope, encouragement, and successful examples of people who were able to arrest their addiction and enter recovery.

In a nation that has eight million "problem drinkers," more than 200 *national* Alcoholics Anonymous-style groups, and more than 2,000 meetings each week of support groups catering to those caught up in "relationship addiction" *alone*—and where millions of others attend groups specifically formed for recovery from problems such as substance abuse, alcoholic families, eating disorders, and obsessive-compulsive behavior—there is no doubt that all these recovery programs that are based on the original Alcoholics Anonymous Twelve Steps have done a tremendous amount of good.

To my knowledge, they are the most effective programs known: Most reputable alcohol and substance abuse treatment centers use the Twelve Steps or some variant of them in their own programs; and many therapists will not work with substance abuse patients unless they attend a twelve-step-style recovery program. For the last 20 years, these programs have done exactly what they were designed to do, to help people free themselves from whatever substance or behavior holds them in addiction.

It's no wonder that a Scripps Howard News Service story in 1989 maintained: "Throughout the country, there is a rush to...Alcoholics Anonymous, Cocaine Anonymous, and Narcotics Anonymous. Nationally, AA membership has easily doubled in the last decade. The country's Cocaine Anonymous groups have seen an even more dramatic rise, from 169 to 1,042 in four years." Ask any experienced recovery counselor, and you'll hear that twelve-step programs definitely work.

But recently, another series of voices has begun to question certain aspects of the program. One of the foremost of these is psychologist Stanton Peele, author of *The Diseasing of America: Addiction Treatment out of Control,* who criticizes the 12-step process as "a religious conversion experience," and terms it "a kind of brainwashing."

"The...AA philosophy...that alcoholics...are unable to control their drinking from birth," writes Peele, means they "...are obligated to think of themselves as having a lifetime condition...alcoholics are taught to believe that they are exactly one drink away from total relapse and the need to start again at day one." Others criticize the program's insistence that "recovery is forever" as undermining self-esteem; the way groups absorb members' time to the exclusion of all outside activity; and the way many members seem to just transfer their addiction to the program without attempting any further growth or progress.

In February of 1990, *U.S. News and World Report* called this "America's addiction to addiction." One social worker I interviewed who is employed by a veteran's hospital alcohol treatment program voiced this concern recently when he said: "We need a Twelve Steps Anonymous to handle peoples' addiction to the program."

In fact, as the number of support groups and the problems they face has mounted, so has the controversy. Concern over whether they are to be viewed as effective methods for arresting addictions or simply as a means for transferring the addiction to a more benign and less disastrous form is becoming more widespread.

This growing doubt has penetrated so deeply among the public at large that it has even become the subject of comic strips. A "Feiffer" cartoon featured a woman worrying because she goes to her support groups "seven nights and three afternoons a week" for her eating, drinking, smoking, and intimacy "disorders." She couldn't "live without them," the woman says, and then concludes, somewhat crestfallen, that she may have a "support group disorder."

Recently, I have noticed that clients who had been in recovery groups and long ago stopped their addictive behavior were also beginning to voice these concerns and felt restless with the program. Among them are clients who have come to me feeling discouraged and disappointed with *themselves* because they couldn't achieve satisfying lives through the recovery programs alone, and clients who—after years spent going from one kind of a group to another (AA to Al-Anon to CoDependents Anonymous to Overeaters Anonymous) as they quit one addiction only to discover they still had others—are kept by the groups from noticing that the underlying *cause* of all these compulsions had yet to be addressed.

Friends also have expressed frustration with being "in recovery" for years, and wanting to get *beyond* it. And colleagues have expressed concern about clients who seem to be stuck *because* they can't transcend their recovery programs. Members of my weekly drop-in therapy group attend to work on issues *not* addressed in their twelve-step programs. Even as I write this, after overhearing a phone conversation about this book, a young man who works for me (and incidentally is in recovery) said, "Were you just talking about a book about something beyond the Twelve Steps? Where can I get three copies?"

Although twelve-step programs have limitations, their effectiveness can or should be discounted. When, in the second chapter, I analyze the problems of misusing the Twelve Steps, I am not attacking the steps or the program. Instead, I hope to show you how to build on the foundation of continued long-term recovery that these groups have made possible and move on to a full, autonomous life free of addiction and the fear of relapse, without feeling dependent on the program's support, whether or not you continue to attend.

My clients are justly grateful for the help they've gotten within these groups. "The twelve-step program saved my life" is a statement I hear often. As a therapist, I am also grateful for the way these groups supply an ongoing, 24-hour-a-day support structure and friendship that is both beyond the scope of, and an excellent adjunct to, private therapy.

But for many long-term recovery group members, it is no longer enough to remain "clean and sober," to learn the Steps, to be a part of the "family." Life beyond the group, beyond recovery calls to them; human beings have an innate need to grow, to accomplish, to achieve.

The recovery program has done its work; its objectives have been achieved, and often successful group members have successfully completed recovery. But there is no culminating celebration, no movement to a new level. When students study diligently and learn their lessons in school or college, they graduate and move on to a higher level. But for members of recovery groups, there is no graduation or recognition that they have completed their work—no *Thirteenth Step beyond recovery to a health and wholeness that transcends any further permanent dependency on the program* to keep them free from addiction.

The philosophy and perspective of the twelve-step programs as they are currently constructed does not acknowledge that permanent recovery of any kind is possible. Members are convinced that nothing like a Thirteenth Step can *ever* exist, and they are convinced that addiction is a life-long "illness" that can never be cured, that there is no such thing as graduation, and that all attempts to leave the group can only end in failure. This prevents them from learning the skills they need to fully enjoy their lives and relationships.

I agree that addiction is indeed a very serious problem, and is very difficult to heal. But just as people doubted the ability of anything to arrest addiction until Alcoholics Anonymous introduced the Twelve Steps and proved its effectiveness in the face of many doubts, there is increasing evidence that once addictive behavior has been stopped through the intervention of a recovery program, many people can recover further beyond the likelihood of relapse.

Because they do not believe in completing recovery, often program members and sponsors actively discourage members from leaving the group. As a result, even members who feel they've gotten all they can from the program and eventually leave feel burdened by a sense of incompleteness, self-doubt, and guilt.

Helping clients, friends, and colleagues resolve these conflicts and find meaning beyond their self-help programs led to the writing of *The Real 13th Step,* which addresses the following questions:

- How do you know you are ready to move beyond the program, and are not just in denial?

- What criteria must you meet to be ready for graduation from twelve-step programs?

- Does graduation mean you must leave the program forever? What is appropriate program participation once you've achieved independence?

- How is self-reliant living different from arrogance and selfishness?

- What is healthy autonomy? Is it lonely?

- Why are some people on a treadmill of self-help group after group, and how do you stop the cycle?

The methods, exercises, and ideas in this book build on what you have already learned in your recovery program, and are based on proven psychological theory and techniques. By following the teachings here, you can both honor the accomplishments you achieved in recovery and effectively move beyond them, to normal, functional living. You can learn how to heal old dependency, old pain, and free yourself to enjoy the challenge of life. Because they are based on time-tested theories (and because this book has been used by so many treatment programs) some of the exercises and teachings may seem familiar. But never before has such a coherent, complete outline of the basic tools been presented in a way you can use *on your own* to effectively learn autonomy and create permanent, lasting recovery from the patterns of dependency that lie embedded in your subconscious mind.

This book's primary audience is those people who, with the help of a recovery group, are recovering from severe problems of addiction and dependency. However, because of the social bias in most societies against independent thought and action, almost everyone develops some degree of dependency and has his or her growth toward autonomy impaired. Therefore, the ideas and exercises in this book will also be useful for anyone striving to achieve a greater degree of personal freedom and autonomy in his or her daily life.

You may never have had problems with obsessive-compulsive behavior, or addiction, but sometimes you might find it difficult to assert yourself in groups, to initiate conversations about painful topics, to ask salesclerks or repairpeople to correct errors, or to confront friends or relatives who need it. If so, by following the suggestions contained in this book, you'll find yourself able to deal with most of life's difficulties with greater ease and self-confidence.

This book is divided into three sections: In the first, you will learn about recovery: what it is, its benefits and problems, and why it is beneficial to move beyond it.

- In Chapter 1, we will address autonomy, what it is, and how to develop it to prepare you to take the Real Thirteenth Step.

- In Chapter 2, we will explore what recovery is, how to know if you have achieved it, why it is a replacement addiction, and how you can progress beyond recovery to full autonomy.

In the second section of the book, you will learn how to complete your recovery.

- In Chapter 3, you will learn how the roots of both addiction and autonomy develop, and begin the process of moving beyond recovery.

- In Chapter 4, you'll learn the basic tools you need to change your deep-rooted subconscious beliefs.

- In Chapter 5, you'll learn specific techniques for completing your recovery and moving on to autonomous living.

In the third section, you'll explore Developing Autonomy. Building upon your twelve-step experience and your completion of recovery, you'll move to autonomous living.

- In Chapter 6, you'll find exercises designed to help you learn what autonomous thinking is, and how to develop it.

- In Chapter 7, you'll learn why dependency destroys relationships, and what autonomous, healthy relationships look like. Here, you'll find guidelines for recognizing and maintaining autonomous friendships and intimacy, and exercises to help you create the proper balance between intimacy and independence.

- In Chapter 8, you'll explore the adventure of fully autonomous living. You'll experiment with discovering your Job on Earth, and learn how to live according to Inner Wisdom, without losing your perspective.

I invite you to turn the page and begin taking the Thirteenth Step toward autonomy, self-confidence, and self-reliance.

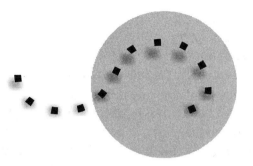

Author's Note

As a member of a twelve-step recovery program, you may have heard the term "thirteenth stepping" used disparagingly to mean having inappropriate sexual intimacy with new members. In this book the phrase "Thirteenth Step" is used to mean completing recovery and achieving appropriate intimacy with yourself.

To me, *taking the Thirteenth Step means taking the next step beyond the Twelve Steps* and graduating from the group to healthy, fully autonomous living. That's why I have chosen to call this book *The Real 13th Step,* and any time I use the phrases "Thirteenth Step" or "the Real Thirteenth Step," it is this healthy intimacy with self, not inappropriate intimacy with others, that I mean.

Although the twelve-step programs are among the best known of the self-help recovery groups, there are many others that are based on the Twelve Steps, such as Adult Children of Alcoholics (ACA), Overeaters Anonymous (OA), Gamblers Anonymous (GA),Narcotics Anonymous (NA), CoDependents Anonymous (CoDA), Debtors Anonymous (DA), and Al-Anon, or that, though they differ in the number of steps or in some details, take basically the same approach.

Many self-help groups, including those for incest survivors, codependents, or adult children of dysfunctional families, and others use a program based on the therapist's own feelings about the appropriate number of steps. But they all are very similar in their focus on a Higher Power, on fearlessly facing the self, and in making amends to those who have been injured. Because they all share the same focus on recovery through the support of the group, I have chosen to refer to them most often as *recovery groups* or *programs.* When you see these phrases, you will know I'm speaking about recovery groups in the most inclusive sense, and not exclusively AA-type twelve-step programs.

Addiction, obsession, compulsion, and dependency all share common elements, because addictive behavior is compulsive, and we become obsessed about anything on which we are dependent. Although therapists and programs consider these to be technically different behaviors, for the purposes of this book I have used the terms "addiction" and "addictive" and related words ("drunk," "dry," "sober," "abstinent") to include all compulsions, obsessions, and addictions.

Part One

Recovery: Stepping up From Addiction

Chapter 1

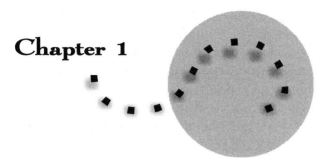

Autonomy:
The Real 13th Step

The trouble with twelve-step programs is that they just replace the addiction—then you're stuck with the program for life. I know people who've been going to three meetings a week for 10 years.

—Wayne Curtis, Psychologist

Through 28 years of doing therapy, I have seen numerous clients who benefited enormously from a recovery program and then came to me for private therapy either on the recommendation of a sponsor or a fellow member, because they still had problems in their lives and relationships. I have also seen clients who gained sobriety through other methods, including Rational Recovery, in-patient treatment programs, religious conversion, and even some clients who have made it on their own, through sheer strength of will. Even though they overcame alcohol, drugs, gambling, compulsive overeating, or overspending, they still had anxiety, depression, broken relationships, and problems with emotional control, so they came to me.

Those who followed the program felt it made them strong in recovery, and they were grateful. Knowing they were strong enough, with the help of the program, to achieve recovery led them to believe that, with effective help, they could achieve even more.

Richard O., age 45, a self-employed professional, says, "The program created a miracle for me, my freedom from addiction. Moreover, I have never seen any other recovery program work the way AA's works. It works! But it took *me* to govern my mind and control my excesses. I am entering my 10th year of being sober. I stopped attending meetings after six months, primarily because they were repetitive. I don't want, desire, nor have a yen for booze and I keep a fully-stocked bar in my home for guests." He discovered the importance of autonomy on his own.

Bob D., age 62, an aerospace engineer who began having heart problems, says, "I'm grateful to AA, I really feel the meetings saved my life. But now that I've been sober for three years, I realize that there's more I need to do, and I can't seem to find it in AA."

Mary L., age 33, a successful real estate agent and divorced mother of two, says, "I found that my whole life—my friends, my activities—were all limited to the program. For a while it felt great, being surrounded by recovering people, but then I wanted more variety. I wanted a life of my own! I'm grateful to the program, more grateful than I can say, but I never felt completely healthy until I left."

Like these people, you may feel you've benefited enormously, but sense that your ability to function on your own in the outside world is limited. Like many other clients, you may feel that the time has come for you to graduate from your dependence on the group, and to develop the additional skills you need to manage your problems and to cope successfully and fearlessly on your own. Even if you don't feel dependent on any group to maintain your sobriety and recovery, you may have many questions about what living a truly healthy life entails.

Twelve-step and recovery groups indeed offer many benefits. The support of the group, the living examples of people overcoming addiction and compulsions, the intelligence and power of the Twelve Steps, and the security of a proven plan for overcoming old thinking and destructive behaviors are all invaluable benefits of following the program. But some experts maintain that the program becomes a replacement for the addiction—in essence, addiction to recovery. What the program does not provide is a way to progress beyond the Twelve Steps.

If you have been a member of a twelve-step program, or if you have achieved recovery by other means, you may be ready to move on to the

Real Thirteenth Step. That is, you may be ready to develop an understanding of the emotional dynamics underlying your original addiction that will enable you to gain true mastery of every aspect of your life.

Moving beyond the Twelve Steps is a gradual process. It does not mean leaving your group prematurely, it does not mean abandoning your personal program, and it does not mean leaving the support of your friends in recovery. What it does mean is gaining new understanding beyond merely maintaining recovery—understanding and information not available within the limits of your twelve-step program.

How do you know if you are ready to take the Real Thirteenth Step? Ask yourself the following questions:

- Have you remained free from your addiction or compulsion for several years?

- Are you realistically confident that your life is no longer unmanageable?

- Are you happy to be in recovery, and particularly, to be clean/abstinent/sober, but still at a loss about how to run the rest of your life?

- Are you tired of being told you are an addict/alcoholic/codependent and will always be an addict/alcoholic/codependent?

- Are you feeling restless and confined in the group?

- Are you beginning to feel you may have just traded one crutch for another?

- Do you feel you are missing out on life because of the pressure to constantly attend group meetings?

- Do you realize that all your former friends were connected to your addiction, all your present friends are involved in the program, and you have trouble forming friends with others outside these groups?

- Would you like to let go of the program and try your "wings" as an independent, fully recovered human being, but are afraid you may slip back into your old, destructive behavior, because you have been told no one ever recovers?

- Do you sense you may be cured and ready for life outside the group, but you're not sure you possess the skills for coping with the world successfully by yourself?

If you can answer yes to most of these questions, you are ready to graduate from recovery, understand the reasons behind your addictions or compulsions, and take the Real Thirteenth Step to self-reliance and freedom from dependency.

Why Graduate?

Although twelve-step-style recovery programs are unsurpassed in transforming destructive addiction, compulsion, or dependency into a much healthier dependency on the program itself, your recovery remains incomplete. It still leaves you dependent upon the group. Your current doubts about the group and feelings of restlessness may be prompted by your inner awareness of this lack of completeness. Your restlessness means you are ready to complete your recovery and graduate to taking full and complete charge of your own life—to achieve autonomy.

Autonomy, which means to be self-governing or self-regulating, may seem cold and scientific, but it represents personal empowerment. Rather than being cold, autonomy is a source of emotional warmth: Only when you feel able to take care of yourself can you successfully take the necessary risks to love and be loved. The exercises and information in this book will help you build the essential foundation you need to create intimacy with yourself and others.

This book contains the information you need to take one more step than your recovery program has provided—recovery from your final dependency on the group. You will learn how to take charge of your own life, and devise your own program to keep yourself from becoming dependent, addictive, or obsessive again. The Twelve Steps are like a tourniquet that stops a hemorrhage; they have saved your life, but the wound itself still needs to be treated. Unless the injury is healed, you will always be, as the programs put it, "recovering" but never "recovered."

Your replacement addiction to a sponsor, the steps, and the meetings is vastly more functional than your original addiction, but limits your ability to live a full and emotionally complete life. Recovery can absorb your time and attention, much as your original addiction did, and prevent you from moving on.

When you first entered recovery, you probably abandoned old friends or left an addictive or compulsive mate or dysfunctional family, because their influence was harmful. Finding a ready-made group of friends at AA or other groups probably produced initial euphoria, but eventually you discover these new friends also have difficulties and problems. Like you, they have the emotional dysfunction that accompanies addiction.

As you progress in recovery, you may long for people who share your interests (such as music, sports, art, politics, or books) rather than addiction. But if you believe you must attend the group regularly to remain in recovery, you don't have the time to make friends outside the group. If your family of origin is dysfunctional, you may be at a loss about *how* to find new friends, and your recovery program probably does not provide information, encouragement, or guidance about how to make friends outside of the group.

After years of dependency and addictive behavior, becoming autonomous, confident, and self-reliant may sound like an impossible goal. Perhaps you have always been afraid you couldn't function successfully on your own. Your dependence on drinking, eating, shopping, sex, overwork, or other excesses may even have been partly caused by your fear that you were too weak or stupid to manage your own life. Ironically, your destructive behavior patterns may appear to you to be the proof you seek to support your false belief that you are incompetent.

But others who have had the same problems have learned to end their addictions—even after years of apparent failure—and so can you! Instead of remaining dependent on a substance, a behavior, or even a self-help program to maintain your recovery, you can learn to manage your own life independently. You can take the same step Carl, a 33-year-old long-haul truck driver, took—the Thirteenth Step, beyond mere recovery to health and autonomy.

Carl

Carl began drinking at age 14. It was the "in thing to do." His buddies would steal alcohol from home, or talk an older guy into buying some beer. At first, it just seemed "grown up" and exciting, but soon it helped him forget his problems at home and school. His father was a truck driver, and was away a lot. Carl missed having a father like the other kids did, but he liked it better when Dad was gone. When Carl's dad was home, with nothing to do, he drank, became angry and violent, and Carl and his mother got the brunt. Because of his inner turmoil about the abuse, and no guidance from his troubled parents, Carl was unable to cope with school. Drinking became his only relief, and a big problem. Carl had hangovers, blackouts, arrests for drunk driving, and disastrous relationships.

Carl tells how he got to AA at age 28: "I went to the first meeting because I was ordered to by the judge after a DUI. I hated it, but they said 'keep coming back,' and I had to anyway." Being arrested for a DUI got his attention, and the court's referral to AA got him moving. "I went to meetings because I had been ordered to, but I never shared [spoke]. When I first said, 'My name is Carl, and I'm an alcoholic,' I began to face my problem. The Twelve Steps changed my life. For the first time, I had some hope."

Carl spent four years in AA, working the Steps, attending daily meetings, and even speaking at hospital alcohol programs to introduce AA. "AA was all I needed—until I fell in love. Suddenly, I had no idea what to do. When that relationship broke up, I was afraid to meet other women. I had nothing in my life to talk about except AA. I discovered that meetings were not a good place to meet women. They were there because they needed to work the Steps—they were not ready for healthy relationships. I got restless. Meetings seemed repetitious, I had gotten what I needed, but I was afraid to leave, because I knew I was supposed to be in recovery forever. I didn't know what to do instead."

Carl had several relapses in his first six months in AA, and he didn't trust himself to stay sober without frequent attendance, but after a year, he wasn't learning anything new. Carl felt he needed more help than his sponsor had to offer.

Carl came into therapy because, although he was a handsome, well-built man, he needed to learn how to relate to women, and how to meet people outside AA. In therapy, Carl learned to confront his feelings, and he discovered his awkwardness and shyness around people he didn't know was a result of internal emotional pain and a poor self-image.

As Carl learned to face his own feelings, he began to heal the trauma of his childhood. His confidence and energy were increasing. His self-esteem grew as he learned autonomous thinking and self-government. He began to trust himself, to discover what was healthy for him, and to take good care of himself. Carl reclaimed his life, from the painful legacy of a dysfunctional and abusive family, from the ravages of out-of-control drinking, and finally, from dependency on AA.

Carl says, "I will always be grateful to AA. Nothing else would have gotten me sober. But I'm glad I found a way to graduate. Now, my involvement is voluntary—I can do it if I want to help someone, or to remind myself of what drinking was like, but I don't need the group any more to stay sober or keep my serenity. Life is more fun, I'm enjoying myself more, I have more friends, and I'm successfully in love."

●

Healing Is More Than Recovery

If you're one of the millions of men, women, and young people who have successfully stopped a destructive behavior—involving addictive substances, food binges, spending, gambling, abuse of others, or codependent relationships—through participation in one of the many twelve-step or twelve-step-inspired recovery groups, you have learned, grown, and with the help of your program, become able to manage the biggest problem in your life: addiction. Through the powerful examples and support of others in the program, you have achieved a status called being *in recovery*—you've stopped an addictive habit, and its devastating effects are gone from your life.

The support of the twelve-step program, and the "family" feeling that develops among members, rebuilt your self-esteem, which was devastated by addictive behavior. This self-esteem begins to develop in much the same way it develops in a small child, based on rewards and approval for "good behavior" (maintaining abstinence or sobriety and attending meetings). For many, it's the first time that their productive, healthy behavior has been rewarded.

Rebuilding self-esteem in those who have had it damaged can be a long-term process. Frequently, the damage began in early childhood, and takes considerable support and encouragement to repair. As your self-esteem grows stronger, your investment in your recovery also grows, and your chances of remaining free of your addiction increase accordingly.

Twelve-step recovery programs are a brilliant combination of factors that help people who are caught up in overwhelming addictions get into, and stay in, recovery. Many components of the programs contribute to keeping members invested in recovery—even when it's difficult.

Twelve-step programs create a strong influence that effectively helps its members combat addiction through:

- The support of the group.

- The accountability of regular meetings, (especially once you have made friends there).

- The constant availability of your sponsor.

- The continuity and encouragement provided by receiving tokens for each month of sobriety (chips), and celebrating each anniversary of your sobriety (birthdays).

- A program of corrective steps that provide an alternative to old, destructive behavior and thinking.

But most recovery programs stop there. They insist you can never move beyond recovery. The underlying emotional shortcomings (such as low self-esteem, lack of self-control, inability to establish intimacy, lack of motivation, and inhibited emotional expression) that made you addictive are not addressed. If you want to move from recovery to full healing (autonomy) you must confront and correct these deficiencies.

There are more accurate ways to measure health than simply by looking at the duration of your sobriety. Factors such as self-esteem, self-awareness, self-control, emotional balance, and how you handle change, problems, and relationships all affect your emotional health.

Beyond Recovery

Overcoming dependency and moving beyond recovery means having the self-confidence to face your problems on your own, learning to think calmly and rationally about stressful situations, and knowing you can handle difficulty without resorting to an addiction to people, substances, or behaviors—in short, achieving autonomy.

A twelve-step group focuses on helping you get into recovery, then simply accepts that you will continue to remain addicted forever. That's why you are told to "keep coming back" and that "recovery is forever." The program does not confront the emotional patterns that accompany the addiction. For example: You may have stopped drinking, but you still have difficulties forming lasting relationships; you may have overcome bingeing, but you are still unable to work out problems on the job; you may have stopped working compulsively, but you don't know how to get along with your spouse and children.

Problems Underlying Addiction

From a therapist's viewpoint, addiction is not the problem but the symptom of greater underlying problems. What are these problems? What are the causes of addiction?

Experienced recovery counselors maintain that addictive behaviors are actually ineffective attempts to heal or relieve intolerable pain. As Anne Wilson Schaef, author of *When Society Becomes an Addict,* says, when we have our addiction to hide in, "we do not have to deal with our anger, pain, depression, confusion, or even our joy or we feel them only vaguely. We stop relying on our knowledge and our sense and start relying on our confused perceptions to tell us what we know and sense. In time, this lack of internal awareness deadens our internal processes, which in turn allows us to remain addicted."

Yet, many people have faced enormous pain and suffering from child-hood on without resorting to addictive behaviors to hide in. People who are disabled, disadvantaged, or from broken homes can often success-fully cope with pain on their own in a healthy, functional manner, every day of their lives. They believe they can cope on their own.

Those who turn to addiction, in contrast, feel that they are not strong, capable, or smart enough to cope with life on their own and need outside help to survive their pain and suffering. Pain does not cause addiction—the conviction that you are *unable to cope* with pain does. When you believe you can't handle difficulty, you look for a place to hide, for a person, substance, or behavior you can depend on to help avoid the problem. Therapists call this belief *dependency* and it, not the pain, is the cause of addiction, compulsion, obsession, and codependency.

To completely overcome your addiction requires that you change the mental attitudes that perpetuate dependency and develop into an autonomous individual dependent only on yourself. These attitudes are:

- *Hopelessness.* Habitually thinking "what's the use" or "I'm not capable anyway"; often accompanied by a belief that you're undeserving.

- *Helplessness.* This is an attitude related to hopelessness, a doubt that you can set intentions and keep them, or that you can take care of yourself when necessary.

- *Dependence on others.* Believing you must get motivation, sup-port, and comfort from outside yourself, because you lack the ability to depend on yourself.

- *Fear of pain.* Not knowing how to heal your old hurts; expe-riencing constant self-criticism; and the inability to face un-resolved emotions such as fear, rage, and guilt.

- *Self-abandonment.* Being disconnected with yourself; not un-derstanding of your responsibility to yourself; and no expe-rience of the security and comfort of self-awareness and self-love.

- *Mindlessness.* Not thinking clearly and not being aware of your own thoughts because you habitually look to others for answers to problems—an inability to problem-solve or consider options, and the resulting lack of choice.

These attitudes create a feeling of powerlessness. (That is: I *cannot* help myself; I am not strong enough to cope with life, fear, pain, helplessness, choices, relationships, and so on.) Dependency is a conviction that you cannot survive without the addiction, person, substance, or behavior that you rely on. When you do try, feelings of rage, fear, and panic begin to emerge, then overwhelm you, sending you back to the "safety" of addiction, which you depend upon to numb or deaden these feelings. Facing your unresolved feelings and painful history seems more terrifying than the ravages of alcohol, abuse, or even the health risks of compulsive smoking, overeating or workaholism—because you believe you can't cope without help.

"An addiction," writes Anne Wilson Schaef in *When Society Becomes an Addict,* "is any process over which we are powerless. It takes control of us, causing us to do and think things that are inconsistent with our personal values and leading us to become progressively more compulsive and obsessive."

One of the underlying pains of addiction is the buried fear of helplessness and dependency that comes from growing up in a dysfunctional family. As Dr. Timmon Cermak, founder of the National Association of Children of Alcoholics, writes in *A Time To Heal,* "In the midst of this unhealthy environment, COAs [Children of Alcoholics] must pass through the critical stages of developing trust, autonomy, mastery, identity, and the ability to separate themselves from those around them." In a healthy family, your parents would help you progress from an infant's normal dependency through childhood exploration and adolescent separation to autonomous adulthood. However, when family dysfunction prevents you from completing this process, you remain stuck in dependency. Because you never feel strong enough or confident enough to cope with life on your own, you look to something outside yourself to help you through it. The result can be addiction to anything from work to religion.

If you had grown up in a healthy, functional family, you would have been gradually encouraged to become increasingly autonomous and more self-reliant. You would have received support when your efforts went wrong, and approval when they turned out successfully. You would have learned you could trust and depend on your own abilities to cope with the problems you encounter in life, and that you do not need to depend on others to do so for you. As a self-dependent person able to face life on your own two feet, you would be far less likely to turn to addiction to help you through painful experiences.

Addiction is a symptom of a dysfunctional childhood, but it becomes so destructive and so all-absorbing that you have to stop the addiction and begin recovery before you can begin to handle the true, underlying problem. As Schaef says, "At some point we must choose to recover—to arrest the progress of the addiction—or we will die." By getting into a program, you have made that choice.

By numbing feelings, addiction also blocks learning and growth for the period of time covered by the addiction. For this reason, the AA *Big Book* defines alcoholism as "a state of being in which the emotions have failed to grow to the stature of the intellect." So, if you are addicted (to gambling, substances, or codependent relationships) from age 15 to 32, your emotional development, attitudes, and reactions when you enter recovery will still be those of an adolescent. When you finally end your cycle of destructive behavior, your social, emotional, and many of your mental skills will not have advanced much beyond the level of development they had reached when your addiction started, as Carl's story illustrates.

Carl

Carl (who drank heavily from age 14 through age 28) had achieved five years of sobriety at age 33, but was left with the social skills and the emotional development of an abused 14-year-old. He did not know socially polite "small talk" or etiquette, the correct approach to ask a woman for a date, or how to develop a lasting relationship. After getting sober, Carl had to catch up with his contemporaries and learn social skills, information, and knowledge that he had missed. He came to me wanting to know "how to talk to women" and was completely mystified about how to make friends, ask for a date, or develop a relationship. He had missed all the skills adolescents and young adults are supposed to learn.

●

To make the difference between early recovery and completed recovery (autonomy) clear, the following chart is a comparison of the related attitudes:

Recovery	Autonomy
Self-control: Overcoming my addiction/compulsion is the most important thing—I still occasionally feel strong urges to revert to old behavior. I need a lot of support and encouragement.	*Self-control:* Addiction is no longer a big issue: A temptation may come up now and then, but I know how to control my impulses.
Gratification: I am focused on instant gratification. I feel deprived when I don't get what I want.	*Gratification:* I understand the value of long-term goals and delayed gratification, and I can motivate myself to keep my long-term goals.
The Program: I work hard at the steps of my program. I do it because it works, but I really don't understand why.	*The Program:* I understand what keeps me emotionally healthy. I've modified the steps and developed my own program to suit my individual nature.
Honesty: I struggle to tell the truth—to myself and others.	*Honesty:* Telling the truth to myself and others is easier for me because I realize my life works better when I do.

Recovery	Autonomy
Competence: I have a lot of unanswered questions: What is functional living? What is a healthy relationship? I don't think I have everything I need to make my life work.	*Competence:* I feel effective in everyday life. I have the skills I need to be successful, and when I need new skills to achieve my goals, I know can learn them.
Change: Changes are scary. I want security, and I'm afraid of disappointment.	*Change:* Change is fun, a challenge, inevitable, an opportunity for growth. Disappointment is a part of learning and growth.
Problems: Problems seem huge and difficult—they might threaten my recovery.	*Problems:* Problems may be frustrating, but they usually can be solved. I can trust myself to refrain from addiction even when things go wrong.
Feelings: I don't know what to do about my intense emotions. They frighten me.	*Feelings:* Emotions are natural, welcome, easy to handle. My feelings are important and I know what to do about them.
Self-awareness: I don't know who I am and I usually don't know what I feel and can't figure out what I want.	*Self-awareness:* I know myself well, including what I want and how I feel. I am my best friend, my own partner in life.

Clearly, recovery can only be a halfway point. It is not possible or appropriate for recovery groups to attempt to fill all of a member's needs. The specific intent of the programs is to steer you into recovery and to halt addiction. It is not the program's job to move you beyond recovery. Restructuring the psychic system that created the behavior in the first place is beyond their scope.

In early recovery, having a definite program of steps to follow was an enormous aid to your progress. It gave you the first concrete plan for dealing with your addiction, and you welcomed the structure, even though you may have struggled with it. You learned and grew a lot.

But if you expected that ending your addiction would create a life-changing revelation, you were probably disappointed. Even after you've stopped your destructive behavior, you still have the same internal problems as before. Frequent meetings and endless talks with sponsors and members help, but when you are alone, your doubt and disappointment are still there.

You need something more than what your recovery program is giving you, but you're afraid to tamper with an effective formula that you don't understand. You've been warned that if you don't follow the Steps, you can have a relapse at any time. "Keep coming back," was encouraging early in the process, but has begun to sound oppressive. You're now feeling better—but you may also be feeling stuck.

Completing Recovery

To move from early recovery—beyond addiction and dependency—to autonomy, you need to replace the dysfunctional models of the past with new skills. The skills you need to achieve autonomy are:

- Effective communication.
- Taking risks.
- Problem-solving.
- Coping with failure.
- Facing pain.
- Learning.
- Forgiveness.
- Independent behavior.

Stuck in Recovery: Does it Have to Be Forever?

Twelve-step programs insist that you identify yourself as a lifelong addict for a good reason. You are far more likely to relapse if you leave the continuing influence of the group before you have mastered autonomous skills and changed your underlying dependency. This is a truth learned from experience, and not as unreasonable or arbitrary as it might seem at first glance. All group members have witnessed many actual relapses suffered when members, even of long standing, leave the support of the group.

Another good reason to identify yourself as a lifelong addict is that people caught up in addictive behavior have a truly astounding capacity to deny problems, to block them out. Addictive people often have learned to rationalize away even very destructive behavior—such as losing jobs and loved ones because of drinking, repeatedly going back to a battering spouse, or gambling away the rent money. Here's what denial sounds like:

- I can stop anytime.
- He/she really needs me.
- I'll win it all back next week.
- It's all my (husband, wife, boss)'s fault.
- I just can't resist a good bargain.
- No one else will get the work done right.
- It's not so bad.
- Everyone messes up.

Causes of Relapse

People in denial often minimize the problem and believe they're cured as soon as the twelve-step program begins to help them gain control and they stop the damaging behavior. They then leave the program's support prematurely, *before* completing the work of the Twelve Steps. Hence, the danger of continual relapses (frequently demonstrated by public figures such as Robert Downey Jr., Charlie Sheen, and Whitney Houston) into the old, destructive behavior.

Former child star, now actress and director, Drew Barrymore, learned this fact the hard way, when she prematurely announced in media interviews that she was "cured" of her alcoholism, then had several public relapses. She told *People* magazine: "The truth is that you are never fully mended. There is no happy ending because there is no end to the struggle for a clean and sober life." She has since been successful in recovery and in her career.

The addict's "quick-fix" mentality is another factor in causing relapses for those who leave the program prematurely. If you have been addictive, compulsive, or obsessive you are probably familiar with this tendency to look for a quick or easy answer.

The twelve-step programs and most of the other recovery groups combat the relapses caused by denial and the quick-fix mentality by reminding you that quitting destructive behavior alone is not enough and telling you that you *will never get beyond recovery.* That's why the twelve-step programs urge you not to refer to yourself as "recovered," but "in recovery." In order to tell your story at meetings, you must first say, "I am a recovering alcoholic (addict, overeater, and so on)...." As an AA pamphlet states: "...alcoholism does not go away...recovery is forever..."

In recent years, sponsors, researchers, and alcoholism counselors within the program are recognizing that there are different stages of recovery. People who have been in recovery for enough time to work a program, gain experience in sobriety, and master all the steps eventually are said to attain "second- and third-stage" recovery. I agree with these stages, and maintain that growth can continue even beyond them.

Recovery only lasts forever when nothing is done to combat addiction's underlying causes—when the emotional problems and dependent attitudes that precipitated the addictive behavior still exist.

One sign of this failure to address the patterns that created the addiction is a condition Alcoholics Anonymous calls a *dry drunk.* This occurs when someone has stopped drinking, but still exhibits "absence of favorable change in ...attitudes and behavior... or the reversion to these attitudes and behavior by the alcoholic who has experienced a period of successful sobriety." A dry drunk is someone who is not recovering from the addictive process and the unhealthy attitudes that created it.

As Dr. R. J. Solberg, alcoholism expert, puts it in the AA publication *The Dry Drunk Syndrome*, "The alcoholic, when drinking, has learned to rely on a deeply inadequate, radically immature approach to solving life's problems. And this is exactly what one sees in the dry drunk." Dr. Solberg describes the "obvious traits" of a "full-blown dry drunk":

- *Grandiosity:* unrealistic expectations of your own abilities.

- *Judgmentalism:* being highly critical of others.

- *Intolerance:* not accepting others' individual mistakes or differences.

- *Impulsivity:* acting without thinking.

- *Indecisiveness:* inability to make up your mind.

- *Dishonesty:* lying, cheating, making false promises.

- *Controlling:* pressuring others into doing what you want.

- *Self-centeredness:* unable to consider others' feelings and needs.

According to Anne Wilson Schaef, the "dry drunk syndrome" means you can be in recovery and still be addicted: "Individuals who are not chemically dependent and yet function in the addictive process are on a dry drunk." Recovery literature implicitly recognizes the connection between relapse and the failure to address the causes of addictive behavior. Dr. Solberg writes that the condition is dangerous because "...every relapse is preceded by a dry drunk [that] was allowed to go untreated."

The remaining reason that sponsors and members of twelve-step programs believe that recovery is forever is that those who created and maintained the program did so as a result of their own involvement with compulsion and obsession. In short, their conviction that recovery is forever may be a symptom of the very lack of self-trust and self-confidence that led to their own difficulties in recovering from addiction. Having spent years unsuccessfully struggling, unable to manage their own addiction without the constant support of a group, they became convinced that no one could either. In fact, their very expertise in the field may be a resolution of a dilemma: How do you continue to grow and challenge yourself and still remain in recovery? The answer is: Become more and more expert about addiction.

However, the constant admonition to "keep coming back" can also mean that a member who has recovered sufficiently to venture out independently from the group will feel guilty for leaving. Members whose developing self-esteem is undermined by the resulting feelings of guilt tend to react in one of two ways: Either they abandon their fledgling impulses toward autonomy and further growth and return to an even more complete dependency on the group; or they escape back into their old addictive behavior.

Because twelve-step programs often feel like "family," they can have a powerful influence. To the degree that you allow them to undercut your autonomy, and keep you dependent, they can replicate your original, dysfunctional family.

Susan

Susan, a 32-year-old recovering from codependency, faithfully worked her program for two years, and began to feel stronger. She sought the encouragement of friends outside the program, and began to realize her dream: to open her own flower shop. Things went very well, at first, because Susan had a flair for floral design, and was personable with customers.

Then, the shop began to get very busy. Susan felt stressed. She was attending three meetings a week, and working constantly at her shop. After being exhausted and stressed for several months, she decided to drop her meetings. This gave her the extra time she needed for herself, but it had consequences: she felt guilty and afraid of relapse, and her friends from meetings began telling her that she needed her meetings and that she was making a big mistake. Soon, they stopped calling her. Susan ignored her fear and stress for a while, but without emotional support, her enthusiasm for her business began to falter. She began overeating and bingeing, she became panicky and disorganized, and she eventually gave up her store lease and moved the faltering floral business into her home. She was in despair, and ready to give up, go back to being a secretary (which she hated), and attend all her old meetings. Susan says: "I was a mess—worse than before I joined CoDA. I even talked to a doctor and tried prescription drugs, but they just made me drowsy. The anxiety was still there. I began to feel suicidal."

A concerned friend, seeing that Susan was overloaded with guilt and self-doubt, suggested therapy. In counseling, Susan got the help she needed to examine her decisions of the past year. Soon, she was able to see that her problems had merely been normal for a new business, and her relapse occurred because she let her guilt and fears override her thinking ability. We worked to resolve her fear of failure, which originally came from a family belief that she was the "pretty one" and "not too bright"; but was exaggerated by her twelve-step friends' insistence that she would fail if she left the group. She gained control of her eating again, made friends among other people in the floral business, and reevaluated what she wanted to do with floral design. This time, she designed her business to meet her needs and desires, kept it smaller to be less overwhelming, took some courses in business, and ignored what friends thought she should do. Susan is now enjoying a small, exclusive, and thriving business, and she has time for a social life, recreation, friends, and romance. She says, "Without advice or help from anyone who knew floral business skills, I got frightened and confused, and stopped doing *what I already knew how to do to keep myself healthy.* I know now that it's my responsibility—not the program's, to keep me doing what I know is right, and to learn what I need to know."

●

Feeling stuck in the Twelve Steps is like being admitted into school to learn a skill, and never told how to graduate, no matter how competent you become. In this (twelve-step) school, a student may turn around and become a teacher (a sponsor), but there are no instructions for graduating honorably and finally.

This lack of encouragement begins to undermine the self-esteem so painstakingly won through the program. Although many people have successfully withdrawn from the program, they generally feel guilty and insecure about their ability to succeed on their own for years after leaving. This guilt and insecurity, coupled with a lack of information about achieving autonomy, can be a cause for relapse, which provides an excuse to return to the safety of the group. The less adventurous never leave at all. To encourage health and growth, twelve-step programs need a provision for graduation and moving on. They need a Thirteenth Step.

Ready for the Thirteenth Step

Recovery is not a quick and easy process, but although the skepticism caused by relapses is understandable, you do not have to be in recovery forever. The experience of many people who have achieved autonomy beyond the twelve-step programs proves that it is possible for a dysfunctional or "radically immature" person to mature, to become functional, and to develop a permanent and enduring ability to remain free from dependency and addiction.

You may already feel that you are ready for graduation and to take the Thirteenth Step to personal autonomy. Or if you still believe that recovery is forever, you may be ready to take the step and not be aware of it—you may have dismissed the restless signs as denial, or further evidence of your own emotional problems. How do you tell if your feelings of restlessness and of having gotten all you can out of the group is simply denial or if it is a legitimate indication that you are ready to move on to healing and autonomy? The following quiz is designed to help you decide if you have completed the work of recovery and are ready for the Real Thirteenth Step. Answer the questions yes or no:

Quiz:
Are You Truly Ready to Complete Recovery?

1. Have you identified and admitted your obsessive, compulsive, or addictive behavior?

2. Have you maintained abstinence or sobriety for six months to one year without relapse?

3. Have you completed each of the Twelve Steps at least once, or completed the steps of another recovery program?

4. Have you been following your program faithfully for at least this time period?

5. Do you have a sponsor, buddy, therapist, or other knowledgeable person with whom you discuss your problems in recovery?

6. Do you devote some time each day to meditation, prayer, or solitary contemplation?

7. Have you become aware of the difference between your conscious personality and the Higher Power within?

8. Have you learned to recognize and handle successfully the triggers and mechanisms that set off your compulsive/addictive behavior?

9. Have you shared your story repeatedly with others, and listened to theirs?

10. Are you able to rely on others for support and ask for help when you need it?

11. Have you had a successful relationship with a sponsor, buddy, or other support person for a significant time?

12. If you are from a severely dysfunctional family, or a survivor of abuse or incest, have you had sufficient therapy, individually, and/or in group, to heal the damaging legacy of your childhood?

13. Have you severed or limited all relationships with people who supported your addictions and compulsions, unless they are also fully in recovery?

14. Can you say no when tempted or pressured?

15. Do you know the difference between instant and deferred gratification, and can you choose intelligently between them?

16. Can you *act* on thoughtful decisions instead of impulsively *reacting* to events and circumstances?

17. Do you have a clear sense of who you are and what your goals are?

●

If you can answer yes to most of these 17 questions, you are probably ready to take the Thirteenth Step.

If most of your answers were no, you need to do further work within a recovery group to overcome the worst of your dependency and addiction while you learn the additional skills you need to complete recovery.

Either way, you'll find that the exercises, guidelines, and case histories in this book will help you understand the underlying causes of your addictive behavior, and help you develop the emotional maturity and psychological tools necessary for autonomy.

Surrendering the Dream of Dependency

What is completing recovery? Of course it begins with entering recovery in the first place, but eventually moves beyond it. "My Wednesday night meeting has so many new people... I need to hear more recovery," says Ava, age 35, in describing her changing attitudes after a few years in CoDA. "It's good for me to go to that meeting and share *my* recovery, that's my Twelfth Step; but I'm also joining another meeting where I can hear less of 'I'm having this terrible problem, and it's awful,' and more of 'I'm having a problem, and here's what I'm doing about it.'" Ava's description pinpoints the essence of recovery—moving from absorption with the problem to focus on the solution. In order to move *beyond* recovery toward a healthy and independent life, you must have laid that groundwork; but there are still hurdles to overcome. "As the price of liberty is vigilance—so the price of independence is self-determination, the price of dignity is self-assertion, and the price of respect is self-respect," wrote psychiatrist Dr. Thomas Szasz.

Self-determination and self-respect are the necessary keys most dependent people need to be able to take full responsibility for and control over their own lives. Without these keys, dependent people are like Teddy, a well-educated and talented man who, when he began to be aware of his internal attitudes, said in frustration, "I'm 36, and I still live my life as though *someone else* is in charge of it." Why does Teddy feel this way? Because he believes others can take care of him and advise and protect him from harm better than he could himself. To feel wholly in charge of himself and his life, Teddy must give up the dream that there is someone else who can make it better, who can take total care of him, who can be responsible for him more effectively than he can himself.

My clients in recovery all exhibit this lack of belief in themselves—it is what I call the Dream of Dependency. This dream is seductive, because it encourages a fantasy view of life without responsibility or consequences.

Clients have this dream for three reasons:

1. When they were children, their parents led them to believe that someone *would* take care of them and make it better.

2. Dysfunctional parents failed to teach them the skills necessary to take care of themselves.

3. Consequently, they never learned to feel capable of being responsible for themselves.

Why Autonomy Is Not Learned in Childhood

Taking care of and being responsible for yourself requires skills that are usually learned in early childhood. However, in a dysfunctional family, you don't always get the healthy positive examples you need to learn these skills. Christina Crawford eloquently describes this condition in her book *Survivor*:

> Maybe I never knew who I was. Maybe I never had time to spend knowing who I was. My life as a child was spent concentrating on saving myself from a crazy person. But when, as an adult, you can't get your needs met because as a child no one was there to validate and love you and you never developed interpersonal life skills, that is how you live.

This is not unusual, or entirely the fault of your parents. If you were gradually taught and encouraged to be self-reliant from early childhood, you would learn the necessary skills and attitudes for autonomous living one step at a time. Unfortunately, many parents were not trained in autonomy either, and could not teach their children. Dr. Charles Whitfield, author of *Healing The Child Within,* notes this fact:

> Rarely does anyone find a mother, other parent figure or close friend who is even *capable* of providing or of helping us to meet all our needs...Many mothers or other parent figures are mentally and emotionally impoverished. A likely reason is that *their* needs were not met as infants, children, and/or adults."

The pressure of growing up dependent upon adults who are them-selves dependent distorts the child's development, writes Timmon Cermak, in *A Time To Heal*:

> Children of alcoholics are forced to crystallize their identi-ties under circumstances that are far from optimal. Their environment lacks a core feeling of safety. Communication is distorted by denial, leading to the deafening silence of secrets. Self-care is misinterpreted as selfishness. Roles become rigid so that the family can protect itself from change. A sense of continuity does not exist. Neither is there any significant privacy. In the midst of this unhealthy en-vironment, CoAs must pass through the critical stages of developing trust, autonomy, mastery, identity, and the abil-ity to separate themselves from those around them.

Even the popular idea of parents' responsibility for children can be counterproductive. Because parents think in terms of *controlling* their offspring rather than teaching them to make choices on their own, most children are taught dependency, not autonomy. The result of this em-phasis on dependency, writes Editor Connie Zweig in *To Be A Woman,* is far-reaching:

> Psychologically, deep within, many of us do not...develop fully balanced egos or a sense of real individuality in our society; we remain dysfunctional in some essential ways. We continue to carry Mother and Father within us, not only following in their footsteps but often actually walking in their shoes. We re-create our parents' patterns, becoming second-generation alcoholics, abusive parents, or compul-sive high achievers. Or we rebel against them, believing ourselves to have broken the patterns, but actually remain-ing unconsciously trapped within them.

Another reason autonomy can seem difficult is because most of our society actively discourages it. Media images of love and caring, a paren-tal "I know what's best for you" attitude among helping professionals, religious and political leaders, and the generally accepted idea of parents' duty create an atmosphere in which autonomy appears to be selfish and alien. Children are taught to value caring for self as self-centered and egotistic. Alice Miller, the famed psychoanalyst who writes about harmful attitudes of parenting, says parents often operate on false beliefs:

- *A high degree of self-esteem is harmful in children.* Such parents punish, denigrate, and belittle their children, producing "good little boys and girls" who learn to look outside for approval. This is the "spare the rod and spoil the child" attitude.

- *A low degree of self-esteem makes a person altruistic.* Such parents often express their belief as: "It is better to give than to receive," with the added idea that you don't deserve to receive anyway.

- *A feeling of duty produces love.* Such parents do not believe that their children will love them if allowed to choose autonomously. It is child-management by guilt: "If you love me, you'll..." or shame: "You're a bad little girl/boy if you don't...."

Such societal and parental attitudes prevent children from learning self-esteem and the pleasure of self-love. As we shall see in the next chapter, children who don't learn self-esteem grow into dependent adults. Children who don't learn self-love and self-control (rather than learning guilt and duty) become addictive adults. Those children who are taught self-esteem and autonomy, and therefore take care of themselves, are viewed with disbelief ("She can't be that good"), suspicion ("Yes, but if we only knew..."), and envy ("Some people have all the luck") by other parents.

Recovery programs are challenging the social attitudes of addictive and dependent adults by defining caring for others without regard for self as *codependency* and *enabling*. Books such as *CoDependent No More* by Melody Beattie and *When Society Becomes an Addict* by Anne Wilson Schaef have popularized a concept long-established in psychology theory: that it is unhealthy to be too dependent on another. However, although all these have indicated that dependency is unhealthy, they haven't yet learned to value *autonomy*.

Components of Autonomy

Autonomy begins when you understand that no one can take care of you better than yourself, that only you are responsible for your life, and when you start to learn effective methods for doing these things yourself. Autonomy is composed of many things:

- *Self-reliance* (this is the dictionary definition of autonomy): Making your own rules and living by them; also called self-governing.

- *Self-determination:* Deciding your own future through planning and careful action.

- *Higher purpose:* A desire to create and accomplish for a purpose beyond outer rewards, for the *satisfaction* of accomplishment.

- *Self-motivation:* The ability to generate your own enthusiasm and find your own reasons to reach your goals.

- *Self-confidence:* The security that comes from having a sense of purpose, and the confidence to accomplish your purpose.

- *Self-esteem:* Appreciation of your talents and abilities, the recognition that you are a healthy, capable, and loveable person.

- *Self-love:* Learning to care for yourself the way you care for your others.

Benefits of Autonomy

When you achieve autonomy, you gain three important benefits:

First, you acquire the emotional strength necessary to free yourself from dependency. Dependent people, when faced with a problem, wait helplessly (or demand hysterically) for someone else to solve it. To be responsible is to be able to make effective decisions and choices for yourself, to weigh alternatives, and to evaluate ethical dilemmas and solve problems. When a problem arises, instead of blaming someone else or escaping through denial or addictive behavior, the autonomous person follows five steps:

1. She faces it squarely.
2. Learns as much as possible about it.
3. Considers many options.
4. Weighs the possible outcome of each option.
5. Often seeks advice and counsel before reaching a decision.

As an autonomous person, you can ask for help, but you remain in charge of how much and what kind of help you accept. In addition, you can make clear agreements about what is expected in return.

The second benefit of autonomy is the creation of a healthy role model: you. This forms a basis upon which you choose appropriate friends and a suitable mate. When you learn to interact in a healthy way with yourself, you create a new pattern of interaction that replaces your early dysfunctional habits and improves all your relationships. For example, if you criticize yourself frequently, you're more likely to stay around others who are critical, because it feels familiar. Conversely, if you are kind to yourself, you'll be more comfortable around others who are kind.

In addition, achieving autonomy helps you recognize it in others. When you are caring and responsible toward yourself, you learn those skills from your own intimate experience, which you can then use in your friendships and intimate relationships with others. The more experienced you are at identifying healthy friendships, the more your circle of good friends grows—beginning with your relationship with yourself, expanding to a few new friends, and eventually growing into a supportive "family of choice" who reinforce your autonomy and independence.

The third benefit of autonomy is responsibility: knowing that *you* must learn whatever it takes to make your life successful, functional, and happy. Dependency is based on the belief that you need someone else to fix the problems of your life. When you learn to be self-sufficient, you gain control over your own well-being and happiness. This becomes an enormous source of self-esteem.

These benefits of autonomy—emotional strength, an internal role model, and responsibility—actually enhance relationships with others, and allow giving and receiving to be truly unconditional. Only a person who is fully capable to care for himself or herself can be able to love and give freely; deprived people give grudgingly. The following chart will help you compare what autonomy is and isn't:

Autonomy is:	Autommony is not:
Knowing yourself.	Narcissism.
Liking yourself.	Being selfish.
Being committed to taking care of yourself, no matter what.	Dependence or neediness.
Being able to enjoy your own company.	Loneliness; hiding out; rudeness; rejecting behavior.
Making your own decisions and carrying them out.	Procrastination, helplessness.
Doing what's important and good for you even when others don't like it.	Codependency, pleasing others at great cost to your well-being or self-esteem.
Enjoying others, but not making them more important than yourself.	Sacrifice and martyrdom; rescuing (helping those who haven't asked for it).
Making thoughtful decisions.	Avoidance.
Thinking clearly in a crisis.	Hysterical panic.
Being a competent adult who can play and be childlike, but always think like a grownup; loving wholeheartedly, but still thinking clearly about yourself, your lover, and your relationship.	Childishness, reacting, acting out, grimness, joylessness, self-destructive love, loving those who are unavailable.

Developing Autonomy

As children, our natural curiosity is powerful. Young children are intensely focused on learning through their five senses. Research shows that children are "turned on" by situations in which they can learn. Their bodies produce hormones such as adrenaline and endorphins—natural substances that produce a "natural high"—the body's own internal motivation and reward system for learning.

When faced with a new experience, young children are highly motivated to explore and learn, as long as they feel safe and unthreatened. Secure toddlers are irresistibly drawn to bright colors, new sounds, and new experiences—they find jingling car keys fascinating. To a child who has supportive, loving, functional parents, the world is a fun, safe place to be, and learning is exciting and exhilarating. Children who feel secure are compelled by their joy in learning to venture forth, to begin to take small risks, and begin to act independently of their parents. By taking such small risks, at first under parental supervision and support, and later as they grow increasingly independently, children gradually learn the necessary skills of independence.

Autonomy grows out of these healthy learning experiences. Through taking risks as children, we learned how to solve problems and how to deal effectively with disappointment and failure. Mastering these skills produced in us a confidence that we can rely on ourselves to experiment, to solve new problems we encounter, to comfort our disappointment, and to correct our mistakes. When we know these things, we know we are capable of autonomy, and we become more successful in life.

A frightened, insecure child, in contrast, is dependent on the adults around him. He will be too unsure to take even a small risk, and he'll look to others to solve his problems and care for his feelings. Growing up insecure leaves you unaware of your motives, feelings, wants, and attitudes toward yourself, thus leaving you out of control and unable to figure out how to satisfy yourself. It is as though you don't own your life, as though someone else must be running it.

Autonomy vs. Dependency

To illustrate the difference between how a dependent person and an autonomous person each handle the same situations, following are several scenarios for comparison:

You find yourself letting your exercise routine go because your new partner doesn't exercise. *Dependency:* You notice this, but you do nothing about it. *Autonomy:* You notice it, and go on to discuss the situation with your partner, explain how important your routine is to you, and discuss possible solutions until you find a mutually satisfactory plan.

Your raise is due, and you deserve it, but it hasn't been mentioned. *Dependency:* You're afraid to ask about it and don't. *Autonomy:* You request an appointment with your supervisor, and calmly remind her of the due date.

You call a plumber to fix a stopped-up drain, and he wants to tear out the whole wall and replace all the pipes. *Dependency:* Even though you think he's wrong and you'd like another opinion, you let him do it. *Autonomy:* You ask him for a clear explanation of why he wants to do the extra work. When you find out that boring the drain out would be a temporary solution, you ask him to do that only, giving yourself time to get another estimate on the larger job. When you have two or three estimates, you make your decision.

You feel anxious, and you go to the doctor to see if your thyroid is overactive. Your physical results come back normal, but the doctor prescribes a tranquilizer to calm you down. *Dependency:* You don't think it's good for you, but you take it because he said so. *Autonomy:* You tell her that you're unwilling to take tranquilizers or relaxants, and ask for alternatives. She recommends therapy, yoga, or meditation. You ask your friends for recommendations and join a class in relaxation techniques.

Your friend, who has had a number of accidents, asks to borrow your car. *Dependency:* You worry about it, but you give him the car keys. *Autonomy:* You say, "I'm sorry. I'd like to help, but I can't loan you my car. Can I drive you somewhere?"

Your brother, who's always in debt and never pays you back, asks for money. *Dependency:* You resent it, but you give it to him. *Autonomy:* You explain that you don't have extra money to give away, and carrying the debt he owes you is beginning to hurt your relationship. You care too much about him to let it go any further.

Your wife always wants to spend Thanksgiving at her parents' house. *Dependency:* Even though you miss holidays with your family, and they complain that they miss you, you give in to keep the peace at home. *Autonomy:* You tell her that you miss holidays with your family, and they complain that they miss you, so you want to talk about other options. Together, you discuss the problem, talk to your respective families, and decide that this year you'll go to your parents on Thanksgiving, and your wife's family the following weekend.

Your husband is much harsher with your children than you think is right. *Dependency:* You say nothing because you're afraid of him. *Autonomy:* You call a child psychologist to get an independent opinion, and when the psychologist says the behavior is abusive, you request that your husband go with you to family counseling. If he refuses, you go to counseling yourself to find out how to protect yourself and your children.

Your former roommate has too much to drink at your party. *Dependency:* You don't think she should drive home, but when she insists, you let her. *Autonomy:* You don't think she should drive home, so you call a taxi and keep her car keys. The next day, you call and make arrangements for her to get her car.

You hear that your friend spread a rumor about you. *Dependency:* You're hurt and confused, but you don't ask her about it; you just let the friendship deteriorate. *Autonomy:* You're hurt and confused, so you ask her to have lunch with you. At lunch, you tell her what you heard, ask her if it's true, and get an explanation that clears things up.

When you understand the difference between dependency and autonomy, and have acquired the skills you need, every situation of your life becomes easier to handle.

Graduating From Recovery

When you achieve a solid sense of autonomy, graduating from your recovery program feels like a natural next step. You begin to choose your friends independently of the group, keeping those friends from the program that enhance your life and making other friends outside the program. Gradually, you will want to do more activities that are not program-related. As your life becomes more fulfilling and active, you will need meetings less. You'll begin to revise and change your original program to a discipline and pattern that expresses your own uniqueness, and incorporates what you've learned about yourself. For example, your Twelfth Step may evolve into sharing your experience of autonomy with others, both in and out of recovery programs, rather than continuing to attend meetings and sponsor people.

Self-regulation and Setting Limits

Many people new to therapy and recovery ask: "Does taking the Real Thirteenth Step mean I can never safely engage in my old addictive behaviors again without relapsing?" No client of mine who has worked a program and been sober for a while has ever asked this question. Their attitude is: "I feel so great without it, why should I hurt myself?" Or, as Richard O. said earlier, "I don't want, desire, nor have a yen for booze."

Mary L. seconds this idea: "The last thing I would want to do is go back to my old, dependent relationships. I'm finally free, and I don't need my old behavior any more."

Susan, when asked if she misses her old overeating behavior, says: "The food I eat now is right for me. It's healthy, delicious, and satisfying. I don't feel deprived at all. Why would I want to mess this up?"

There are many addictive substances: cocaine, cigarettes, alcohol, fat, sugar, salt, caffeine, marijuana, some over-the-counter medications, and prescription and all street drugs. In small doses, some of these are not a serious health problem. But unless prescribed by your doctor, you don't need them, so why ingest what's not good for you? Dr. Andrew Weil, professor of addiction studies at the University of Arizona, in a lecture on our confusion about drugs, gave an excellent overview of the autonomous person's attitude toward substances with a potential for abuse:

> Drugs, sex, and food are the areas most concerned with pleasure and the areas of human experience that I see emotion most strongly affect...Think of the psychological effects...Does it make you calm and centered? Does it make you jangled? Does it make you sexually aroused? Do you

feel like going out and beating someone up? Pay attention to those kinds of things...try to be aware of how they affect you and make some conscious choices about what happens to you. Make conscious choices about how and with what you nourish yourself.

Like many other aspects of taking care of yourself, setting limits with substances can be difficult. Achieving autonomy means knowing your sensitivity and capacity, being realistic about them, and acting accordingly. When you understand how to handle the inner dynamics that underlie your struggle, you will acquire the self-confidence and self-reliance you need to cope with and overcome the temptation of a relapse without the need to go to a meeting or call a sponsor every time. Learning to set your own limits is part of completing the Real Thirteenth Step.

Denton Roberts, a minister and psychotherapist, describes autonomy in his book *Able and Equal*:

> Autonomy is the knowledge that we are the *owners* of our lives. We are not owned by parents, bosses, government, church, neighbors, spouses, children, or cars....We are not, sometimes much to our dismay, victims of people and institutions. No longer being a victim means we determine our lives and what to do with them. Our ability to respond to life is both an asset and a challenge. Without the indulgent feeling of being victimized by the world or circumstances, we take possession of life.

After completing the exercises and processes in this book, you will have enough experience in what autonomy feels like to build upon what you know, and, with practice, take full and complete responsibility for your life. You will also begin to be aware of how well the people around you have developed their own autonomy, and how to choose appropriate partners for friendship and intimate relationships. You will have a sense of your value to yourself, your worth within the society, and your power as a healthy individual. As Roberts writes, "When we possess a healthy sense of our autonomy we are no longer willing to define ourselves by what we are against; instead we define and direct ourselves by what we are for."

Personal power that comes from taking care of yourself feels so good that it becomes quite easy to develop the motivation you need to maintain it. Any lack of personal power quickly becomes obvious. It is similar to the experience of serenity you found while working your recovery program. Once you feel serenity, a sense of inner peace, you can tell when it's missing. Once you feel the joy and power of taking full responsibility for yourself, and the satisfaction of a life you have carefully chosen for yourself, your motivation to maintain the feeling will be high.

Internal Resistance

Getting to that feeling of motivation, though, requires overcoming resistance. As you take steps toward autonomy, you will encounter internal emotional resistance, which will cause you to feel embarrassed, discouraged, anxious, helpless, and often hopeless. There are three main reasons for this resistance:

1. *The fear of pain of emotion.* Because dysfunctional family experience creates emotional pain and hopelessness where self-confidence and self-esteem should be, this pain must be faced and cleared in order to move on to autonomy. Because you were overwhelmed and underequipped to deal with this pain as a child, you will tend to feel inadequate to handle it as an adult. Therefore, you will resist bringing it into your awareness.

2. *The fear you can't learn, will fail, aren't worthy.* Toxic families prevent the development of healthy risk-taking, problem-solving, and self-confidence—all of which are essential to learning. The fear that you can't learn, and the belief that learning is painful or impossible, interferes with your thinking. This fear will come up when you begin to learn the new tools and techniques necessary to attain autonomy.

3. *The belief that you can't succeed.* This type of resistance causes you to feel discouraged, hopeless, and helpless: "What's the use, it won't work anyway." It is another mechanism to avoid the expected pain of risk-taking and learning, and is based on the false belief that learning is too hard for you.

Overcoming Resistance

Internal resistance can be overcome by replacing the old, toxic experiences with new supportive and encouraging attitudes. By correcting the hopeless, helpless, and mindless attitudes you developed while growing up and learning new skills, you can attain the self-confidence you need to overcome your reluctance. There are three skills that correct and remove resistance:

1. *Awareness.* By learning to pay attention to your thinking, you can become aware of your resistance and other destructive thoughts or behaviors when they occur, so that you can begin to correct the old, frightening, false thinking with new, reassuring information.

2. *Learning.* Through exercises and information, you can create a new internal environment in which you support yourself in the three skills necessary for learning: risk-taking, problem-solving, and self-confidence. Once you develop these skills, learning will no longer be frightening, and your resistance will fade.

3. *Forgiveness.* If you never have experienced forgiveness, you never learned to forgive yourself. Not forgiving yourself creates and perpetuates your toxic shame. Learning what healthy forgiveness is, how it is different from just accepting destructive behavior, and how to create it, removes the last of your resistance to autonomous thought and living.

Together, these three skills give you the confidence you need to face the self—the internal toxic shame and pain resulting from your childhood. By doing this, you will find your true self—the innocent, enthusiastic, loving, healthy, and autonomous person you really are, when the underlying causes of your dependency and addiction are resolved.

Chapter 2

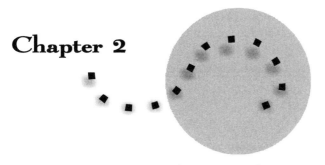

Dilemmas of Recovery

I loved drinking. The most difficult part...is admitting: "I have a problem I can't control..." In this area you have to be willing to give up, willing to be helped...you will get nowhere, until you are ready to admit defeat...and thereby win a victory you may never have thought was possible.

—Jack Lemmon

Have you joined several twelve-step programs, each designed to help you overcome a different addiction, yet still feel your life is somehow seriously out of control?

Recovery programs don't provide a context for achieving healthy, independent living. As a result, members are left with no alternative but to remain with the group if they are to avoid relapsing to their old addictions. Having spent years developing destructive habits, it is very easy for members to let their addiction to the group become equally destructive. Members who were rigid, dominating, and overcontrolling with family and loved ones before can become equally so in the name of the Twelve Steps, demanding that everyone under their influence join groups or follow the program. People who were insecure and frightened remain that way, except when they are surrounded by the warmth and support of the group, attending meetings almost every free moment, or moving from program to program in a vain attempt to solve every problem they have through the Twelve Steps.

This pattern has led many therapists and addiction counselors to believe that something is needed to help twelve-step members who cannot get beyond constant meeting attendance or cope with life on their own. Therapist Bob Holder wrote to *New Age Magazine:* "In my work as a consultant, I have observed clients becoming addicted to the twelve-step programs and unable to transcend [them]." Some experts feel that a Twelve Steps Anonymous is needed to handle peoples' addiction to the program.

Undoubtedly, you have heard something of the controversy about the Twelve Steps and the ultimate effect of recovery programs reflected in the conflict among professionals. For example, Dr. Stanton Peele, author of *The Diseasing of America,* believes that the program is emotionally destructive: "The chief innovation in AA philosophy is the idea that...alcoholism is inbred...also irreversible...alcoholics are obligated to think of themselves as having a lifetime condition...they are exactly one drink away from total relapse and the need to start again at day one." Many medical professionals agree with him.

In contrast, Gerald Goodman, director of the UCLA Self-Help Center, takes the opposite view and sees the program as an important benefit: "If you look beneath those controversial Twelve Steps into actual AA method, you'll find a remarkable set of psychological mechanisms that have changed the way the world thinks about repairing the addict."

The Twelve Steps were designed to help you overcome your addiction and achieve sobriety, serenity, and recovery. Although you can overcome substance abuse, correct some dysfunctional thinking, and establish a foundation for self-esteem by completing the Twelve Steps, you cannot learn independent thinking or techniques for choice-making, self-reliance, or healthy relating. Eliminating alcohol or other addictive substances or compulsive behaviors is essential, because it makes it possible for you to think clearly enough to learn; but the information given in the program is not sufficient to retrain and reeducate the habits of a lifetime, or to replace destructive, dysfunctional family patterns with healthy habits. Restructuring the mental patterns and healing the often abusive history that create obsessive-compulsive/addictive behavior is beyond the program's scope.

Ironically, the same Twelve Steps that help you recover from your addiction—allowing the growth that has prepared you for autonomy—can also undermine that autonomy even before it can begin to develop.

If you misinterpret what the steps are intended to teach you, you can use them to keep yourself dependent on meetings and the steps. The program keeps you involved long enough to overcome your denial and resistance to sobriety and serenity; but once you are far enough along in your recovery, that same dependency that was helpful in early recovery may be holding you back from further growth.

Let's look at how the recovery programs, so effective at putting a stop to your original addiction, can also work to foster dependency on the group—thus creating an addiction to recovery—and how you can overcome the limitations of the program and "kick the habit" of recovery.

The Power and the Peril of the Twelve Steps

The steps quoted here are adapted from the original Twelve Steps, as formulated by Alcoholics Anonymous. (Although exact wording of the steps can vary slightly from group to group, they remain the same in essence.) Except for the additions in brackets, they're quoted from *Alcoholics Anonymous*.

Step One

We admitted we were powerless over [your addiction: alcohol, gambling, drugs, food, others, and so forth]—that our lives had become unmanageable.

Why this step aids recovery: Step One was created to help confront the four forms of denial:

1. *Grandiosity:* I'm in control. I can stop drinking/smoking/ shooting up whenever I want to. I don't have a problem.

2. *Blaming self:* He doesn't mean to beat me up, I really deserved it. He'll change. He loves me.

3. *Blaming others:* I drink because she nags me. If she left me alone, I wouldn't have a problem.

4. *Despair:* Oh, what's the use, I'll never change. Nothing can be done.

Until you confront and accept the fact that your addictive behavior *is* your problem, no healing can occur, because your mechanisms of denial keep the truth out of your awareness and your addictive behavior too well-defended.

As Jim Munsen writes in his article "From Denial to Surrender," addictive behavior "is a disease of denial. If you confront a practicing alcoholic with the possibility that he is an alcoholic, the response will be 'No, I'm not!' ninety-nine times out of a hundred." Denial can still be at work even when you get to the program: "I didn't come to AA to stop drinking, I just wanted to stop getting into trouble. I knew that every time I got into trouble alcohol was involved, but I never considered alcohol to be the cause of the trouble." This is typical alcoholic thinking.

Those familiar with addictive people know that no addict will be motivated to do something about his habit until he hits bottom. In your own life, you know that something forced you to face your problem and finally get to a meeting. Whether that was loss of a relationship, a drunk-driving arrest, bankruptcy or debt problems, or just the realization that you didn't approve of your own behavior, for you, it was hitting bottom.

Step One begins there, at your first awareness of the trouble, by asking every member to admit he or she is out of control. Thus, the initial step toward hope and healing becomes acknowledging reality. Life is unmanageable.

How this step impedes autonomy: Once your denial is overcome (which takes time and experience) and you have attained the later stage of recovery, continuing to believe you are powerless over the addiction becomes counterproductive. Failure to realize your *own* growing power prevents you from achieving anything beyond arresting your addictive behavior. Taken uncritically, Step One prevents you from acknowledging the strength and power you need to overcome denial and admit your real problem.

By interpreting this step to mean that you are powerless to change your behavior and take control of your own life, you will always feel dependent upon the group to keep you from relapse, and you can never leave or grow beyond the program to autonomy, independence, and full adulthood.

Step Two

We came to believe that [only] a [Higher] Power greater than ourselves could restore us to sanity.

Why this step aids recovery: For years you struggled to control your addictive behavior and failed, until you no longer believed in your ability to control your life and restore it to sanity. Whatever it took to control this obsession, you knew it would have to be wiser and more powerful than you are. By visualizing such a power in terms of God, Inner Wisdom, the Unconscious Mind, or a Higher Power and turning the problem of your destructive behavior over to it, you gained the psychological support you needed to face the truth at last. This freed you of an intolerable stress and allowed you to turn your energies toward the remaining steps of recovery.

The Higher Power concept also helps to handle the overwhelming nature of problems created by your addiction and dependency: the ruined relationships, emotional pain, and financial chaos you may have caused. Once you have taken the first step and admitted the damage addiction has done, its actual extent becomes apparent, and this often leads to despair. Step Two acknowledges the impossibility of your handling it all at once, all by yourself. That's why "Let go and let God" and "Turn it over to God" are phrases heard often in self-help programs.

People of faith know that strong belief in a Higher Power is life-changing. Anyone who lives according to spiritual beliefs and principles will tell you of many transforming and transcendent experiences. Research has shown that people who live according to a strong faith and belief in a Higher Power (however they interpret that) are healthier and more successful than those who do not.

How this step impedes autonomy: Relying solely on an outside force to help you stop your addiction and restore you to sanity reinforces the kind of dependent behavior that made you and kept you addicted in the first place. Ultimately, it can only cause you to transfer your addictive tendencies to this Higher Power. As long as you go through life believing you are not powerful enough on your own to control your addictive behavior, you will never feel confident enough to stand freely on your own two feet. This belief also can become a convenient excuse for relapse: "God didn't help me, so I couldn't help drinking again." While faith in a

Higher Power is important, it is more valuable to see your faith as a partnership rather than a dependency. Think in terms of "the Lord helps those who help themselves."

Step Three

We made a decision to turn our will and our lives over to the care of [Higher Power], as we understood [it].

Why this step aids recovery: The first and second steps ask you to acknowledge that you are powerless over your own addictive behavior, which you may have been denying for years, and that only a new perspective (Higher Power) could help you change. As difficult as this may be, now you are asked to go a step further in a more profound acknowledgment, and admit that you are not only unable to control your addiction, but that there are other things beyond your control as well.

Like most addictive people (in reaction to the chaotic, dysfunctional, and unreliable circumstances in which dependency usually develops) you probably have been obsessed with control. You may have tried to make others act in ways you were sure would prevent trouble or pain for you, blaming them for your troubles in order to deny responsibility or avoid feelings you were unable to face. Or a dysfunctional family system may have led you to believe that you can or should control the world around you.

Your denial may have been strong, but when you face reality, you realize the number of things that are beyond your control are as endless as the world is wide—the weather, accidents, other people's actions and reactions, your own feelings, and so on.

If control was important, the pain and disappointment created by your inability to control everything in your life was probably one reason you began to engage in addictive behavior—to blot out the pain of disappointment and failure. So, accepting your inability to control everything can help remove a powerful motivation to continue the addictive cycle.

Step Three also allows you to relax and discover that acting in harmony with life, and making the best of what comes along, works better than trying to force life (and others) to be responsive to your desires.

Carla

Carla, 55, a petite, shy, quiet lady who was battered and then deserted, says: "I was hysterical when my lover left me. My therapist suggested CoDa, but I was reluctant, until my friend Mary went, and it really helped her. So, I decided to try. Finding out that I was powerless over others was a relief. I had spent years trying to do or say the magic words that would control my lover. I prayed to God, but God didn't stop him either." Carla worked her program, and learned a lot about herself in the process. After a few months, she had a disastrous return to her former lover, where she was lied to and mistreated once again. "I see now how easily I would fall for a line. I learned a good lesson: I participate in the unhealthy relationship by being gullible and wishing, instead of paying attention." Carla then got back into meetings and worked her program, and simultaneously came into therapy. She says: "I learned how to recognize people as they are, rather than trying to make them the people I want them to be. Now, I find people I can enjoy without needing to change them." Carla is now living happily on her own, healing her relationships with her children, and developing a new, loving partnership.

●

How this step impedes autonomy: Turning problems over to a Higher Power is, at best, a temporary expedient to assist you through a period when you have not yet developed the confidence and ability to face and solve them yourself. However, to continue to leave your sanity *completely* in the hands of a Higher Power can reinforce your old habit of depending on something outside yourself to help you cope with your life.

It is more effective (and better for your self-esteem) to consider that you have a partnership with your Higher Power. You can then cooperate with your Higher Power in an autonomous way, making decisions according to your spiritual or ethical precepts and values, but accepting responsibility for the results. Once you have cleared away the worst of the damage and made your life more manageable, continuing to leave your sanity solely in the care of your Higher Power is an abdication of your responsibility to think for yourself, and therefore it becomes denial.

Gene

After three years in AA, Gene, a 35-year-old Catholic who was educated in religious schools, had an emotional crisis when some issues in his life were not solved by "turning them over to his Higher Power." He came into therapy because he kept asking God to create a healthy, committed relationship for him, and his relationships kept turning sour and falling apart. These bitter defeats, combined with his childhood history of begging God in vain for deliverance from a brutal father, brought up overwhelming rage against God and life. He began drinking again, and his drinking frightened him enough that he overcame his reluctance to therapy. Gene says, "The Second and Third Steps confused me. I never realized how angry and helpless I felt about God. I needed help to evaluate my own behavior, and see how I was creating my own mess. As long as I left it in God's hands, I wouldn't change. Now I have a new faith, a partnership in which I take care of my responsibilities, and trust God to take care of the rest."

●

In order to achieve successful, independent, and autonomous living, you must learn how to evaluate your behavior, and how to place Inner Wisdom or Higher Power—in proper perspective.

Step Four

We made a searching and fearless moral inventory of ourselves.

Why this step aids recovery: This is probably the most difficult of the early steps, because it asks you to confront all the defects in your own character. But in order to bring the addictive cycle to a stop, it is necessary to be able to look at your own life from an objective viewpoint. Like most people in recovery, you probably had a tremendous amount of fear about facing yourself, your own negative feelings and thoughts, and unmet responsibilities, so you probably have been blocking them out for most of your life. Only through facing the extent of the damage your addiction has done, do you find the motivation to abstain.

The Fourth Step helps you take an eye-opening look at how you are *creating or perpetuating* your own pain. It begins the process of rational self-evaluation that must be at the foundation of taking responsibility and control over your own life.

If you grew up in a dysfunctional or abusive family, taking a dispassionate, detached inventory is a brand-new skill. In the past, the only options you learned for evaluating your mistakes were either to deny your defects, or to mercilessly castigate yourself for having them. In a functional family, you would have received years of training in this mental skill, as your parents helped you learn to evaluate your actions and their consequences with questions like the following: "Do you like it when someone hits you? How do you think Johnny would feel if you hit him? Do you like having Johnny for a friend? Do you think he would want you for a friend if you hit him? Is there a better way to settle your argument?" Children from healthy families are taught repeatedly, through example, experience, and explanation, to evaluate their own behavior. The Fourth Step is a beginning to learning these skills.

How this step impedes autonomy: While this step was created to help break the cycle of addiction and denial, in actual use, members and sponsors often focus exclusively on faults. If you come from a dysfunctional family, you may already carry a tendency to overemphasize your faults. When facing yourself, you may tend to forget that objective review includes *both* what you do well *and* what you do wrong. To move beyond merely arresting destructive behavior to the ability to evaluate yourself objectively and honestly, you must learn to include the *positive* in any self-review.

Step Five

We admitted to [a Higher Power] to ourselves, and to another human being the exact nature of our wrongs.

Why this step aids recovery: If, like most dependent people, you have been placing the responsibility for your destructive behavior outside yourself most of your life, this may be your first experience with accepting responsibility for your own actions. You may never have believed you could do this before, and doing it can make you feel stronger and less dependent.

You may also have carried an overwhelming burden of guilt (a result of what you did "under the influence"). Because most models of a Higher Power include the compassion to forgive the sincerely repentant, Step Five may also have been your first experience with the hope of forgiveness. *Twelve Steps and Twelve Traditions* says, "It was only when we resolutely tackled Step Five that we inwardly *knew* we'd be able to receive forgiveness and give it, too." Being able to accept forgiveness from a Higher Power is directly related to forgiving yourself. You may never before in your life have been ready to give up your addiction, which is one reason why earlier attempts to quit may have been unsuccessful. This change of attitude alone constitutes one of the main cores of recovery. Addictive behavior is often a result of the pain of being unable to forgive yourself. Taking this responsibility off your shoulders removes one more motivation to continue your addiction.

Through the time-honored catharsis of confession, you are freed from your guilt and granted permission to change. "This practice of admitting one's defects to another person is, of course, very ancient," according to *Twelve Steps and Twelve Traditions*. "It has been validated in every century...Psychiatrists and psychologists point out the need...for discussion...with an understanding and trustworthy person."

How this step impedes autonomy: There is another opportunity here, as in Step Four, to overemphasize the negative. Joseph Campbell wrote in *The Power of Myth*: "Ramakrishna once said that if all you think of are your sins, then you are a sinner. And when I read that, I thought of...going to confession...meditating on all the little sins...Now I think one should go and say 'Bless me, Father, for I have been great, these are the good things I have done this week.'"

Concentrating too much on the negative induces despair; too much emphasis on the positive can become denial. Independent, healthy self-evaluation requires keeping a balance.

Step Six

We were entirely ready to have [a Higher Power] remove all these defects of character.

Why this step aids recovery: At the beginning, it was a big step for you just to acknowledge that you couldn't handle your problems and to turn them over to a Higher Power. Now, having faced the extent of those faults, taken inventory, and admitted them to another, you are finally fully aware of the damage they have done and actively want to have them removed.

This is true forgiveness, which allows a fresh start. This is different from denial, which says, "Oh well, it can't be helped, just forget it."

How this step impedes autonomy: Being willing to stop your addiction and being willing to have someone else do it are two different things. Being willing to live without an addiction is one thing and being willing to take responsibility for your own life is another. As long as you rely on a power other than yourself to help overcome your flaws, you will remain dependent on God or the group. Remaining dependent on God or the group leads you away from learning to depend on yourself to do it instead. Accepting a Higher Power as a partner in your quest to change your attitudes and behavior is a much more effective option.

Step Seven

We humbly asked [a Higher Power] to remove our shortcomings.

Why this step aids recovery: After realizing you have shortcomings and deciding to change them, you are now ready to do what you have probably been fighting all along: Humble yourself enough to ask for help in ending your addictions. What you once denied was a problem, you now acknowledge that you need to change. You have changed from being passive and defensive to taking the first active step to help yourself overcome addiction.

How this step impedes autonomy: You may not realize how much strength you have developed by taking this step, and continue to believe it has all been the work of a Higher Power. You may think that you do not have the power to quit on your own. As long as only God or the group can remove your addiction, you will believe you need God and the group to keep you free from your addiction. Again, it's a partnership with God that will work best.

Step Eight

We made a list of all persons we had harmed, and became willing to make amends to them all.

Why this step aids recovery: If you habitually see yourself a helpless victim, you focus only on the pain you have suffered. You may have failed to realize the pain you inflicted on others. This step helps you reevaluate relationship problems in terms of your own contribution to them.

Step Eight also introduces the concept of *amends*, meaning the possibility that old hurts you have inflicted can be healed. The idea that mistakes can be corrected, that you can *do something* about old problems, and that your relationships can be repaired, is essential to achieving recovery. If you can never make amends for your mistakes, then you are required to be perfect. Because it is normal to make mistakes in life, an attempt at perfection makes successfully running your own life impossible. This step removes another motivation to continue addictive behavior because it reinforces the truth that no one is perfect, leaving you no reason to need to escape from failure at perfection.

How this step impedes autonomy: As in Step Five, the danger here is that the emphasis is entirely on the harm *you've* committed. Because many twelve-step members have been victims of neglect and abuse as children, it is important to be able to acknowledge any harm that has been done *to you.* In order to have control of your own life, you need to be able to ask for amends when they are due you. You also need to address the harm done to you. Otherwise, as Dr. Timothy Cermak writes in *A Time to Heal,* "The irony is that when ACAs fail to validate their own feelings as adults, they are guilty of *precisely* the same neglect toward themselves they received from their parents."

Step Nine

We made direct amends to such people whenever possible, except when to do so would injure them or others.

Why this step aids recovery: The Eighth and Ninth steps separate contemplation from action, and remind you to think before acting. The Ninth Step forces you to stop running away from responsibility for your actions and provides practice at rebuilding your damaged relationships—which often results in an experience of healing and redemption.

Making amends (and deciding when it's appropriate) gives you a chance to apologize to others for the pain your past actions caused them, and to begin the healing process.

How this step impedes autonomy: By placing all the emphasis on you in the amends-making process, this step reinforces your old pattern of feeling that you have to control situations. Being autonomous means learning to acknowledge the autonomy of others, too. Only others know how much they feel you've harmed them and how you can best make amends to them.

When Carla, whom we met in Chapter 1, tried to make amends to her grown children, their reaction was hostile and unreceptive. Carla says, "AA didn't teach me how to listen to what *others* felt. I learned from my children that I couldn't heal the relationship by telling them *my* version of my mistakes. I had to learn to hear their stories, too." Healing relationships requires emotional awareness and competence. You can begin to respect the autonomy of others by asking them if they felt harmed or offended, and finding out what *they* think would make amends.

Step Ten

We continued to take personal inventory and when we were wrong promptly admitted it.

Why this step aids recovery: This step helps you incorporate the personal inventory of the Fourth Step as an ongoing part of your life. The Tenth Step can help create a daily habit of paying attention to your own behavior, attitudes, and actions in a non-judgmental, solution-oriented way. If, like most people whose lives were ravaged by addiction, you have deliberately stayed out of touch with yourself for years, learning to take frequent inventory can help prevent your problems (particularly, relapsing back into your old, addictive behaviors) from getting out of hand. This is excellent groundwork for building a healthy relationship with yourself. One AA pamphlet advises that, for those who have worked this step, "self-searching becomes a regular habit...Admit, accept and patiently correct defects...When the past is settled with, present challenges can be met."

How this step impedes autonomy: Because the twelve-step programs focus on destructive behaviors that must be arrested, this inventory can become another list of problems and defects. To move from recovery to health also requires an equal emphasis on admitting what you do right. Otherwise, if you don't learn to encourage and acknowledge your positive qualities, you remain dependent on others to validate which traits are worthy of praise. Because only you can truly judge what is best for you, this dependency can keep you from following your own best course, unable to live according to your own ethical standards.

Step Eleven

We sought through prayer and meditation to improve our conscious contact with [a Higher Power] as we understood [it], praying only for knowledge of [its] will for us and the power to carry that out.

Why this step aids recovery: Daily focus on the wisdom available from a Higher Power helps you gain much-needed support in remaining free of addictive behavior. Research has also shown that meditation is calming and is an aid to thinking clearly. Meditation can provide a process for examining your ideas more objectively, an opportunity to consider higher motives before acting, and a time of deep relaxation and/or healing, all of which can reduce the stress levels previously hidden by your addiction.

How this step impedes autonomy: As in other steps, the focus on the will of your Higher Power can play into your tendency to depend on the will of something or someone else to help you through life, and not on your own. Alternatively, this something else can lead you to expect meditation to solve your problems without action. If you think about meditation in this way, you never develop a will strong enough to make decisions and achieve goals.

Step Twelve

Having had a spiritual awakening as the result of these steps, we tried to carry this message to alcoholics and to practice these principles in all our affairs.

Why this step aids recovery: The Twelfth Step helps challenge the chronic feelings of being powerless that led to your becoming addictive. It gives you a new sense of your own worth by affirming that whatever problems remain for you, you are powerful enough now to help someone else. It changes your point of view from "Who will help me?" to "How can I help you?"

With this, a member becomes a *sponsor*, begins to reach out to help others who have suffered the same problems, and learns the personal satisfaction that comes from helping another halt his or her own destructive cycle of addictive behavior. Sponsoring and spreading the word provides a powerful peer support system to help ensure people won't relapse, by encouraging group interaction and keeping members involved even after they have worked all the Twelve Steps. All teachers know that learning to effectively teach something requires understanding the subject on a new level. The challenge of sponsoring people new to recovery is a way to gain a deeper, more powerful understanding of your own recovery process.

How this step impedes autonomy: Having members who have been in recovery continue their involvement in the program as sponsors can work against the development of autonomy in several ways. First, interaction with persons you sponsor can replicate old, toxic family patterns, and become emotionally painful and damaging to both you and your charge. Second, the member whom you sponsor is dysfunctional by definition and may have severe emotional problems beyond your knowledge and scope. This can be damaging to your self-esteem, and impede the member's emotional progress.

Next, the sponsoring process can put the sponsor in a powerful position, emotionally, similar to that of a parent or therapist. For addictive people who are often controlling, it can become a way to avoid healthy peer relationships. Finally, sponsoring and maintaining ongoing involvement in the program can be a way of avoiding the challenges of life on the "outside". You do not learn independence, time-structuring, or how to create your own sense of purpose, because all these life skills are provided by the program. In addition, everyone is not emotionally suited to be a sponsor—and if sponsoring is not comfortable or desirable for you, you may feel that you've let the program down. The concept of "giving back" is too limited if it focuses solely on staying in the program.

The learning processes of all twelve steps lead you toward independence; but they stop short of the goal. To achieve autonomy, a Thirteenth Step is needed, one that would emphasize your responsibility for yourself, emotional self-awareness, independent thinking, and functional life skills.

Addiction to The Program

Addiction to the twelve steps is fostered by the fact that the programs as presently constituted do not address these critical issues:

- Lack of healthy replacement habits.
- Lack of information about functional living.
- Lack of models for healthy relationships.
- Replication of dysfunctional family patterns.
- Dependency on the group.

Indeed, because they are given no assistance in living successfully outside the group, people who leave, such as Jack, often do fail and begin to drink or exhibit other compulsive behaviors again.

Jack

Jack, a married 45-year-old executive, entered a treatment program when his long-term daily drinking began to interfere with his career. The six-week hospital stay ended with an introduction to AA and a strong recommendation to attend meetings. Jack attended for a few months, until he became sure he wouldn't drink anymore, then he dropped out—without completing the Steps. The first time he experienced a lot of stress, from marital trouble and job pressure, he had "just one beer" at lunch, and within two weeks, his problem was worse than it had been before he entered the hospital. Jack learned the hard way that he needed to complete his recovery before being on his own. He went back to AA, got a sponsor, and completed the Twelve Steps. In therapy, he learned how to negotiate and communicate with his wife, his business associates, and himself. Once he had learned to be truly autonomous and to manage his life, he could reduce his dependence on meetings and still stay sober.

●

Even if *you* don't try it alone, the examples of others who did and failed are numerous. Perhaps your sponsor remembers how he fell off the wagon several times; or your new friend Paula remembers how she went back to her destructive relationship once and got beaten up again. The *Big Book (Alcoholics Anonymous)* is filled with such stories. People who leave too early get pushed back into the old patterns by the strength of their original habits, the fear that they cannot remain in recovery without the group, the isolation from friends and supportive people, and the guilt they feel for leaving the program. AA interprets these relapses to mean that leaving the group is impossible, and coming back is the only way to maintain sobriety and health. In the Real Thirteenth Step, however, achieving autonomy means learning to maintain your emotional health and support yourself effectively in living a satisfactory life.

Lack of Healthy Replacement Habits

The many self-help groups help you stop a destructive habit. They function in a spectacularly successful manner to make your life less chaotic. What they don't do is take you all the way to healthy! As the old saying goes: The absence of a negative does not create a positive.

Although your life became more manageable, you are not moving forward. You no longer drink, or work, or spend, or love too much, but you do not know how to fill the time that once was consumed by your addiction. In fact, when you do find yourself with time on your hands, you probably feel the old habit reasserting itself, and are tempted to occupy yourself the way you used to—by engaging in your former addiction again. In his book *Heresies,* Dr. Thomas Szasz explains why: "Habits in personal conduct are like energy in physics; so long as we remain alive, we cannot get rid of habits by annihilating them, by making them disappear; we can only change or transform one habit into another."

To avoid relapsing into your old addiction, you probably decide to fill the time instead amid the safety and support of the group. This is certainly preferable to returning your addiction, but is it hardly normal, healthy living as other people you know experience it.

In order for your life to be actively better, you need to do more than merely stop a bad habit. You need to develop good habits to replace it. The only real difference between people who become dependent and those who become self-dependent or independent, is that the independent people were fortunate enough to have good role models and learned healthier ways of coping with problems, stress, and feelings than the addictive people did.

As children, autonomous people learned the healthy habits of honesty with self and others, effective thinking and problem-solving, and self-reliance and self-trust. You *learned* the dependent ways of thinking and acting that led to your addiction—you weren't born with them. So it is possible both to unlearn them and to learn new, more effective ways of thinking and acting. Hopping from program to program, as new addictions arise to replace the old ones is another sign that twelve-step programs members desperately need to learn new replacement habits.

Recovering alcoholics will join Overeaters Anonymous, Al-Anon, CoDependents Anonymous, Narcotics Anonymous, Adult Children of Alcoholics, or Debtors Anonymous, perpetually repeating the Twelve Steps for each new replacement habit as it arises. It is very common in kicking a habit to replace it with another habit in this way. Compulsive people often move from addiction to addiction. Do you remember being surprised, as a newcomer, to walk into an AA meeting and see a heavy pall of smoke, lots of coffee being drunk, and sweets and junk food in abundance?

John Bradshaw writes of his own experience in *Bradshaw on the Family*: "When I put the cork in the bottle, I still had to deal with what Vernon Johnson calls the *ism* of alcoholism. I was still a compulsive personality. Consequently, I soon developed other addictions. I smoked, drank 12 cups of coffee a day. I became addicted to the adrenaline rush of working and making money. I struggled with sugar binges and dieting."

Why isn't successful attendance at AA enough to stop this cycle? Because it doesn't teach autonomy and self-management. The strength of the Twelve Steps is that they help stop destructive habits, but the ongoing addiction to the program demonstrates that complete healing has not yet occurred. As Anne Wilson Schaef explains: "The primary addictions...are the addictions to powerlessness and nonliving...all secondary addictions lead to these two primary addictions." As we shall see, powerlessness and nonliving are the opposites of autonomy.

A few groups do attempt to address these issues, mainly by recommending literature and encouraging members to get therapy in addition to the program. Like others in these programs, perhaps you are becoming aware that handling the root causes of addiction requires more than just achieving sobriety and serenity. Taking the Real Thirteenth Step will help you confront those underlying causes, and free yourself from the underlying mental patterns behind addiction and dependency.

Lack of Information about Functional Living

Unfortunately, because the programs are so tightly (and necessarily) focused on overcoming your self-destructive behavior, most of the information they provide is about maintaining your sobriety and serenity "one day at a time." Even when some of the newer programs, such as ACA and CoDA do recommend reading about handling the pain of your past, most of the information is still focused on the emotional *problem* and how to overcome it. Yet without such vital living skills, you will never feel confident to face life outside the group on your own.

If you grew up in a dysfunctional family and spent many years ravaged by addictive behavior, you have probably had little opportunity to learn competent everyday living skills as these:

- How to think clearly and rationally, evaluate people and situations, and make choices.

- How to create a sense of purpose in your life free of addiction.

- How to handle change and the normal upsets of life.

- How to create your own ethics and guidelines for living.
- How to learn to trust yourself and make commitments you can keep.

Just managing your budget, deciding where and how to live, or finding a better job may feel like more than you can handle. No wonder many people fail to make it on their own outside of group, when the lack of these skills can keep you trapped in the recovery process and keep you unnecessarily dependent on the program by making it feel safer and easier for you to remain in your group.

Lack of Models for Healthy Relationships

Adequate relationship skills are critical for creating happiness in your life. The lack of skills and tools has been responsible for much of your current misery. Without relationship expertise you get involved with "toxic" people, overburden the ones who care, and create chaos instead of love. Failed relationships are endemic in the lives of addictive people, and numbing the pain of lost love is probably the most common excuse for addiction relapse. Because other group members come from similar backgrounds, they may provide no better role models for how to have healthy relationships than your own family did.

Yet, recovery programs teach us almost nothing about relating in a healthy manner:

- What to do about trusting people.
- How to replace old, toxic relationship patterns with new, healthy ones.
- How to end loneliness and create internal intimacy.
- How *functional,* healthy intimacy with others works.
- How to successfully deal with the *other* relationships in your life: your boss, siblings, co-workers, neighbors, friends, and so on.
- How to find a healthy relationship in the first place.
- How to set limits, say no, have fun, get close, create space.

With no mental picture or model of what healthy relationships look like, and few skills to build that model in your life, your chances of forming a successful relationship outside the group remain small. Additionally, your dependency on the group to supply all your relationship needs can make building an independent, autonomous, *happy* life all but impossible. When you know what healthy relating is, and you have the skills to accomplish it, your chances for complete recovery from addiction are excellent.

Replication of Dysfunctional Family Patterns

Although the "family" atmosphere created by twelve-step and other recovery groups is of value in providing the support and reinforcement that help you stop your addiction, in many respects, the kind of family that the group will foster and recreate will have many of the same damaging family patterns that led to the members' addictions.

The lack of information about healthy living and lack of models for healthy relationships means, in many cases, that members have no other guide for how to interact with one another than the same addictive models they learned as children. When this happens, even the good that the program has already done can be undermined and the recovery group can actually drive members back to their addiction by re-creating the conditions they tried to escape through addiction in the first place.

John Bradshaw's experience illustrates the dynamic involved: "The group was my new family...my family of affiliation." Often, program members enter therapy because this "new family" has become very painful and toxic for them, and they don't know where to turn if they can't trust their recovery program. The fact is that without other strong models, each of us has a tendency to re-create our original family whenever we become close to others, even though those early relationships made us very unhappy.

According to family therapist Virginia Satir, people will usually choose the familiar over the healthy. When we encounter familiar patterns, no matter how painful they may be, we know what is expected of us, and we know what the results will be. Even when we are sure the results will be painful, they are less frightening than the unknown results of dealing in a new way with unfamiliar people. Often, when in the presence of someone who evokes a parental role, we feel childlike, small, powerless, and helpless: "I couldn't help it—he made me do it."

This is as true within recovery groups as it is elsewhere. In this new environment, after spending some time with the same people in the program, interacting in the only way we know, we may reconstruct our original family without realizing it, complete with shaming, control struggles, fighting, mixed messages—sometimes even including violence and inappropriate sex.

The "family system" is imprinted on everyone's subconscious, childlike mind, so we have a tendency to interpret and respond to the world according to that system. Aggressive people may be perceived as and reacted to "just like" an angry father; passive people as "just like" a weak mother.

Martha

Martha, an overweight woman of 64 who had to lose weight to protect her health, attended a special program run by her OA sponsor, Bill. At first, the program went well, with Bill assigning lots of writing and homework exercises, and Martha began to find it easier to stick to her eating program and lose weight. After a couple of months, Martha's old rage at her abusive father arose, and she yelled at Bill during one of the special meetings. Because Bill had no training or ability to deal therapeutically with her rage, he got angry in return, and banished Martha from his program. Martha was so upset that she dropped out of OA altogether. In therapy, Martha was able to express her old rage safely, and her compulsion to eat to repress the rage lessened. She went back to OA, and learned to manage her own eating.

●

We also gravitate toward people who replicate our original family members because they seem familiar. Within the group, a sponsor may take on a parental role, and other group members may function like siblings, increasing the feelings of powerlessness and dependence that were familiar from childhood. To the degree that the members of your self-help group, or the Steps themselves, undercut autonomy, they are like original families—partially dysfunctional.

Child abuse expert Alice Miller explains this pattern as a search for a way to correct the old family environment: "What if a person has never had the good fortune to experience his early dependence on his parents and the accompanying separation anxiety...they resort to a...re-enactment of their dependency and obedience in early childhood. Even very brief contact with a group can give one a feeling of maternal warmth...never experienced before, which makes one feel secure...But...the group is only a substitute, the search for what is missing can never stop...Every form of addiction, instead of doing away with the old longing, simply perpetuates the tragedy by repeating it...Someone who was not allowed to be aware of what was being done has no way of telling about it except to repeat it."

This problem is compounded when program members are not re-covered enough to be objective about themselves or their interaction with you. They may be projecting their early family experiences on you, as you project yours on them. Your sponsor may be wise enough to help, or may unintentionally make the problem worse. If early rage or shame erupts, an untrained sponsor, like Martha's sponsor Bill, may not have the tools to deal with it. Together, you can re-enact the old feelings of anger, fear, hurt, rejection, and shame—and not even real-ize it, because those feelings are so familiar. Unless you've been taught the tools to deal with painful emotions from the past, you may find yourself sliding back into old, destructive behavior. It is both painful and enlightening to discover that you have re-created your dysfunc-tional family from scratch, in a brand-new environment, when no one else from your original family is there.

Of course this happens in other aspects of life besides the program. People recreate family patterns wherever they go—at work, at school, among friends. "Not only do we become accustomed to the manner in which our parents have always treated us," explains Dr. Sonya Fried-man, "but we recreate that...with the men we marry. Most women who are unhappy in their relationships with their parents are unhappy...with their husbands in a remarkably similar way."

If your underlying belief is "This is how it is" or "This is what I deserve," you can continue to repeat your initial family experience without realizing it.

Twelve-step members are often enraged when the past is replayed, and seek others to blame. At first, Martha blamed her leaving the program and going off her diet on Bill, because he got angry at her, just as her father had in the past. But by working through her rage and other underlying feelings, Martha used her experience with Bill to learn more about herself. You, too, can use difficult relationships to get a better understanding of old beliefs and how they perpetuate old problems. Using life experience as a mirror of your dysfunctional process is an autonomous way to gain power and understanding of healthy relationships.

Dependency on the Group

Because it is difficult for those who struggle to control an addiction to accept advice from people who do not have firsthand knowledge of the experience—even from therapists, counselors, and clergy—the fact that recovery programs surround you with the support and encouragement of others who have also suffered this adversity makes them particularly powerful and effective. But in the later stages of recovery, the program's peer support resource, so effective early in recovery, often becomes just another family dependency. If you have been attending as many as seven meetings a week for several years, and have turned your life around with the help of the group, you may now feel that you're incapable of success *without* the group.

To control your behavior, it was necessary to cut yourself off from the people who helped reinforce or tacitly support your addiction. Your twelve-step friends may have become your only friends. For the first time in your life, you find yourself surrounded by others who have suffered with the same addiction as you have—and they have been able to quit. As someone with a dependent personality looking outside yourself for relief, you naturally want them to think well of you and even to feel special by quitting, too. Once you have entered recovery by stopping your addiction, you naturally want to keep their approval by remaining in recovery. In a sense, what you are doing is transferring your dependency from a worse alternative to a better one. In essence, at this stage, the group is still functioning as little more than a substitute addiction.

Part Two

Completing
Recovery

Chapter 3

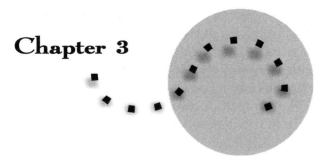

Beyond Recovery:
From Dependency to Autonomy

The stages of human development are the same today as they were in the ancient times. As a child, you are brought up in a world of discipline, of obedience, and you are dependent on others. All this has to be transcended when you come to maturity, so that you can live not in dependency but with self-responsible authority. If you can't cross that threshold, you have the basis for neurosis.

—Joseph Campbell

Before you can successfully take The Thirteenth Step, learn the healthy skills of autonomy, and move beyond the program, you must complete your recovery by going deep within yourself to heal the pain and to *unlearn* the negative beliefs that made you—and kept you—dependent. If all of your previous efforts to stop your addictive behavior on your own (without the support of a recovery group) have ended in relapses, it is because you don't know how to address the childhood factors that created, and still drive, your dependency.

Like anyone else who has suffered from a long illness, you must first heal completely before you attempt to build yourself back up to optimal fitness. Otherwise, you will inevitably find yourself suffering a relapse back into your old, addictive behavior.

Until you repair the damage of being raised in a dysfunctional family, you will always live with the possibility of relapse, even within the support of a group. You can't permanently recover from the dependent behavior that has devastated your life without correcting the self-defeating belief that you are not good enough to handle problems and face painful circumstances on your own. To complete recovery, you must replace the old, dependent patterns with the awareness that you were born with all the talents, intelligence, and ability it takes to meet whatever challenges or difficulties life might bring your way. You can affirm your right to be a healthy, autonomous individual and gain confidence in your ability to meet life's difficulties, cope with setbacks, and be self-assured in your relationships with others.

The good news is that once self-defeating thought patterns are replaced, it becomes much easier to successfully manage. When you are familiar and comfortable with the dynamics of autonomy, self-control feels good. It becomes a question of self-care, of doing good things for you because you deserve to be well-treated, because you deserve a happy and functional life, and because you enjoy doing nice things for yourself, including taking care of yourself. For a healthy, self-reliant person, autonomous behavior comes easily, and is not forced or difficult.

To be free from dependence, you need to understand the key skills that foster independence and autonomy—risk taking, problem solving, and coping with disappointment and failure; how they develop in healthy families; and how dysfunctional families undermine your early efforts at developing these skills. Armed with that understanding, you can begin to reverse your early negative experience by identifying old beliefs and replacing them with positive new ones.

Autonomy and the Dependent Child

Although we all begin life entirely dependent on our parents or caretakers, we are supposed to learn independence, self-reliance, and self-confidence by progressing through a series of gradual stages. With the proper support and training, children grow into healthy, fully functioning adults able and eager to meet life's challenges in an autonomous fashion. Healthy, fully competent parents prepare you to become autonomous and competent by being a constant source of encouragement during your early ventures at independence. Likewise, they support you when these attempts go wrong. When, as a small child, a parent makes you feel secure, you use that parent as a "home base"—venturing out and experimenting with the world for brief periods, then running back for reassurance and encouragement. This stage of learning can be seen in the way toddlers in a new environment grab onto a parent's legs and hide, then peek out and venture around, only to dart back to safety and hide themselves again when they feel overwhelmed or frightened.

If you have confident, supportive parents, your adventuring becomes more widespread, and of longer duration as you grow older, and your self-confidence grows: As a child of 7, you might stay overnight with a friend for the first time. As a teenager, you might get your first job working at a hamburger stand. After high school graduation, you may leave home for the first time to live on your own or attend college.

When this process fails to take place (as it so often does in dysfunctional families), you never learn to depend on yourself and never feel strong enough or able enough to manage life's challenges. Instead, you become insecure and depend on others to help you cope.

Developing the Skills of Autonomy

When a child's early ventures are supported and encouraged, he or she gets the opportunity to master the three skills involved in meeting challenges or taking any autonomous action: risk-taking, problem-solving, and coping with failure/disappointment.

Risk taking. To venture forth and act on your own in any new and difficult circumstance is to take a risk. To take a risk means facing uncertainty: an outcome or consequences that you cannot predict or control, with the possibility of things going wrong, of being hurt, or of failing. In a functional family, you learn to view this as a challenge or an opportunity to learn from mistakes. In a dysfunctional family, you learn to see this possibility as something to be feared and any situation that creates it as something to be avoided. "Forbidden the risk-taking and exploration essential for healthy development," writes psychologist Nathaniel Brandon, in *Honoring the Self*. "The child intuits that he or she is inadequate to the normal challenges of life, is inherently unfit for independent survival." With competent parents, a child learns how to handle this fear gradually, in stages, so that it never becomes overwhelming.

Problem solving. In healthy development, small children experience very small risks, surviving them and being praised and encouraged for taking them (whether or not mistakes are made). This experience gradually increases the child's confidence in his or her ability to cope and then move on to taking larger risks. Through this trial-and-error learning, coupled with parental teaching and natural physical and mental development, the child begins to build self-control and competence—and eventually masters the skill of problem-solving.

Handling disappointment and failure. The risk of disappointment or failure is inherent in any autonomous action. Risk implies that you cannot be sure that your actions will result in a successful conclusion. Inherent in any new venture is the possibility that the outcome will be negative, a mistake will be made, or you will have to cope with failure.

Recovery expert John Bradshaw, in *Homecoming,* maintains that developing a healthy, fully functioning adult mind requires making "mistakes, which are an integral part of being human. Mistakes serve as warnings from which we can learn...To live in dread of making a mistake causes you to walk on eggs and live a guarded, shallow existence."

The History of Dependency

Ideally, through positive role modeling by adults, learning from experience and gentle encouragement, a child progresses from dependency to autonomy. But the truth is that few people grow up fully autonomous, even when they are not from dysfunctional homes.

Because of a strong, long-standing social bias against independent thought and behavior, many parents were not raised to be autonomous and independent themselves, and so cannot model it for their children. Historically, in most earlier societies, especially those living in primitive or marginal conditions, independent behavior was viewed as threatening to the close group cooperation and fragile routines that insured group survival. In later societies, it was often viewed as weakening or threatening a leader's control and power over the group.

You can still see this bias in the way public schools focus more on robot-like "good boy and girl" behavior than on encouraging independent thought and self-confidence. In both family and school environments, a child exhibiting these autonomous qualities is often met with hostility, ridicule, and punishment. Children who challenge a teacher or parent (who has low self-esteem and a fear of autonomy) by presenting a different idea about how to solve a geometry equation, or how to make the bed, are likely to be met with ridicule of the new idea or to be told "Do it my way because I said so." The crucial values that produce autonomy (independence and experimentation) are rarely valued or rewarded, thus blocking the path to autonomy.

This patronizing behavior fosters dependency rather than autonomy. Parents, teachers, and other adults take responsibility for the children's actions rather than encouraging and helping the children to be responsible for themselves. Adults are viewed as all-knowing, all-wise, and all-powerful; the children are ignorant, foolish, and powerless. In short, children are seen as dependent on adults and unable to make sound decisions or to take responsible action on their own. When children are regarded and treated this way by adults, they grow up believing they are powerless.

This attitude creates a tendency to invest all power and importance in the parent, and to make the parents' feelings and reactions the focus of the child's life. "Our culture," says Dr. Susan Forward in *Toxic Parents*, "and our religions are almost unanimous in upholding the omnipotence of parental authority." Children raised this way begin to feel unimportant and powerless, thus creating the roots of dependent behavior. As a result of these social biases, most parents are unable to teach autonomy to their children, because they were never taught it themselves. Instead, they tend to err either on the side of protecting or restraining them too much, or pushing them forward too hard and too critically early on during their first childhood venturing at independence. Either extreme undermines their fledgling attempts at autonomy and prevents them from completing their growth beyond dependency.

We are so familiar with the idea that parents are responsible for their children that it sounds reasonable. In practice, it creates dependency and prevents healthy development. We are all familiar with the example of parents who force their children to do homework or chores "because I said so," rather than helping the children to understand why homework is valuable to learning. Such parents give their offspring the idea that they are to do things unquestioningly—to keep their parents happy or because they're ordered to. They don't learn to perform difficult tasks on their own in order to learn and grow from the experience. On the other hand, children who are encouraged and supported in taking the responsibility for homework, and who see the benefit of chores done well, feel proud that their efforts count and as a result, learn self-motivation.

Parents who try to make things perfect, try to protect children from reasonable risk, or who are themselves overwhelmed by life or worry about how they look as parents—in other words, parents who do not feel fully autonomous—cannot model autonomy for their children, encourage them to be independent, or help them develop beyond dependency. "ACAs often do not know what normal adults are supposed to be like," according to Dr. Timmon Cermak in *A Time To Heal*, "because their vision of mature behavior, which most people get from watching their parents, is incomplete. Their families have not provided them with all the models of healthy, or even civil, adult behavior that are needed."

If parents try to protect children with "smothering" love, or to motivate them with guilt, or prevent them from experimenting, the children grow into fearful, uncertain adults. If parents withdraw support and demand too much from a child—withdrawing love to motivate, criticizing instead of encouraging—the child is convinced he or she is not good enough or that love must be "earned." As an adult, he or she feels mystified about being loved, and becomes dependent on others to feel worthy of love.

Some children grow up with a combination of "smothering" and criticism (one overprotective parent, one overly critical parent). This compounds and multiplies feelings of fear and inadequacy. Whichever family situation you had, you are left incomplete, and never developed self-confidence, ability for independent action, and autonomy. Instead, you became stuck in dependency.

Dependency and the Dysfunctional Family

If your family, like those of most people in recovery groups, was severely dysfunctional (unpredictable, angry, physically dangerous, frightening, hysterical, or chaotic and confusing) it compounded the social beliefs that already inhibit autonomy. For example:

- The toddler, who is severely chastised, criticized, or frightened in the experimentation stage learns to anxiously and dependently watch the adults for cues rather than venturing out autonomously into the world to learn.

- The 7-year-old who has been neglected does not feel secure about proper conduct when out of the home.

- The high school student who is criticized and made to feel dependent and inadequate at home may feel discouraged and overwhelmed by school, and may never make it to college at all.

- The young adult who feels his dysfunctional parents "need" him, may never leave home and try his luck in the world because he remains dependent on their approval.

Growing up in a dysfunctional family sets the stage for dependent adult behavior, as Dr. Susan Forward explains in *Toxic Parents*: "Whether adult children of toxic parents were beaten when little or left alone too much, sexually abused or treated like fools, overprotected or overburdened by guilt, they almost all suffer surprisingly similar symptoms: damaged self-esteem, leading to self-destructive behavior. In one way or another, they almost all feel worthless, unlovable, and inadequate."

A child who is trapped in an emotionally dangerous dysfunctional family becomes overwhelmed, enraged, and/or terrified. The family denies any safe outlet for these devastating feelings, and may even punish the child for expressing them. As a result, the child begins to grasp compulsively for anything that can numb the pain of having to bear them. Finding a relationship, substance, or behavior that can block out this pain creates an insatiable craving—a craving we call *addiction, dependency,* or *compulsion*.

Growing up with frightened, confused, or incompetent parents can also set the stage for *codependent behavior*. When parents feel inadequate, are addictive, and lack self-confidence, children cannot depend on them. Instead, children are rewarded with the greatest love and approval when their parents can lean on the children. In effect, the normal parent-child roles are reversed. The child becomes the parent and caregiver, with tragic results: A child who receives love when catering to the parent becomes dependent on or addicted to *the parents'* addiction. The child grows older and leaves home convinced that to be loved, he or she must take care of others. This leads to a cycle of looking for troubled people—usually those who have their own problems with dependent behavior, who love out of neediness rather than healthy motivation.

The 3 Skills of Autonomy

The foundations of autonomy or dependency are laid in the early exploratory stage of childhood. It is impossible to overemphasize how important this stage is to individual development. In the development of a basic attitude about life, there may be no more critical passage. A child who successfully learns self-reliance will have the confidence and skills to meet life's challenges. Conversely, a child who does not learn to rely on himself will become fearful of challenge and will learn only dependent, unproductive methods of reacting to it.

One reason our initial explorations in life are so important is that they represent our first real attempts to experience ourselves as independent beings separate from our parents. When our early experiments are positive, we learn to expect success and look forward to independence. We grow up motivated toward autonomy, and life seems full of promise and excitement.

Early attempts at independent activity are critical, because during this stage we develop our first crude, and in most cases characteristic, skills for dealing with challenging circumstances. If this early exploration goes well, a child learns to cope with challenge *without being dependent* on others, and will be able to live life as an autonomous individual. Later, when presented with new or difficult experiences, he or she has the self-confidence necessary to cope and to successfully manage new situations.

This ability to cope with life's challenges independently serves as the basis for all later positive attitudes toward self: self-esteem, self-confidence, and self-reliance. The positive reinforcement of each success and the excitement and pleasure of learning entices a person farther and farther beyond the original parental dependency—until, one day, he or she has become an independent, autonomous individual. Making this transition successfully requires mastering the stages leading to autonomy and developing the required skills of risk-taking, problem-solving, and coping with disappointment and failure.

Risk-taking

Throughout life we face situations that we cannot predict or guarantee, in which risk is unavoidable, such as when we are forced by circumstances to change jobs or meet new people, or when we must differ with those we love. In addition, there are times when experimentation and risk-taking are desirable, as when you leave the job you know to get better conditions or a higher salary. Successful risk-taking requires learning to evaluate risk before acting, and weighing the advantages of success against the disadvantages of failure. Functional homes teach children how to evaluate risk through trial and error, from watching the behavior of others, or with the guidance of healthy and supportive adults.

Five-year-old Tommy takes the risk involved in making friendly contact with a new neighbor child. From experience, he learns to weigh the possibility that he will make a new friend against the possibility that they won't get along, or what the new child will be mean or selfish.

Healthy, supportive parents will help Tommy learn how to evaluate potential new playmates by discussing positive signs (a friendly disposition, a genuine smile, ease in playing with others) and negative signs (pushing, not sharing, yelling, teasing). Tommy weighs these possibilities as best he can, and makes his choice. If the encounter turns out well, Tommy's parents will be pleased for him, will encourage him to play with the newcomer again, and to continue to meet new potential playmates. If the outcome is negative, good parents will sympathize while offering the encouragement needed to ensure that Tommy continues to meet new people. Properly supported and encouraged, Tommy will soon learn how to evaluate the risks involved in meeting new people, and the majority of his experiences will be positive—and he will feel emotionally secure about handling his failures. While he is mastering risk-taking, he is also learning important social skills.

As Tommy grows older and is able to think more abstractly and clearly, he will become better and better at evaluating the disadvantages and advantages in the risks he wants to take. Knowing how to evaluate which ones are worth taking makes the venture easier.

However, if Tommy's parents are dysfunctional, they will express their own fears about encountering someone new and emphasize the potential dangers beforehand. Even if the outcome is positive for Tommy, unsupportive parents will often criticize the other child or continue to emphasize other negative possibilities ("He looks stupid" or "Be careful, he might break your toys"). If things go wrong, as they predicted, they will be sure to emphasize how correct their original fears were or warn against future attempts ("I told you kids can't be trusted" or "Don't get your hopes up, a lot of kids are like that").

Without the ability to calculate risk, Tommy would either be too afraid to attempt any new behavior, and therefore be dependent on others to tell him what to do, or would be trapped in addictive behaviors to block out and avoid his fears. The latter might cause Tommy to take unreasonably dangerous risks and experience disaster after disaster.

●

Problem-solving

Problem-solving is a basic autonomy skill because it applies to almost every aspect of life. As soon as we venture beyond the easy reach of those who advise and counsel us, we are faced with problems. Naturally we want to do our best in every new situation and bring it to a successful conclusion for ourselves and others. The moment we encounter something new, we are presented with the challenge of unknown and unfamiliar elements.

In order to solve problems, we need to learn the four elements of problem-solving: 1) evaluating the problem, 2) considering possible solutions, 3) deciding which to try first (which calls on our skill at evaluating and taking risks), and 4) trying out the solution by taking action.

Eight-year-old Mary visits her friend Rose and stays away from home overnight for the first time. When bedtime comes, Mary discovers that Rose's mother doesn't leave the light on in Rose's bedroom, as Mary's mother does at home. At first, Mary is worried, and thinks about the situation (evaluating the problem). Then she considers what she can do to make it better (considering possible solutions). Before the visit, Mary's parents discussed proper behavior and possible problems that might arise. They told her if she needed advice, she could ask Rose or Rose's parents, or she could call home. Mary chooses to talk to Rose first, suggesting what she would like (deciding which to try first and taking action). Rose says that they can ask her mother if the closet light could be left on, and the door ajar. When Rose's mother says yes, Mary has solved her problem and learned an essential skill of autonomy. Without the advance support of Mary's parents, who helped her weigh the risks, acknowledged that they wouldn't criticize or overreact if she made a mistake, and prepared her for her first night away from home, Mary might have felt dependent on her unavailable parents to solve the problem, been insecure to ask for what she wanted, and remained frightened all night long. Had this happened, Mary would have been reluctant to try sleeping over at a friend's house again.

●

When dysfunctional parents smother or criticize our early efforts at problem-solving, we are unable to properly develop the skill. As a result, we are more likely to fail at coping with new situations by ourselves. Convinced by experience that we are inadequate to solve life's problems on our own, we begin to fear the world is too complex and frightening to handle. Thus, we look outside ourselves for something or someone we can depend on to help us through anything new, difficult, or challenging, while our progress toward autonomy is blocked.

Coping With Disappointment and Failure

Problem-solving doesn't always lead to success on the first try. Even when we have mastered the four skills of solving problems, we are not guaranteed every attempt will prove successful. Your attempts at risk-taking can still result in disappointment or failure. Otherwise, there would be no risk.

When children who have functional parents make a mistake or fail, the healthy support and guidance of their parents helps them cope with mistakes so they are not discouraged from taking future risks. Proper support helps them learn to understand and manage disappointment, anger, self-criticism, and frustration, and reassures them that their feelings are a natural reaction to circumstances that don't work out as planned. With support, disappointment and frustration pass away quickly, rather than remaining repressed inside, where they can develop into toxic shame. Then, by focusing on what can be done to correct the error or how to begin again, supportive parents helps generate hope for the next try.

Twelve-year-old Bobby learned this skill on his paper route. On Saturday, Bobby, who delivers the papers on his bicycle, misses hitting the steps with a paper and breaks Mrs. Smith's window. First, he feels fear: "Uh-oh. I've done it now. Mrs. Smith will be really angry when she gets home. Maybe I should run away before anyone finds out I did it." Then, he feels disappointed: "I really messed that up." Next, he blames himself: "I'm too clumsy. I should have been more careful." Then, he remembers what his supportive father told him: "Everyone makes mistakes, Bobby. That's a normal part of learning. If you make a mistake, you can almost always correct it. And if you can't, at least you can learn how to avoid making the same mistake again." So, instead of giving up, running away, blaming himself, or losing his confidence, Bobby gets off his bike, goes up to Mrs. Smith's door, and admits he broke the window. He offers to pay for it and asks her to find out what it would cost. After Mrs. Smith says she will, Bobby finishes his route and goes home.

When Bobby gets home, he's still upset and tells his father what happened, and how bad he feels. Bobby's dad remains supportive and reassuring: "Don't worry, Bobby. It was just a mistake. You didn't break the window on purpose. I know you're still upset. That's natural—I would be upset, too. Because you've done what you can to fix your mistake, I'm proud of how you handled it. Now, why don't you consider what you could do to prevent it from happening again, and when you've figured that out, let go of it, forgive yourself, and go on to something else." With the guidance of supportive parents, Bobby learned how to resolve—not suppress—his feelings, and applied his problem-solving abilities to correct the problem on his own.

Without the support of his parents, especially if they were overly critical and he feared punishment, Bobby might have tried running away or lying to solve his problem, adding further to his burden of guilt and shame. On the other hand, if his parents had rushed right in and fixed the problem without allowing him to solve it himself, he would not have learned how to deal with failure at all, and his paper route experience would have become a negative memory in which he had to depend on others to help him cope, and left unable to assuage his guilt.

●

When supportive parents give both guidance and the necessary information to understand mistakes, work them out, and handle disappointment, the child learns problem-solving. As an adult, he or she has the necessary confidence to meet most of life's challenges without having to depend on others, and knows how to cope with failure. Those who develop autonomy are no longer afraid of the new and the challenging.

In fact, they feel smart and skillful enough to venture forth independent of parents or anyone or anything else. Such people never need to become dependent on people, substances, or behaviors to face life's risks and problems. They never develop the behaviors and attitudes that are the foundation of dependency, because they don't experience fear and pain when confronting situations calling for autonomous action.

The 3 Attitudes of Dependency

When we are prevented from developing the skills of autonomy, our growth toward independence is blocked and we learn to react to new situations in ineffectual ways that actually *increase our dependency.* Being prohibited from or perhaps even punished for early, independent childhood venturing inhibits the development of autonomous skills. If we also learn ineffective behaviors, the foundations of dependency are laid. If we lack the ability to successfully handle new circumstances on our own, we are forced to turn to something outside ourselves to help us through these challenging events, and we fail to progress. As we grow older, who or what we depend on may change—from Mommy and Daddy to a significant other to addictive substances or destructive behaviors.

As John Bradshaw writes in *Healing the Shame That Binds You:* "Shaming experiences...are recorded in a person's memory bank. Because the victim has no time or support to grieve the pain...his emotions are regressed and the grief is unresolved...imprints remain in the memory...of the shaming scenes...forming collages of shaming memories...Shame as an emotion has now become frozen and embedded into the core of the person's identity. Shame is deeply internalized." Internalizing shame in this way means that risks become too painful to take, problems too overwhelming to solve, and failure too terrifying to risk, so it's easier to turn to addiction to mask the pain.

Instead of learning to solve problems and gaining confidence, we decide we are not smart enough to handle them on our own. When faced with problems, we begin to panic and stop thinking. In other words, we learn *mindlessness* and depend on the judgment of others rather than ourselves.

Instead of developing confidence in our ability to cope with failure and disappointment, we simply feel incompetent, stupid, and ashamed of our inadequacy. We begin to despair and give up: We feel *hopeless* that our own efforts will never be good enough.

Instead of developing the ability to think clearly and solve problems effectively, we feel *helpless* and anxious, and look for someone or something else to take care of us.

These three attitudes, or negative coping skills, keep you dependent. They are at the core of all addictive behavior, obsession, and compulsion. They prevent you from growing beyond dependency on substances, behaviors, people, and your recovery group itself. As long as you still have these negative beliefs, you will never be or feel able to independently cope with life's challenges, and you will never be able to perceive yourself as strong enough to stand on your own.

Mindlessness

When young children are taught that taking risks is frightening or dangerous, they feel incompetent to handle new situations. Consequently, they want to avoid becoming aware of anything new, such as opportunities to learn, challenges, and potentially painful situations— in short, anything that requires them to cope on their own. It's a downward spiral: The less aware they become, the more risk they avoid, the more things go wrong, and the less aware they want to be. Because most of life presents some challenge, children eventually narrow their focus to just the day-to-day or even moment-to-moment events of their lives and have to depend on others to help them through anything new or challenging.

Thus, if little Tommy has been made to feel that the risk of meeting new people is too great, rather than seeking out his new neighbor, he may ignore the child (not be aware of him). Even if he does make contact, Tommy may be ready to break the relationship off and run home as soon as any difficulties occur between them, convinced that his parents' dysfunctional fear was right, and lacking any idea of what to do when problems arise. Soon, Tommy may even begin to ignore most possibilities for developing new relationships, and all other challenges and risks, until the attitude has become so habitual, he is no longer even aware when such possibilities exist, or that he is ignoring them.

●

Helplessness

If early attempts at problem-solving are smothered or harshly criticized, the outcome of any situation will almost always be unsuccessful. Even when the child is successful, he or she is made to feel inadequate, that "you could have done better" or that "you were just lucky this time," and that next time things will very likely turn out worse. In a dysfunctional family, no matter what the outcome, childhood efforts are made to feel like disasters. As a result, the child begins to feel helpless, dependent, and unable to solve life's problems without help. Rather than feeling turned on and excited by the prospect of trying new experiences, he or she becomes turned off and discouraged. If your experience was like this, you eventually became so convinced of your own helplessness that you're no longer willing to try to solve problems, and instead depend on people and substances to make you feel better.

If little Mary had come from a dysfunctional family, rather than trying to figure out what to do about feeling fearful at Rose's house without a light, she would have been convinced that there wasn't an answer, or that if there was, she couldn't be smart enough to find it herself, and would need to turn to someone smarter, like her parents, to fix it for her. If they were unavailable, she would be paralyzed, unable to find a possible solution.

●

Hopelessness

Once such experiences make you feel that mistakes and failures can't be corrected, you have no reason to hope you can make the situation better. Rather than being a natural, temporary, resolvable reaction to failure, feelings of shame, incompetence, and disappointment become so constant that they deepen into despair. You become convinced there is nothing you can do to improve or better yourself or your skills, and that you and your life are both hopeless.

If Bobby's parents had been discouraging, rather than support-ive, he could have become so hopeless that he probably would not have been courageous enough to take the paper route in the first place. If he did risk the paper route, and broke a window, he would have been sure nothing he could do could make it better, and most likely would run away or lie about his responsibility for the broken window, and the situation would have become much more of a di-saster. Both Mrs. Smith and Bobby's parents would have been an-gry with him. With no help or support, Bobby would be left unable to correct his error and convinced it was safer to just give up, not to try anything challenging in the first place.

●

Toxic Shame, Magical Thinking, and You

The damage parents' negative reactions do to a child's daily learn-ing process is even more devastating because it occurs at an age when the ability to think is still imperfectly formed, and children are extremely vulnerable to believing whatever adults say. A child has no way to evalu-ate whether criticism is valid, because his or her ability for abstract and rational thought (understanding non-concrete concepts such as *far away, next year, good, evil, frustrated*); the ability to evaluate; ("Spilling my milk isn't *that* bad; Mother is overreacting"); and the ability to project future likelihood from current events ("Father is very tired, and his boss gave him a difficult time today, so if I get whiny, he's going to blow up") are undeveloped.

In the early years (some experts say before age 5, some before age 8), thinking ability is only partially developed, and events seem to hap-pen magically. Children, wide-eyed, believe that the Tooth Fairy really left the quarter, or that Mommy's kiss heals a bumped knee, or that the Santa in the department store is really going to bring the toy they ask for down the chimney on Christmas Eve. Small children love to play peek-a-boo, because they believe they can't be seen when *their* eyes are covered up.

Children cannot see the cause-and-effect connection between events (a small child cannot understand that planting a seed will produce tomatoes weeks later); they think in very concrete ways, and they cannot understand abstract concepts (such as *near and far,* and *left and right*) until about age 5. They are the center of their tiny universe, they believe everything that happens relates to them, and they perceive their behavior to be the cause of every event (when Mommy smiles or frowns, baby feels responsible).

Connecting unrelated events and behavior in this way is what psychologists term *magical thinking,* the stage in a child's thinking in which we believe we are the cause of physical phenomena. In *Imaginary Crimes,* psychologists Lewis Engel and Tom Ferguson show that magical thinking begins as part of normal childhood development: "As children we are ignorant of the laws of cause and effect, and may at times come to irrational conclusions...Magical thinking is the child's belief that she has the ability to make things happen by simply thinking about them."

In the film *Home Alone,* when the young hero awoke to find himself alone in the house, he concludes that it's because the night before, he wished his whole family would disappear. The more prosaic truth, that he's been accidentally forgotten by his rather disorganized family amid the chaos of leaving for vacation, simply doesn't occur to him. It is this quality of childhood thinking that makes fairy tales, fables, and magical stories so believable to children. In their eyes, they are as real as many other "unseen" events: Daddy's work, older brother's school, germs, "when you grow up." If a child cannot experience something with her own five senses, it is not real to her and seems like magic.

Children begin their first autonomous ventures into the world while still in the magical thinking stage, so they are particularly vulnerable to the negative, critical, or fearful parental reactions, especially during early trial-and-error efforts. Because the natural limitations of magical childhood thinking make it impossible to evaluate situations objectively, children are vulnerable to whatever adults say. A child will simply accept, without question, that adults' behavior, teachings, and evaluations are correct. If adults are overcritical and say, "you're bad, useless, and worthless," in response to every normal childlike mistake, the child naively comes to believe this overly harsh evaluation.

This childhood inability to differentiate between *doing* something wrong (making a mistake) and *being* something wrong (a bad child) leaves each one of us vulnerable to believing we are bad, stupid, and unworthy. After a while we constantly feel ashamed of our inadequacy, as if we ought to apologize for existing and deserve to live in an environment of criticism and abuse.

Contempt for your own existence is, perhaps, the single most destructive feeling you can have about yourself, because it makes you feel unworthy to cope, unfit to exist, and completely dependent on the effects and opinions of others. Therapists call this feeling *toxic shame,* (a phrase popularized by John Bradshaw) because it is so strong and so deeply imbedded that it devastates and poisons all of life.

In *Healing the Shame That Binds You,* Bradshaw explains the effect toxic shame can have on children when it is fostered during the critical period of magical thinking: "when shame has been...internalized, nothing about you is okay...you have the sense of being a failure...you are an object of contempt to yourself." Toxic shame forms one of the major roots of dependency, one source of the inner pain you try to subdue with addiction and compulsion. Bradshaw explains why: "When you are contemptible to yourself...you turn your eyes inward, watching and scrutinizing every minute detail of behavior. This internal critical observation is excruciating."

This internal criticism or toxic shame, learned in childhood, is tied to every effort, activity, or thought you undertake—all your efforts are deemed unsatisfactory. The belief that nothing you can do on your own is ever good enough becomes painfully embedded in your mind as a child, and doesn't go away. It remains locked there, where it keeps you mindless, helpless, hopeless, and dependent until you learn how to reach it and re-educate it.

To sum it all up, if your parents treat you lovingly, if things go well, you (the child) are okay. But if you are led to believe that making mistakes is wrong, you become dependent upon others—your focus is on anxious observation of how the adults expect you to do things.

Your Dependent Inner Child

If you grow up in a dysfunctional family, you do not outgrow your original dependent childhood personality or the negative judgments you made about your ability to cope with life autonomously. Instead, your childhood mind forms the basis of your adolescent mind and then your adult mind. Because the negative attitudes you learned in childhood guarantee that your subsequent attempts at independence and self-control will be unsuccessful, your childhood personality (which many psychologists call the *inner child* or the *subconscious*) becomes convinced by experience that you are unable to manage life on your own.

The attitudes and the skills that keep you dependent were formed in the childhood magical mind, and lie so deeply buried that they are very difficult to change or unlearn. It's as if there are two different aspects of you: the rational grownup and the magical child. You gave up using that magical thinking process long before your earliest memories began, so it is difficult for your adult self to become aware of or communicate with this key part of your inner child. Even when you do manage to get in touch with it, you may not be able to communicate with it effectively, because it still perceives and thinks about the world magically while you tend to think and communicate as an adult.

You may never have understood why it seemed so agonizingly impossible to end your addictive behavior, why you felt so helplessly unable to control yourself for so much of your life, or why you have always been dependent on something other than yourself to help you cope with risk and pain. You know from your personal experience just how hard it is, how much you have struggled to change, how many countless times you have failed, and how much you and those around you have suffered as a result. The problem is not that you are weak or haven't tried hard enough. Rather, you have been putting your effort into the wrong places.

As an adult, you may know that your addictive behavior is destructive and that you are a worthwhile person who no longer needs to depend on others for support and guidance. But your inner child is buried so deep and thinks so differently that your message can't penetrate. This is one reason why you have heard yourself and other support group members make statements like: "I know I shouldn't do it, but I just can't help myself."

Unless you know how to communicate with your subconscious child mind in the same "language" it speaks, in a way that it can understand, you cannot work with it to change the attitudes and habits that first made you dependent. When a message from your adult mind does penetrate, your child mind doesn't understand it because you put it in adult terms. To your inner child, your attempts at communicating, though they make perfect sense to you, simply may seem like senseless gibberish.

To complete your recovery and unlearn the attitudes and skills that keep you dependent, you need to bridge the gap between your adult self and your inner child—to communicate in the kind of magical terms it understands. Establishing this effective connection between your rational adult mind and your magical child mind is essential to your recovery. Only when you have your inner child's full and willing cooperation are you able to correct the damage of your childhood.

Without a way to communicate with your child mind, you can try to overcome your dependent behavior by asserting your willpower or trying to act exclusively from your adult mind. But if you cannot reach the inner child, all you accomplish is to create an internal struggle between your child beliefs (which have the power of years of experience and repetition behind them), and your adult mind, whose ideas and knowledge mean little to the inner child. Without this communication, the minute you get stressed, overloaded, or confused, your child mind reasserts itself and takes over, causing you to revert to old, familiar modes of behavior. For example, you might have decided to give up drinking because you realize, rationally, that it is bad for you. Logically, you know how to handle each temptation that could arise: what to say if a friend offers you a drink, how not to drink at a business lunch, how to stay out of the bars on Friday night. But then, let's say, your spouse fights with you, and suddenly you're too upset to think rationally. Immediately, your child self reacts with dependent behavior and you find yourself drinking again, and you don't really understand how it happened.

A recovery group would probably tell you to go to a meeting to get help to fight the impulse. And *if you make it to a meeting*, you will probably calm down enough to maintain your sobriety. However, in both cases, something *outside you* strengthens your behavior and keeps your underlying dependency controlled.

Twelve-step Programs and Childhood Dependence

The worldwide success of the twelve-step and other self-help recovery groups is in part due to the way that the solid support of regular meetings and contact with program members provides new members with a supportive family-like atmosphere. Regular attendance supplies many of the skills and tools necessary to overcoming dependence—which many members never experienced as they grew up in dysfunctional families. Twelve-step groups can provide:

- Unconditional love and support.

- Reliable, predictable influences you can count on, perhaps for the first time in your life.

- The acceptance of being welcome, whoever you are, and whatever state you are in.

- People who will listen, without arguing or interrupting, as you tell your story.

- Human warmth, and the support of being around others who understand your problems.

- The encouragement of seeing others overcome addiction and problems like your own and make it into recovery.

Thus, recovery groups provide a safe environment for experimenting, taking some risks, foregoing your addiction, and facing the pain and fear that you previously screened out with addictive substances or behaviors.

Recovery groups do not, and cannot as presently constituted, help members develop the skills that build autonomy. Because they focus on the importance of the group over the individual, they could possibly undermine your attempts to grow beyond your childhood dependency. Addictive people often have long histories of being abused and/or abusive, and habitually discount or ignore the feelings and needs of others, so the twelve-step programs counter by asking members to focus on the welfare of the group. By placing emphasis on caring about each other, they maximize the group influence and make their system of rewards more effective. Through this system of support, reward, and example, groups help people who are used to destructive behavior find a reason to control it. To make this point, one of the Twelve Traditions of AA is that "Our common welfare should come first; personal recovery depends upon AA unity."

This focus on group unity can be a tremendous help to those in early recovery who were alienated by uncaring, chaotic families—because they learn to consider the welfare of others. But it also has some drawbacks. Unfortunately, the emphasis on the "common welfare" can also reinforce dependent attitudes developed in dysfunctional families, where it is common for individuals to be told that they cannot do what they want because the family as a whole or the parents are more important than the children, and what they want to do (go to college, go out with friends, dress as they like) is not good for the family. Believing that others are always more important than you leaves you feeling powerless and helpless. This powerless feeling, in turn, leads to a conclusion that you are not strong enough to take action on your own.

In other words, the group, like your own dysfunctional family, reinforces a lifelong tendency to view yourself as what psychologist Nathaniel Brandon calls a "family asset"—whose life, by right, does not belong to you, but to them, and who has no legitimate entitlement to independent action. In *Honoring the Self,* Brandon asks: "Did your parents encourage you to feel that your life belonged to you? Or were you encouraged to believe that you were merely a family asset...?"

One of the important functions of effective parents and teachers is to encourage children to realize that their lives belong to *them,* which helps children feel important enough and powerful enough to master the skills of autonomy. It also makes them feel equal to, and therefore not dependent on, the others around them. Such attitudes are discouraged in twelve-step programs, as they are in dysfunctional families and schools, where too much independence is suspect as detrimental to the group unity and survival. If you attempt to develop autonomy within the group, you may find yourself criticized for not attending meetings, or rejected by friends within the group, or even accused of relapsing. You may be encouraged by the group to let go of a destructive outside relationship, but paradoxically rewarded and encouraged to be dependent and other-oriented with twelve-step group members. Asserting your independence within the group (by challenging the rules or offering a dissenting opinion) often meets with hostility or disapproval.

John

A client, John, a hair stylist who was recovering from abusive relationships, attended CoDA for a year and became the group secretary. After a few months, John began to feel ready to take some healthy risks, and decided to go back to school. He asked for someone else to take over his duties so he could attend a college class that met at the same time. After meeting, members of the group warned him that he "needed them" and told him tragic stories of others who had left the group when they began feeling better, and then relapsed into old behavior. No one congratulated or supported him on taking classes to improve himself.

●

Of course it is important for people caught in addictive behavior to learn to acknowledge the importance and existence of others, to care about their welfare, and to regard them as important. Addicted people often lack socialization skills, and being an accepted member of the group enhances self-esteem to a point that makes it easier to give up destructive behavior.

What is *not* always understood by members of twelve-step programs, their members, or society in general is how critically recovery from dependence rests on finding the necessary balance between caring for others and caring for self. It is difficult for most people to understand how autonomy, independence, and caring for yourself *blend with* and *enhance* caring for others. We can genuinely care for others, as opposed to being focused dependently on them, only when we care for ourselves. We are not emotionally prepared to receive anything from others or give anything worthwhile to others (close friendship, respect) if we are not familiar with feeling it toward ourselves. We cannot be emotionally willing to receive any of these unless we already feel them toward ourselves, and accept our right to deserve them.

From his unique perspective as both a minister and licensed therapist, Denton Roberts shows how autonomy and self-esteem are essential to caring for others in his book *Able and Equal:* "... How I relate to myself determines what I am willing to give and receive from others... *I will not let in from others that which I am not giving myself,* and *I am not adept at giving others what I am not giving myself.* The way I relate to me prepares me internally to give and receive. Until I have an appreciation of myself I will not fully receive another's appreciation."

Your relationship with yourself is your most intimate experience of how personal interaction feels—this internal experience is the one against which you compare all others. Whether you are aware of it or not, how you treat others and how they treat you are measured against the criteria of *how you treat yourself.* Therefore, the more healthy and autonomous you are, the more your chances increase for having healthy relationships with others, including the members of your twelve-step program.

One reason recovery programs have only helped you stop your addiction but not your dependency is that most recovery workers have only recently become aware of the importance of the inner child and the techniques for communicating with it. Even when they have known about the inner child, they have rarely focused on issues of autonomy and the forces that undercut its development during its critical formative stages. Instead of empowering the inner child and helping it become stronger and more independent, they have focused on healing its hurts—curing the symptoms but leaving the causes untreated.

Another reason that recovery programs have not been able to correct the root causes of dependency is that once you are old enough to have entered the stage of rational thought, others can no longer directly influence your subconscious without your active participation. Once you acquire the ability to think abstractly, pass judgment, and make evaluations, you no longer believe the events of the world take place in a magical way and do not believe information unless it sounds reasonable and makes sense to your adult, rational mind.

To move beyond mere surface recovery of this kind to deep inner recovery requires making a connection with your subconscious, childlike mind, bringing it into your present, everyday life, and working cooperatively with it in a way it can understand. Otherwise, it will resist any positive, healthy decisions for change your adult mind makes that run counter to its years of negative experiences and beliefs. Recovery programs and therapies, unless they recognize and work with this fact, can do no more than arrest and stabilize addictive and compulsive behavior by influencing your adult thinking.

Because you are the only one who has direct access to your mind, once you learn the language of magical thinking, you gain an ability no one else can ever have—to work with, influence, and change your childlike, creative, subconscious mind. Therefore, the most powerful person in your recovery, growth, and healing will always be you.

Chapter 4

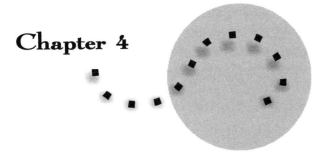

Deep Recovery: Learning How to Change

If you...study and learn the techniques, you diligently follow all the instruction...then comes the time for using the rules in your own way and not being bound by them. You can actually forget the rules because they have been assimilated. You are...one...who has been...transmuted.

—Joseph Campbell

You have learned how growing up in a dysfunctional family blocks autonomy during the early vulnerable period of magical thinking and creates dependency that becomes buried deep in your subconscious, childlike mind. To change the dependent patterns you were taught and to create new, autonomous patterns, you need to learn the special language your childlike inner mind uses so you can communicate with it.

The language your magical child mind speaks is, like most languages, acquired through practice and use. First, you learn the various words and what they mean, and how to put them together correctly in order to convey meaning to someone else. Then you must practice until you become fluent. The special language of the subconscious, childlike, magical mind is learned in a similar fashion, but by using processes instead of words. Because of the power of these processes to create change when properly used, and their ability to effect magical thinking, I call them the *magical tools*. These six magical tools are:

1. The Senses: The power of experience.
2. Imagery: The power to change events.
3. Self-Love: The power to heal your hurts.
4. Self-Image: The power to be your own hero.
5. Environment: The power to create support.
6. Repetition and Memorization: The power to effect your beliefs.

In essence, these six tools are the basic elements that underlie all our early childhood learning. Unless you can communicate in this "magical thinking" language, you cannot change what you learned through that language—from your senses, your environment, memorization, imagination, self-image, and the way you love and are loved by others. As you grow throughout life, your early learning can hold you back unless you know how to change it. Only through learning to "speak" to the child mind with these tools can you change early learning. Although logical thought and reasoning play an important part in adult learning, the child mind can only take in and learn new information by the application of these six tools.

The exercises in this chapter will show you how to use these processes to learn the language of the childlike mind and apply it in order to accelerate learning, change old habits, mentally practice sports or dancing, teach yourself new skills, and motivate yourself to exercise, eat healthier, relax, or learn something new. Practicing these exercises will form the foundation for the deeper work to come.

At this point, you are not actually beginning to change your old, dependent thinking to build autonomy, even though the exercises will produce some "side effects" of changing old beliefs and learning new, autonomous skills. Instead, the purpose of doing these exercises is to become familiar with the tools and to learn to use them to communicate with your subconscious, childlike mind.

Learning these tools in itself enhances your autonomy because they give you the means to heal and alter your own subconscious, which—by giving you the knowledge of what creates the changes, and the choice of what changes to make—makes you independent of any system of change and emotional healing, including this book. Once you master these tools, you can create and design your own system of change, without having to depend on others.

6 Magical Tools for Reaching the Child Mind

By nature, each of us learns differently. Some of us tend to learn more through one basic process than another. To effectively reach your own childlike mind, you must find out which combination of these tools works best for you, You must also learn how they work and how to use them effectively. Each of these tools will help you to influence ingrained beliefs and ideas in a different way.

Knowing which tools work best for you will help you evaluate books, workshops, therapy, and meditation or learning techniques, according to the tools they incorporate, and to know which ones suit you best *before* you try them. For example, if you are contemplating a new kind of meditation, and you know that the sensory experience of hearing is important to you, you can choose a meditation that involves background music. If you know that physical touch or movement is important, you'll choose a meditation that is based on movement, such as Tai Chi. If visualization is your favorite, you'll choose a corresponding technique, such as guided meditation.

The Senses: the Power of Experience

When we were very young children who had not yet developed the capacity of abstract thought, our only source of knowledge about the world around us was what we perceived directly through our senses: sight, touch, hearing, smell, and taste. Many of our earliest experiences, including those first autonomous ventures out from behind mother's skirts, occurred when we still related and responded to the world almost solely in terms of the senses. Although we develop other methods of learning about the world later, as adults we still continue to learn much of what we know about the world in this sensory way. Sensory experience becomes the hidden foundation on which all later learning is based. Information and impressions that come to us through the senses still exert a special influence over us, like the smell of a fresh Christmas tree, hearing the song that was playing when you met your first love, or the sight of a rainbow. More important, when we did begin to develop the capability to think, we thought first in sensory images, and only later learned to think in words—babies recognize Mother's face long before they know the word *Mama*.

All this suggests that the part of your mind that receives and thinks in images and impressions is more basic and its influence stronger than the part that thinks and reacts in terms of words, and that sensory impressions underlie much of the original magical thinking of childhood. The child first has a "sense" of what it has experienced, and then tries to connect events to her sensory experience with limited thinking ability. Therefore, if a child has a mouthful of strained spinach when Mom and Dad have a fight, she may never eat spinach again throughout her adult life. That makes sensory impressions and memories a powerful tool for bypassing your rational conscious mind, and for speaking directly to your subconscious child mind. By working with your inner mind, you can correct the damage that growing up in a dysfunctional family did to your development as an autonomous person. When you talk to your child mind in the language of the senses, you contact an important aspect of your contemporary adult mind as well.

You may have experienced already the power that the senses have to put you in touch with your child self. For example, when some aroma or sound or flavor has suddenly recalled the memory of a long forgotten experience. Perhaps the scent of flowers has reminded you of a favorite place, or an old song reminded you of a time when you were sad. That is why once the adult experience has covered over the child self, it can still be effectively reached through invoking the senses.

A vivid "flow of thoughts you can see, hear, feel, smell, or taste" is, as oncologist Martin L. Rossman, M.D., writes in *Healing Yourself*, this "interface language...[which] can help you solve practical problems, develop insight...enhance your self-confidence."

The following exercise will show you how to use your sensory experience to communicate with your own subconscious, childlike mind and create mental and physical changes. You learn how to use your imagination to invoke sensory images through building a personal "retreat." With practice, this will then become a place you can go to for psychological and physical relief from stress and for emotional healing. With practice, it becomes a quick way of gaining access into your subconscious child mind, an excellent setting for future mental work, and the basis for many of the other exercises throughout the book. Repetition of this exercise will give you valuable experience in invoking the power of your senses. You will also develop your ability to create imaginary mental images, which will become the basis of many other skills you will learn in this book, such as creative thinking.

In doing the exercise, you should take great care to imagine and develop your sensory impressions vividly and in as much detail as possible. You will be asked to notice how everything looks, feels, smells, sounds, and tastes. The more completely you can experience all of these sensory details, the more effective you will be in reaching and impacting your child mind. For maximum results, take plenty of time to get your senses involved in the process.

If this kind of mental imagery is new to you, you may, at first, have trouble in recreating everything in vivid sensory detail. If your early childhood experience was overwhelming and negative, you may have learned a habit of blocking as much sensory information as possible. Because of this blocking, you may be out of touch with your senses and thus have difficulty in building a realistic sensory image that invokes all five senses.

Don't discourage yourself by trying to do each step perfectly, or you will make it much more difficult than it needs to be. Instead, do the best you can to start, knowing your skill will improve as you repeat the exercise. If you patiently and regularly do this exercise, your ability to create realistic and vivid sensory impressions will quickly improve. You will gradually become more aware of your own sensory experiences in your daily life. The sights, sounds, feelings, smells, and tastes of the world around you will become more vivid and will begin to have more impact.

Even though you are being asked to picture details and get your senses involved, you probably will not see pictures as though you were watching a TV or movie screen. It is enough to know what your scene looks like, to be able to describe what you're picturing, and remember colors, smells, and feelings. Your own individual way of seeing the scene will work, whether you do it in words, pictures, or impressions.

As you master Magical Tool 1: The Senses, you'll acquire a basic skill for affecting your subconscious magical thinking. In future exercises, this becomes a tool you can use to contact your inner childlike mind; to change unhealthy attitudes and habits into new, healthier behavior; or to heal and resolve old, painful childhood memories. In later chapters, you will learn to use it specifically for replacing dependent thinking and skills with those of autonomy. Many of the exercises and guided meditations later in the book begin by invoking your senses as we do here.

Even though the six basic tools are designed to be used over and over again throughout your lifetime, you don't need to repeat them too much in the beginning. As you are learning them, simply do each one two or three times to familiarize yourself with it, and go on to learn the next. Because they interact and build on each other, and because they are so powerful and continuously useful, you will be motivated to use them over and over until they become lifetime habits.

You may find it works best to read the instructions for this exercise and those that follow into a tape recorder, or take turns with a friend and read them aloud for each other. Read slowly, pausing between sentences. Then you will be free to let your imagination roam, and to picture scenes in ever-increasing detail without having to stop and interrupt yourself to read each new instruction.

Exercise For Magical Tool 1: Using The Senses to Build a Retreat

1. **Choose a scene.**

   Think of a favorite place where you have enjoyed being alone, one that feels relaxing and private enough to be yourself. It might be a beach at a vacation spot, the attic in Grandma's house when you were a child, a waterfall on a camping trip, sitting on a porch at night, a luxurious hotel suite, or even a favorite spot in your present home. Or choose an *imaginary* place you would enjoy relaxing in: a restful room you have seen in a magazine, or an appealing scenic landscape from a calendar, or perhaps a place from a novel or movie. As you think of the scene, notice whether it feels real to you, because you'll contrast this to how it feels later. You will probably feel distant from it, and somewhat detached at this point, before you use your senses.

2. Develop your visual image.

Sit in a comfortable chair, relax your body, close your eyes, and use your imagination to *see the scene* you have chosen in as much detail as possible, but don't strain or struggle to see it. Just allow the scene to unfold, and add details as you think of them. It's not important to create a perfect, lifelike picture. At first, just strive for a clear impression of the scene. Think about what it looks like. Is it outdoors or indoors? Is it day or night? What colors are there: green grass and trees, brown carpets and flowered wallpaper? Are there flowers and rocks, furniture, or decorations? Though you have stopped consciously trying to picture the scene, you may be surprised to discover that as you invoke the remaining senses with the subsequent steps of the exercise, the scene becomes clearer, seemingly by itself.

3. Picture yourself in the scene.

Now use your imagination to see *yourself* in your scene, as a living participant, wherever you feel most comfortable and at ease with yourself. Are you standing, sitting, or lying down? What objects in the scene are near you? Which ones are at a distance? What are you wearing? What are the colors? How do you look? When you have pictured yourself as part of the scene as completely as you can, go on to the next step.

4. Use your sense of touch.

Use your imagination to *feel the scene* around you. Are you lying on grass, sitting in a favorite chair or standing on a city street, or perhaps dangling your bare feet in a running brook? What does the air feel like? Is it clear and rich, the way it is after a rain, or is it the close, heavy air of summer? Is a breeze moving against your skin, blowing your hair? Are you warm or cool? Are your clothes rough or smooth, tight or loose? Or are you wearing clothes at all?

5. Use your sense of hearing.

Use your imagination to *hear the sounds.* Is there traffic noise, a radio, music, voices in another room, floors creaking, a fan whirring, birds chirping, water running, or wind blowing?

6. Use your sense of smell.

Use your imagination to *smell the air* around you. Can you smell something cooking, flowers, animals, rain on the breeze, cleaning products, pipe tobacco?

7. Use your sense of taste.

Use your imagination to taste any flavors that may accompany the smells: the mouth-watering taste of good food cooking; the dusty taste of an old attic; the sweet, metallic flavor of rain; or the mouth-watering aroma of coffee.

8. Reinvoke all your senses.

Take an extra few moments to use your imagination to notice the information reaching *all your senses*—sight, sound, touch, smell, and taste. Absorb the sensory feelings of your retreat and relax fully into the scene, so you can experience your retreat in as much sensory detail as possible before going on to the next step.

9. Modify your retreat to suit you.

Now that you have clearly established a private retreat, look around it and see how it suits you. If you can think of any improvements you'd like to make, change it to your liking. This is your personal haven, and it is important that it be as comfortable and pleasant for you as possible. Would you prefer more privacy? Less sound? More light? More green grass and trees? A cozier place to sit? Try various combinations out; you can change them back if you don't like them. Customize your retreat until you feel it is just the way you want it before going on to the next step.

10. Notice the difference in how you feel.

Notice how you feel at this point. You may be surprised to discover the difference in your scene from the first time you thought of the retreat. Perhaps as you developed the sensory images of your retreat, the sounds and sensations of your real world have receded. You may even feel more present in your mental retreat than in your actual surroundings. Do you feel more relaxed, calmer, and more secure? Have your thoughts slowed and become quieter? Do you feel emotions you have not felt for a while, such as nostalgia, peace, sadness, happiness, love for others or yourself? Relax a few moments and let these feelings sink in before moving to the next step, to get the full benefit of the calm, relaxing peace of your retreat.

11. Preserve your retreat for future use.

Observe the scene you created one more time to fix it in your memory. Review all the sights, sounds, and sensations until you could describe it clearly to someone else. Select a small object from your scene, one that you can hold, touch, and see. The object you choose should be in some way symbolic of, or remind you of, your retreat, because it will become your key to return— an object to focus on that will bring the whole scene back to your memory in full sensory detail. For example, a colored pebble from beside a brook, a key to the door of a room, a branch from a flowering bush, a doll or teddy bear from a bed, or anything else that immediately suggests the whole scene for you. Hold the object in your hand, concentrate on it, and observe every detail of it carefully enough so you will remember it later. When you have done this you have mentally preserved your retreat and completed the exercise. It is time to slowly transfer your attention back to your physical surroundings. Because you're coming out of a dream state, bring yourself back into the present by moving your fingers and toes a little and slowly and gently open up your eyes.

12. Repeat to become fluent.

The relaxation you experience during the exercise demonstrates the actual physical and mental difference that sensory imagery can make. As you become more proficient, the images you create will become clearer and more vivid, and the power of their effect will grow stronger. The more you repeat this exercise, the easier and faster it will be for you to invoke your senses in imaginary settings (the basis for many of the exercises that follow in this book). In addition, you have created a mental and emotional haven to which you can retreat any time you need a break from life's stress and strains. In future exercises, you will find that this is only the beginning of what you can use sensory imagery to accomplish.

This safe haven also will become a place you use when you have inner healing work to do. When you want to return, simply choose a quiet, uninterrupted time and place, relax, close your eyes, and visualize your key object. As you picture the object, the image of your retreat will probably arise automatically in your imagination. If not, repeat the steps from Step 2 or until you have re-created the scene completely. Each time you complete the exercise, refocus on your symbolic object, to increase its usefulness as a key that can invoke the scene immediately.

●

Other Uses for This Exercise: You can use this tool to give yourself the equivalent of physical experience, and teach yourself new behaviors and skills. For example, if you tend to crave foods that are not good for you (fats, sweets, or salt) and you want to learn to eat healthier foods, use the above steps to enter your retreat, and there imagine yourself eating healthier foods, such as vegetables and fresh fruits, and enjoying them. Use your sensory input to make the healthy foods look, smell, and taste wonderful. By repeatedly imagining the colors, tastes, textures, and smells of these healthy, delicious foods, you'll find that your tastes in actual eating gradually begin to change. You'll notice and be attracted to different items in the grocery store and on menus.

If you are anxious about an upcoming meeting with your boss, mentally rehearse the meeting by inviting him or her into your retreat first. In your sanctuary, you'll be the host or hostess, and you'll have the upper hand. Using all the sensory information you can: the smell of your boss's cologne, the color of his or her business suit, the sound of your voices. Once you've established the sensory data, picture the meeting going well. Imagine serving coffee or a snack, and present your program, or listen to your employer praise your work. Repeat several times, until you feel calm throughout the entire process. You'll find that when you get to the actual meeting, you'll feel less anxious.

If you believe you are clumsy because during childhood, everyone told you that you were, use the method in this exercise to picture yourself as a child, then see yourself gracefully running and dancing until you feel confident.

Once you become fluent in using the power of your senses as a language to communicate with and change your subconscious thought patterns, you can apply it to coping successfully with many different situations.

Imagery: the Power to Change Events

One of the most powerful ways to reach back into your childlike mind and change deeply buried dysfunctional and/or destructive thoughts and attitudes is through your imagination, using what many psychologists know as *imagery* and others call *visualization* or *mental rehearsal.* Everyone is familiar with imagery to some degree: It is our mental ability to visualize or picture scenes and events without being there—what most of us call having a daydream or fantasy, something you have been doing all your life.

Here, you are going to learn how to put it to use in a powerful form of deep, inner healing. Visualization, imagery, and fantasies are powerful in their effect because the mental impressions they create are similar to the magical language of childhood thought processes. "Imagery is a window on your inner world, a way of viewing your own ideas, feelings, interpretations," writes Dr. Rossman in *Healing Yourself,* "...a means of transformation and liberation...." Remember how real your sanctuary came to feel as you practiced the last exercise, and the profound physical and psychological changes it created? Experiences and activities imagined in the same amount of detail can feel as real. Properly used, imagery allows you to learn from visualizing as you would from the real experience. Coupled with the use of your senses, imagery duplicates actual, physical experience closely enough to make a similar impression on your subconscious mind. "Through imagery," writes Dr. Rossman, "you can stimulate changes in many body functions usually considered inaccessible to conscious influence. In the last 20 years, we have learned that imagery is the natural language of a major part of our nervous system."

Research shows that when we imagine an activity in complete sensory detail, nerves and muscles are electrically activated in similar way as when we actually perform the activity. That's why when you remember angry or happy events, you re-experience your original feelings; why remembering tastes (imagine biting into a lemon) can make your mouth water; or the memory of something that smelled rotten and disgusting can make you feel nauseous. Many competitive athletes now routinely use imagery to practice for events because of this measurable physical effect—visualizing themselves going through the motions until they feel they have the moves "down pat," which gives them an equivalent of actual physical practice without overtaxing their muscles and stamina.

Imagery has more than just a mental effect. Correctly used, imagery is a way to create imaginary experiences from which to learn, and a way to learn the skills of autonomy by taking risks in your imagination without real-life consequences. Later, you will use the power of imagery to heal old, painful childhood memories, to release yourself from the dependency and low self-esteem they created, and to rehearse autonomy-building experiences. These uses of imagery develop your creative ability to forecast positive options and future developments, a basic skill of autonomous thinking. In your imagination, you can create experiences that never occurred in real life. You can even return to an old scene and visualize it happening differently.

Although some elements of this exercise may seem childish or silly, remember that we are seeking to communicate with your childlike mind. Often, nonrational "magical" thoughts, processes, and rituals—because they are so similar to early magical thinking—will change mental patterns, and thereby heal lives where logic and conscious thought have failed.

In the previous exercise, you already used one form of imagery—visualizing a scene in order to practice using your senses to reach the subconscious. The exercise that follows will help you sharpen your skill at creating and changing vivid images, and will show you how effective imagery can be.

The focus here is on taking a scene that is problematic and creating a positive outcome. Once you have become familiar and comfortable with using imagery in this way, your childlike mind will have a useable pattern to follow in changing deeply buried beliefs. In later chapters, we'll use this tool to rerun early scenes of your childhood in which negative experiences formed the root cause of your addiction and dependency. Imagery can also be used to anticipate future events, and minimize risk-taking by rehearsing the events in advance.

Again, taping this exercise or asking a friend to read it will allow you to experience it without distraction.

Exercise For Magical Tool 2: Using Imagery to Create a Fantasy

1. Choose an event or story.

Select a story you know well, where you can be the main character who changes a sad ending and makes everything turn out okay. Use a story you have read or have been told by a friend, a fairy tale, a plot from a TV show or a movie, or a dramatic sports event. The story should have an unhappy ending that you can change. For example, you can be Donald Trump facing his creditors. By rerunning a campaign, you can turn your favorite political candidate from a loser to a winner. Or you can be the heartbroken heroine or hero in a soap opera and win back the lover who has just left you. Did your favorite sports team bungle last Saturday's game? Be the coach or the athlete who saves the day. You can even be the princess who saves the knight by outsmarting the evil wizard, or the understudy who takes over for the star who broke his leg. When you've chosen your story, go to the next step.

2. **Involve your senses.**

As you did in the first seven steps of the previous exercise, use your senses to build your retreat; relax, close your eyes, and develop all the sights, sounds, sensation, and people in the scene of your story until it is as real and vivid as possible. Again, once it is established using all five senses, imagine yourself in the scene as the main character of the story. Be sure and picture yourself dressed for the part. Take as much time as you need to develop the scene and the characters around you as fully as you can. Then, go on to the next step.

3. **Make silly changes for practice.**

Once your scene is fully established, change the people and events several times to practice using this tool, and to experience how easy it is to change a mental scene. Be silly, have fun, and let yourself enjoy using your imagination. Redecorate the room, or change what the people are wearing. Stand people on their heads. Change maple trees to palm trees, turn everyone blue, shrink buildings into little toys, or turn the clouds green. Make at least three changes in the scene, and then change everything back to the way it was before going on to the next step.

4. **Change the events and make a happy ending.**

After you're comfortable using your imagination on these small changes, you are ready to move on to bigger things, such as creating a new positive ending for your story. Imagine you are the main character, the hero or heroine, and figure out what you could do differently to change the ending to a happy one. Then visualize yourself acting out these changes until you have brought the scene to a successful conclusion. As coach, you can run different plays, or even pull in better players from other teams or from sports history, or even have Rambo play on your football team! As the soap opera character, you can have your lover storm out, then return, having realized there is no one else in the world but you. As Donald Trump, you can decide not to buy the Atlantic City casino, or conjure up a fantastically rich foreign investor who bails you out.

5. **Make changes until you are satisfied.**

   Stay with your story and change it any way you like until you feel are completely satisfied with it. The more changes you make, the more you learn about making choices, and the better you develop your capacity to create and forecast options and alternatives.

6. **End the scene.**

   When you feel finished, find a way to end the scene—you can have all your characters take a bow, and bring the curtain down, or allow your story to fade or float away—and slowly come back to your normal consciousness as you did at the end of the previous exercise.

7. **Repeat to become fluent.**

   Practice this exercise several times, using different stories and characters, until it becomes easy. As you practice, you will become familiar with the techniques of imagery and visualization, and stretch the power of your imagination.

●

Self-love: The Power to Heal Deep Hurts

Most dependent and addictive people are confused about love. Babies first learn about love not from what they feel *for* their parents, but from the feeling of warmth and tenderness they receive *from* them. If your parents were so emotionally damaged themselves that they could not give you enough of the qualities of healthy love—warmth, caring, support, or tenderness—you will have trouble understanding how love works as an adult.

It is hard to allow yourself to be the object of your own love and caring if you grow up in an atmosphere where self-love is often mistakenly thought to be selfish and uncaring. Because we carry toxic shame, it's hard for many of us to believe that we deserve love, even from ourselves. Many people don't even realize that such a thing as self-love is possible, much less a powerful healing tool.

Learning how to love yourself is the safest and most effective way to begin to learn how to love others. The following exercise uses platonic love or friendship to help you learn how to love yourself. The focus is on friendship because you probably (like most people) have healthier, clearer ideas of what it is to love a friend than to love a family member or a romantic partner. It also focuses on friendship to separate the concept of love from romance and sexuality. With practice, this exercise will teach you to treat yourself as well as you treat your friends, to become your own best friend, and will help establish a healthy pattern for all your future relationships.

In the following exercise you'll use self-awareness to learn how to become your own best friend. Once you have mastered it, you can create the inner security your inner child needs to complete your recovery, overcome dependency, and achieve autonomy.

You don't need to record these instructions, but you will need a pen or pencil and a notebook, journal, or writing paper.

Exercise For Magical Tool 3:
Using Self-love to Be Your Own Friend

1. What kind of friend are you?

In this step, you will become aware of your patterns of giving friendship, and begin to develop a description of them. Take a moment to consider what kind of a friend you are. How do you treat your friends? Consider especially those friends you met in your self-help group while in recovery, when you were beginning to develop somewhat healthier behavior patterns. Without being critical of yourself, seek to discover what you can about how you treat others. Chances are, you will find that you treat them with as much respect, kindness, and caring as you can manage. If a friend needs you, you probably try your best to do what you can to help. Most likely, you also care about whether your friends are happy, and you try not to hurt their feelings or upset them. You probably even attempt to be polite and considerate, when at all possible.

To get a detailed idea of what kind of friend you are, make a list of the ways you treat your friends. Title the list "My Friendship Style." You can use your answers to the following questions to get you started; others may occur to you as you go along: Are you a casual or more formal person? Are you affectionate, or would you prefer a good conversation to a hug? Do you like to send greeting cards and letters? Would you prefer to talk on the phone or meet for coffee? Do you like to be with several friends at once, or do you prefer one at a time? Try to be as specific as you can. ("I want them to be nice to me" is not as informative or useful in the later steps as "I want them to listen to me, and not criticize me.") Add as many other details as possible to your list about how you act with friends. This list will describe how you offer friendship.

2. How would you like your friends to treat you?

In this step, you will examine your patterns of receiving friendship, and further develop your description. Now consider how you would like your friends to relate to you. Don't be concerned if it differs from what you do for your friends, or even if it differs from what you do for yourself. Make another list called "How I Want My Friends to Treat Me," and again, try to be specific. Keeping your uncritical attitude, write down in as much detail as possible how you like to be treated, using the following questions to guide you. What would you like from your friends: To be listened to? To be invited to go places? To have quiet time together? To be hugged? Do you want them to respect you and keep their agreements? Do you like to get presents, cards, and letters, or are hugs and being listened to more important? This will tell you how you would like to receive friendship. When your list is long enough to satisfy you, go to the next step.

3. Compare your lists.

Review the first two lists, comparing the way you treat your friends, and the way you want your friends to treat you. Place the lists side by side, and see what is similar and what is different. Again, *do not criticize yourself.* Your objective here is to learn more about friendship and what it means to you. Think about what the items on your lists mean: How does the way you want to give friendship differ from the way you want to receive it? Many people give differently than they would like to receive: Some send lots of cards and letters, but prefer receiving phone calls. Some people would rather listen to others, and don't worry as much about being listened to. Knowing whether your giving and receiving are similar or different will help you understand how you want to love and be loved. At this point, you have already learned some things about your ideas of friendship, and you may find that you want to add to or change either one of your lists. For example, if receiving phone calls is on your second list, you may realize that you like to make them, too, so add it to your first list. Make as many changes as you like. When you feel your lists are ready, and you understand the similarities and differences, you are ready to go on to the next step.

4. **Develop your definition of friendship.**

Draw up a third list called "My Ideal Definition of Friendship." If your examination of the other lists tells you that you like having deep conversations with your friends, and you like them to call you on the phone, you know that conversation is an important sign of caring to you. If you like to play golf or tennis or football with friends, then sharing athletic activities, challenge, and competition are probably an important expression of caring for you. If you like hugging and lots of caring attention, then warmth and affection are important to you. Or you may like friendship to be more formal and have enough distance that you don't feel smothered. Make this list as complete a description of friendship in its ideal state as you can, based on what you've learned. Then, read it and ask yourself, "If my best friend treated me like this, would I feel cared about, loved, and happy?" If not, make the necessary adjustments. If your answer is yes, go on to the next step.

5. **Determine how you relate to yourself.**

Now, consider how you treat yourself. Do you treat yourself the way you would like to treat others? Do you treat yourself the way you would like your friends to treat you? How does it compare with your definition of friendship? Make a list called "How I Treat Myself," containing statements like "I'm critical of myself" or "I break agreements with myself," or "I like being alone with me."

6. **What kind of friend are you to yourself?**

   Now compare your definition of friendship with your list from Step 5. You may be dismayed to find out how very differently you treat yourself from your ideal of friendship. Perhaps you don't keep your promises to yourself as you would to a friend. You might not treat yourself with kindness and respect. Maybe you mentally nag or criticize yourself. Although you never break a date with a friend, you may keep putting off your time with yourself, or avoid caring for yourself with exercise or relaxation. The best test of your friendship with yourself is: If someone else treated you the way you treat yourself, would you want to be their friend?

7. **Becoming a friend to yourself.**

   Now that you have discovered the kind of friendship you enjoy, and compared that with how you treat yourself and how friends should treat one another, you have some more thinking to do and some choices to make. First, decide how you want to improve the way you treat yourself. Develop three simple ways you can be a better friend to yourself. One way to do this: If you have a friend you feel good about, treat yourself as you would treat the other person. Ask yourself, "How would I respond to Maggie in a similar situation?" Chances are, you will find you are usually kinder to her than to yourself. How would you speak to your friend if you thought she forgot to do something? Now, do you treat yourself more harshly? By comparing the way you treat yourself with the way you treat your friends, you will begin to develop clear guidelines about how to change the way you treat yourself. Write down your ideas about befriending yourself.

8. **To develop trust, be consistent.**

   Once you begin changing the way you treat yourself, you must be consistent in order to develop a habit of being nice to yourself.

Just as you learn to become friends with others because they consistently treat you well, you can build a friendship with yourself by consistently treating yourself as you would a friend. Once you develop your ideas about how to be a better friend to yourself, post your list of guidelines somewhere visible. Renew your plan for being a better friend to yourself every week for at least six weeks. At the end of that time, you'll find that treating yourself well becomes much easier and feels more comfortable.

●

Self-image: The Power to Be Your Own Hero

One of the first things children begin to learn is an inner self-image. Self-image is the way we imagine ourselves to be: attractive, unattractive, competent, incompetent, happy, scared, angry, friendly, lucky, unlucky, lovable, unlovable, and so on. Self-image is partly developed from abilities, experiences, role models, peer groups, and your own perceptions. However, the largest part of this image is developed and modeled from the attitudes and character that parents have toward their children.

When parents are healthy and functional, the self-image a child learns is primarily positive and promising. Children of functional families feel that they will be able to learn or do whatever they need to and they aspire to develop good qualities like kindness, honesty, and courage when they grow up. Visualizing themselves in this way encourages children to aim high in life and not to be afraid of challenge—because it is what they expect of the person they see themselves being.

When parents are negative and unsupportive, the self-image a child internalizes is also basically negative and dysfunctional. The child's resulting sense of self and of his or her own abilities and potential is negative and stunted. Such a child may feel stupid, like a loser, or may fear becoming a victim, addicted, or abusive, like his or her parents. Such a negative self-image limits your expectations of what you might be and can accomplish. If you lack trust in yourself you will learn to give up before you try or to adapt to negative expectations without really trying to succeed. You can replace these damaged, dysfunctional elements in your self-image with positive, healthy ones by using imagery to access your child mind and help it learn a new self-image. Picturing yourself positively can provide you with self-confidence, the motivation to venture forth into life, and enthusiasm for living. This, then, also provides powerful images that access your subconscious magical thinking and permit healing and change to take place. At the same time, you are acquiring magical tools that can be used to heal the dependency and the damaged self-esteem of your early childhood.

The following exercise will teach you how to use the power of self-image to visualize yourself as the heroine or hero of your own life. Creating this image will help generate courage and provide the model you need to confront the issues of your life more effectively.

One classic heroic image that is useful in this process is that of a warrior who challenges the old patterns and ventures forth into an unknown new way of living. Others include the magician, the saint, and the good witch. Danaan Parry, in an article about his work with war veterans who suffer from post-traumatic stress disorder, called "Peace and the Warrior," explains the power of the warrior image in aiding healthy growth: "Warriors...are...able to embrace the unknown...a pretty scary place. Not just the physical unknown...It's going into their own psyches....those dark places...the ability to face the darkness...puts them in the class of warrior." You can learn how it feels to have personal power by using imagery to visualize your own heroic image of a warrior. You can become a warrior, writes Lucia Cappacchione in *The Picture of Health,* "in the psychological sense of one who battles with his or her own destructive patterns and tendencies...to confront anything that blocks our creativity and growth...[with the] vigilance, discipline and courage...to face the negative habits that keep...us from fulfilling our goals and dreams."

Thinking of yourself as a warrior provides a new concept within which you can redefine "self" in your subconscious thinking. For example, Fred, who feels stupid and inept, can imagine he is James Bond to experience being a man of intelligence and action.

Psychologists know that "acting-as-if" something is true often makes it true. Here is an example:

Marguerite

Marguerite, a pretty 27-year-old client of mine whose mother had been afraid to go out in the evenings found herself similarly afraid, and unable to talk herself into going out socially. I suggested she pretend she was the glamorous, self-confident Loretta Young (a TV personality she admired as a child). She tried it the next time she wanted to go out, and it worked. By pretending to be Loretta Young, she felt much more enthusiastic about going out, and handled the situation the way her heroine would have. A few days later, she called me, laughing, "This is 'Loretta'—Dahling, it worked! I had a marvelous time." The "heroic" image of Loretta's behavior provided a role model for confidence in social situations, and replaced the timid, insecure model of Marguerite's mother. Having a more self-confident image to emulate was the tool that Marguerite used to overcome her subconscious fear. After a few times of pretending to be Loretta, Marguerite began to feel strong and capable enough to go out as herself.

●

In this exercise, you'll learn how to use the power of self-image to rehearse and develop desirable character traits you don't believe you now possess. For best results, read these instructions onto tape, or have a friend read them for you.

Exercise For Magical Tool 4:
Using Self-image to Create Your Inner Warrior

1. **Choose a model.**

   From current life, history, or fiction, find characters you admire. You can use friends or public figures; comic book or movie heroes or heroines; storybook characters; figures from Greek, Roman, Native American, Celtic, or other legends; mythic figures; saints; angels; or any other powerful model.

2. **Determine what you find heroic.**

   Study these role models and try to determine what it is about them that makes them heroic to you. Is it kindness in the face of difficulty? A high moral character? Serenity and inner peace? Physical courage? Special intelligence? Questing for knowledge? Helping the needy and/or helpless? Write a definition of heroism that incorporates that aspect of your heroines or heroes. For example, "My heroine is a strong, wise woman who uses her intelligence and awareness to take care of herself, who is caring and generous to those who need help, but who also knows how to say no so she does not get used or taken advantage of." Or "my hero is a clever man who outsmarts his enemies and uses his wits to succeed at his goals." Or, "my heroine is a warm, nurturing, motherly woman who is strong enough to protect herself and her children from violence and danger." Chances are your definition will also include independence, self-confidence, and self-reliance—in short, autonomy.

3. **Create an image of your warrior.**

   Using these qualities, put together a composite mental picture of your hero or heroine. Give your heroic figure a name you like, either a regular name you've always liked, such as Rebecca or Harrison, or a descriptive name, such as Power Woman or Loving Man. By doing this, you separate the heroic qualities from the original stories, and make them more flexible and useable in your own life. For example, if your heroic figure is James Bond, you can make a new character called Jason who has all Bond's intelligence and savoir faire, but omits the violence. Use sensory imagery to develop a mental picture of your heroine or hero, including clothing, facial features, body type, lifestyle, and living space. For example, Jason might be blonde where James Bond is dark, and Jason might have a different car, clothing, and apartment, all of which are more to your taste.

4. Imagine the effect of your heroic image on your daily life.

Once your mental picture of your heroic image is complete, picture your hero or heroine living *your* life. (Picturing someone else, who feels more powerful than you do, allows you to have more objectivity and a new perspective on how the challenges of your life might be met differently from your usual habits and ingrained ideas.) What would it be like if your heroine or hero showed up at your job disguised as you? How would she or he get along with your friends? What would change about the look of your home? How you wear your clothing? Begin by imagining your heroine or hero waking up in your bed, having her or him look around your room, and developing the sensory detail: sights, sounds, and sensations. Then, move your heroic image through an average day, seeing what he or she would eat, wear, say, and do, in each activity of your normal day. Notice how others react to and treat your heroine or hero. Make corrections as you like. If your heroine or hero is too overpowering, make her or him a little more gentle. If he or she is too perfect, give her or him a few minor flaws, less beauty, or allow her or him to make a few mistakes, to make your heroic figure more real. Play with the scenario until you are comfortable enough with your heroic image to imitate it.

5. Bring your heroic image into real life.

Now that you've imagined how this powerful, courageous heroic image would live your life, try adopting some of her or his attitudes and actions for yourself. Practice living your life as your ideal hero or heroine would live it. This may seem difficult or scary at first, but if you take it one small change at a time, you can improve the quality of your life and your interaction with people a lot. To begin, just try adopting some of your hero or heroine's attitudes. For example, you could be more cheerful in the morning, or more confident at work. Use your heroic image as a model. You can try out the changes before you actually act on them by using imagery. When the need to make decisions arises, imagine how your heroic image would handle it. When problems occur, what solutions would your warrior consider?

6. Develop a habit of consulting your heroic image.

Once you have developed a clear picture of your heroine or hero, you can also invoke him or her at any time as a counselor. If you're facing a problem or dilemma, you can meet your hero or heroine in the mental retreat you developed in the first exercise and talk about the problem before making a decision. You'll find the discussions give you a clearer picture of the problem, because you have to present it in such a way that someone else can understand. You will also be surprised at how effective your heroic image's advice will be. Often we possess insight in our subconscious, childlike mind that can only be reached through the aid of a magical tool, such as talking to an inner warrior, hero, or heroine.

●

Environment: The Power to Create Support

All children learn some of their behaviors from mimicking those around them. You can easily see this in young children as they play house, or play teacher, and imitate exactly the adults they know. If you grew up in a dysfunctional family, you learned many of your dependent, destructive attitudes from the role models your parents provided you.

You can put the power of role models to work to help you change many of your own behavior patterns and replace them with more healthy ways of relating with others by using Magical Tool 5: The Environment, to surround yourself with people who interact in healthy ways, providing positive role models for each other. A group of friends who provide healthy, functional models of your new beliefs and attitudes in action can be a powerful support in your attempt to develop positive new attitudes. Oncologist Bernie Siegel, who understands the emotional as well as medical aspects of healing, describes the value of group interaction in *Peace, Love and Healing*: "Through our pain we can find others to love and to heal. That's what groups like Alcoholics Anonymous and Exceptional Cancer Patients (ECaP) are all about. In fact, I always say that if you're fortunate enough to be an alcoholic or drug addict or have a disease, you can find a group to be part of, and you'll have lots of people to love and be loved by. We need to start groups for people who just enjoy living." The role models in support groups can be a very beneficial in your healing process. Conversely, dysfunctional role models can set you back or block your healing.

A network of friends is what Bernie Siegel might call a group "for people who just enjoy living." It consists of people who care about you and treat you with kindness and respect, and for whom you also care and treat with the same regard. The following exercise teaches a controlled, gradual process you can continue to build on and develop lifelong as you become increasingly autonomous. If you follow it, you will eventually build your own network of friends. In such an environment, you can experience the new attitudes with all your senses, seeing, hearing, feeling, smelling, and tasting the atmosphere as the people around you interact. You'll learn how to find, choose, and establish friends of your own who will provide you with the support and encouragement you need to grow and change. The sensory experiences of being surrounded by healthy, loving, supportive friends will also support your childlike mind in maintaining healthy, new ways of thinking.

In the following exercise, you'll learn how to build on your recovery group experience and learn to create your own individual group of mutually supportive role models. Once you have learned how to form a support group and keep it going, you can use it as a prototype for all your future networks. By following these steps, you can change dysfunctional, dependent patterns of relating to others, and begin to develop a healthy pattern in their place, which will help you move from dependency on the group toward more autonomous group activities.

Exercise for Magical Tool 5:
Using Environment to Build a Support Network

1. **Identify others who have similar goals.**

   Select a specific goal you want to implement that, ideally, would be easier if done as part of a support group, and find several people who share these goals. Perhaps your common interest is looking for new jobs, learning a foreign language, creative writing, or even an interest in a craft or hobby you can enjoy together. To find them, you can talk to friends and family, or put an announcement on a bulletin board at work or school, your recovery group, a community center, the Laundromat, or the market. You can even place a small ad in a local paper. (Note: If you are contacting strangers, don't give out your address. Instead, arrange to meet in a group in public places until you know each other a little more.) When you have found at least three or four others who express interest in your project, go on to the next step. You may not believe you can find anyone who is interested in your project at the start, but if you discuss your interest with others, you may be surprised to discover just how many are enthusiastic.

2. **Agree to meet.**

   Arrange a time and place to meet *specifically to support each other in achieving your goals.* At your first meeting, discuss your purpose as a group, and work up guidelines. What is the intention of the group, and what are the responsibilities of each member? Set an agenda, a schedule of what you want to accomplish, for the first few meetings. This agenda is just a beginning guideline; the group will alter it to suit its needs as the meetings go on. Determine how often and how long your meetings will be. Ask members of the group to make a commitment to meet together on a regular basis (for example, once a week for two months), any frequency, as long as they are regular and reinforce the habit of meeting as a group.

3. **Work together toward your goal.**

   If your group was formed as a support for those who want to find better jobs, you can get together to discuss career possibilities, read and share job-search articles and books, look for job openings for yourself and each other, work on resumes together, role-play job interviews, encourage each other when things are not going well, and celebrate when one of you is successful. If it was formed because you share an interest in needlework or art, you can share ideas, work together on your projects for a specified time each week, and pool resources to get supplies or special equipment (buy a quilting frame, hire a model). To work on developing your autonomy with this book (or to accomplish the goals of any other how-to book), you could read and discuss a chapter at each meeting, and do the exercises all together or in smaller groups.

4. **Live what you are attempting to learn.**

Use your meetings as an opportunity to practice what you are learning. If you are learning French together, make an agreement to speak only French for at least part of your group time. If you're learning to be more autonomous, agree to practice saying what you want and what you think in group, and to support each other in taking risks and solving problems by noticing and encouraging each other's moves toward independence. Whatever your goal, make it a practice in the group to be as positive and encouraging as possible.

5. **Discuss your satisfaction with the group.**

Set aside 10 minutes of each meeting to discuss how well your group is working, whether the meetings go the way each member wants them to, how well you're meeting your goals as a group, and what can be done to make it more effective. If you like, you can do a round: each person, in turn, says a sentence or two about how well the group is meeting their needs, and what, if anything, should be changed. To encourage attendance and build closeness, make feeling good and having fun together one of your group's priorities.

Strive for balance in giving and getting support. Are you as supportive to yourself as you are to the others? Remember, the most effective and lasting network is one where giving and receiving feels balanced for everyone involved. You can support and encourage each other's optimum learning (and autonomy) much better with praise, information, and caring. As an individual, observe each member's behavior and attitude. Seek to discover which make the best support team for you. If you see dysfunctional patterns developing, such as pressure to perform, criticism, and power struggles, speak up and work together to correct the problems.

6. **Develop problem-solving guidelines.**

One way to avoid recreating old, toxic family systems is to agree in advance on a method your group will use to handle problems when they arise. All group interaction eventually requires some problem-solving, so pick a system that all members of the group can agree feels productive to them. Work out a system by yourselves, or decide to solve any problems that arise by taking a vote, using *Robert's Rules of Order,* trying discussion and agreement, or any other method all members agree to abide by. Having this worked out in advance will prepare you for coping with problems as soon as they do arise, and provide a healthy model of interaction, so members can avoid slipping into old, unconscious, and dependent patterns. Follow your group agenda and use its problem-solving process as necessary, until the group completes its goal.

7. **Review your experiment as a group.**

When the group has achieved its goal (most of you have gotten new jobs, or learned belly dancing) or substantial success, have a meeting to review the whole experience together as a celebration of your accomplishments. Ask each person to say what he or she learned as you worked together, and have each person make suggestions about what, if anything, they would like to do differently next time. In what ways was it supportive? What were the problems? How did it feel to have a support network that met regularly? What would you do differently next time? Decide as a group if you would like to continue getting together. Seek to understand the pros and cons from everyone else's point of view. Because there are bound to be different opinions, some in exact opposition, about what went well and what didn't, you'll all have an excellent opportunity to learn about how differently people perceive group interaction, which will give you practice in dealing with diverse attitudes and solving interpersonal problems.

8. **Review the process for yourself.**

Before you continue or repeat your group experience and go on to build a network, be sure you understand the personal value of your experience. Review how well the group worked for you, and how you relate to the others. Can you say no if the group wants to do something you don't want to do? Who is easiest for you to talk to? Why? Who is the most difficult? Why? Did you enjoy working with these people? Who did you enjoy most? Why? Was there someone you had trouble with? Why? What kind of influence did interacting with the group have on your attitudes and ideas? If you were to do it again, what would you do differently? Would you like to maintain contact with anyone in the group? If so, let them know and ask them if they're interested in exploring a personal friendship.

9. **Repeat to develop a network.**

If the group decides to continue, the odds are good that you will begin to become an ongoing network. To do this, just begin at Step 2 again. If the group disbands, you can continue to enjoy any friendships you made on an individual basis, or you can build another group, repeating this exercise from Step 1. By doing this several times, you can eventually build a permanent support network with the people you enjoy most from these single-purpose groups.

●

Also, you can begin to look for new friends everywhere you go, using the relationship skills you learn here to help maintain those relationships and begin to build a more informal group of friends.

Repetition and Memorization: The Power to Effect Your Beliefs

One of the first ways children learn ideas and behaviors, is through practicing them repeatedly until they are locked in memory—whether they are learning about riding a bicycle, writing a first alphabet, or adopting negative beliefs like "I am stupid." Memorization and repetition influence the childlike, subconscious mind because they are based on our original way of learning. As children, we learn by repetition of ideas and activities, and by hearing what is said to us over and over. As an adult, if you repeat a statement or paragraph enough to memorize it, it becomes a part of your automatic thinking—the thoughts that arise, unbidden, into your awareness. Repetition continues to be a way we learn new skills and information as adults.

When you have repeated a thought enough for it to take effect on your child mind, it becomes part of your subconscious belief system. These repetitions suddenly produce a cumulative effect where new awareness and abilities seem to "click" in a particular moment, and at that point you make a quantum leap from being new and awkward at the task or idea to doing or believing it as though you had done it forever. That moment is visible to others as measurable change. This magical quantum leap of change takes a long-term commitment to practice, but is eventually achieved in a moment of realization.

As children, we often learned negative ideas about ourselves because our parents, peers, and others repeated them to us: "You're a bad boy," "Girls aren't smart," "You're a problem child," "You'll never get what you want," "Life is miserable." Reinforced by repetition, these negative ideas become part of a litany of programmed instructions that repeat in your subconscious child mind, and later affect your attitudes and behaviors as an adult.

You can use the same process by which you learned the negative beliefs to replace them with healthier, more positive beliefs. As simplistic as it may seem, repeating a positive phrase over and over until it lodges deep in your child mind and takes effect can counteract this subconscious negative programming. Although the effectiveness of repetition as an aid to learning has probably long been known to you, you may never before have realized that it might be applied to changing your own inner programming. You can confront your internal negative thinking by using affirmations, prayers, poetry, proverbs, wise sayings, quotations from literature, and other positive statements, and making them a part of your mind through repetition and memorization. You may find, as you begin to repeat a positive statement, that the old programming in your subconscious child mind reacts quickly and your first impulse is to argue with the positive statement. If your statement is "I am lovable," as you begin to repeat it, your inner child mind may react with internal comments like, "Oh yeah? Then why did Harry leave?" These arguments are an indication that the statement is beginning to have an effect, because it's reaching deeply enough to raise an argument. Just keep repeating your positive statement, and you'll find that the negative arguments subside after a while.

With this exercise, you can change negative thoughts such as, "I'm not lucky, nothing good ever happens to me" or "No one will ever love me" to positive, self-supporting statements. This is a simple way to use the power of repetition, which is one of the earliest ways we learn—by doing or hearing something over and over, until it becomes automatic. You have already used the power of repetition in all the previous exercises, and you will become more capable and confident of your ability each time you repeat an exercise. Here you will learn a method of verbal repetition you can use to counteract and change deeply buried negative attitudes you learned in childhood.

Exercise for Magical Tool 6:
Using Repetition and Memorization to Plant New Seeds of Consciousness

1. Choose a positive statement.

Choose a one-sentence statement, preferably just a few words, that would help you to feel better about yourself or your life. Select a quote that feels positive, encouraging, and supportive to you. Simple lines like, "I am okay today" or "I am smart and capable" or "Today is my lucky day" are sufficient. Or find a positive quotation from poetry or literature, a quote from the *Daily Word* or other meditation guide, a biblical quote (for example, from the 23rd Psalm), a song lyric, or a quote from philosophical writings. Other good sources are books such as Shakti Gawain's *Creative Visualization* or Sondra Ray's *I Deserve Love*.

2. Copy your statement.

Copy the statement you have selected several times onto file cards or pieces of paper. You can make these decorative or simple, but try to make them easy to read.

3. Post your statement.

Place these copies of your positive idea where you will be sure to see them: at your desk at work, in your wallet, on the refrigerator door, over your kitchen sink, on your bathroom mirror, beside your bed, on the dashboard of your car, in your gym or school locker. By doing this, you will be reminded often of this positive thought.

4. Repeat your statement.

Each time you see your positive thought, read it to yourself to become familiar with it, and memorize it. The more you repeat this statement, the more effect it will have on your childlike, subconscious mind. If it's a longer quote consisting of several sentences, read the whole thing over each time. Then, focus on one sentence per day until that phrase is memorized. You can make it a point to commit it to memory immediately if you wish, but it's not essential. Simply repeating it by reading it daily will do the trick after a while. (Note: Repeating the statement may create some internal agitation. Your old, negative thinking may become very clear to you. This is actually good; it means the positive message is getting in. Just keep repeating your statement, and allow the negative thoughts or feelings to pass.)

5. Change your statement when it is memorized.

Once memorized, this new positive statement will become part of your natural attitude and thinking process. After a while, you will find that your statement begins to repeat itself, like a chant, in your mind whenever you're bored, tired, or overloaded. You will begin to make all your decisions from the basis of this new attitude, rather than your old, negative thoughts. Shortly after you notice this, you will also notice that things you do are beginning to change "all by themselves." This is repetition and memorization at work.

You now have six powerful tools with which you can gain access to your own subconscious thinking, reeducate your childlike magical thinking, and heal old toxic shame. The magical tools of the senses, imagery, self-love, self-image, environment, and repetition and memorization are the keys to your subconscious. By practicing these tools until they are familiar and easy to use, and by using them in the exercises of this book, you can create a model of autonomy and health for yourself that transcends your toxic past. Mastery of the magical tools gives you the power to face your inner fears, establish contact with your inner self, and develop autonomy.

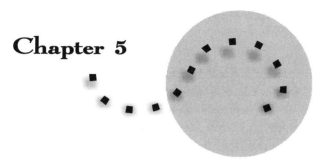

Chapter 5

Completing Recovery: Facing Self

As Freud discovered, and as Jung, Rank, and later Rollo May elaborated and refined, when the conscious and the subconscious become acquainted with each other, a new persona is born. A whole, awake, compassionate person steps forward from the one who was previously fractured, incomplete, and at war within himself or herself. Those early analysts observed, as do therapists in general, a sudden burst of enthusiasm for living in such cases, a quickening of the senses, an acceptance of the self as it is and the world as it is.

—Peter London

Once you have learned how to use the tools that speak directly to your subconscious child mind, you are ready to complete the process of recovery through facing and changing your deepest self. As you replace the attitudes of dependency—mindlessness, helplessness, and hopelessness—you can move on to achieve autonomy through learning the skills of risk-taking, problem-solving, and handling failure and disappointment.

Replacing dependency and achieving autonomy happen simultaneously. You don't really *unlearn* old habits, ideas, or ways of performing tasks.

Instead, you *replace* them with new knowledge that corrects or takes the place of the old—like learning new computer skills, better dance moves, or a more efficient way to do your job. You may remember an old idea or behavior for a long time, though most likely you will eventually forget it from disuse. You just don't act on it or think much about it because now it seems irrelevant, inconvenient, and wrong .

Completing recovery involves laying the foundations of autonomy, which simultaneously replace and heal the last vestiges of dependency.

Correcting old behavior is very much like re-teaching a child: If 4-year-old Sally is severely punished for spilling her milk, she feels flawed—she believes she was "bad" to spill the milk (actually normal behavior for a child her age), and she is also frightened and pained by the punishment. If this happens often enough to Sally, she will begin to change: She may become distrustful of herself, her environment, and the people around her. She will become afraid to try anything she is not certain she can do perfectly, to avoid punishment. She will probably learn to look to others anxiously for constant approval and reassurance that they are not going to punish her.

To correct this problem, help Sally overcome her fear, and return to her normal, self-confident state, a more competent adult would have to intervene, teach Sally what to do about spilled milk: Get a sponge and clean up; get another glass of milk; fill it less full; and hold it more carefully when she drinks. In addition, to lessen her fear, Sally would need to be reassured that she would not be punished in the future, that the best way for her to learn is to correct her mistakes. In this way, Sally's emotional hurt would be healed, and she would learn how to behave differently in the future. Sally will soon forget the spilled milk, although she will probably remember how to handle milk properly. If this benevolent teaching process is followed in every area of Sally's life, her fearfulness will eventually fade, and she will once again be a happy and confident little girl.

But if no corrective action is taken, even years later as an adult, Sally's experience will be active in her subconscious childlike mind, undermining her self-esteem and hampering her risk-taking, even though she spilled the milk and learned to think of herself as "bad" years ago. As an adult, she must correct the learning that occurred in childhood before she will be free of the dependency created there.

Being aware of your subconscious child mind and how magical thinking works gives you the ability to face yourself in new and powerful ways. For the first time, you can confront the hidden motivations and conflicts recovery programs don't cover. In this chapter, you will learn how to use the magical tools you developed in the previous chapter to simultaneously resolve and correct the childhood emotions at the root of your dependency, and build a new foundation of attitudes and behaviors upon which autonomy can grow. In addition, you will learn how to create the inner safety your child self needs to let go of old, hurtful experiences and forgive yourself and others.

Awareness, learning, and forgiveness are adult, corrective versions of the three skills that build autonomy: risk-taking, problem-solving, and coping with failure and disappointment. Replacing your dependency with autonomy requires understanding the negative experience and learning of childhood, focusing on helping your child self begin to accept and develop healthier attitudes and behaviors, and doing so with a supportive, caring attitude. Now that you have the tools for replacing dependent attitudes with the skills necessary for autonomous living, your old, addictive behavior might seem easily conquered. But often it isn't.

The Internal War:
Resistance Against Autonomy

As you apply the tools of autonomy to complete the work of recovery, you may find yourself encountering inner fighting and resistance, as your deepest self attempts to defend what seems safe and familiar (dependency). If, in your childhood, the adults around you viewed your childish attempts at independence as rebellious or dangerous, they taught you that dependency was safer than autonomy. Without support, many of your childhood attempts at risk-taking failed, which confirmed the adult's fears and your own.

You may feel your resistance as emotional symptoms—such as fear, panic, shame, hysteria—and even physical ones—such as headache, nausea, or sleeplessness. Change naturally creates some resistance, because it requires extra thought and work. For example, we all groan at the thought of moving house, even if we're excited about the new home, because we know we'll have to pack, move, and then get used to a new place. Change involves taking risks—it presents us with a lot of new situations for which we will have to find new solutions (such as how to get to work from a new home). Emotional change is risk-taking, too. No matter how difficult your old, dependent behavior is, it is familiar to you, and you know how it feels. At the mention of change, your child self, who like any little one is easily frightened and hurt, and who feels helpless and hopeless because he or she tried many times and has had many failures, will balk, stall, and go into hiding. No matter how enthusiastic you are about completing recovery and gaining autonomous control over your own life, you will still encounter some internal resistance to the necessary changes.

Although most formerly addictive people discover that they have a lot of resistance to overcome on the path to self-awareness, if they persevere, they find that there are many rewards for overcoming that resistance. It truly takes the self-image of a warrior, at times, to continue the hero's journey toward healing.

Your Internal War

Because of the difference between your subconscious, childlike thought patterns (also called our *intuitive, feeling aspect* or *our right-brain thinking*) and your rational, adult, reasoning thought patterns (also known as your *thinking aspect* or *left-brain thinking*) you may feel that there are two (or more) "voices" in your mind—each with a different attitude and opinion. As the child of dysfunctional parents, your subconscious (and still dependent) side—which is still locked in addictive thought patterns—is often in conflict with your rational adult side—which knows it is in your best interest to learn.

When you begin to work to actually change your inner child's thinking, this struggle can escalate, and you may find yourself caught in an internal "war" between these parts of your inner self.

Being at war within yourself may sound absurd, but it is common and psychologists are very familiar with the phenomenon. M. Scott Peck, author of *The Road Less Traveled,* describes how common this resistance is: "It may sound strange to laymen, but psychotherapists are familiar with the fact that people are routinely terrified by mental health. A major part of the task of psychotherapy is not only to bring patients to the experience of mental health but also, through a mixture of consolation, reassurance and sternness, to prevent them from running away from that experience once they have arrived at it." Signs of this internal struggle or warfare are:

- Feeling obsessive, compulsive, or addictive.
- Procrastinating.
- Fighting and arguing with others.
- Depression.
- Dissatisfaction.
- Irritability.
- Exhaustion.
- Anxiety.
- Tension.

Depression and exhaustion are very common symptoms of this internal struggle. It is as depressing and exhausting to fight with yourself as it is to constantly bicker and argue with someone else. The arguing, turmoil, and destructive negative interchanges of an internal war damage your sense of a healthy, unified, whole self and absorb almost all your energy.

This inner warfare also produces a constant noise in one's mind, as the voices of these two sides of your mind become locked in never-ending argument, which makes clear thinking almost impossible. As long as the war continues, you will continue to use poor judgment in the important decisions of your life, because a substantial part of your thinking ability is hampered by the war. Just imagine trying to think in a room where two people are arguing about everything, most of the time! When you can't think clearly, you are not aware of the information you are receiving that could tell you who is trustworthy and who is unreliable; you are not able to evaluate all the options available to you and make clear decisions; and you cannot sort out the difference between realistic options and options that are too pessimistic or too optimistic to serve as the basis of a good decision. In addition, the exhaustion resulting from constant turmoil causes you to "forget" or feel unable to think clearly about your circumstances and your actions, which leads you to be dependent on others to do your thinking for you.

This internal war is not winnable, because both sides feel equally right, and equally powerful. Even if one side *could* win, *you'd* lose, because either your childlike feeling, creative, expressive, and intuitive (subconscious) side would be defeated, or your logical, thinking, result-oriented, adult (rational) side would. Either way, you'd be operating at half power, unable to think clearly, or unable to feel feelings—which is what happens to many people. Just as in wars in the external world, both sides inevitably pay a heavy price.

Judy

Judy, 55 and attractive, was battered by her husband for more than 20 years. Her children were also battered. She tells why she remained in the marriage after being close to death from battering several times. "I couldn't think. Every time I tried to decide what to do, my mind would jump around from 'This is awful—I have to get myself and the kids out of here' to 'How would I live without him earning the money?' to 'This is what I deserve anyway.' I could never think clearly enough to figure out what to do. After a while, I would get tired of trying to think about it, and not do anything."

●

When you learn how to get both sides to negotiate and work together, then everyone wins—you create a problem-solving team that is both intuitive and rational, creative and practical. Only when your internal war is settled, and the two sides form a working partnership, do you attain the capacity to use the full power of your thinking ability.

Overcoming Resistance

Your resistance can be overcome, because it's only a result of your old, magical thinking. To overcome your resistance, start by taking small steps. When feelings of embarrassment, unworthiness, shame, or fear arise, just slow down, and remind yourself that your resistance is built into your subconscious, dependent thought. Pause whenever you feel resistant, to give yourself a chance to relax. Don't push yourself, or criticize yourself, but use your magic tool of self-love to reassure and encourage yourself past the problem.

Discussing issues with yourself, asking yourself questions, and comforting yourself are hard concepts for a dependent, childlike mind to understand, because being dependent means being focused on *others,* not on yourself. Even once you understand how to confront your inner feelings, you may resist at first, because you feel confused, ashamed, or embarrassed. The old, ingrained subconscious beliefs that your feelings are frightening, and that you're unworthy of attention are fighting with your new, rational, adult knowledge that *you* are important to you.

Most people with addictive and dependency problems encounter this resistance when they attempt to change their behavior, as the following story illustrates:

Barbara

Barbara is 38, intelligent, educated, attractive, and frustrated. She sits in my office, saying, "Why can't I do what I know I need to do? I know when I'm doing something self-destructive, like overeating, and I know when I'm *not* doing something good for me, like looking for a better job—but I just can't seem to make myself do what's right."

I suggest, "Barbara, have you asked yourself what the problem is?"

Barbara: "I don't know. I get confused when I think about it."

Me: "Will you try something right now? Will you ask Barbara inside you what's going on?"

Barbara: "You mean, talk to myself?"

Me: "That's right, go to the source of the confusion and ask."

Barbara: "Oh, I couldn't do that—that's crazy."

Barbara's embarrassment, confusion, and objections are all versions of resistance, which takes understanding, patience, and effort to overcome. After some work on her inner confusion and the belief that she didn't deserve the attention she was asked to give herself, Barbara does get into the dialogue, using *Barbara 1* and *Barbara 2* as names for the two voices at war inside her. (The following dialogue actually took about 20 minutes, and is condensed here to save space.)

Barbara 1: "Why won't you do what's good for you? Why do you eat the wrong foods? Why don't you exercise like you should?"

Barbara 2: "Why should I? It's no fun, you make me eat weird food and do boring exercises and you'll just make me do more crummy stuff after I do that."

Barbara 1: "Wow! I didn't know you were so angry at me about it. I'm only wanting you to do what's good for you. I know the food is weird, but that's how diet food is. And exercise is boring."

Barbara 2: "Well, Susie is thin, and she eats regular food, and I'd rather walk or dance than go to a smelly, boring old gym."

Barbara 1: "I guess you're right. I haven't been thinking much about this. I think we can find a way to eat regular food that's more fun. I guess we don't have to diet like my mother did. Nowadays, there's non-fat frozen yogurt, and we can eat fresh salads, fruits, and vegetables. I guess if I feel like munching while watching TV, I could make plain popcorn, and eat fresh fruit, graham crackers, or carrot sticks. Do you think we could do that?"

Barbara 2: "Yeah, that doesn't sound too bad—as long as we can have a special treat sometimes."

Barbara 1: "Now, what about exercise? What can we do if we don't go to the gym?"

Barbara 2: "Some of those dance exercise classes are okay, and I like the Jacuzzi at the gym, but I hate the machines. I want to go for a walk, or roller skating with friends, or take some dance classes."

Barbara 1: "Gee, that not only sounds like it might work, but like it might be fun for a long time."

Barbara 2: "Okay, let's do it, but let's make it be about fun more than about losing weight. I don't care about what I weigh, I care about feeling good. And don't get crabby with me. I won't do even the fun things if you yell at me."

Barbara 1: "Okay, you're right, I do get crabby at you, and that's not fair. How about if we make a deal? You help me figure out how to make being healthier fun, and I'll be more encouraging and praise you more often."

Barbara 2: "Okay, you've got a deal. I'll let you know if you get crabby."

●

Like Barbara, you may have old, toxic, childhood beliefs that you're not worthy of attention, that confronting your inner turmoil is confusing, and that your feelings don't count, which makes it impossible for you to think clearly enough to see the inner struggles that hamper you. Like Barbara, you may have been taught that talking to yourself is crazy.

You can overcome this resistance by doing internal dialogue exercises like those that follow in this and later chapters. Try "Finding Your Trouble Spot" (page 162) to begin. Once you negotiate an internal truce, you can become a new kind of person, within whom both the intuitive, feeling part and the rational, acting part work together for the common good, without a "good guy" or "bad guy," or winner and loser, but seeking to solve problems so that both sides are satisfied. Negotiation, communication, and partnership become an integral part of your relationship with yourself, producing a sense of wholeness and power that give you the confidence to take risks and to be autonomous.

Awareness, Learning, and Forgiveness

To complete recovery and build the self-confident base you need to learn autonomous thinking and behavior, you must master three essential elements: Awareness, learning, and forgiveness.

All internal change requires these three elements. When you are proficient at all three, you'll find that making permanent changes in your old dependent attitudes, learning to take care of yourself in an unpredictable world, and freeing yourself from the tyranny of your past behavior is not only possible, but also very rewarding. By making the changes, you can discover true inner peace (freedom from your internal war and turmoil), satisfaction, and a sense of competent teamwork with yourself.

To find out what you need to change, you must be aware of your internal turmoil, confusion, and dependent thinking. Next, you'll learn how your inner struggle operates and what triggers it, and what you need to do to make the changes you believe are necessary. Finally, forgiveness will ensure that you can let go of the pain, suffering and struggle your addictive and dependent behavior (and the out-of-control behavior of others) has caused you.

Awareness

Change begins with awareness, because you cannot effectively change something you do not know about. Until you become fully aware of your subconscious inner beliefs and the patterns that keep you dependent, you cannot bring them out of the past and into the present, where you can work to correct them.

At first this awareness may be difficult, because if your childhood was painful, you probably spent years trying not to be aware of how you felt and what you wanted. If your every effort to experiment as a child ended in pain or humiliation, it became painful to be aware of your desire to learn new things, to have new experiences, and to take risks. Potential risks were everywhere: In being aware of your thinking, you risked thinking independently; in being aware of your feelings, you risked feeling stifled, outraged, and explosive; and in being aware of thinking and feeling, you risked having to take action. Eventually, to avoid risk, you stopped being aware of anything, and began to focus instead on others who became your central focus in life.

When you avoid awareness and risk, you don't get a chance to develop positive skills:

- You don't learn to evaluate negative clues from yourself, your environment, and others that would help you anticipate and avoid problems.

- You miss promising opportunities because you can't evaluate positive clues from the same sources.

- You don't master clear, logical thinking and problem-solving.

- You miss learning relationship skills, such as anticipating problems that could develop, analyzing what causes them, and solving them before they become entrenched.

- You avoid making choices and decisions because they seem impossible, when you aren't aware of all the options available to you.

- You aren't objectively aware enough to be able to evaluate others for reliability, safety, and emotional stability.

Awareness of self is a normal, natural attribute of a healthy personality. As children, we go through a time of fascination with ourselves, including our fingers, toes, and body functions, and eventually our thought and feeling processes. If we are allowed to grow in a supportive environment, we gradually develop awareness of the world outside ourselves—others and ourselves as separate from our sensations and feelings. To a young child, the idea of self is fascinating—a child is eager to learn what feelings mean and how they are similar and different from those of other people. In a healthy environment, this natural self-awareness would be encouraged, and lead to curiosity, risk-taking, and eventually, autonomy. But in the dysfunctional family, it is stifled through criticism, ridicule, and shaming.

When responsible adults are unable to manage or express their own feelings, children learn to be suspicious and ashamed of their feelings, reactions, and impulses (the basic elements that define self). If, as a child, you expressed strong emotion, your parents may have felt helpless and frightened. They viewed your childish feelings as evidence that they were not parenting correctly. To a child, a parent's negative reaction to feelings would mean that those feelings are bad. Therefore, you would block them out, turn off your awareness, and treat feelings as something to be avoided and afraid of. As you grow up, this childhood habit of avoiding feelings is so strong that you accept it as truth, and believe that awareness of your feelings is terrifying and dangerous. This fear forms the basis of your reluctance to become self-aware. It becomes what psychologists call *resistance.*

This damage is particularly acute when it comes to emotion. To think clearly or function in life, you have to face emotions that seem terrifying, and so you avoid them. Most clients in therapy encounter these fears as they begin to look at their mental process. John, an M.D. who had never in his 45 years been aware of what he was feeling, began to sweat and tremble when he did the "Trouble Spot" exercise. Judy, the battered wife quoted earlier, cried from fear for several consequential days before she was able to begin facing her inner feelings. Both John and Judy, as they eventually became self-aware, found that their fear of feeling was far worse than any of the actual repressed emotions.

When you are unaware of your own emotions, you become dependent on others to tell you how you feel, or on substances and behaviors to keep your own feelings submerged, as your internal stress and the pressure from repressed feelings grows constantly stronger. Most people from dysfunctional families have had their feelings squelched as children by the following statements:

- Don't cry, I can't stand it when you cry.

- Shut up, or I'll give you something to cry about.

- Don't you get angry at me, young man (lady), I'm still the parent in this house.

- Don't tell your father (mother) it will just upset him (her).

- Don't get so upset over nothing.

- Don't raise your voice in this house.

- Don't get too excited—you'll just be disappointed.

- If you get too happy, something bad will happen.

The result of all this denial and fear of emotions is that we become *emotion-phobic:* deeply afraid of our own feelings, for the reasons mentioned, and even of others' feelings, for fear they will tempt our own tightly held feelings to burst forth. Even if you have been unaware of your emotions until now, they still exist. The evidence that you are feeling them, and that they are acting in your life, is your addictive and dependent behavior, the internal stress and tension you probably feel, the mental turmoil of your inner war, and probably occasional uncontrollable outbursts of rage, hysteria, or ongoing depression. Being unaware of your feelings can cause you to be destructive and out of control; and the pain of suppressing them is a major reason for depression and addictive behavior.

Fear of Self-Awareness

Clients commonly give many reasons for not allowing themselves to feel their feelings. No matter how rational or sensible these reasons sound, each one represents the fear of self-awareness. The good news is that fears and concerns about feelings are groundless. Handled appropriately, your feelings, when you become aware of them, not only won't hurt you, but can also help you heal old problems. Such negative beliefs as: "If I start to cry, I won't be able to stop" or "My grief is so powerful, it will hurt me" or "My anger is too scary" or "Feelings are too painful" or even "If I get too happy, something bad will happen," are just evidence of fear. Here are answers to common myths about feelings:

You will be able to stop crying. The worst that can happen is that you'll cry yourself to sleep, perhaps for several days in a row. By allowing this to be okay and crying all the old tears that were held in, you can eliminate depression, making it easier to think clearly, heal old pain and hurt, and achieve a sense of inner peace. Research shows that crying reduces stress and boosts the immune system. Once you have cried out all the old backlog of inner tears, you will find that you react more appropriately to sad and tender situations, and you are effectively able to respond to others who are sad.

Acknowledging your grief and disappointment when you suffer loss will not damage you. Grieving a lost opportunity or allowing yourself to feel disappointed at a failure allows you to acknowledge the loss and move on. Without expression, your grief and disappointment can keep you stuck and unable to let go. Faced and accepted, it can become an opportunity to change direction, and give yourself a new opportunity.

You won't become more impulsive or violent if you express your anger. Expressing old, repressed anger and learning to manage it in effective ways has helped many people change from unemployable to successful, move from isolation to warm, loving friendships; and lose mysterious and debilitating aches and pains. Releasing blocked feelings also brings anger at small irritations down to more appropriate levels, because such small annoyances no longer become the excuse to vent old, forbidden rage.

Expressing feelings reduces pain, it does not increase it. Because repressed feelings are so painful, you are far more likely to be pushed into old, addictive behavior if you *don't* express your feelings. If you learn to release them appropriately, you'll remove a lot of the internal pressure that causes you to seek relief in old, addictive behaviors.

Feeling positive feelings will not get you in trouble or get you hurt. Love doesn't get you into emotional trouble, dependency (based on old, toxic shame) does. Excitement is not dangerous, it is motivating. Feeling positive feelings makes life feel worth living, because it's more fun. Remember, feeling your feelings is not the same as *doing* anything. You can still choose your actions wisely, even when you're happy, excited, or in love.

Awareness as Risk-Taking

If you were taught to deny and repress your feelings, internal awareness becomes a form of risk-taking. If you grew up in a dysfunctional family, becoming fully aware of yourself and your feelings will feel risky for two reasons:

First, as a child in an unpredictable, toxic environment, you learned (like young Sally) to focus all your attention on pleasing and placating the adults around you. Surviving within an over-critical or over-protective family requires that you be anxious and vigilant, constantly looking to others for approval and reassurance that you're doing okay. You learn to ignore and suppress awareness of your own needs, feelings, and wants, because they are viewed as disruptive by parents, teachers, and others. In dysfunctional families, caring about yourself is believed to be "selfish" and cold, and people who are selfish are believed to be unworthy of love.

Second, the internal pain of toxic shame makes self-awareness seem frightening because children who have internalized shame are convinced they're going to do badly at whatever they do, including handling their feelings. In addition, your toxic shame created a backlog of stored up "unacceptable" feelings—rage, grief, despair, and terror—which have never been acknowledged or expressed. These repressed feelings and the shame connected with them are painful, and avoiding them is often the driving force behind the need to escape self through addictive or dependent behavior. Because these feelings were held in and not properly expressed, managed, or faced in childhood, later on they seem painful, overwhelming, and unmanageable.

Not knowing how to manage feelings safely and appropriately keeps you in helpless bondage. Until you face your inner pain, the best you can do is to remain in recovery, because your inner pain is too great for you to leave the safety of a recovery group. To move beyond recovery means making a heroic journey to self-awareness. This journey is heroic because as you begin to challenge your old, dysfunctional beliefs about your feelings and desires, you will probably encounter all the pent-up and suppressed emotion. Your embarrassment, procrastination, reluctance, and fear can become intense. Facing your inner feelings means heroically encountering and overcoming your resistance.

The exercises that follow will help you discover and develop self-awareness of your internal voices, and of the struggle inside. Each exercise uses a combination of magical tools—particularly, the senses, imagery, self-love, and repetition—to help you end this conflict by directly influencing your subconscious, simultaneously healing old, dependency-creating beliefs; and building new, autonomous skills. The "Finding Your Trouble Spot" exercise will help you zero in on your inner conflict and establish clear communication with your subconscious, child self. When you experience tension, depression, or other signs of the inner war "The Negotiating Table" uses visualization to help you turn your internal war into an inner partnership.

When you begin to become aware of yourself and your feelings, the first thing you may discover is your own inner tension, anxiety, or troubled feelings. The energy it takes to stifle or repress your feelings, and the resulting stress, are usually experienced in your body as muscle tension. This tension can be felt as a headache; a stiff neck or tight upper shoulders; lower back pain; an upset or queasy stomach; a clenched jaw; or tenseness, tightness, or pain anywhere in your body. The majority of people in recovery whom I've worked with have had a sensitive or tense area in the stomach or chest, along the breastbone.

Barbara, the young woman we met earlier who was reluctant to talk to herself, came into a session and said, "I feel anxious and uptight, and I don't know what's wrong." I asked her to focus on her body, and tell me where the tension seemed to be. After a few minutes' thought, she said, "My chest feels tight."

Barbara then did the "Finding Your Trouble Spot" exercise that follows to find out what was creating the tension. The first thing Barbara's spot "said" was, "I'm angry at Fred because he reminds me of Dad." Barbara's response was," Oh, Fred's not so bad. Maybe he didn't mean it," which discounted her inner feelings, as expressed by the spot. Barbara was amazed to realize that she had this argument with herself about Fred frequently, but she had never noticed before. She realized, as she became more aware of her feelings, that she was feeling frustrated in her present relationship because she wasn't being treated well. As she allowed her inner feelings to come out, she was able to trace them all the way back to her childhood. She remembered early experiences with her father, from whom she couldn't get time or attention or any expression of caring, no matter how hard she tried.

Once these feelings were out in the open, and Barbara knew what they were, we were able to clear up her early childhood issues through adult/child dialogue, and as Barbara began to feel less upset, more in control of her own life and better about herself, she began to see her current relationship more clearly. She realized that Fred was mildly neglectful, and somewhat thoughtless, but not as cold and cut off as her father, and she began to learn how to ask Fred for what she wanted. Not only did her relationship with Fred improve, but Barbara's relationships with other men, like her boss and her brother, also got better. Through focusing on her "spot," Barbara learned what caused her tension, dealt with the feelings, and learned some new skills. She began to think more clearly and to satisfy her own needs independently. Her relationships became more satisfying, because she felt less needy and dependent on men. The men she dated could relax and enjoy her company without feeling pressured, so they viewed Barbara as more attractive.

Doing this focusing exercise accomplished three things for her:

- It helped her to separate Fred's mildly forgetful behavior from the serious neglect of her father.

- She saw the importance of working on her issues with her father.

- It helped her clear up her confusion about whom she could trust and with whom she could be friends.

●

Like Barbara, you can become aware of the specific causes of your inner conflicts by tuning in on your trouble spot. When you're no longer struggling to repress feelings, but learning to cooperate with them, your "spot" will become a source of valuable subconscious information. It is a place where you collect the tension from unexpressed feelings, and will soon become a portal for easy access to them. If getting your trouble spot to open up and let your feelings out goes slowly at first, remember that you may have repressed those feelings a long time; be patient with yourself and the process. Before long, you will understand many things about yourself that are new to you, such as why you overreact to certain people and situations, or what is causing your depression. You can use this "Trouble Spot" exercise any time you feel body tension or internal stress, to locate the causes of the conflict, resolve them, and ease your stress or tension.

Note: For most people, the problems that this exercise will bring to your attention will be quite easy to handle by following the instructions. If, as you try contacting your trouble spot, you become concerned about what you're finding— such as a history of incest and child abuse, or overwhelming rage—talking with a counselor may be helpful. Remember that even with tough inner problems, the worst part is already in your past. There is nothing inside you now that can harm you, if you learn how to cope with it in a healthy, functional fashion. "Finding Your Trouble Spot," once mastered, becomes a way to create quick and easy communication with your subconscious—which means you will be instantly aware of your intuitive feelings about people, events, and situations. It will help you learn to evaluate new situations before you enter them, because your intuitive feelings will be available to you. Your judgment about people, situations, and events will become more accurate, and your emotional risk-taking more successful.

Have a friend read this to you, or record it on tape, so you can do the exercise uninterrupted.

Exercise:
Finding Your Trouble Spot

1. Find your tension spot.

Sit in a comfortable place, where you won't be interrupted. Close your eyes, and take a few moments to focus on your body. Mentally go over your body to find the place where tension or upset seem to be most strongly concentrated. You may discover tension or tightness in your chest, stomach area, head, neck, shoulders, arms, legs, or back. When you have found this spot, put your awareness on that part of your body. If you discover several tension spots, choose the one that feels most intense and begin there. If you discover none, try focusing on your chest area. Focus your attention there and use your power of imagery (Magical Tool #2) to visualize soothing, relaxing warmth beginning to surround and penetrate it and ease the discomfort. After a few moments you will probably feel the tension let go a little. To help yourself feel the warmth better, gently place your hand there.

2. **Be a good listener.**

   Place your attention where your hand is, and say gently to your spot (to increase the chances that your emotional attitude is helpful and caring): "I'm ready to hear what you have to tell me." Listen for a while to what your subconscious, inner self has to say, holding your attention on the spot. Your spot will communicate to you in words, images, or physical feelings, whichever comes naturally to your subconscious. For the purpose of this exercise, whatever method your spot uses to communicate we will call *talking*. Do not censor or reject any thought that comes into your mind now. Just pay gentle attention, and allow whatever images, ideas, physical sensations, or thoughts you may have surface into your awareness.

3. **Allow plenty of time.**

   Allow enough time (about 10 minutes in the beginning) for the images and/or sensations to emerge from within you. If you get restless, remember that it's just resistance, caused by your old self trying to avoid change and convince you that your feelings don't count. Remind yourself that you care about you, and be patient with the delay. When you begin to get images and sensations, don't argue or agree with them, just let them come. If your inner voice says, "I don't know" or "I don't want to tell," say something like, "I'd really like to hear, I know I've neglected you, but now I realize you're there, and I'd like to hear what you have to say." Or just sit quietly and patiently for a while, to demonstrate that you are willing to listen. Accept whatever information you get, however meaningless or silly it seems. You probably have an old childhood belief that your feelings aren't important, so counteract that by assuming that what you get is meaningful, even if you don't understand it.

   You may get physical sensations: warmth, cold, your pulse beating, a tightening, or a relaxing. You may receive symbolic images:

a wall, a knot, fire, whimsical creatures, dragons, teddy bears, little boys or girls, religious or fictional characters, or wise teachers. You may remember early scenes from your own history. You may just "hear" your inner self talk in a matter-of-fact way. Whatever you receive, maintain a "this is interesting—tell me more" attitude, as you would if a friend were telling you his or her inner secrets. This friendly interest will help the information flow faster, and prevent the blockage caused by criticism or argument.

You are creating a new awareness of your self and your feelings as you do this, so allow yourself enough time for this new attitude and method, and be as open to learning new things from your inner self as you can.

4. **Begin a mutual dialogue.**

After receiving whatever your trouble spot has to share with you, you can begin a dialogue. Offer suggestions ("I will ask Fred to listen more carefully, if you like") and ask questions ("Why do you think Fred is scary?") but don't argue right or wrong. Your objective is to become aware of and understand the issue that your inner self is trying to bring to your attention. If your spot says something you don't like such as "You like Fred more than you like me," you may have trouble listening to it. Try not to attack or discount what you learn ("How could you say that?"), but strive for understanding ("Why do you think I love him more?"). Your magical mind, the subconscious, speaks in its own language, the language of your dreams and intuition. It may take you awhile to understand it. Keep in mind that this is a part of you "talking," and you already know everything you need to understand what your spot is saying.

Learning to listen to your inner voice is much like prayer or meditation—an open mind, focused here on your tension spot, instead of on your Higher Power. Once you become proficient at this, you can bring up specific issues to discuss with this inner voice, and give and receive counsel as you would with a friend. This makes you less dependent on others to help you "talk things out" when you're contemplating a new move, or beginning a new relationship, or meeting new friends.

Knowing your inner self's intuitive and emotional reactions to new people and situations gives you needed information to help you take risks more successfully, and cope with the feelings that come up when you do, which are skills useful in attaining autonomy.

5. **Repeat for proficiency.**

   The more you make contact with your trouble spot and practice listening and dialog, the easier this exercise will get. After repeating it four or five times, you will find that you can "check in" with your spot more easily. After 20 times, you'll be able to do it on a moment's notice, without closing your eyes, and even while you're doing other things. This ability to be quickly aware of your inner prompting gives you the autonomous power to take care of your own feelings on the spot.

●

Once you have established this internal communication, you have a technique that can be expanded to end your internal war. In addition to communicating with one inner voice, as in the previous exercise, you may find sometimes there seem to be two or three voices taking different positions on the issue. The following exercise will teach you how to handle them all at once.

At one time, hearing voices in your head was thought to mean you were crazy, but several decades ago, many modes of psychotherapy—including psychosynthesis, transactional analysis, Gestalt and Jungian therapy—recognized that inner voices are normal, and that everyone has some kind of mental commentary going on most of the time. These therapies began to focus on these "arguing aspects" of the mind and developed methods for dialogue. Using these methods, it is possible to create inner harmony by resolving the conflicting ideas into cooperating parts of a mental team, as you will see here. This exercise is a simplified and modernized version of such techniques and is especially effective in resolving your internal war, which is indicated by the signs mention earlier, such as tension, depression, and irritability.

Exercise:
The Negotiating Table

1. Listen for the voices.

Whenever you feel anxious or tempted to return to addictive behavior, or you're having trouble making a decision, assume there *is* an inner struggle between various parts of yourself—an internal war. Arrange some uninterrupted time to sit quietly, close your eyes to help you concentrate, and listen to your inner self. Chances are, you will become aware of several voices that are arguing in your mind. At first, you may hear nothing, or a confusing babble of several inner voices talking at once, but if you allow some time, and patiently wait, as you did with your trouble spot, what they say will begin to come clear. You may have inner voices saying: "I want to take the new job, I need a change."; or "I'm scared. Everything will be new and unpredictable."; or "I better stay where I am. If I try it, I'll fail."; or "I'm too stupid to make this decision myself."

2. Name your voices.

To most people, these voices usually begin to feel as though they have personality characteristics or attitudes such as grown-up and child (grown-up: "You have to get a job."; child: "I don't want to."); dreamer and pragmatist (dreamer: "Wouldn't it be nice if we won the lotto and didn't have to work?"; pragmatist: "We'll never win, and we shouldn't waste the ticket money."); or male and female, procrastinator and nagger, or memories of the voices and attitudes of your actual parents. When you have distinguished two or more voices, give each one a name to help you keep them clear. The names can be people's names (Joe, Mary), or descriptive, like those above. One of my clients has two main arguing voices he calls the Rebel and the Visionary. Another woman has a whole crowd, with whimsical names such as: Hysterical Harriet, Angry Amy, Pleasing Pauline, Critical

Carl, Depressed Debra, and Rusty Resistance. Choose whatever names you like, or ask the voices if they can tell you their names. Having names will help you keep track of who's talking, and therefore give you more control over the "conference."

3. **Seat everyone at a table.**

Visualize the characters your voices represent seated at a conference table. Give each one a turn to talk, and listen to that point of view. Becoming aware of what issue your internal "voices" or "characters" are arguing about makes it possible for you to mediate, and come up with solutions that satisfy all parties.

4. **Take charge of the conference.**

In order to take charge of the confusion and end the internal war, you must be a moderator, and not get drawn into the argument. If bedlam breaks out and all your internal voices begin talking at once, call your imaginary meeting to order, just as a moderator does. Ask questions of each voice, just as you would at an actual meeting. Try to get them to make useful suggestions about how they could solve the problem at hand. Keep focused on your goal of getting your internal warring voices to cooperate with each other. Your attitude here, as moderator, should be much more active and directive than in the previous exercise.

5. **If you get confused, write it down.**

If you have too many voices arguing over a particular issue, keep them separate. If doing this strictly in your imagination feels difficult, try writing the different points of view on paper, where you can be aware of them in an orderly fashion. Make a column or a page for each voice, and briefly write that voice's opinion on the issue. After you get all the voices written down, go back into your conference, and again work toward a cooperative solution to the problem, using your written notes as reference. For example, you might write as follows:

Rebel: I won't work. You can't make me.

Dreamer: I know my prince will come and rescue me from drudgery.

Taskmaster: You have to look harder! You're not doing enough.

Pessimist: It's no use, I won't find a job anyway.

6. Be aware of should's.

While sorting out the struggle, look for *should, ought,* and *have-to* on one side, and *won't, can't,* and *you can't make me* on the other. They are the keys to your internal struggle, because these words polarize and antagonize a discussion. Direct the voices who are saying *should* to use *could* and to explain their reasons for wanting it that way. Direct the ones who are saying *won't* and *can't* to say what they want, and why. This will establish a more cooperative, less antagonistic feeling.

Make it clear, as moderator, that the committee's job is to reach a mutual agreement, not just to fight. Insist that each voice offer *solutions,* and don't allow them to just complain. In the previous examples, you could instruct the Rebel to say, "Instead of working, I want to play my music," and the Taskmaster to say, "We could find a job if we looked more."

7. Reach agreement.

Continue the session until you reach an acceptable agreement that feels like it satisfies everyone. If there are too many problems to be dealt with at one meeting, create an agenda (a list of topics for discussion), write it down so you won't forget, and have several sessions until you solve each item on the agenda. If your committee began working on a job issue, but then issues about money, the kind of work you do, car repairs, and your expensive shopping habit came up, you need to have a separate meeting for each issue, and stay focused on the job issue for now.

8. Repeat to build cooperation.

The first time you do this exercise, it may be chaotic. But by doing it several times, you will become more comfortable with your inner voices, know how to handle them better, and therefore be more in charge of your committee. Each time you repeat these steps, your inner voices will follow the negotiation routine more easily, until soon you'll find that your thinking is more organized. Even when you are considering several conflicting ideas, you will be able to negotiate internal problems very quickly. After repeated use, this exercise will virtually eliminate the internal noise and anxiety that inner conflict can create. With this constant din gone from you mind, you will be able to think much more clearly, weigh the pros and cons of various solutions, and make decisions a lot more easily.

●

As these exercises illustrate, attaining self-awareness doesn't have to be mysterious or difficult. Being aware of your thoughts and feelings brings inner problems out into the open, and helps you resolve inner conflicts, but awareness by itself is not enough. Without new information, you would lack anything but the old, ineffective solutions.

Learning

To move beyond awareness to change, you must learn new options. Learning changes people, because once you learn something new, your perception of yourself and of your environment is different. The difference can be profound, as when you first learn that you can stop drinking by following your recovery program, or subtle, as when you learn a new way to cook a meal. Learning the six magical tools in the last chapter and doing the exercises in this chapter have already changed you. You know how to use your senses, your mental power of imagery, and self-love to make changes within your mind. You are also beginning to understand the power of self-image, environment, and repetition, which means that you view the world about you and your own mind differently. You have more information about, more understanding of, and therefore more control over these aspects of your life. Awareness increases your motivation to learn, and through learning, you obtain new options and solutions to old problems.

Self-awareness is an emotional form of risk-taking, because you are risking learning new things about yourself. Learning is the equivalent of problem-solving, because in learning you develop new answers to new questions. If, as a child, your risk taking and self awareness were blocked just as you were attempting to develop autonomy, you never got the opportunity to learn problem-solving skills, especially in regard to your feelings. Solving problems in connection with your inner awareness and your feelings requires that you learn new attitudes, because the old attitudes that created the problems to begin with.

Counselors know that a large portion of helping people to heal their lives and develop autonomy is simply helping them *learn* practical techniques for living. For example, if you were prevented in childhood from taking risks and making new childhood friends, you will lack social skills.

Denton Roberts explains the importance of learning new options: "Psychotherapies tend to focus primarily on pathology, illness and the restoration of healthy functioning. Once we have corrected any historic mistakes we still need a method to assist us in maintaining health and staying on our side."

Learning new autonomous modes of behavior, thought, and action is essential if you want to maintain new attitudes, because the success you gain by using new skills reinforces your new beliefs. Like many addictive and dependent people, you may be convinced that you cannot learn, because your early experience discouraged risk-taking and problem-solving, encouraged dependency, and did not help you acquire learning skills. Learning new skills now will free you from depending on others to think for you.

No matter how incapable you believe you are, and no matter how automatic your behavior and feelings seem, you have *learned* everything you know. As an infant, you weren't habitually afraid, angry, discouraged, or hopeless. Whatever helplessness and dependency you had at that time was a *real* limitation of abilities, not a set of beliefs. As an adult, if you are hopeless, afraid, angry, discouraged, helpless, or dependent, all those attitudes were learned because of *environmental influences* (Magical Tool 4). If you understand that automatic behavior is learned, then you'll realize that you can learn new ways of thinking, new emotional tools, and create new patterns of behavior.

Simply by reading to this point in the book, and doing the exercises as they were presented, you have already learned a great deal. Learning involves risk-taking. Whether you realized it or not, when you opened the covers of this book you took a risk that you'd have a new experience that would change things about your life. Your old attitudes and beliefs are being challenged and changed by new information, the experience gained by doing the exercises, and the realizations you have had as a result of this experience. By now you have already learned to use your imagination to practice new skills, and may already be exploring some new hobby or skill you first tried out in your imagination. Or you may be using your private retreat from the very first exercise to relax you on a daily basis. Every exercise and paragraph in this book is a learning opportunity.

If you have ever held a job, driven a car, gone to school, played a sport or a game, or ever found your way to a new friend's home, you have proved yourself capable of learning. If you ever made a change from using a dial phone to a push-button phone, or used a computer, a video game, or a VCR, you are indeed capable of learning, and of changing long-standing behavior patterns.

Because you have conclusively proved that you can learn, and indeed have already learned a lot in this book, the question is not to teach you *how* to learn, but to help you discover how you *naturally* learn, what I call your *learning style*.

Learning How You Learn

Learning becomes easier and more effective when you become aware of *how* you learn. People receive information in different ways: We are auditory, visual, tactile, and imaginative in different proportions. That is, spoken words (hearing), pictures (sight), touching, and imagination are more or less important to you depending upon your learning style. Your learning style consists of two parts: *sensory preference* and *attitude.* Sensory preference is merely a description of which senses you naturally use more than others. Attitude is a more complex description of how your personality traits, learning history, and prejudices affect your approach to learning. Together, they create your learning style.

Sensory preference refers to the senses through which you learn most easily and with the deepest understanding. There are four main types: auditory, visual, tactile, and imaginative. Often, we use a combination of these.

Auditory: If in visualization exercises you are more likely to think in words than in pictures, and you are highly verbal, then you are probably an auditory learner, and you know you have learned a new idea when you can explain it clearly. It would be most effective for you to talk, hear, or read about new ideas, and lectures and audio tapes may be a good way for you to learn. You may enjoy listening to the radio. You'll probably use a phrase like, "I hear what you're saying" or "It sounds like..." to mean you understand someone.

Visual: If you tend to picture things rather than capture them in words, you are probably a visual learner, and know you've learned something only when you can visualize the steps or imagine yourself using it effectively. Visualization techniques, videos, watching someone else, or seeing diagrams and pictures are probably the most effective ways for you to learn. You may use visual phrases like, "I see" to mean that you understand, or "See that?" to mean, do you understand?

Tactile: If you lean toward the physical, like to touch things, and learn best by doing or tinkering with things, then you are a tactile learner, and you know you've learned something when you "feel" it more than see or hear it. "Walking through" a new skill or habit, acting it out physically, and "hands on" learning could work well for you. For you, "I feel it" or "I've got it" are ways to say that you understand.

Imaginative: If you are able to *see* in your mind's eye things you have never seen in reality, including the landscapes of fiction or fantasy books you read, you are an imaginative learner, and you can daydream vividly—to you, those fictional landscapes become *real*. Visualization and imagery are powerful techniques for you, and "I can picture it" or "I can imagine" are ways to say that you understand.

You may prefer more than one of these styles in different circumstances. No matter what kind of learning style suits you best, if you take advantage of your sensory preference, learning will be easier for you. You will not have to struggle against or translate the method you're learning from into your own preference before you can absorb the information.

172

Attitude is the other component of your learning style. Your attitude is heavily influenced by your early environment and experience, and refers to the pre-set ideas you have before you encounter new information. Some people are enthusiastic about learning, because their experiences in the past were rewarding; some people are more cautious, and still others are resistant, because to them, in the past, learning meant failure (as from a bad school experience). Your learning attitude also includes preferences (you like to learn quickly or slowly, alone or with others) and prejudices (such as "Formal education is more prestigious than learning a trade"). These attitude differences can be incorporated into your learning just like your sensory preferences are. For example, if you like to learn with others and you think "book learning" is best, you can form a book study group. If you like to learn alone, and you value "practical" learning (skills you use), you'll enjoy "how-to" video or audio tapes or books.

Some learning attitudes can create problems. If you come from a family where education is positively emphasized, then your attitude toward organized learning will be positive. You'll be proud of formal, organized learning (schools, courses), anticipate it with excitement, and seek it out. However, your family's emphasis may cause you to miss out on the other kinds of learning, such as sports, current events, mechanics, and arts.

In contrast, if you come from a family where education is put down, or where you're told you're stupid, then book learning is negatively emphasized, and you'll fear it. But you may be much better and more relaxed at other things, such as auto mechanics or dance, and may not realize that they count as kinds of learning, too.

Your attitude determines whether you approach learning new things with enthusiasm, procrastination, composure, or anxiety. Positive attitudes toward particular kinds of learning make those kinds easier: "I love school, and it's fun and easy" or "I love to work with my hands." Negative attitudes toward particular kinds make them more difficult: "I hate getting my hands dirty," "I'm afraid of hurting myself," "I'm no good at anything mechanical," or "I hate books, I was never good at school."

Although it's impossible to avoid learning, if your family made you feel too pressured about school grades or that learning was for sissies, you may try to avoid that rigid definition of what learning is. If you attempt to avoid learning, you may wind up learning many new things the hard way, through being forced by negative experiences. That is, if you don't learn about your car, because it's "dirty work," you may be cheated by mechanics, or find yourself stranded on the highway until you learn enough to know the danger signs of a failing car. If this is the case, you can use the tools you are learning in this book to change attitudes that are getting in your way. Or if you don't learn to cook because "it's for sissies," you may find yourself spending a lot on food, eating unhealthy fast food, or missing foods you really like.

The two quizzes that follow are intended to help you discover your learning style—the first one deals with sensory preference, the second with attitude. After taking them, you'll combine them both to form a complete learning profile, which you then can use to make all future learning easier.

These questions are designed to help you understand your learning process. There are no right or wrong answers. You may have more than one choice per question, or a more appropriate, original answer. Remember, nobody is 100-percent auditory, visual, tactile, or imaginative. All of us learn in all four ways, but we have preferences.

Quiz:
Your Sensory Preference

To discover your sensory preference for learning, take a sheet of paper, and make four headings across the top. Down the left hand margin, write the numbers 1 through 5 like this:

Auditory (A) Visual (V)   Tactile (T)   Imaginative (I)

1.

2.

3.

4.

5.

For each answer to the following questions, place a check mark in the proper category. When you're done, tally up your totals. The category with the most checkmarks will indicate the sensory mode through which you learn most easily. The columns with the highest number of check marks indicate your natural learning modes (the ones through which you learn readily), and those with the least checks indicate modes that are less easy for you to use.

By using these results, you can see what your most natural, habitual, and effective learning styles are, and you can tailor your own learning to take the best advantage of them.

1. **When you think, do you:**
   - ☐ Hear words in your head? (A)
   - ☐ Draw or visualize pictures? (V)
   - ☐ Write things down or touch related objects? (T)
   - ☐ Daydream fantasies and visions? (I)

2. **When you were (are) in school, did you learn better from teachers who:**
   - ☐ Explained in interesting ways? (A)
   - ☐ Wrote or drew diagrams on the board or showed movies and pictures? (V)
   - ☐ Gave you hands-on experiments or homework? (T)
   - ☐ Asked you to imagine or guess what the situation was like? (I)

3. **When you want to learn something new (for example, operating a computer, cooking a new cuisine, playing a new game or sport) do you:**
   - ☐ Take a class or read a book? (A)
   - ☐ Watch someone else do it first? (V)
   - ☐ Experiment and learn as you go? (T)
   - ☐ Dream about knowing how to do it? (I)

4. You feel confident you've learned something when you:

- ☐ Can explain it to someone. (A)

- ☐ Can see the results or watch yourself do well in a mirror or video. (V)

- ☐ Do it with your own hands, or when it feels easy. (T)

- ☐ Can see yourself doing it well in your imagination. (I)

5. You do a lot of:

- ☐ Reading and writing. (A)

- ☐ Watching TV, movies, and people. (V)

- ☐ Physical activity. (T)

- ☐ Daydreaming and fantasizing. (I)

●

Discovering your attitude is more ambiguous than finding your sensory preference and does not lend itself to columns of check marks. On a piece of paper, write the heading: "How I Learn." As you read each of the following questions, write your answers out completely as statements. This will give you a more useful, narrative description of your attitude. For example, if your answer to the first question is "Oh, boy!", write it out as: "I approach learning something new with an 'Oh, boy!' reaction." When you've written out all the questions and answers, you'll have a paragraph that describes your learning style. At the end of the quiz there are a sample paragraph and instructions for how to use it.

Quiz:
Your Learning Attitude

1. **You approach learning something new with which of these reactions:**
   - ☐ Oh, boy!
   - ☐ Oh, dear!
   - ☐ Uh oh!
   - ☐ So what?

2. **In reading this book, do you feel:**
   - ☐ Skepticism?
   - ☐ Acceptance?
   - ☐ Resistance?
   - ☐ Enthusiasm?

3. **When you first encountered this exercise, did you:**
   - ☐ Read the whole thing through without doing it (so you knew what you were getting into)?
   - ☐ Plunge right in and do it as you went along?
   - ☐ Share it with a friend to get support in doing it?
   - ☐ Ask others what they thought of it?

4. **Do you feel learning is:**
   - ☐ Work?
   - ☐ Helpful?
   - ☐ Fun?
   - ☐ Like solving a puzzle?

5. **Do you often:**
   - ☐ Get lost in learning something new and forget what time it is?
   - ☐ Learn something new just to make life more fun and interesting?
   - ☐ Have to have a logical reason to learn something?
   - ☐ Resist or procrastinate about learning?

6. **In learning new things, are you most motivated to:**
   - ☐ Prove you can do it?
   - ☐ Compete with someone?
   - ☐ Beat your own previous effort?
   - ☐ Try something new?

7. **When you face a brand-new task, do you prefer:**
   - ☐ To be left alone until you figure it out?
   - ☐ To be led, step-by-step through it until you know it?
   - ☐ Watch someone else do it first?
   - ☐ A combination of guidance and hands-on practice?

8. **The things that seem most valuable to you are:**
   - ☐ Things people learn from books, teachers, and/or school.
   - ☐ Things people learn that are called trades, such as mechanics or carpentry.
   - ☐ Office and business skills.
   - ☐ Practical skills, such as driving or cooking.
   - ☐ Fun skills, such as sports, the arts, or hobbies.

9. **Rank the options in question 8 in order of their value or importance to you as follows:**

   ☐ Most important

   ☐ Very important

   ☐ Somewhat important

   ☐ Not very important

   ☐ Least important

10. **Now rank the same five options in question 8 in order of their usefulness as follows:**

    ☐ Most useful

    ☐ Very useful

    ☐ Somewhat useful

    ☐ Not very useful

    ☐ Least useful

11. **You know that you have learned enough for a session when you:**

    ☐ Feel overwhelmed and confused by new information.

    ☐ Have mastered the new task or skill.

    ☐ Are told it's time to take a break.

    ☐ Get bored and restless.

    ☐ Feel ——————————————— (fill in the blank).

●

At the end of your paragraph, add the information from the first quiz. (This will give you your learning profile.) Here's an example of Mary's result from the two tests:

How I Learn

I approach learning something new with an "oh, dear" re-action. Even in reading this book I feel resistance. When I first encountered this exercise, I read the whole thing through without doing it, because I was nervous about it. I feel learning is helpful, but I often resist or procrastinate about learning. In learning new things, I am most motivated to beat my own previous effort. When I face a brand-new task, I prefer to be led step-by-step through it until I know it. The most valuable things to me are things people learn from teachers and school. The most important things to me are things people learn in school, the least important are things people learn that are called trades. The most useful thing is business skills and practical skills, such as cooking and driving. The least useful are trades. I know when I have learned enough when I feel overwhelmed and confused by new information. My learning style is mostly visual, some-what imaginative, and not auditory at all.

●

Now begin to use your sensory preference. If you found out that you're auditory, read your paragraph out loud to yourself, or discuss it with a friend. If you are visual or imaginative, read your paragraph onto a tape, and as it plays back, close your eyes and make a mental picture of your profile. If you're tactile, act it out. If you have more than one strong preference, use more than one method.

When you've got a clear idea of what parts of your learning attitude are positive and helpful, incorporate them into your learning in the rest of this book. You can use your magical tools and other exercises to change the attitudes that you find problematic, or that might get in your way.

If you find that your learning style is making you avoid learning, or making learning hard for you, you can change it by using the "Finding

Your Trouble Spot" or "Negotiating Table" exercises to reach you sub-conscious child mind and counteract the dysfunctional information that's in there with new, more correct ideas. When you do this, make learning, and specifically how it feels, the topic of discussion. Your objective is to correct old, negative attitudes that your childhood experience taught you (such as, "I'm stupid, and learning is hard for me") with new, positive information (such as, "I have been learning all my life, without knowing it; I am smart, and I can learn whatever I want to know"). Using Magical Tool 6: Repetition and Memorization is an excellent way to replace negative attitudes and beliefs about your learning abilities.

After reviewing her paragraph and picturing in her imagination how her learning style would look in action, Mary realized that she was visual, very tentative and hesitant in learning, would do best with a guide or teacher, and most respected institutional (school) learning, although she used practical things more. Thinking about this for a while, Mary decided that using a support group or learning with a friend (Magical Tool 4: Environment) or taking classes were the easiest ways for her to learn; that she should take the time to visualize the subject she was learning, watch someone else, or use pictures (such as videos or a picture cookbook) to make learning easier. She also decided to encourage herself more about being able to learn by using the exercises for Magic Tool 3: Self-Love, and Magic Tool 6: Repetition. She did this by having discussions with her "trouble spot" to change her attitudes and make learning less intimidating, and by repeating affirmations (such as, "learning is easy for me"). Because she's a visual learner, Mary cut out some magazine pictures that represented the things she wanted to learn, added encouraging captions to them, and hung them near her desk where she could see them.

Understanding your style of learning and becoming comfortable with it can renew your pleasure at seeing old things in new ways. Once you begin to replace your old skills of dependency with the creative skills of self-awareness (risk-taking) and learning (problem-solving), there is only one thing that can keep you tied to your past: the need for forgiveness—the way to correct the childhood circumstances that prevented you from learning how to cope with mistakes and failure.

Forgiveness

Now that you feel reassured about your ability to learn and know how to best apply your innate learning abilities, it's time to learn how to handle failures and mistakes. Learning to handle mistakes means learning to understand that mistakes are natural and normal, and even helpful (not disasters or signs that you are hopeless and stupid, as you came to believe in childhood), and discovering how to forgive yourself for making them.

Learning forgiveness begins with learning to forgive yourself for the damage you did to yourself and others with your old, destructive habits, and for allowing others (perhaps within your family or later adult relationships) to be abusive to you or take advantage of or undermine you in the past.

My definition of forgiveness is a bit different than you may have been taught. The dictionary defines *to forgive* as "to give up resentment of," which I have found is nearly impossible for people who grew up in problem families—often there are too many real injuries to forgive. It can also be unwise, because resentment functions like a reminder to yourself to "watch out—this hurt me before." Ignoring the past and forgiving others who may still be abusing you now ("He didn't mean to beat me up, he was just drunk") gets you hurt or mistreated over and over again. Dependency is often perpetuated by forgiving and forgetting that someone has hurt you, and not confronting the person or ending the relationship.

Forgiving yourself for past destructive behavior ("It wasn't my fault, I had a rough childhood," "I can't help it, my anger just takes over."), if not based on a real, inner change of attitudes, turns into excuses, indulgence, and self-pity. Forgiving yourself without learning from your destructive behavior, and without determining how to change, is aptly termed *denial* by recovery programs. If you don't recognize the consequences of your destructive behavior, and accept responsibility for it, you have no incentive to change.

Hanging on to resentment will not really protect you or allow you to let go of the past and move on in your life, either. As long as you hold onto the blame and resentment, you will feel like a helpless, hopeless, dependent victim of your past history. You do need to learn to forgive, but just giving up resentment is not sufficient. A new model of forgiveness is necessary.

As a person from a difficult background, and one who has been controlled by addictive and dependent attitudes and behaviors, there are a number of things you may need to forgive:

- You may need to forgive yourself for doing emotional, mental, or physical damage to others.

- You may need to forgive yourself for doing emotional, mental, or physical damage to yourself.

- You may need to forgive yourself for letting others damage you in those ways.

- You may need to forgive others (parents, children, spouses, friends) for hurting themselves in all the above ways.

- You may need to forgive others for doing emotional, mental, or physical damage to you.

Creating Safety

Safely and honestly forgiving all these past hurts is not accomplished by simply giving up resentment. First you must find a way to be safe from future damage and abuse. Once you have learned how to create safety that you can rely on, and you know how to protect yourself from further damage and to prevent yourself from causing damage, you are no longer threatened, and forgiving past destructive behavior (your own and others') becomes easy.

When your reasons for resentment, both against others and against yourself, are based on real damage, only the assurance that you can take care of yourself so that you won't be hurt or that you can be sure you won't get destructive makes true forgiveness possible.

Recognizing the consequences of your own destructive behavior and taking responsibility for it does not mean punishing yourself. It means becoming aware of the dependent ideas and feelings that are behind your behavior and learning how to change them. It is possible to love and approve of yourself now, yet be aware that you have allowed yourself to be damaged by yourself and others in painful and destructive ways. If you've caused yourself pain in the past by being involved with abusive people, you can learn to understand your inner reasons for feeling dependent on such uncaring people. By using your inner awareness exercises and your magical tools, you can change the beliefs that keep you helpless in such relationships.

It is not necessary to blame and punish yourself in order to remember the consequences of destructive behavior. Instead, you can use your inner awareness exercises and magical tools to find the deep inner feelings and beliefs underlying your behavior and make the necessary changes.

Although it is often not possible to stop others from being abusive or violent, you can take steps to see that their rage and destructive behavior does not threaten or damage you. Remembering who hurt you is not the same as condemning them. You don't have to condemn others as bad people to be wary of their out-of-control or problematic behavior. You can recognize that they are fallible human beings, too, and often more damaged by childhood experience than you were, and that until they repair their own damage, as you are repairing yours, you must keep a safe distance.

In fact, to an abuser, the possibility that they might lose a relationship, or that their destructive behavior causes you to keep a safe distance, is often the confrontation that will make him or her look at their own behavior.

The following exercise will help you to learn new ways to cope with situations where you were hurt by others, beginning in your childhood. Through the power of imagery (Magic Tool 2), you can learn to protect yourself from others by rehearsing and changing old painful scenes as many times as you need to make sure you know how to take care of yourself.

It is not easy to be sure that an old behavior problem (your own or someone else's) is gone forever. Even when you or the other person has done inner work to correct the problem, in a situation of enough stress, it may return. This exercise will help you learn how to take care of yourself in difficult and painful situations, and give you a chance to practice various solutions and responses until you find the ones that work, without risking any real-life consequences. Learning to care for yourself in very realistic terms begins with healing old, painful scenes from early childhood.

A big problem for many addictive and dependent people as they complete their recovery is the fear of recurring destructive behavior, on their own part or from others. With this exercise, you can rid yourself of that fear by assuming control of events in your subconscious past, and unlearning some of your old, dependent decisions about life and replacing them with new, more autonomous ideas. It is also a wonderful way to learn the skills of early risk-taking, problem-solving, and handling disappointment or failure. I believe "Time Travel" is the single most powerful exercise you can do to clear out old traumas, remove the roots of dependency, and build autonomous skills, including the ones that keep you safe from emotional, mental, or physical harm. The "Time Travel" exercise helps you develop the self-protection needed to achieve forgiveness and let go of damaging behavior, situations, and people.

After you have learned this exercise (and the ones that follow) with consistent use and practice, you will no longer need your resentment to protect you, because you have learned how to ensure your safety. You will be able to release and forgive old hurts, recognizing that the people who caused them (yourself included) didn't know any better ways of behaving at the time. As you learn how to stop dysfunctional adults in your past from hurting your child self, and to protect and care for yourself, you will also learn how to recognize when people in your life today are uncaring or out of control, and what to do about it.

In the form shown here, this exercise is most effective whenever a memory of emotional, physical, or psychological pain from your childhood is troubling you. But with minor changes, you can use it for other inner work, too. For example, if you're having a recurring dream that troubles you, you can use this exercise to replay the dream, and it won't bother you anymore. By using scenes from times other than your childhood (a quarrel with your current mate, or an encounter that you're afraid will happen with someone who's angry at you) you can use "Time Travel" to practice risk-taking (rehearse in advance social events where you'll meet new people, or talk to someone around whom you've been shy).

To allow yourself the full impact of the exercise, without interruption, read the following steps into a tape recorder and play them back.

Exercise:
Time Travel

1. Invoke a childhood scene.

To begin, sit quietly by yourself, and close your eyes. Visualize yourself as a small child (Magical Tool 2: Imagery) in a painful scene from your childhood. You will learn how to correct the scene, take care of yourself and then forgive whomever created the problem, and forgive yourself, for your own participation. Allow the troubling scene from your memory to appear around your child self. You may get a mental picture, or if not, just imagine the scene as you remember it. Remember to use Magical Tool 1: Your Senses, to establish your scene clearly. If, however, this is a scene of childhood abuse or incest, you may find it too painful or stressful to use all the senses, so allow yourself to keep your distance by just thinking of the scene, and not developing as much sensory information. If your scene is very painful or frightening, view the scene as objectively as you can, as though it is a story about someone else, or a movie.

2. Enter the scene as an adult.

Like a time traveler from the future, visualize yourself in the scene as the grown-up you are today. There will be two of you present, the small child you were, and your modern, adult self.

> When Tom, 29, a talented musician and owner of his own business, did "Time Travel," he went back to a birthday party he had attended at age 5. His parents had dropped him there and he had felt abandoned. The other children made fun of him, and he had been afraid at parties and gatherings ever since, convinced that he was socially inept, and no one at a party would like him. He visualized the scene of the party as vividly as he could, and then imagined his adult self sitting down by little Tommy.

3. **Take charge of the scene.**

   Now it's time to take charge of the scene—as you did in the Magical Tool 4 exercise (self-image)—and protect your child self. Do whatever is needed to stop the adults or other children from upsetting, hurting, or neglecting your child self. If the other children or adults are too badly behaved, you can make them leave if you want to—you have total power here, in your imagination. Use that power to make a safe environment and to provide protection for your child self. If you like, you can also surround your child self with loving people.

   > Tom helped young Tommy in two ways: First, he realized that Tommy was dressed much more formally than the other kids, so he helped him take off his tie and suit jacket, and roll up his sleeves. Second, Tommy was too shy to join the other kids, and the grown-ups there were too busy to notice, so Tom helped Tommy find a game to play. Soon other kids joined them.

4. **Take care of your child.**

   As the child in this scene, you may be frightened, angry, confused, feeling helpless, or overwhelmed with grief—the "adult you" can use Magical Tool 3: Self-Love, to be rational, effective, competent, and reassuring. You may encounter some resistance in the form of feeling incapable of taking care of your child self. But remember, you can do this over and over in your mind until you get it right. You can try to fix the situation in several different ways before you decide which is best.

   Visualize removing your child self from danger; comfort and reassure; correct any lies your child self was told (that he was stupid, or it was her fault) by telling your child the (positive) truth (he is intelligent, no child causes her own abuse); and take time to begin to establish a friendship with your child self. If you see that your child self needs some information or help, provide it. Promise that your child will never be left at the mercy of ignorant, malicious, incompetent, or uncomprehending people again.

When another child began teasing Tommy, Tom imagined intervening. He comforted Tommy, gently corrected the other child, and got the other child involved in the game. He told Tommy, "I love you. You're okay, that little boy is just teasing."

5. When your child self feels safe, discuss forgiveness.

When you have corrected the scene enough that your child is out of danger and feeling safe, talk with your child about what happened. Discuss what went wrong and who made mistakes, and decide how to avoid being the victim of those same mistakes again. Once you and your child both know he or she will not be hurt again (because you'll do what it takes to protect him or her), you'll find that your child will be ready to forgive the people who hurt him or her, and will understand that they just don't know how to behave. Help your child see that whatever happened was not his or her fault, and your child self doesn't have to make the same mistakes the others made, or repeat the mistakes he or she made.

> Tom and Tommy talked about the party, and decided that Tommy's parents should have gotten more information before the party about how Tommy should dress, and they should not have dropped him off, but stayed with him until they knew he would be okay. The grown-ups at the party should have watched what was happening with the children more, and Tommy himself could have been less afraid and not taken things so seriously when he was teased. Tom promised he would check out social situations in advance from now on, and not leave Tommy stranded among strangers without Tom there.

6. Take your child to a safe place.

Close the scene by visualizing your child self in a safe, secure place, completely out of danger. Reassure him or her that you'll be there when you're needed, and tell him or her how to get your attention when he or she feels in danger. This means that your adult, rational self will not leave your emotional, child self alone, dependent, and at the mercy of people who are hurtful. Do not leave the scene until your child self feels calm and secure.

> After their discussion about the party, Tom visualized taking Tommy back home, where Tommy felt safe, and tucked him in. He hugged Tommy, told him goodnight, and said Tommy could call him whenever he needed him for protection.

6. Repeat regularly.

After you have done "Time Travel" the first time, you can keep your promise to keep your child self safe (and build self-trust) by time traveling back to your child self as often as needed, until it becomes an unconscious habit (Magical Tool 6: Repetition). Once you've done this many times and become proficient, you will not need to close your eyes to be in instant contact with your child self; you will be able to imagine being with your child self at any time. Doing this exercise repeatedly, whenever old, painful memories arise, will eventually clear out your childhood traumas, and correct the damage done within your dysfunctional family, while helping you practice the autonomous skills needed to take care of yourself. You'll find that you instinctively know when someone or something is hurtful to you, and when you're being hurtful to others. You'll also know what to do to correct the situation, (don't be alone with violent or emotionally hurtful people, don't allow yourself to be in tempting situations, and so on) and you'll feel safe enough to forgive those who are confused and behave in hurtful ways, because their behavior will not be dangerous to you.

> With practice, and by going back to other scenes where Tommy was uncomfortable around people, and helping him cope, Tom found that he was much more comfortable in crowds and at parties. He had new ideas of what he needed to do to have a good time, and how to take care of himself if something began to go wrong. Tom found that he saw other people differently, too. He could keep his distance from people who didn't treat others well, and he

could easily recognize the people who were safe and healthy for him. Once little Tommy, his child self, knew when and how to join in appropriately, Tom could have fun, be playful, and feel more relaxed.

●

Once you have overcome your resistance and made the journey within, made contact with your inner self, and learned to be aware of your inner feelings and beliefs, you have begun to learn how to care for yourself effectively, and to release the hold that the past has on you. In short, you have completed recovery and entered autonomy.

The more adept you become at self-awareness, learning, and forgiveness, the more autonomous you can be. The hurts of the past can be healed, and the dependent beliefs you learned as a child no longer have the power to prevent you from feeling capable of taking care of yourself. With practice, you will master these new skills, and be able to apply them whenever needed. Your old hopelessness and helplessness will gradually fade away, and you will be able to live independently in the world, in charge of your own life.

Part Three

Achieving
Autonomy

Chapter 6

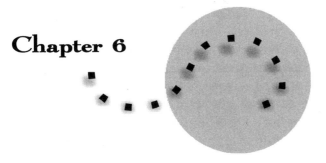

Autonomous Thinking: Weighing Choices in Everyday Life

Autonomy can be described as the power we possess, used or unused, to direct our energy to create our individual lives. The question of whether we will to take advantage of it, claim it as our own, is the most persistent and recurring issue we face. Claiming this power is both a difficult and rewarding task.

—Denton Roberts

Up to this point, you have been learning how to complete recovery by changing the old, negative, subconscious thought patterns, perceptions, and the internal dialog you learned in childhood. This in itself is a life-changing experience, because as your perceptions of yourself and your reactions to situations change and become more effective, your life automatically begins to feel freer, healthier, and more hopeful.

Now you can further develop your autonomous skills by shifting your focus from your internal world to the outer world. Now you will learn to apply your new skills and ways of thinking to helping you cope effectively with the problems and challenges of everyday life.

The Most Important Choice of Your Life

The biggest challenge of autonomy is giving up the dependent dream that someone else will take care of you or can make it better, and accepting responsibility for running or governing your own life. "Ever since we relied on our mothers to make a bruised knee better with a Band-Aid and a kiss," writes Harvard's Dr. Ellen Langer, in *Mindfulness,* "we have held on to the assumption that someone out there, somewhere, can make us better."

> Not accepting the responsibility to take care of ourselves is dependency. Accepting the responsibility, and taking care of our own lives, is autonomy.

Realistically, no one else can or will take proper care of you, because each person has all he or she can do to run his or her own life properly. We can give love and caring to one another, but it is impossible to effectively take over responsibility for someone else. No one else can make it better for you because another person cannot know your needs, wants, thoughts, and circumstances intimately enough to make effective choices for you.

You are responsible for your life already, whether you accept it or not, because even avoiding a decision is a decision. You alone will bear the consequences of making or not making this choice, as you bear the consequences of all your decisions. Every choice you make or avoid, and every action you take or postpone, produces some effect in your life.

Like it or not, you will experience the result of all your choices, decisions, and actions *even if you choose to remain dependent.* The key to successful, autonomous living is accepting the responsibility and learning how to make choices effectively, rather than relying on others or trying to avoid responsibility altogether and leaving your life open to chaos and turmoil.

When you rely blindly on others and are dependent on their reactions and decisions, you create codependent and destructive relationships with inappropriate partners. When you are dependent on someone else and you feel helpless and hopeless, you cannot choose an appropriate partner or say no to an inappropriate one. You quickly become too entrenched to firmly reject a partner's abusive or irresponsible behavior.

Deciding to make your own choices and take responsibility for them is critical, because before you can do anything, you first have to *choose* to do it. Choice and decision-making precede everything you do and every action you take, every course you set, every relationship and interaction. Before you can begin to take healthy, effective action, you need to learn to make effective choices.

After the initial decision to recover from addiction, this is the most vital decision of your life, the most important choice you will ever make or avoid, because in deciding whether or not to choose autonomy, you are also deciding whether or not your life will remain in chaos and pain or whether you will move on to achieve satisfaction and success. Relinquishing dependency and accepting responsibility for yourself and your life is a choice only you can make; no recovery program, therapist, workshop, exercise, or book—including this one—can make it for you.

It is a *vital* decision you must make for yourself, by yourself. And it is *not* a decision you can put off if you wish to move beyond the dysfunctional dependency on recovery groups that keeps you in the bondage of recovery. It is a decision you must make if you want to be in charge of your own tomorrows.

There is no doubt that making your own choices and taking responsibility for your life requires dedication, commitment, and effort, but when you consider the alternatives, it is easy to see that autonomy is by far the least painful choice. If you choose to remain in dependency, you can be certain of these consequences:

- You will repeatedly find yourself at the mercy of people who attempt to control you, smother you, or abuse you.

- You will often feel out of control, and in danger of relapse.

- You will have difficulty making decisions, and be troubled with procrastination and bad choices.

- You will not feel good about yourself, your life, or your actions.

- You will not be able to distinguish healthy people from addictive/dependent people, or healthy love from codependency, and will repeatedly find yourself in destructive relationships.

- You will not be able to achieve your full potential in life, or set and accomplish your most cherished personal goals.

- You will not know the true joy, contentment, and security that result from learning to make your own autonomous choices, or the self-confidence of knowing that you can successfully rely on yourself.

Life Without Dependency

When you understand that only you can make life better for you and only you are responsible for your choices, you encounter the world from a new perspective: Your view of yourself and everything around you completely changes. Instead of dependently hoping or expecting others will take care of you, which keeps you powerless, you meet them as someone who expects to take care of yourself and who expects others to take care of themselves.

In a relationship, both of you remain independent and retain the right to ask for what you want, the power to say yes or no, and the responsibility to make good decisions on your own behalf. This may sound less romantic than being taken care of, but it actually gives each of you the room you need to fully be yourselves, and makes your sharing free of painful, damaging *strings* or the weight of hidden dependency. You mutually support and care for each other on a new level where neither of you is drained or deprived by the unmet dependent needs of the other. Instead, love and support flow freely between you, and you look forward to sharing the pleasures and solving the problems of life together, as equals.

When you are fully autonomous and equal, you also gain the security of knowing that you are loved for yourself, for the unique person you are, with your talents, skills, feelings, successes, and shortcomings— not for how much you need, or how much you can give, but because you are a delight and a joy to your partner and your partner is an equal delight to you. The result is a *sustainable* relationship, with constantly renewable joy, sexual pleasure, satisfaction, and mutual regard.

The way that you relate to situations is also changed. Free from dependency, you no longer see yourself as a helpless, hopeless, victim of circumstances, but as a capable individual who encounters challenges and problems confident in your ability to meet them and make effective choices. You know you can rely on yourself to think clearly, and respond effectively and creatively to unforeseen circumstances.

The 6 Elements of Effective Choice

To become fully autonomous, you must be capable of taking care of yourself effectively. Caring for yourself and learning responsibility for managing your life requires making constant choices, some large, some small; but the more effective your choices are, the more success, confidence, and self-respect you will experience.

There are six elements that constitute effective choice:

- Paying attention.

- Being creative.

- Evaluating options.

- Making choices.

- Committing to your choice.

- Adapting to the unexpected.

1. Paying attention. You deliberately and consciously choose to focus your awareness on both the internal and external information that can let you know when making a choice is necessary.

2. Being creative. When faced with a problem, you use a combination of your intuitive and your practical thinking to develop options and solutions from which you can choose the best.

3. Evaluating options. You consider both short- and long-term probable results of each selection and weigh them for effectiveness and possible drawbacks.

4. Making choices. Based on these three preliminary steps, you then make the best choice you can. But your work is not finished.

5. Committing to your choice. Once your choice is made, you must commit to it and follow through on it. If you don't take the appropriate action after making your choice, you probably didn't commit to it.

6. Adapting to the unexpected. Even after committing to a choice, it may not work out as you thought because of circumstances beyond your control or events you did not foresee. So you must be capable of adapting to the unexpected, which includes coping with your surprise and disappointment, and then overcoming any resistance this creates to making another choice.

Harry

Harry, who has mastered the skills of autonomy, begins to notice (internal awareness) that he feels cramped and uncomfortable in his apartment, that he's making more money and can afford to move, and that his landlord is advertising the building for sale (external awareness). So, he begins to search for options (being creative): First, he does the "Reality/Fantasy" exercise (later in this chapter) to find out exactly how he wants to live. Then, he looks in the right neighborhoods and the papers and lets friends know he wants to move. When he has enough options to choose from, he compares them (evaluating options) against what he wants, what he can afford, how close to work they are, and so on, until he knows which is his best bet. At this point, the choice is obvious, and Harry decides (making a choice) that he's going to put a deposit on the new place.

Now comes an unusual and crucial step. Harry talks it over with himself one last time: "Is this choice okay with me? Have I checked it out thoroughly enough? Do I understand the probable advantages and disadvantages? *Even if it turns out that I'm wrong, can I accept that I made the best decision I could? Okay, I'll stick with my decision.*" From this point on, all the possibilities have been discussed and agreed upon, and Harry makes sure he doesn't allow himself to waffle, procrastinate, second-guess himself, scare himself, or doubt the move. He is committed to his choice. However, life is not predictable, and two months after Harry gets into his new apartment, he finds out that the city has declared his block will house a new Civic Center, and all residential buildings will be torn down. Harry is angry, life feels unfair, and he thinks he did all that work for nothing. He allows himself awhile to feel this frustration and disappointment, releasing them in a healthy way by complaining to friends and calling the city to object.

Then he decides: "My decision was a good one. There was no way I could have foreseen this. It's upsetting and unfair, but I have six months to enjoy this apartment before I have to move, and that's plenty of time to find an even better one. Besides, I may even get some compensation from the city for my inconvenience." He adapts to disappointment and is ready to make a new choice.

●

Paying Attention

In order to make effective choices, you must pay attention to yourself and the world around you. If you are aware of both inner and outer clues, you will notice when you need to make new decisions, and have the information you need to make an effective choice. Paying attention is a conscious choice in itself, a commitment to find a *new, more effective way* to think about events and ideas.

To understand what I mean about paying attention, think of any small children you know: Whether they're asleep, playful, noisy, or angry, even when their faces are dirty, or they are upset, they are still loveable. When children are small, they have not yet learned to be self-conscious, ashamed, and wary of others.

If you look at a photograph of yourself as a baby or child of 2 or 3, you will probably see an open, wide-eyed, curious person, not frightened or damaged by the world, and your heart will go out to that child. You'll want to keep your child self safe and secure. Responsible parents deliberately and consciously keep their attention focused on the actions of a small child, anticipating and responding to needs and problems to ensure the child's well-being. Similarly, to take responsibility for yourself, you need to deliberately and consciously keep some of your attention focused on your feelings and actions so you can anticipate your needs and developing problems.

This does not mean that you must be aware and alert 100-percent of the time. If you set your expectations too high, you'll defeat yourself.

When we're under stress, extra tired, anxious, or otherwise overloaded, our thinking ability is hampered. It's fine to take breaks from paying attention—little breaks, including meditation, naps, reading, television, or recreation, and larger breaks, including vacations and days off—when we don't have to maintain as high a level of awareness. When you're relaxing on the beach, at home, or with friends, and there is nothing you need to accomplish immediately and no problems facing you, mindlessness is fine, even healthy. It gives you a vacation from thinking, and refreshes your mental powers.

As long as you know how to pay attention when it's needed, you're vigilant enough. However, when you are making an important choice or setting goals (such as when your health, safety, emotional well-being, financial security, or personal happiness are involved), you need to be able to be fully aware and paying attention. Paying attention in these circumstances means considering both your internal feelings and the external factors that affect your decision. If you pay attention to all these factors, your choice will be much more effective.

"Mindful awareness of different options gives us greater control," writes Ellen Langer in *Mindfulness*. "This feeling of greater control, in turn, encourages us to be more mindful. Rather than being a chore, mindfulness engages us in a continuing momentum." In other words, mindfulness produces its own excitement. In fact, the human mind *thrives* on alertness. Langer reports that in experiments in which elderly people were asked to perform tasks that required them to pay attention and think, they actually stayed healthier and showed fewer signs of aging than unchallenged, disengaged, or bored seniors.

When you pay attention, you are exercising your mind. The more often you pay attention, the easier it is to maintain the habit, until eventually you realize that you pay attention to your inner world and the world around almost all the time. You notice circumstances and situations that call for choices as they arise, as well as the information needed to make your choices.

Being Creative

To make effective choices, you need to consider and imagine as many options for yourself as you can. This challenges your ability to be imaginative. Every new invention or idea is a result of rejecting the old, proven, conventional ways and taking a risk by trying something new. Creativity is connected to your ability to think *non*rationally—to fantasize, daydream, and envision—and is therefore more like play. Creativity, being childlike, is often silly or nonsensical, and it can be irrepressible. You can block out your awareness of it, but you cannot stop doing it.

With the exercises and magical tools you have learned, you have already begun to release pressure and remove the blockages to your creativity and to reactivate your ability to fantasize and use imagery. Through "playing" with these fantasies and images, and through using scenarios from your life in fantasies that you can alter at will, you can become aware of your creative thinking. You'll find that this familiarity with creative, nonrational thinking will be a powerful help when you need to come up with new ideas. With practice, you will be able to come up with at least five solutions or options whenever you are faced with any problem or choice.

No one needs to tell you precisely *how* to be creative, because creativity comes naturally to your childlike, subconscious mind. Small children do more creative thinking than any other kind, because everything in their environment is new and must be figured out through experimentation and guesswork. Children use fantasy and imagination much as you did in the magical tool exercises—to try out new ideas without having to take risks.

Evaluating Options

Once you have developed several options, it is time to evaluate them and to know which seems likely to be the most effective. For example, you may want to live in a $500,000 house, on a $30,000 yearly income. There are several possible ways to resolve the disparity, from finding a way to change your income to choosing a cheaper house. What usually works best, however, is to examine all the options you have been able to imagine and decide what is important to you.

You may want that house for status, because it's lovely to look at, because it's big enough for all your projects and friends, or because it overlooks the ocean. If you only require some of the components of the house—the ocean view, a front porch with columns, or more room than you have now—you may be able to get them elsewhere in your price range. If you want the prestige, maybe you can get some of that by being active in your community. If it has to be *that* house, in *that* area, maybe you can start your own business, or become a real estate agent, and find a way to afford it. In Harry's case, he checked his options against a list of requirements: Is it quiet enough? light and airy enough? close enough to work? within my price range? and other considerations.

Evaluating options is not difficult if you are supportive of yourself in the process. If you remind yourself that you are smart enough to figure it out and that you deserve to have what you want, you'll be able to think clearly enough to do a proper evaluation. In childhood, you may never have learned how to evaluate options effectively and may have thought you weren't smart enough or it was too difficult. As a result, you may be uncertain about what criteria to use when you evaluate options. The following checklist of considerations might make it easier for you to feel confident that your choices sound and healthy:

- Is it practical?
- If not, are there parts that are practical, or can you make it practical?
- What are the benefits?
- What are the drawbacks?
- Do you know the steps you have to follow to bring it about?
- How do the rewards compare with the problems?
- Do you presently feel good about it?
- How does your inner child self feel about it?
- Does it make sense—can you explain it clearly to someone else or on paper?
- Would you advise a friend to do it?

Making a Choice

Surprisingly enough, when you have covered the first three elements of choice-making, actually making the choice becomes simple. When you have sufficient information and you've evaluated your options, one or two best choices will stand out. Only if you have a rigid, dependent definition of the "right" way to do things, and are not open to considering new and different solutions, will your choices seem limited or blocked. For example, if it's cheaper, faster, and less stressful to take the new rapid transit system to work, but you insist that, for prestige reasons, you have to drive in your Mercedes, your prejudice will prevent you from making the soundest, most effective choice.

Committing to Your Choice

After you have made your choice, you must commit to acting on it. No choice is really made until a commitment is made to it. Without making a commitment to your choice, you will find yourself procrastinating, wavering back and forth, or criticizing yourself endlessly about your decisions. Without commitment, you can focus endlessly on the potential "what if's" of making choices—"What if the roof falls in?" "What if I haven't thought of everything?" "What if I'm wrong?"—and never get to making any choice at all. If you do that, each decision becomes an invitation to an internal war of self-recrimination, argument, and doubt.

If you learned to fear making mistakes and believed that your early decisions were disasters, committing to your decisions may be difficult at first. Dysfunctional families focus more on who's at fault than on how to fix the problem, and you get used to blame, because when a decision goes wrong, everyone accuses everyone else.

In the past when you made a decision, you probably were unable to commit to it and wavered back and forth. You may have given yourself excuses ("I'm too stupid to make this decision by myself" or "I'll think about that tomorrow") to avoid the commitment. But you don't need to fear making a poor choice or one that doesn't work out as well as you hoped. Making mistakes is natural, everybody does it, and no one can know every factor before making a decision. Sometimes you don't do all the preliminary research perfectly, or perhaps you don't make as effective a choice as you might like. Yet once you have generated and researched options and evaluated them sensibly, there is no reason to be afraid of taking responsibility for your decision.

Committing to your choice becomes easier when you have the confidence that you thought it out as best you could, and that your choice was made as well as you could make it. To commit to your choice, first check with yourself, as Harry did, to make sure "all of you" is in agreement with the decision, with no reservations. Using the "Negotiating Table" exercise from the previous chapter is a very effective way to make sure you are ready to commit to your decision without second-guessing yourself after the fact.

Committing to your choice means you can choose not to argue with yourself over it, doubt your judgment, or put off acting any longer. It means not blaming or accusing yourself if things go wrong, but rather focusing on how to fix the problem. Committing to your choice is the point at which you choose to stop focusing on solving the problem and begin focusing on implementing your solution.

Adapting to the Unexpected

No matter how carefully you evaluate your options, or how satisfied and pleased you are with your choice at first, sometimes things don't work out—you can even outgrow your former choices. To effectively run your life, when you find you've made a mistake or an earlier choice no longer suits you, you must be able to start the whole process over again and make new, healthy choices in its stead.

None of us has total control over what happens in our lives. Other people can let you down, move away, or fall ill, or circumstances can change unexpectedly. Your employer might lay you off because of a business recession, or you might come into unexpected money, become ill, fall in love, or be offered a job opportunity you couldn't have anticipated. Often life thrusts choice upon you when you are not expecting it, and you are required to make choices you didn't anticipate.

Adaptability is the willingness to handle change and to choose again when our choices do not work out, without wasting a lot of time and energy in resistance or resentment. Once you have made a commitment to a choice you like, being faced with the need to change it is disappointing. In addition, sudden, unanticipated change that you did not initiate (particularly if the change is unpleasant or creates difficulty) can produce some internal struggle. You can use the same techniques you learned to help you cope with disappointment and failure to cope with these feelings.

When failed decisions cause you to feel frustrated, angry, resentful, or disappointed, use the "Finding Your Trouble Spot" exercise on page 162 to discharge your feelings and acknowledge your disappointment. If your disappointment is overwhelming because the loss is a death or other tragedy, you can use the "Discharging Your Feelings" technique in Chapter 7 (page 263) to help you cope.

Once you have fully acknowledged the feeling of anger or disappointment, remind yourself that you believed in the choice when you made it, and that you are capable of making another choice. Now, look for any "silver linings" in the change, as when Harry saw the possibility that he would be reimbursed by the city, or that he would find an even better apartment.

The combination of acknowledging your feelings, supporting yourself unconditionally, and looking for silver linings will help you feel more hopeful, and generate the energy you need to begin the process of making another, more effective choice.

The Importance of Making Choices

Accepting full responsibility for your life means learning to make careful, effective choices. When you make your own choices, you affirm that you are important enough to yourself to care what happens. Every thoughtful choice you make improves your life, affirms that you feel your worth, and demonstrates that you care enough to think carefully about what affects you. In taking responsibility for your life, by your willingness to pay attention to the need to make choices, by creating and evaluating options, by making the choice, by committing to it, and by adapting to the unexpected, you develop the skills to take care of yourself in any and all circumstances. You no longer need to be dependent on anyone else but *you.*

You now have the tools to enable you to take charge of your own life and circumstances. This makes it possible for you to be responsible for yourself, and also gives you the opportunity to arrange your life and circumstances to suit your individual, unique needs. You can now choose, perhaps for the first time in your life, how your life will be.

You no longer have to do things you don't want to do to because your dependency on someone or something else demands it. Instead, you are able to do what pleases you, and you will find that you feel more generous toward others. You will give to them or do things for them because you *want* to, because it makes you happy to make them happy. You will be able to choose to be around people who treat you with respect and kindness, and who are enthusiastic about you. You can build an autonomous life, designed and planned to enhance your own well-being and satisfaction, and to enjoy the friendship of others.

Living autonomously produces its own dilemmas, poetically described by Rev. Virginia Greeley, an ordained minister in the Christian Church, Disciples of Christ:

Choices

The choice comes not one time—or two
   but every day, in all I do.
Every day when I awake
   I choose the prize—and what's at stake.
Then every moment through the day
   I choose again, what games I'll play.
No choice is really a wrong turn
   it might just bring me more to learn.
Voices speaking at each ear
   which one will I choose to hear?
First one speaks and then the next
   I could choose to be perplexed!
But in-between is not much fun
   besides, it leaves nowhere to run.
Will I stick with pain and fear
   and stagger through each passing year?
Or will I dare to make the choice
   and listen to the other voice?
I'm the one who must decide
   that's one choice I cannot hide.
No one else can choose for me
   what I do and who I'll be.
So every moment every day
   I must choose again my way.
Will I stay with fear and doubt
   or will I take the other route?
The route which says that I'm OK
   that I can do great things today.
Great things for me may be no more
   than going out my own front door!
But day by day, and choice by choice
   I strengthen the supportive voice.
It really is a daily chore
   to get up, and choose once more.

●

As you make effective choices in your daily life, you learn new skills and new ways of being. When you are open to experimentation and learning—not criticizing yourself for the old methods, but making corrections where necessary—a world of new ideas opens up. Friends, books, workshops, and classes can provide new ideas about functioning successfully in business, relationships, and everyday life. All these sources can provide options (a better way to save money, a new recipe, a new way of evaluating your options) but *you* are the one who gets to make the final choices. One of the problems your effective choice making and autonomous thinking will open up is that some of these new alternatives will be good, and some will be bad, for you.

In order to know what new options are good for you, you apply your system for effective choice: experiment to find new options, think and evaluate, and choose. Whose ideas suit you best? Which methods, if applied in your own life, will be most effective?

Knowing how to choose well is perhaps the most important difference between dependency and autonomy. Being able to make self-aware and effective choices also frees you from the limits of "What will people think?" and makes what *you* think more important. Because you have learned to pay attention, you no longer need to depend on what others think to know THAT your decisions are as sound as they can be.

The ability to think for yourself in this way is one of the great gifts of autonomy. It means that your life becomes undeniably *yours*—you are the one responsible force behind it. Creative thinking is one of the most enjoyable talents of your magical, childlike mind. It's fun! As Peter, a 22-year-old who learned autonomous thinking, said, "This is playing 'like the big kids'—I get great glee in challenging popular views of 'the way it is' and reexamining the facts for myself. Finally, I feel competent and grown up."

Meeting Your Resistance to Inner Change

You may find yourself resisting autonomous thinking because it creates an enormous change and disruption in your belief system and lifestyle. When you are operating in dependency, everything you do—your work, family, friends, and intimate relationships—is based on your old, helpless, hopeless addictive feelings. Making the inner change to autonomy and high self-esteem also changes the basis of these same things. Family relationships that were based on guilt and duty begin to change, and after everyone is reassured that they can be loved for being themselves, become more open and honest.

Social relationships that were based on superficial façades or false images crumble, and you begin to let your real self show, which gives you a stronger, more independent image. Intimate relationships based on dishonesty and withholding—in which both partners struggled for control—become based on mutual respect, love, and negotiation.

These changes are uncomfortable because they are unfamiliar. They are somewhat frightening because each change represents a risk: You cannot predict the outcome, and you will be presented with new situations about which you must then make effective choices. Sometimes you will fail or be disappointed.

If as a child you were prevented from learning risk-taking skills, the emotional child part of you will find these changes scary, because it is hard to trust that you can solve all the problems that may arise, make effective choices, or handle failure and disappointment. That inner child self is still afraid and is now dependent on you, and wants you to "make it better." And you, as an adult, *are* capable of taking risks, solving problems, correcting mistakes, and handling your feelings. You can use all the skills and exercises you are learning to handle problems as they arise, and also calm, comfort, and reassure your child self.

Change requires us all to take risks; there is no way to guarantee that the outcome will be what we want it to be. On the other hand, as you learn to think more autonomously, you'll see that this new way of thinking helps you to evaluate the risks and anticipate the outcome with a high degree of accuracy. Autonomous thinking actually makes risk-taking far less risky, because by boldly facing problems and considering options, you make far more effective choices than when you avoid them or look to others to tell you what to choose.

If you frighten yourself or discourage yourself in advance by fearing that you can't handle change, your adaptation to the change will be much harder. The truth is that you have been facing change all your life, no matter how hard you tried to resist it or block it out with addictive behavior. Resisting change is what creates chaos, because when you resist it, you cannot be aware of it enough to make effective decisions; so you wind up having things change on you without your control or participation.

Change is a basic fact of life. We grow older, seasons come and go, people move away, change their minds, or die, and the circumstances we live in are constantly in flux. Once your resistance to autonomous thinking is resolved, you'll find the experience of change becomes exciting and exhilarating, and you'll look forward to it.

Meeting Challenges from Others

Once you break through your internal resistance to autonomous thought and begin to express your individuality, you will probably encounter some external resistance from some of those around you. People with sufficient self-esteem of their own will realize how positive your changes are, and encourage and applaud you, but dysfunctional, dependent people will often challenge, test, or even attack you if they see you as more independent or stronger.

People who are close to you form a type of "family system". That is, close friends, lovers, and sometimes even business associates (if you work very closely together, have been working together for a long time, or work for a small company) act somewhat like family members and duplicate old family patterns, even if you are not related.

Dependent people are threatened by independent behavior because it jeopardizes the entire "family system," where each person depends on the other's dependence to maintain the status quo. In other words, such a pseudo-family is based on the belief that if you don't *need* one another to function in life, why would you stay together? Anything that threatens this neediness feels dangerous, so sometimes they will escalate their needy, critical, and/or abusive behavior to try and eliminate the threat that you will become independent and abandon them. This is similar to the way dysfunctional family members create and maintain dependency by attacking behaviors that appear to be independent. As you become more autonomous and learn to think for yourself, you come into conflict with those who *depend on your dependency,* and also with society's prejudices.

Most people, especially those with dependency problems, are upset by change and try to resist it. People who are insecure and only understand dependent love become fearful when someone they care about becomes independent. As you change your behavior, your friends, family, and co-workers may react with criticism or fear, because at first all they can see is that you're different. It will take them awhile to see that the difference is an improvement. When you get negative reactions from your friends and others, they may invoke old, childhood memories of being criticized, attacked, abused, or rejected by your dysfunctional family.

Suzanne

Suzanne, a 27-year-old legal secretary who was recovering from bulimia and compulsive overeating, used to take her father (a Fundamentalist Christian alcoholic who had neglected her as a child) out to lunch every week. At one lunch, when he was complaining about how big a problem he had with drinking, she suggested that he try the same therapy that had helped her. He shocked her by replying, "If therapy turned me into an unloving person like you are, I don't want any part of it." Suzanne was understandably upset and hurt about this remark. In her therapy session, she was able to see that her father was just frightened at the thought of facing his problems, and because he knew that being loving was important to her, he attacked what he instinctively knew was a tender spot to distract her from his problem. Using Magical Tool 3: Self-Love, Suzanne evaluated her own behavior, decided that she was a loving, caring person, and was able to recover her inner calm. By the next time she saw her father, she knew that if he was mean to her, she would tell him that he wasn't allowed to talk to her like that. In his irresponsible way, he had forgotten his earlier remark.

●

As a child you were dependent on the approval of others, so you may find the negative reactions of others frightening or upsetting. Keep in mind that no matter how hard you try, your choices and actions can never be approved of by everyone all the time. Wanting constant approval from everyone is just a sign that you are experiencing some last vestiges of dependent behavior. The price you pay for trying to please everyone is tremendous—a loss of self-esteem, being out of control, emotional pain, uncertainty, and, eventually, return to dependent, destructive behavior.

One of the tasks you undertake when you accept responsibility for yourself and choose autonomous, independent living is to nurture and protect your new attitudes and abilities until you grow strong enough to withstand a more confrontational environment. By reinforcing and supporting your autonomous thinking in this way, you become your own sponsor (parent, adult, guardian) and no longer remain dependent on a group, friend, lover, sponsor, or relative to support and encourage you. You are still free to discuss events and ideas with others, but evaluating them yourself ensures that you can listen to advice autonomously, and choose to use it or ignore it.

Healthy human beings have to learn to live with the disapproval of others. In order to be fully yourself, you must learn to be comfortable with occasionally being the center of both positive and negative attention from others. If your self-esteem doesn't feel strong enough to withstand the negative reaction of those who are threatened by specialness, you may be tempted to give in and try to stifle your individuality.

Through the work you did in the previous chapters, you've already begun to handle this problem. By using your Magical Tool 5: Environment, you can choose to surround yourself with people who will support your autonomy, individuality, effective choices, and autonomous thinking. Also, by working to resolve your internal war, and learning to use Magical Tool 3: Self-love, you have attained the ability to protect yourself from those who attack, criticize, or disapprove of you, as Suzanne did with her father. You can recover from others' disapproval and criticism by supporting and comforting yourself as you would a friend. With sufficient internal support, and an independent group of friends who will help you to encourage yourself, you will easily be able to withstand the occasional frightened, dependent person you encounter who lashes out and criticizes or devalues you.

There's no need to get upset over these attacks, or let them divert you or change your commitment to your choices. *You* are the one who is responsible for your life, and the one who has to live it. You needn't take attacks personally either, if you remember that they are based on the subconscious fears and childlike magical thinking of people who have not yet taken control of their inner, dependent beliefs and fears.

Challenging Your Recovery Group

As you complete these final chapters and move into fuller autonomy, you may find that you no longer need to depend on your recovery group to be your support system. Although you may still *choose* to maintain friendships you began in your group, or choose to sponsor others or continue to attend meetings at your discretion (going back whenever you *want* to), you'll find that you possess all the skills and abilities necessary to make clear, effective choices about your own life, and about what behaviors are right for you, independent of the opinions of the group or its members. Instead of relying on the group or a sponsor to be responsible for you, think for you, or take care of you, you now know you can rely on yourself.

As you become more independent, you may find your perceptions of and reactions to your recovery group and its members changing significantly, and theirs to you. In the beginning, you needed them to model healthier, non-addictive behavior, and many of them were much farther along in recovery than you were. Now you may begin to see flaws and weaknesses you never noticed before. You may discover that though they have stopped their addiction and been able to remain in recovery, many of them are still caught up in dependent attitudes and addictive behavior.

Instead of feeling critical of group members, or upset that your relationships are changing, you can choose to view your observations as evidence that you are growing and changing, and increasing your own possibilities for satisfaction and happiness by learning to take care of yourself.

Group members may also react negatively toward you, and perceive your ability to remain recovered and free of addictive behavior without the group as a threat, because the program has taught them to perceive it so. You'll find that if you don't react negatively, but stay calm and reassure them that you're doing well, most of them will relax.

Pam

Pam B., a successful businesswoman in her 30s who had been sober for several years, and had done her work on her feelings and learned autonomy in therapy, stopped calling her sponsor very often, and only attended meetings occasionally, as she wanted to. One day, her sponsor called her, and, in an angry manner, began giving her orders: "You're risking a relapse. You must attend at least three meetings a week. You must call me every day." Pam calmly said, "I'm sorry, you've helped me a lot as my sponsor, and I should have told you how well I am doing. My life is going well, I have no temptation to drink, my job is great, and I feel fine. What works for me is going to an occasional meeting, but I don't need such regular attendance." Pam got no more trouble from her sponsor, and a few months later, at a meeting, her sponsor hugged her and congratulated her on her success.

●

You may also find some group members looking up to you to model autonomous, healthy behavior for them. If this is your first experience at being viewed as a role model, you may find it surprisingly uncomfortable. Being in the spotlight can be scary if you grew up dependent, because in a dysfunctional family environment, being the focus of attention often means being criticized, made to feel guilty, belittled, or punished. Once you get used to it, you'll find it's good for you and you deserve it.

Autonomous Thinking and Individuality

When you take responsibility for yourself and begin to think for yourself, you begin to discover your own individuality. Once the childlike part of you is reassured, and trusts you to care for him or her as your parents did not, and once you master the magical tools, and make the commitment to being responsible for your own life, an interesting thing happens. When you take care of yourself completely, and create internal and external support for yourself and your individuality, you will have the secure base you need to blossom and grow, and to express what you have been longing to express all your life—your own special, inner, individual self.

As you come to accept the previously hidden parts of yourself, and learn not to depend on others for approval or acceptance, you will discover your true individuality. You will begin to look at the world with a new sparkle in your eye, a creative, individual approach, a way of looking at the world, at life, and at other people that you've never seen before. Both your secure and loved inner child self and your competent and effective adult self will be facing life together, as a team. The adult you, by using clear thinking and effective choice, provides the safety the child in you needs to take risks, experiment, and express himself. Your child self will keep the adult open to creative, new ideas, and aware of your feelings and reactions. The combination of this team—and the cooperation between the child's fantastic, magical thinking, and the adult's rational, practical thinking—will give individuality what it needs to begin to express itself, in a way that is attractive to others and productive for you.

Perry

Perry, a 45-year-old computer programmer, needed to make some career changes. He felt paralyzed—although he knew what he should do, he was unable to begin. Perry was terribly afraid of any new, untried situations. When he examined his fear and the resulting helplessness in therapy, a memory arose: When he was 11 years old, he took ballroom dancing and deportment lessons, which he usually enjoyed. One day, proper introductions were taught. The boys were to say: "Hi, my name is ____, would you like to dance?" When his turn came, he said, "Hello, my name is Perry..." and the 80 children in the hall broke out in derisive laughter because he did not say "Hi." Perry was humiliated. Although he admitted that he enjoyed the classes when he got there, he resisted going, and eventually stopped. The possibility that he might be laughed at was too terrifying. Perry realized it was this terror that was stopping him from searching for a new job. Using "Time Travel," Perry went back to that scene, and adult Perry told child Perry (and the whole class) that saying "Hello" was not only acceptable, it was admirable, because little Perry had taken the lesson and individualized it. Once that early scene was resolved, Perry's resistance to meeting new people and trying new situations faded, and he was able to make his career change.

●

When you take an idea or event and place your own unique stamp on it, you are displaying your individuality. When you have satisfying relationships that are quite different in form from your parents' marriage, or from those of your friends, you are making your own choices and customizing your relationship to suit you and your partner. You may, for example, prefer to live separately, although you are in a committed, monogamous partnership, or you may be more conservative and traditional in your relationship than your friends are.

When your work is satisfying but different from what your parents and friends think you should do, you are making individual choices. You might give up a job they approve of for something you love doing. You express your individuality when you have friends who enhance your life, and to whom you can say no if they tempt you to do something you think is not good for you. Your friends might be an unusual mix of people, different from your family.

As an autonomous person, you eat, wear, and do what is right for you, regardless of the fads and trends of the day. When your home suits you well, and you enjoy being there, then it and its decor reflect your own individual taste (perhaps combined with that of a partner). As an individual, you get to express yourself as you wish. If you have a talent (such as art, acting, sports, writing, public speaking, caring for pets, crafts, cooking), you make room for it in your life.

To stimulate your individual thinking, try this mini-exercise:

Exercise:
Tapping Your Individuality

1. **Ask your own opinion.**

   At frequent intervals (about five times a day) during your regular workday, ask yourself: "What do *I* think about this? Do I like it? Does it make sense to me? Do I agree or disagree with the others? If I had unlimited power, what would I do?" By doing this, you'll get used to asking *your own opinion* of ideas and events.

2. **Listen to the answer.**

   Listen to your opinions as you would to the ideas of a respected friend. Consider them, weigh them, and even discuss them with yourself from time to time. Allow them to influence your daily thought. If you feel, for example, that your work is not satisfying enough, just accept and allow that feeling to be there, and it will eventually create a need to act, and many exciting ideas for how to act. There is no need to act on your ideas yet; just practice listening to your own opinion for now.

3. **Repeat to make decision-making easier.**

   After you practice asking your own opinion faithfully for a few weeks, it will become automatic to have personal opinions about everything around you. If you don't pressure yourself, but let your ideas incubate at their own pace, this awareness of your own opinion will have a profound effect on what you do and how you act. Activating your individual thinking ability will gradually increase your options and choices, and make decision-making faster and easier.

●

When you're faced with a choice you have to make, or you have a new idea you'd like to try, you can use two different types of thinking—

subconscious, creative, childlike fantasy, and rational, practical adult evaluation—together, to develop creative and effective choices. Your child, magical mind has feelings, intuition, and the creative ability to fantasize about options. Your adult, rational mind has life experience, wisdom, and the ability to evaluate your ideas for practicality. Using them both in cooperation will make sure you're being as creative as possible, imagining the largest number of options, yet making sure they are considered in a logical, practical manner.

In the following exercise, I'll use the example of Harry, who was trying to decide if he wanted to move, to illustrate.

Exercise
Reality/Fantasy Dialogue

1. Use your favorite method of dialogue.

Select a favorite form of adult/child or rational/subconscious dialogue (time travel, hitting the spot, adult/child dialogue, inner voices) to use for discussing a problem or new idea with yourself. *Harry used an adult-child dialogue.*

2. Fantasize.

Your subconscious, childlike mind is creative and fantastic—new ideas abound, without constraint. Let yourself freely fantasize about what you would like to have happen. Be sure you don't get practical at this point, because that cuts off the creative flow— it's okay if your fantasies aren't possible, they'll still contain useable ideas, and some new things your practical side wouldn't think of. Allow your creative self to be as silly, whimsical, impractical, or fantastic as it wants to be. *Harry's child self, when asked to think about where he wanted to live, came up with the following ideas: Moving is scary, I want to stay here. I want to live in a castle. I want to live in Paris. I want to go live in the woods.*

3. **Begin a dialogue about the fantasy.**

   Begin a dialogue between your creative, child mind, and the more rational, adult mind. Remember, this is not a fight, an argument, or a contest, it is a brainstorming and problem-solving session. Make sure both aspects of your thinking show interest in the other's ideas, and keep the dialogue focused on solutions. If you don't understand an idea, ask questions and don't criticize. For instance, if you're facing a decision about moving, your dialogue might sound something like this:

   Harry: What do you want to do about moving?

   Child: I don't want to move. I want to stay here forever.

   Harry: Well, I thought you wanted more room, and a place for a cat.

   Child: You're right! I do. Let's move to a castle.

   Harry: What do you like about a castle? Aren't they cold and drafty?

   Child: A warm castle. I want lots of space, and a place to be alone. Like in a tower room.

   Harry: Oh, I see. How about an extra bedroom with windows and maybe lots of cupboards and closets?

   Child: Yeah! That's it. And a moat.

   Harry: A moat?

   Child: Yeah, water for me to play in.

   Harry: Oh, I see. How about a hot tub or a big bathtub?

   Child: Yeah! And I want to live in the woods!

   Harry: In the woods? Why?

   Child: Cuz I want trees and grass and maybe even a dog.

   Harry: Oh, I see. Would a place near work with lots of trees and grass be okay? And can we try having a cat, before we decide about the dog?

   Child: Okay, if we can see about a dog later.

This dialog may sound a little trivial, but Harry is really uncovering longings he has had for more space, contact with water, more green surroundings, and a cat, and all of those are possible to realize in practical terms, if not in the child's fantastic ideal. With information like this, flowing uncensored from the child and translated into practical terms by the adult, Harry can know what kind of home would really feel like his "castle."

4. Translate child dialogue into adult terms.

After you have discussed the idea for a while, use your adult, rational thinking ability to translate from childlike magical thinking into real-world terms, remembering that your child mind sees everything in magical, exaggerated, and fantastic ways. To Harry's child mind, a home with a whole extra room *would* seem as big as a castle, and a nice, big bathtub or a hot tub *could* become a moat. Harry could also check with his child mind and see if living by a beach or a lake would meet his wish to play in water.

5. Write down translated ideas, and review.

When you have some ideas that both your creative side and your practical side can agree on, summarize them in writing and let them sit for a few moments, or even a day, so you can get some perspective, and then review them. Use "Playing Chess" (next exercise) or the considerations in the Evaluating Options section (page 201 of this chapter) to make your decision. You'll like your final decision better if both sides of you have participated, and you'll feel more certain you made the right move. *When Harry went apartment hunting, he kept his inner child wishes in mind, and he recognized the light, airy, large apartment, in a garden complex, with a pool and a big Jacuzzi bathtub, the minute he saw it. Because the rent was within his budget, he took it right away.*

6. For big decisions, repeat several times.

If you're facing a momentous decision, such as health issues, a big move, or a relationship commitment, doing this exercise several times will help reassure you that your decision is sound, and will build self-confidence.

The next exercise will help you to further evaluate options by teaching you how to look ahead for possible consequences and outcomes. Like a chess master, you can use foresight in your own life to evaluate the results of decisions before you make them. The great masters of chess are masters because they, too, have developed this ability to look at the chess board, work out every possible move that might be made, and then consider all the possible consequences.

Exercise:
Playing Chess

1. Think creatively and fantasize.

Visualize yourself (Magical Tool 4: Self-image) as a chess master, using your life as the board. Whenever you're facing a choice or decision, take the time to visualize (Magical Tool 2: Imagery) about each option available. Suppose you have two job offers. Before deciding, take the time to gather as much information as you can about each job, then try to picture what the work and the job environment would be like. Imagine getting up in the morning, going to work, interacting with the people there, being in the work environment, doing your assigned tasks. Imagine the positive aspects of the job. Imagine the drawbacks. Do this with each possible choice, creating as complete an image as you can. Remember to consider the long-term possibilities as well as the immediate ones.

2. Evaluate the possible choices.

Ask yourself questions to learn how you feel about each choice, discussing it with yourself as if you were a friend of yours who cared about your well-being and happiness (Magical Tool 3: Self-love). If it's a new job, your questions might be: Is the drive too long? How about your potential co-workers, the company atmosphere, the work itself? Is this a job you could do for a long time, or is this one that would be difficult to sustain?

3. **Sort and evaluate your choices.**

If the choices you have to make are many or complicated, use what you know about your learning style to help you: If you're auditory, try discussing it with a friend, talking out loud to yourself about it, or write a page about each option and read them out loud. If you're visual, you might find that arranging your list of pros and cons into two columns on a page makes seeing which one is better much easier. If you're tactile, try acting out going to work and doing the job to see how it feels.

4. **Get expert advice.**

To verify the reality of your ideal images, and provide environmental support (Magical Tool 5) for your search, locate some real experts who have firsthand knowledge about the information you are seeking. If it's a job search, find people who worked for that company, or in that field, and ask them what you should look for. When you go in for an interview, instead of just letting the interviewer question you, have some questions ready that will help you make your choice. You might ask: Is there smoking in the office? What is the policy about sick days, holidays, and vacations? What are the opportunities for promotion? Is the company financially stable? What is the retirement plan or health insurance?

5. **Allow yourself ample time.**

Perhaps most important, allow enough time to be able to *make* a choice. Waiting until the last moment to make decisions deprives you of the opportunity to find out what your options are, or to gather sufficient information to think about them. The whole point of "Playing Chess" is to take the time to work out and consider all the possibilities, which gives you more autonomous control and a better chance to make a great choice. In the example of a job, don't wait until you can't stand your old job a minute longer, or until unemployment is about to run out, and then take the first thing you can get. Begin *early* to look and compare, to give yourself time to choose, so you can find a job that is ideal. Playing chess works wonders in relationships, too.

Molly

Molly, a 37-year-old professional woman, explains how "Playing Chess" affected her relationships: "Since learning to 'play chess' I find that when I meet someone new, I think: How would we be together? What kind of a friend or mate would this person be? Can I trust them? What would it be like to spend a lot of time with this person? Where are we likely to have problems? Where would we agree? Am I comfortable introducing him or her to my family and friends? It makes a huge difference in who I decide to spend more time with. For the first time in my life, I feel like I'm making a choice about my companions."

●

Autonomy is also called self-governing. Part of a governor's job is to analyze problems and develop various solutions, decide among them, and put them into effect. A governor is responsible for taking care of a state the way you are responsible for taking care of yourself—you both try to use your resources to their best advantage, foresee problems, and prevent them if possible. To accomplish this, a governor spends time before an election focusing on the current problems and designing a campaign platform—a proposal of solutions. Similarly, the following exercise will help you make and define the choice to be responsible for your life—it contains a ceremony for committing to that responsibility.

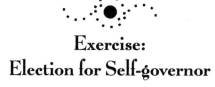

Exercise:
Election for Self-governor

1. **Analyze the situation.**

    As candidate for self-governor, analyze where your life needs new management, more effective or efficient techniques, and damage control. View your lifestyle as though you were just about to take over, and decide where you would like to change it. For example, you might feel that your budget is seriously out of balance, or you might think your personal health and welfare (diet, exercise, dental care) are not as well managed as they might be.

2. **Propose some solutions.**

   Propose a "platform"—a plan, which may encompass a few months or a few years, for improving the governing of your life. Consider proposing:

   - An economic platform: if your budget is in trouble, propose some budget cuts, or a new source of income.

   - A social welfare platform: for increasing your circle of healthy friends, or bringing your social life into balance.

   - A health and well-being platform: to improve your physical condition, adjust your eating habits, or take care of neglected doctor or dentist appointments.

   - An environmental platform: to improve your surroundings, your house and/or yard, to get involved in more environmentally aware activities, or to surround yourself with healthier people.

   - A mental and spiritual health platform: to take classes, try a new meditation, read some appropriate self-help books, or have stimulating and thoughtful discussions.

3. **Put your platform in writing.**

   When you have a plan for each item, write out your entire platforms ("As governor of life, I will make the following changes:") and then post them where you will see them on a daily basis (Magical Tool 6: Repetition). After your election (see next step), do your best to keep your campaign promises.

4. **Make a commitment.**

   Design a simple ceremony to approve your platform, elect yourself governor, and induct yourself into control of your life. This ceremony will add power to your commitment by invoking your senses and using imagery to speak directly to your child mind.

Make it a ceremony that is meaningful to you, and take your promise to govern seriously—giving up all dependence on anyone or anything else to do it for you. This is your official entry into autonomy. For example, you might engage sight by having a flag or campaign posters, and touch by putting your hand on a symbolic object, such as a Bible or the AA's *Big Book*, and promise to do your best to carry out your platform or program. To engage your sense of hearing, you might play a tape of some dramatic music, such as "Pomp and Circumstance" or a Sousa march. The more your ceremony engages your feelings, and stirs you, the more powerful it is to your child self, or subconscious mind.

5. **Review your performance.**

    Periodically, every six months or once a year, check your progress against your campaign platform to see how you're doing. If your platform needs changing, or part of it is not working out as you hoped, as reigning governor you can propose new solutions by going back to steps one and two.

●

The next exercise will help you learn to adapt and be flexible whenever you're trying to accept a change that you didn't choose, plans you had that fell through, or when you become aware of any rigid attitude you'd like to eliminate.

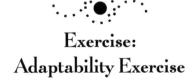

Exercise:
Adaptability Exercise

1. **Choose a method for inner dialogue.**

    Pick your favorite of the "Trouble Spot," "Time Travel," "Negotiating Table," or "Adult-Child Dialogue" exercises, and use it to discuss the upcoming change or the old, rigid belief with yourself and find out what your feelings are.

2. **Give yourself a chance to complain.**

   If you're facing a change, voluntary or not, you may have some resistance to it. If you're challenging an old, rigid belief, you will have some objections to changing it. Allow yourself some time to complain and be unhappy about the change. Express as many of the negative feelings and thoughts as possible, either verbally or on paper.

3. **Evaluate your complaints.**

   Allow yourself some time to consider the points you made in your complaining. Is there anything that you can do differently? Do you want to? Have you made all the choices you can? Are you thinking clearly about the problem? Are you angry at anyone specifically? Are you resisting unnecessarily? If you have a choice, do you still want to change things? If you don't have a choice, can you see some alternatives? Do your options look different to you now?

4. **Befriend yourself to build trust.**

   Discuss the problem with yourself as you would with a friend. Brainstorm for ideas, realistic or even silly, about what you could do to make things better. For example:

   - I could move to Timbuktu and avoid the whole thing.
   - I could talk to Harry and see if this is really necessary.
   - I could ask Martha to help.
   - I could find a genie and have him make my wish come true.
   - I could win millions in the lottery and not have to worry about it.
   - I could come up with three other plans, present them to my boss, and maybe get him to change his mind.

5. **Play chess.**

   Do whatever you can to check the facts about this change. Use "Playing Chess" to consider all the possibilities.

6. Review and decide.

Once you have expressed your anger and disappointment, evaluated your feelings, brainstormed ideas, and checked the facts, you will feel much more in charge of yourself and of this change. Review the things you have discovered and make some decisions.

7. Sell yourself on your new idea.

Once you've decided how much of the change is really necessary, pretend it's your own idea and sell it to yourself. Think of all the possible great outcomes of the change. Consider what you will learn from it. Figure out how you can maximize the benefits of making the change. When you've convinced yourself, make a commitment to your plan.

8. Post and follow your plan.

Draw up a plan for making the best possible results come out of this change. Put the plan where you can see it and read it every day (Magical Tool 6: Repetition). Do your best to follow the plan when the change is made.

●

Thinking autonomously sheds new light on your life, including your relationships. Once you know how to think independently, you are freed from any need to be dependent. Even if you need someone's help, you can clearly consider all your options, decide on the most creative solution possible, and arrange to get the help you need on a clear, mutually satisfactory, independent basis. Remember, it's your choice.

Chapter 7

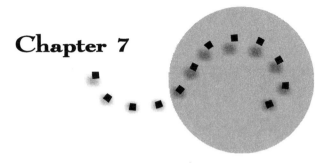

Autonomous Loving:
Creating Healthy Relationships

The more whole you are, the more you can bring to a relationship. When you attempt to have the relationship fill in the gaps and incomplete places inside you, you are bound to become frustrated...Taking time to nurture yourself is an essential ingredient in the nurturing of your couplehood
—Dale Gershon and Gail Straub

One reason it is so hard for us to free ourselves from dependent attitudes and behaviors in relationships is that almost every model and concept of relationships we have ever known is based on the ideal that the other person we love is supposed to take care of us, to "make it better" for us. Even after learning to take responsibility for our lives and to make more effective choices and finding we can successfully handle most situations autonomously, when it comes to relationships (particularly intimate relationships) we can still find ourselves caught up frequently in our old, dysfunctional, destructive, and dependent attitudes and behaviors.

We may find ourselves inexplicably obsessing on someone who isn't available or interested, or even feeling so needy or helpless that we are unable to object to being criticized, abused, or degraded. This behavior is a result of being bombarded with images that imply that love and dependency are the same thing: Lovers should depend on each other to supply their needs, to take care of them, and "make it better," that they should *need* each other ("You are my happiness, I'd die without you"), that they are incomplete without each other, and that two should "become one"—losing their individual personalities, friends, interests, and opinions in the process.

This dependent, dysfunctional image of love has been reinforced by generations of songs, poetry, plays, books, movies and television soap operas—from *Romeo and Juliet* to *Dynasty* to *Twin Peaks*—that have celebrated a dependent model of romantic relationships that is neediness, desperation, and the idea that only the beloved can take care of us. Like an idealized parent, this ideal lover is supposed to love us no matter how unreasonable we are, always be there when we want or need them, always know exactly how to soothe our hurts, always know (and be prepared to give us) precisely what we want (even if we're not sure ourselves), and put our needs before his or her own. Dependent people in relationships are like the unsocialized, dependent infant, who wants what he or she wants when he or she wants it, without expecting to have to return it, and they experience rage and hurt (like the red-faced, bawling infant) when the needs aren't met.

This "romantic" image of love is really a continuation of the search for a perfect parent to "make it all better." The problem with it is that it is based on powerlessness and helplessness. In this romantic image, you have to give up your power to take care of yourself in order to be taken care of, or to take care of someone else. This dependency-based romantic image, although it seems exciting and fulfilling at first, is not sustainable. The relationship cannot flourish, because, since no one else can ever care for you as well as you can yourself (he can't know your needs and wants as well as you do, she can't tell what her care-taking feels like to you, and he has his hands full with his own needs), one or both of you will wind up feeling cheated, used, neglected, unloved, and generally dissatisfied. Dependency creates dysfunctional relationships in which the ground rules are: You can't talk about it (it might upset the other person), it's hopeless (since you can't talk about it, you can't solve it together), and we're both helpless (we can't control our own behavior, or outbursts of anger, or make effective choices).

Dysfunctional relationships happen because your first experience (and basic model) of intimate relationships was with parents "who made it better" and took care of you as a child (and perhaps did not encourage you to become self-sufficient and autonomous), or with parents who were *not* fully there to take care of you (as you felt they should be). Even the best parent/child relationship is unbalanced, with the parent having all the power of experience and ability, and the child being dependent on the parent for survival. Because of this pattern, you either assume that there will always be someone there to take care of you and make life better, or you look to replace the care you never got, and make the pain of neglect or abuse go away. Although your adult mind may outgrow this belief and know better, your subconscious child mind does not. When this happens, you unconsciously expect that whomever you fall in love with will be an ideal "parent"—just as your real parent was or should have been.

On the surface, your adult, rational mind is looking for someone you can enjoy and have fun with. The dependent, wounded, subconscious inner child mind, however, is secretly searching for a substitute for the parent you never had, for someone who will take care of you, make your old wounds better, care about your feelings, and accept you for who you are. If you grew up in a dysfunctional family where you suffered rejection or abandonment at an early age, when you begin to search for a romantic partner, all too often you find a substitute parent who is *too much* like the real parent who let you down, and you wind up repeating the old, subconscious patterns.

Warren

Warren, 34, a computer programmer, came into my office very upset about his relationship. He had grown up in a family where his father was alcoholic and abusive, and his mother was given to uncontrollable rages, which had nothing to do with his good or bad behavior, but of which he and his sister received the brunt. Warren had a lover who, after a few months of happiness (right after they moved in together), became angry and abusive, punching holes in the walls and threatening Warren. Although the lover was male,

Warren realized that he had wound up in a relationship with some-one just like his mother, with some overtones of his father. War-ren believed he had based the relationship on old dysfunctional patterns and was frightened enough by this to leave the relation-ship, and get into therapy to examine and correct his expectations about relationships.

●

Expecting a mate to be the perfect parent you always wanted is un-realistic and places pressure on the other person. Because it is inappro-priate and impossible for your partner to be your parent, disappointment becomes inevitable. When neither of you can live up to these unrealistic expectations, on the one hand you feel inadequate, pressured, and used, and on the other, you feel unloved, uncared for, and abandoned.

You begin to learn about family, love, and relationships in early child-hood during the critical period of magical thinking. You learn from ob-serving your parents in their relationship with each other, and their relationship with you and your siblings. Because you absorb this infor-mation so early, before you can evaluate whether it is healthy, it is as difficult to change your old, dependent relationship habits as it is to change your other dependency habits. What you learn about love, home, and family becomes deeply embedded in the subconscious child mind. Later, it takes over and creates your first reactions to solving relation-ship problems and challenges. When later you fall in love, and are faced with the stressful relationship complications of conflicting wants and needs, you'll have a tendency to fall back into the old patterns. You learned them so early that they feel natural and instinctive.

At the root of most problems people have with adult, intimate rela-tionships lies the mistaken belief that someone else should take care of us—the mistaken expectation of parent/child love, in which the child is dependent and powerless and the parent is in control and powerful. This is how inappropriate dependency in adult intimate relationships can go wrong—resulting in abuse, misunderstandings, anger, or smothering.

Even the most competent parents never take care of their children the way the *children* would want them to. As children, we are supposed to learn, with the help of encouraging parents, to take increasingly more autonomous risks and learn to be competent in life through those experiences with risk. Ideally, the parent/child relationship matures to one of mutual respect and caring, where the child is obviously as capable, functional, and autonomous as the parent. If we let go of the dependent, childish view of love, and use the more mature model, we get a more autonomous picture of familial love. This kind of love is mutually caring, mutually giving, and mutually responsible, without the dependent, needy, or controlling imbalance of power present in the child/parent model. Remaining dependent robs us of our power to receive and give love at full capacity while retaining our self-esteem and sense of competence.

It is easy to be misled by our romantic excitement and attraction. A romantic relationship—with the partner whom you hope and expect will provide you with love, joy, and fulfillment of your dreams—that turns into a miserable and disappointing failure is a very painful experience. Not only is it a terrible disappointment of very high expectations, but it's also a reminder of early childhood rejection and abandonment. The hurt of the failed relationship, coupled with the early childhood despair, can become the type of overwhelming pain people use addiction to escape. Most therapists and recovery counselors report that the pain of a troubled or failed relationship is cited by twelve-step members as the single greatest cause of many alcoholics' relapses.

Romantic relationships are not the only ones that are difficult; you can find yourself repeating early patterns whenever you get close to family, friends, and even co-workers. As soon as you feel you care about someone, or want someone to care about you, your old patterns and models of how people who are supposed to care about each other (our family) come into play. These early models, held in your deep inner mind, create dependent, problematic relationships, and must be changed, if you are to be able to love autonomously.

The Skills of Autonomous Intimacy

The good news is that while relationships are the most difficult aspect of our lives, learning the skills that make them work is one of the easiest. All the skills you have learned so far, in confronting and building an autonomous relationship with yourself, are precisely the same skills you will need to create and sustain autonomous intimacy with others on a long-term basis. Your inner relationship with yourself becomes your new model (and also the standard or criterion), upon which you can build all other relationships. As you create this model within you, you can test it, correct it, and revamp it as needed. Building functional, dynamic and rewarding relationships simply means learning to apply the skills you already know—risk-taking, problem-solving, and effective choice-making, coping with disappointment and failure, awareness, learning, and forgiveness—to relationships.

Risk-taking

A relationship that is not based on playing old, dependent roles, but instead designed to actually *function* in your life, requires taking at least several risks. The first risk is letting your partner know who you really are. If you don't, you run the risk (although you're usually unaware of it) that you'll never feel loved for who you are but because you've learned only to please your partner. When you're maintaining a façade, you live in fear of being found out, that your beloved would reject you if he or she only knew the truth. As this fear eats at your self-esteem, the pressure and resentment build, leading eventually to an outburst of rebellion that can destroy the partnership.

In being yourself, you also risk being honest about your wants and preferences. When you drop the façade, and are your authentic self, you begin to be honest about your wants and preferences. That is, instead of guessing what your partner's wants and needs are, and hoping your partner can guess yours, you ask directly for what you want, and allow your partner to ask for what he or she wants. When you ask directly, you take the risk that your partner will not be willing or able to meet your needs, or that he or she will ask you for something you cannot give. Both of you risk being disappointed. Taking this risk gives you a chance to find out whether the two of you can negotiate mutually satisfactory solutions, and if so (by realizing you both can give and take no for an answer), you lay the foundation for the freedom to give out of generosity, rather than obligation.

It is also necessary to risk being honest about what works for you; even when it's different than the accepted role models. We all have different needs for closeness and space, for communication and silence, for accomplishment and relaxation. Squeezing yourself into a closer relationship than is comfortable for you, or feeling deprived in a distant one, leads to inevitable relationship failure. Feeling badgered by someone who is more verbal than you are or shut out by someone less verbal, or pressured by someone more driven to accomplish, or frustrated by someone more inactive, inevitably becomes intolerable, unless you can discuss your differences and work together to find a mutually satisfactory solution.

These are personal risks of the most challenging kind, because you are exposing the most private aspects of your personality to the other person, and you risk being rejected. If you can do this before your investment in the relationship is too great, your risk of disappointment is diminished. You already know how to cope with failure and disappointment, through feeling your feelings and then working on a new goal. On the other hand, the possible rewards are that you will build a *sustainable* relationship. A relationship you fit into naturally, that suits your needs and talents, and that makes only reasonable demands on you, will remain pleasant, satisfying, and functional in your life and the life of your partner. An autonomous, sustainable relationship—precisely because it is more easily managed and involves less struggle than a dependent, dysfunctional one—frees your energy for having fun together, building toward your future, and enjoying your present life.

The best you can achieve in a dependent relationship is approval for being "acceptable"; but in autonomous intimacy, you can actually be valued and loved for your unique and different qualities.

Problem-solving and Effective Choice-making

In dysfunctional, dependent relationships, problems are solved through struggle. Either one person wins and gets her way, but then has to deal with covert anger continuously expressed by the other; or through passive sacrifice or denial, in which problems are endured or ignored in the vain hope that they'll go away. In the "struggle" relationship, the partners fight a lot, usually about the same issues; one gets her way, and her partner then "snipes" at her, making sarcastic remarks when they're with friends. In the "sacrifice" relationship, a wife might insist that her husband give up golf and spend more time with her, which he does without complaint. Then, however, he comes home later and later, perhaps having had a few more drinks, from the office each night.

In autonomous intimacy, problems are treated as opportunities to reach a new level of success: They are seen as challenges that, when solved, will yield a new and better way of life. Autonomous partners are willing to talk about what's wrong, what they want, and what they're willing or not willing to do, and use effective choice-making together to find a solution.

Coping with Disappointment and Failure

In intimate relationships, as in all aspects of life, you will make mistakes and encounter disappointment and failure. Even with the most well-intentioned, loving mate, you will not always get the response you want. Your sexual advances will be turned down occasionally, your need for sympathy will be met with irritation, your boundless enthusiasm for a cherished activity will be quashed by a mate who's disinterested, irritable, or exhausted; it happens in the best of relationships.

In a dependent relationship, these disappointments are often the cause of stored resentment, arguments, and major battles, because the basic promise of the relationship ("I'll make it better for you") has been broken, and the partners feel angry and helpless. In autonomous relationships, where each person assumes the responsibility to take care of his or her own feelings, cope with disappointment, and develop another creative idea (for example, when your partner isn't enthusiastic about your achievement, you call a friend who will be). The problem remains a small, temporary setback, with no lingering aftermath.

Awareness

Dependent people tend to block out problems and live in denial because of their high level of fear and hopelessness. In their relationships, this means that small problems can accumulate and eventually become years' worth of resentment, anger, and frustration. As an autonomous thinker, making the choice to be responsible for yourself, be aware of yourself, and evaluate your circumstances prevents this from happening.

Once problems accumulate and build up, they take much more energy and effort to correct. Acting autonomously in intimate relationships means being aware of problems when they are small and, thus, easily solved. Using your self-awareness to know when a problem is imminent, you can communicate what you feel, and open the problem up for discussion with an observation or a question: "You seem tense and anxious. Is anything wrong?" or "I'm sorry I got angry when you were too busy to listen to me last night. Can we talk about it?" Being aware and acting on it means that your relationship problems can be solved early, when they are minor, and before the frustration of an unsolved problem causes resentment to build.

Learning

Autonomous relationships do not follow predetermined patterns, so they are a continuous learning process. Dependent relationships, built on trying to meet others' expectations, are run by old, rigid mental patterns, with little room for learning anything. Dependent people defend themselves when there's a problem and see learning new things as dangerous and frightening.

In comparison, autonomous thinkers welcome the opportunity to learn, which gives them the power to know a partner on an intimate level and to learn to communicate in ways unique to them. Partners in autonomous relationships don't fear problems because they are confident they can solve them with effective choice-making. Negotiating and effective choice-making cannot only find the solution to the problem, but can improve the status of the relationship as a result. When you have experience with successfully solving your relationship issues and problems as they arise, you will begin to see each one as an opportunity to learn something new.

Forgiveness

The power to resolve and let go of old hurts, while learning to protect yourself from being hurt again, is one of the most useful skills in intimate relationships. No matter how much you care, and how hard you try, when you get close to your partner, occasionally you are going to get hurt. Even people who are responsible and care about each other make mistakes, because no one can be 100-percent aware, and because you and your partner will not always perceive situations the same way. This emotional clumsiness can hurt, even when it's unintentional, so you need to know how to clear up hurts when they happen.

By knowing how to express your feelings, and figuring out a way to prevent a similar hurt from happening again, you can make it possible to forgive each other. In true forgiveness, there is no lingering resentment, because the problem is solved. You have learned how to heal the hurt and prevent its reoccurrence, so you can forgive and wipe the slate clean. With forgiveness, autonomous intimacy can become like starting over with a clean slate.

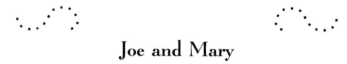

Joe and Mary

Joe and Mary, a married couple in their late 20s, were having a problem because Joe forgot Mary's birthday, and she was hurt. Joe apologized, and that helped, but Mary still felt unsure. After they talked awhile, Joe realized that when he was a child, his family didn't celebrate birthdays, while Mary's family made a special occasion out of them. He "forgot" Mary's birthday, even though he knew it was important to her, because he didn't know what to do, and he helplessly "blanked it out" of his mind. After realizing how important it was to her, he agreed that next year he would ask Mary's friend Sue to help him buy a card and pick out a gift. Mary also decided to make sure her other friends knew when her birthday was so someone would be sure to remember it. Once she decided this, and she heard Joe's plan, she was able to relax, forgive, and forget his mistake.

●

When you use the skills of risk-taking, problem-solving and effective choice, coping with disappointment, awareness, learning, and forgiveness in your relationships, it becomes quite easy to maintain a loving, caring relationship of two equal, independently healthy partners who mutually share their lives and enjoy each other. The more you use these skills to make your relationship more mutual, more successful, and healthier, the more the relationship will display dynamics that are characteristic of autonomous intimacy.

The Characteristics of Autonomous Intimacy

There are four basic characteristics of autonomous intimacy: intimacy with self, non-dependent intimacy with others, warmth, and humor. When these characteristics are present, autonomous intimacy is also present. When these characteristics are not present, it is because dependency and dysfunction have blocked our ability to care for ourselves, be generous with each other, and be relaxed and open enough to enjoy each other.

Intimacy with Self

One reason for feeling dependent and powerless in romantic relationships is fear of loneliness. The belief that "I would rather be in a relationship than be alone," indicates confused, dependent thinking; because that statement could mean: "I would rather be in a relationship— with an addict, with someone violent and abusive, where I'm miserable, with someone who disgusts me—than be alone." This confusion is based on fear of loneliness and a mistaken idea that your sense of loneliness results from a dependency on other people. This fear can be so powerful that people *do* stay in toxic situations, believing it's worse to be alone.

How does this belief develop? We get confused because often being rejected or ignored by others can cause us to reject ourselves. For example, if Mary wants Bob to call her, and he doesn't, Mary criticizes herself: "I'm too fat, that's why he didn't call. No one will ever love me." When she does this, she feels frightened, alienated, and lonely, which she assumes is because she's alone. Confusing the hurt caused by her own self-criticism and self-rejection with loneliness, Mary feels miserable, and blames it on being alone. Her fear makes her vulnerable to a destructive, unsatisfying relationship. Believing that she doesn't deserve to be loved, and that it's painful to be alone, she's vulnerable to the first person who flatters her. She's too panic-stricken to think clearly and make a thoughtful choice.

Mary's loneliness and pain are not the result of Bob's neglect, or of being alone, but a reflection of the quality of her inner relationship. Your interaction with yourself determines whether you feel good or bad, whether you are alone or with someone else. For a short time, the excitement of a new relationship can distract you from your inner pain, but the distraction is temporary. Sooner or later, even in a relationship, the pain will come back, unless you use your magical tools to correct your internal environment. It is not autonomy that creates loneliness, but inner alienation from yourself. Solitude can actually feel fine, and sharing your own company can be joyful. With the internal companionship of autonomy, you never need to feel lonely, because when you're alone, you know how to be a friend to yourself.

When you know you can count on yourself to be a friend, and you have mastered being intimate with yourself, fear of loneliness disappears. When you can enjoy your own company and meet your own needs, loneliness is no longer something to be afraid of. Without the fear of loneliness, you have a choice about when, where, and how you want to be with others. Instead of feeling panicky, desperate (which can cloud your thinking), and dependent on others to keep you feeling okay, you can depend upon internal intimacy to help you feel relaxed and more able to make good, clearly thought out choices about whom you want to be with.

Healthy intimacy is closeness, a feeling of trust and safety that occurs between people (or your child self and your adult self) when they have had enough successful experience together to demonstrate that they care for each other and can rely on each other. True intimacy grows deeper as you realize that you can handle problems successfully together. Intimacy is your confidence in your partner, yourself, and the relationship.

Intimacy with yourself develops in a similar fashion. When your experience intimacy with yourself, it shows you that you can count on yourself for care and support, inner security, peace, and trust, and that your internal intimacy will develop. The difference between intimacy and dependency is that intimacy happens between equals; dependency is based on one individual feeling powerless. When you choose true intimacy, you must give up the dependent dream that someone else (stronger and more capable than you are) can make it better, and accept responsibility for taking care of yourself.

In recovery groups, *thirteenth stepping* means having inappropriate intimacy with a new member (sex with someone newly into recovery); but *The Real Thirteenth Step* as developed here means having appropriate intimacy (caring, responsible contact, and communication) with yourself. Here, as in moving from dependency to autonomy, the focus is taken off the other person and placed on yourself. When you make contact and communicate with your inner child in a loving, caring way, you soon become intimate with yourself. As this internal intimacy develops, you experiment with different kinds of internal dialog and learn what works best for you, and you learn from experience what true intimacy feels like. This, then, becomes the pattern upon which you base the intimacy that you develop with another person.

Neediness and dependency often scare people off, because they have their hands full meeting their own needs, and they know they're too overloaded to carry any further burden beyond their own. Paradoxically, once you develop self-reliance and intimacy with your inner self, the ways you act and relate show others that you are well taken care of, and that you will not place the burden of neediness or expectations on them. Without any additional effort, you'll find that you get more positive attention from autonomous, happy, and successful people.

Would you rather join someone who's having a great time, or be responsible for taking care of someone who's in a mess? Would you want to be partners with a person who's *proved* they can have positive, successful experiences with intimacy (internally, and with friends and family), or with someone whose experiences have been negative and unsuccessful? "Self-image and Self-love," writes clinical psychologist Catherine Solange, are "the key to romance... The state of your love life very accurately reflects your willingness to love yourself and allow others to love you.... Self-love is *Attractive!*"

Healthy, self-confident people recognize your self-esteem because it feels similar to their own. Because you have your inner relationship as a model, you can recognize self-esteem in others.

Intimacy with Others

Once you've developed and enjoyed companionship with yourself, autonomous intimacy with others is much easier. Because your own inner intimacy, caring, and responsibility form the model for your relationships with others, you now have a criterion against which to measure your other relationships. In other words, to determine how well you are doing, you compare the quality of your outside relationships with the quality of your inner relationship, and negotiate with your partner if you see a problem. The success of many of these minor negotiations is what ultimately tells you whether the two of you can work out a viable, sustainable relationship.

When two autonomous people meet and begin communicating to find out if they're a match, and whether they can create a sustainable, satisfying, and successful relationship, they are comparing their external interaction with internal interaction they have already proven works for them. As the relationship progresses, both parties collect more and more evidence that this new person is emotionally healthy, and can relate honestly and reliably. The more success they have with each other, the more trust and intimacy they build together.

This mutual trust and intimacy form the foundation for a love that feels free, generous, and flowing. Here's how Riley Smith and I described autonomous love in our guide to non-codependent relationships, *How To Be a Couple and Still Be Free:*

> Love doesn't limit the beloved.
> Love is not possessive.
> Love encourages growth and satisfaction in the beloved.
> Love rejoices at the beloved's joy.
>
> Let us support one another.
> Let us teach one another.
> Let us love one another—without expectations.
>
> It's okay to take whatever closeness or distance we need.

When you are open and honest with each other, you each feel truly loved for who you really are.

Characteristics of Autonomous Intimacy

There are several characteristics of autonomous intimacy that stand out from the old, dependent model of romantic love.

First, you are willing to make careful selections of the people you become close to, using effective choice techniques to determine if they are reliable, and if your relationship is sustainable. You are not in the relationship out of fear of loneliness, need, helplessness, or so someone else can "make it better," so you can take the time to get to know your partner *before* becoming emotionally invested, and be selective. It is a relationship of *choice.*

Second, you are aware that you are attractive because of your true internal qualities, and not because of surface attributes or behavior. Your intimacy with and reliance on yourself creates your attractiveness.

Third, you value the content—that is, the connectedness, caring, commitment, and satisfaction—of your relationship over its form ("being in love," "being married," "being in a relationship"). It is not the fact of the relationship that is important, but its results: you and your partner feeling mutual love, respect, teamwork, and reliability.

Fourth, you work out problems and issues on the spot, according to what works best at the time, rather than trying to follow a preset pattern or model. You deal with issues and problems as they arise, figuring out the answers as you go along, looking at long-term as well as short-term results, and adapting to new situations as they happen in a by-the-seat-of-the-pants operating style. For example, if one of you gets a great job offer in another city, and the other doesn't want to move, you might decide to try living apart for a few months, or try the new city for a few months, to see what works best, and discuss how it feels as you go along.

Fifth, you value honesty and clear communication above protecting yourself or your partner from hurt feelings, although you take care to express the truth as kindly and gently as you can, and still be understood.

Sixth, you consider your relationship to be an agreement or contract, in which each party has responsibilities and benefits, and which clearly states, in advance, what happens if the contract is broken. This contract might state: "I will stay with you as long as it is healthy for me, and you agree to do the same; if either of us feels that some part of our relationship is becoming unhealthy or uncomfortable, we will bring it up for discussion. If we cannot solve the problem ourselves, we agree to bring in an objective third party to help. If nothing will fix it, we will renegotiate whether we want to stay together." That is, you recognize that your relationship will not survive "no matter what," and you must take responsibility for keeping it worthwhile for yourself and for each other. If either of you feels that your relationship is becoming detrimental, your responsibility is to say so as soon as possible, to give yourselves an opportunity to work the problems out.

Seventh, as with any viable contract, problems, confusion, and changes are resolved through discussion and negotiation. Either of you brings up whatever feels like a problem, and then you discuss it, use effective choice-making techniques, and work it out together.

Eighth, you understand that, in order to be functional, your relationship must be sustainable: that is, you (and your partner) must be able to do what is necessary to keep it going for a lifetime. You recognize that if you must ignore your needs or wants, or act in ways not natural to you to please your partner or society, that you will not be able to sustain such uncomfortable, atypical, self-depriving behavior for long. At the same time, you balance your need to be yourself with other considerations of what is good for you. (For example, you know you won't happily deny yourself classical music forever, but your partner prefers country-western. So, in the interests of sustainability, you find ways that you can listen to classical sometimes, and your partner can listen to country-western.)

Autonomous love is always inviting to others because it puts no pressure on them to take care of you. You can both relax and enjoy yourselves and have fun together, because each of you is meeting your own inner needs, you are not pressured to "make it better" for each other, you take care of problems as they happen, and you don't let them pile up into years of resentment.

Warmth

People often say that autonomous relationships—in which each person is responsible for taking care of him- or herself and not the other person—sound cold, because the fantasy of romantic love doesn't include the clear thinking of effective choice-making or the responsibility of autonomy. But the actual experience of autonomy in loving relationships is anything but cold. Taking care of yourself creates inner security, and the absence of struggle allows you to feel warmth toward each other. Your inner security and comfort radiates out from you as the feeling others describe as "warmth." In this way, autonomously taking care of yourself generates intimacy that feels warm and inviting.

The freedom to love each other without obligation, coupled with mutual trust (based on real experience of each other) and lack of pressure, allows warmth to flow between you. Warmth is a spontaneous feeling of goodwill, respect, pleasure, and satisfaction that arises when relationships are based on autonomy. As equals, together out of choice, demonstrating and experiencing your love of yourselves and each other, you both take responsibility for yourselves and your actions. You solve problems as they arise rather than allowing them to accumulate, and you are free from struggle and frustration. So, when you think of each other, your thoughts will be mostly of the good feelings you have when you're together. It is an accumulation of these good feelings, or emotional successes, over a period of time that we call *warmth*.

Warmth arises out of successful intimacy. In autonomous relationships, you will feel warmth both toward yourself and toward your partner. You can also have warmth in autonomous family relationships or autonomous friendships. As long as the successful history of autonomous loving is there, the warmth will be there, too.

You can tell you're experiencing warmth if you find yourself smiling with pleasure and appreciation when you think of your partner. This warmth is, to me, the greatest reward of autonomous loving and living. To go through days being able to smile to myself about my experience of me, my experience of my spouse, and my experience of friends, makes life feel very worthwhile, and pleasurable—even when outside things go wrong. For example, one day when I was having a difficult time with this book, three of my friends called to tell me they loved me, they were "rooting for me," and they knew I could do it, and my husband came home with a bouquet of flowers. The warmth of those gestures, and the mutually supportive history they represented, made any problems I was having seem minor. Living and loving autonomously is not always easy, because it requires a high degree of self-awareness and self-care. You must take responsibility for thinking about your actions before you do them, but you will also be surrounded with loving, spontaneous warmth every day. Expressing this kind of unpressured, generous warmth feels equally good to the receiver and the giver.

Warmth is also the foundation of autonomous commitment, which is not something you do because you promised or you should. Autonomous commitment is much easier than that. When such warmth and goodwill are present between you and another person, that relationship becomes very precious. You are willing to expend considerable effort to protect such a source of good feelings. That effort is the measure of your commitment. You are not feeling the warmth because you're committed to each other, you feel committed to each other because the warmth is there.

In a dependent relationship, with its attendant feelings of powerlessness, hopelessness, and helplessness, the memories are not as pleasant because the relationship is based on struggle or sacrifice. Our frustration level is higher because we don't get what we want, and the experience of warmth is very fleeting. Some warmth is usually there in the very early days of the relationship, often based more on our fantasy of what we *want* the relationship to be than on our actual experience of what it is. Often the first rush of passion and pleasant feelings fades as frustration grows. Without the foundation of warmth, commitment feels like hard work, and is not sustainable. Although people manage to stay together, they remain so out of obligation or fear of risk-taking, and the relationship loses pleasure and meaning.

Humor

It may seem odd that one of the characteristics of autonomy is humor, but people who are unafraid to be different and individual are also free to be humorous. People who have a solid feeling of self-love and self-worth feel free and secure enough to laugh at silliness in life and in themselves, without being sarcastic or negative. Autonomy is a function of the secure child mind, and children who know they are loved feel secure and become playful.

The most joyous and beloved comedians of all time—such as Sid Caesar, Jonathan Winters, and Lily Tomlin—make us laugh without criticizing or attacking others or themselves. This kind of humor is closely connected to warmth, and it is characteristic of autonomous intimacy.

It takes a certain amount of self-acceptance to create healthy humor, rather than the hurtful kind; but then again, this loving, shared laughter also enhances your degree of self-acceptance. The paradox seems to be that having permission for childlike play also gives permission to be responsible and self-accepting. We laugh *together,* and it feels good.

Just as humor and merriment arise out of the freedom of autonomy, grimness arises out of dependency and obligation. In our parents' youth, relationships were believed to require sacrifice and compromise. We were taught, by word and example, to think of others' feelings and wants, seldom about our own. From a viewpoint of dependency, if we focus autonomously on being healthy ourselves, it seems to eliminate caring about others and to deny these venerable teachings:

- Others' feelings and wants must come first.

- Sacrifice and love are synonymous.

- To care about your self is "selfish" and "stuck up."

- We are incomplete alone, and need another person to make us whole.

- You can only care about yourself or others; not both at once.

But viewed from a healthy, autonomous position based on self-esteem, these old ideas no longer make sense.

Instead, autonomous self-aware people know that no one can be truly generous unless he or she feels secure. If we are deprived, we will (consciously or unconsciously) resent giving. We know that sacrifice and martyrdom are counterproductive to healthy interaction—that it produces guilt to receive benefit at the expense of others' well-being, and that sacrifice is not truly loving because it is unloving toward yourself.

The more you learn about being intimate with yourself and autonomously intimate with each other, the less you struggle; the less you struggle, the more you laugh and play. When an overwhelming feeling of warmth and caring flows over you, often you will laugh. Both the warmth and the laughter arise spontaneously from the childlike inner self, when you treat yourself and your partner with kindness, respect, and caring—in short, when you are autonomously intimate.

A Model for the Autonomous Relationship

The basic attribute of an autonomous relationship is caring, because each partner cares about him- or herself, and each partner cares about the other. Caring about yourself is not selfish, but the foundation of true generosity of spirit and joy of giving.

Self-love creates the inner security that makes generous love possible, and internal intimacy combined with effective choice-making enables you to choose people who are healthy and reliable to love, so when you are autonomous you have an abundance of love to give to others. You realize that you cannot only love and care for yourself and love others at the same time, but that the only functional love is that in which you love yourself as much as you love others.

Operating from this abundance-based belief system, in which we are each fully able to care for ourselves, we are free to be individuals, and we are able to share with each other to our mutual benefit and enjoyment. The desperate, helpless, and dependent attitude that another person should focus his or her life on "making it better" for you, or "making you whole," when examined in the light of this contentment-based, freely shared love seems a selfish and greedy attitude.

This new, autonomous model for relationships gives you a different outlook on life:

- Your ideal of love becomes much more unconditional and free.

- Love is based on cooperation, not martyrdom or sacrifice.

- Problems are solved through cooperative *negotiation,* where you and your partner have equal investments in *both* of you being satisfied.

- Relationships are unique and fulfilling for each individual within a couple and/or family.

- You understand that loving yourself is the necessary foundation for loving anyone else.

- Change and problems are welcomed as opportunities to learn.

- Love is seen as dependable—it is not necessary to try and trap or hold it.

- Trusting oneself becomes more important than trusting others.

- Every event of life is viewed as a challenge to respond in a positive, caring, and healing way.

- Self and others are accepted as fallible, imperfect, yet beautiful human beings.

- Jealousy, possessiveness, dishonesty, and coercion are seen as destructive—traits to work on and overcome.

- Hostile competition feels wasteful and ineffective.

- Cooperation is seen as the ideal way to interact.

- Families become open systems, in which love, honesty, and communication flow freely—both to members within the family and to others.

- Commitment becomes a voluntary, and, therefore, reliable *expression* of an emotional attachment that has grown out of successful interaction, rather than a forced, guilt-based, and unrealistic *promise* based on fantasy and wishing.

As autonomous partners, you create your relationship to suit yourselves and each other. Each relationship is therefore unique and different from all others because the partners are different from everyone else. Autonomy allows you to express your individuality. Partners with healthy self-esteem do not have to distort themselves or deny who they are for fear of not pleasing a partner, or to fit some idea of a relationship.

Because each person involved is unique, there are no rules that apply to all people and all situations. Therefore, a universal model of the roles people play in the "traditional" autonomous relationship is not possible. It is difficult to formulate one-size-fits-all models for autonomous relationships because each new relationship is different from the others.

It is necessary, therefore, to learn to build each relationship from scratch. Rather than following old, dependent, childhood patterns, you can relate "by the seat of your pants"—paying attention to the signs that potential conflicts may be developing, exploring options and weighing the short- and long-term consequences, and choosing your actions consciously with an eye to taking care of yourself and providing mutual satisfaction.

Trouble Signs

In an autonomous relationship, each partner is responsible for expressing his or her wants and needs, and for self-monitoring for signs of resentment, disappointment, or deprivation. These signs indicate a problem either internally or in your relationship with each other.

When these signs occur—usually when we become stressed, are too busy to pay attention, or some problem activates an old, dependent behavior—it is the individual who *feels* them who is responsible to for initiating the effort to make them better. For example, if you're feeling irritable, anxious, and frustrated, it is not appropriate to blame your partner. Instead, you first use an inner-awareness exercise (such as "Finding Your Trouble Spot") to figure out what's wrong; then, if you want your partner's help in solving the problem, you can calmly discuss it. ("I realize that I haven't been getting enough sleep because I've been staying up too late watching TV with you. Can we talk about it?") If you are too upset to talk calmly, you handle your feelings first (on your own) with "Discharging Your Feelings," or "Taking Time Out" (see pages 261 to 264) until you are prepared to talk reasonably. Yelling, screaming, accusing, or rage are never appropriate responses. Instead, they are indications that you are out of control and need help.

An autonomous couple regards fighting as a mistake, not an inevitable part of relationships, and uses effective choice-making to find other ways to handle problems. If Joe and Mary have a fight, they break it off as soon as possible, take a time out, and when they've calmed down, they discuss two problems: what they were fighting about, and why it became a fight and not a discussion. When you are comfortable with your internal relationship, you don't begrudge or resent this responsibility, you embrace it because you know it is the best way to care for yourself, and, at the same time, to ensure a healthy, growing relationship with your partner.

Taking responsibility for yourself in an autonomous relationship means that it's up to you to handle any problem that makes you uncomfortable by following these steps:

1. Become aware of it.

2. Discuss it with yourself and find possible solutions.

3. Implement those solutions that require only your action.

If this solves the problem, fine. If not, go on to step 4.

4. Decide if you want to discuss it with your partner.

5. Discuss the problem and ask for what you want.

6. Negotiate for a *mutually satisfactory* solution.

If you can't find a mutual solution in a reasonable time (an hour or so), you may need to make a temporary decision that you both can agree to, and come back later to try again, until the problem is satisfactorily solved.

Commitment

"I'll love you forever" is a promise that may be unrealistic and impossible to fulfill—it is based on romantic fantasy. It's difficult to predict how you'll feel in five years, never mind forever. While it's romantic and pleasant to speak about love, the true commitment in self-governing love is about negotiating, respect, and fairness, because these activities increase and maintain the warmth in your relationship, which is the best guarantee of relationship commitment and lasting love.

When an autonomous couple commits to having children, or making long-term investments and decisions, they "play chess" with the decisions before they are made, and provide for future possibilities as well as they are able. For example, if they want a baby, they consider their competence as parents (by taking classes and babysitting for friends to learn more) and their financial responsibility, and they research the realities of child-rearing, including arranging for guardians for the children should they, the parents, die. They realize that these serious decisions require serious thought, and that they are not taking care of themselves (or their future children) if they decide based on fantasy alone: "Wouldn't it be nice to have a baby? Babies are so sweet and loveable."

When you are committed to caring for yourself, you value honest communication, so you are unafraid to tell a partner when you are dissatisfied with something. Your mutual guarantee that allows you this honesty actually is: "No surprises—if I'm dissatisfied or unhappy, I'll let you know and give us both a chance to correct it. If we can't, then we get help, and if that doesn't fix it, then we renegotiate what we'll do about the relationship." This is a realistic, sustainable commitment that you can actually expect to meet, and gives you the best possible chance of success. Promising to love "until death do us part," as we can readily see in the divorce rate, is not realistic without effective planning and advance problem-solving to back it up.

Truthfulness

Autonomous people don't waste time ignoring developing problems and being "nice" until they can't stand it anymore, and then blow up with the frustration, saying, "You never listen to me!" or "You always do that!" Autonomous relationships are based on truth. Because partners tell the truth to each other as much and as often (although as gently) as possible, the devastating surprises ("I've had it! I'm leaving you!") do not arise. If there are unsolved problems, you will discuss them for a long time before they could damage the relationship, and the worst possible thing that can happen is that you'll mutually agree that the relationship is not sustainable, and part as friends.

One aspect of this truthfulness is that as an autonomous person, you can also admit when you are wrong, forget, or make a mistake, because you have confidence that you are capable of handling failure and then finding a new solution.

Freedom from Dependent Relationships

As you become less dependent, your love of others becomes less possessive and less needy, more generous, more intimately connected, and more free and flowing. Your newfound autonomy is self-perpetuating, because the old, dependent ways become too difficult and painful in contrast. Once you know how to meet your own needs, and to ask for what you want from others, going back to old, self-effacing, dependent methods of getting what you want, or back to denying yourself, is not at all appealing. As autonomous individuals, each of you recognizes that you are fallible humans who make mistakes, who can admit when you're wrong, and are capable of learning better ways of handling problems and difficult interactions.

For people who can take care of themselves easily and confidently, being taken care of is not an ideal of love, but a type of unpleasant bondage, suitable only for small children and the physically handicapped or mentally ill. In fact, people who truly need care report that being so helpless and dependent is the most difficult part—because it undermines one's self-esteem.

Learning the basic skills of personal autonomy—the magical tools, risk-taking, problem-solving, coping with failure, awareness, learning, and forgiveness—is the foundation for learning the skills necessary for autonomous relationships. Applying those skills to your relationships, and then adding the techniques and exercises that follow in this chapter, will give you a complete model for how to develop the autonomous relationship that is perfect for you. As you practice the techniques and exercises that end this chapter, and add them to the tools you have already learned, you acquire expertise with the techniques and tools needed to reframe your definitions of love and relationships.

Creating and Maintaining Autonomous Intimacy

You already have mastered several skills to help you maintain your autonomy in your relationships, and you can recognize when you have achieved the characteristics of autonomous intimacy. There are several techniques that you will find very helpful for *maintaining* the autonomous intimacy you have created. These techniques help you reclaim your own internal intimacy when you have lost it, communicate better with your partner to make negotiating and problem-solving easier (as well as improve your general communication), and deal with people who are still living by dependent beliefs and patterns.

Setting Boundaries

Living autonomous love is not automatic or easy in a social atmosphere that doesn't support these values. Establishing the difference between what is good for you and what others want, need, or think about it is called *setting boundaries*. "The world is full of people," Joseph Campbell writes in *The Power of Myth*, "who have stopped listening to themselves or have listened only to their neighbors to learn what they ought to do, how they ought to behave, and what the values are that they should be living for." The ability to develop these values for yourself, and to communicate your limits to those who attempt to overstep them, will help you keep others from attempting to impose their beliefs and values on you. Setting boundaries is another aspect of what you have already learned: governing your own life, acting according to what you know is right for you, *even if your family, friends, or lover don't like it.* In short, although problems usually can be negotiated, taking care of yourself sometimes requires saying no.

"Boundaries," writes Jody Hayes, author of the codependency recovery book *Smart Love*, "represent the dividing lines between us and other people. Boundaries are important because they allow us to maintain a healthy sense of self as an individual, separate from everything else. Without this sense, you cannot achieve balance or maintain your own values and goals while encountering the influences and emotions of others." Boundaries and limits, of course, are only needed when you feel your rights are being denied, or the situation is physically, emotionally, or mentally unhealthy for you.

You may need to set the following boundaries for yourself:

- Insisting on privacy and time alone.

- Setting limits to physical contact ("Please don't tickle me. It doesn't feel good to me, and I don't like it.").

- Setting limits to emotional excess ("I won't talk to you if you yell.")

- Setting limits on giving time, attention, money, sex, etc. ("I'm sorry you spent your whole paycheck and don't have your rent, but I can't loan you money.")

- Saying no to requests or demands.

- Refusing to associate with certain behaviors, habits, attitudes, and actions. ("I won't listen to racist jokes. Please don't smoke [or drink] in my house.")

Often, simply knowing what you want, and communicating your wishes to your friend or partner is sufficient to set your boundary. Most other people want to know your preferences so they don't have to guess what your limits are, but in some cases, especially with people who are still in addictive and dependent behavior, setting boundaries is more difficult. When your limits and boundaries aren't respected, you need to let the other person know it. Boundaries are not demands—they do not require the other person to change—they are statements of your intent—the changes *you* will make if your boundaries are not respected.

Steps for Setting Limits

Although your limits are not negotiable, some details are. When someone behaves toward you in a way that you find unacceptable, it is most effective to:

1. Tell them gently what you don't like: "I would prefer it if you didn't smoke in my car." With many people, a simple request will solve the problem.

2. Offer to negotiate: "Your smoking is unpleasant to me. Can we talk about it?"

3. If the other person will not negotiate, make a decision about how to fix your part of the problem, whether the other person likes it or not.

4. In severe cases, you will have to make a unilateral decision: "I'm sorry, but if you won't stop smoking in my car, I can't drive you anymore."

Because it requires *no action at all* on your partner's part, setting your boundaries is not a demand. You can invite your lover or friend to negotiate the details with you, or to express an opinion, but your limits stand *no matter what the other person says*. Setting boundaries and honest communication go hand in hand, because healthy boundaries are an autonomous expression of your true needs (what is healthy for you), rather than a dependent adaptation to (or rebellion against) your partner's (real or imagined) wants.

Maintaining Autonomy With People Who Are Unaware

Once away from the insulated environment of family, friends, or twelve-step programs, (and sometimes even in those venues) we encounter people who don't understand the ground rules we have adopted. Perhaps you are concerned that once you are aware and autonomous, you won't be able to relate to people who have not yet taken the real thirteenth step. This is not true, because being more aware and in charge *increases* your effectiveness, even with those who are still addictive or dependent. The variety of people with whom you can be successful increases, too.

Being autonomous and having self-esteem and the capacity to govern yourself, means you are not at the mercy of others' emotional confusion or uncontrolled behavior. You can let their problems be *only* their problems, and not take them on as your own. Here are some of the more common problem personalities and how to handle intimacy with each type.

Ambivalent personalities. Creating intimacy with potential friends or lovers who give mixed signals—first they seem to invite, then to reject you—can be frustrating. However, getting close to them is easier if you pay attention to *both* signals. The mistake most people make is to believe the invitations, and then get hurt by the rejections.

Handling ambivalence is a lot like taming a wild animal. It takes patience and inner calm. Go slowly, remain relaxed, move closer only when invited, and just stand your ground when rejected. Don't take the ambivalence personally: it's just that your new friend has a difficult time knowing what he or she wants. In this case, emotional autonomy means not becoming more emotionally invested (more in love or caring more) than the other person can match. You are being dependent if you become too invested and *then* demand that the other person match your investment.

Because your prime objective is to take care of yourself, you can only do this as long as it's not emotionally painful. If you find yourself getting hurt feelings, resenting your companion's ambivalence and lack of commitment or energy for the relationship, you're getting too invested, and in danger of being hurt. In that case, it is healthier to back off a bit, let this be a somewhat distant friendship, and look for someone who's more readily available and more definite about his or her interest in you.

Dependent personalities. Surprisingly enough, creating intimacy can be difficult with clingy, overattentive people. The paradox is that you have to have enough separation to create intimacy. A person whose whole world is centered on you, and who tends to give up his or her friends, activities, and lifestyle in favor of yours, loses her or his individual identity, and is not really available for autonomous intimacy. That person wants a parent—not an equal partner—to make his or her life better.

Developing intimacy with dependent people requires boundary-setting and resolve. It's easy to be fooled in the first rush of romance and passion, because for a short while, all that closeness feels okay, and it's what we've all been told love is about. But before too long, you will begin to feel smothered by the other person's needs, unless you set careful limits.

If you realize someone you're in a relationship with is focusing entirely on you, and losing his or her identity in the process (he or she stops seeing friends, waits by the phone, changes schedules and activities to be constantly available) talk about it right away. Let your partner know that individuality is important, and encourage your partner to keep or develop a separate identity, too. The sooner you do this, the easier it is.

Passive personalities. People who resist by doing nothing (they agree to do it, but they're late, or they procrastinate) can be the most frustrating to be around, but they really are very easy to handle, if you know how. To fix this problem, all you have to do is interpret, out loud, what you think their inaction means. If your friend is silent, for example, you can say, "You're not saying anything, and I think that means 'no'. Is that what you mean?" or, "If you don't have a suggestion, I'm going to...(present your solution). Let me know if you think of a better solution, or you have some ideas." or, "You're agreeing with me, but you've agreed before, and I'm afraid you won't keep your part of the bargain. Will you tell me if you don't want to do it?"

If your partner is passively not participating, maintain your autonomy: Figure out what you want to do for yourself, *and communicate it out loud or in writing.* If a friend is habitually late, you can say: "You agreed to be here at 7. If you're late, I'm leaving at 7:15." This gives your friend the choice, clearly states your intent, and minimizes your inconvenience. When dealing with someone who is passive, ambivalent, or reluctant, simply take care of yourself, and don't try to please or control your partner. You'll find their passive behavior eventually disappears, because it becomes more of a problem for your friend than for you.

Calming the Abandoned Child

Most violent arguments and emotional blowups between people, particularly between partners in intimate relationships, occur because both parties involved have (often unconsciously) chosen to allow themselves to become so upset that their inner turmoil interferes with their thinking ability. They cease thinking or using effective choice, and *react* to each other, to the past, and to current events. When upsetting events prevent you from thinking clearly, it is as though your unconscious child mind is *abandoned* by your rational, adult mind, and can only helplessly follow old, childhood patterns. Observing couples with relationship difficulties is often like watching two little children fighting: "You did so!" "I did not, and anyway you stink!" Or, "You did so!" "Well, you did it first!" Actually, fights are just loud, dramatic disagreements about something that could be solved if both parties remained calm and thoughtful. When we get upset, we stop thinking rationally and *interpret* events according to what happened in childhood; *respond* as we did when we were powerless children in a world of adults; and *react* with childlike fear and helplessness. This helplessness often takes the form of rage, resentment, and frustration.

If you grew up in a dysfunctional family where children were told what to do, but not helped to figure it out for themselves, and you have not learned to parent your child self, you have no other choice but to abandon, shut out, or ignore your inner child self (your feelings, reactions, and magical thinking) because it's the only thing you know how to do. Even when you've done your inner work, used adult–child dialogue, and developed internal intimacy, you can still abandon your child self if you get upset and stop thinking, and your autonomous ideas may get bypassed.

There are several unmistakable signs that stress and conflict in a relationship have led to abandonment of your inner child self: Blaming, helplessness, repeating old patterns, and addictive, obsessive, or compulsive behaviors.

Blaming. Blaming is accusing your partner, yourself, other people, or other circumstances for your relationship problems, rather than looking for solutions. As an autonomous adult, you know how to solve problems and that blaming doesn't help, but your dependent child self forgets if the adult part of you is not alert, present, and in charge.

Helplessness. Helplessness is the passive form of blaming. "I can't do anything, because it's their fault." When being upset has caused you to stop thinking, you may feel your old powerlessness, frustration, and helplessness, because without thinking, you cannot solve problems. For example, if you find yourself yelling just the way your alcoholic parent did, or having the same argument with your mate, without resolution, over and over again, you are probably reliving old helplessness.

Repeating old patterns. When you find yourself repeating old patterns, and reacting in old, familiar, dependent, or destructive ways after a fight or problem, your panicky, overwhelmed, and abandoned childlike self is probably inappropriately in charge, and you're not using autonomous, adult thinking to solve your problems. Your child self is acting on the only patterns that are familiar. This will happen less often after you use your magical tools to develop and practice new patterns, and give your child self alternatives.

Addiction, obsession, compulsion. If you begin to feel in danger of reverting to your old, addictive behavior, consider whether you have been listening to your inner child self or are aware of its needs. When inner communication shuts down, problems you could easily handle with autonomous, adult thinking become completely overwhelming to your child mind, which brings up the old hopeless and helpless feelings. When you've completed recovery and developed the skills and attitudes of autonomy, relapse only happens when you forget to use autonomous thinking (when you're under stress, or because you haven't practiced the exercises enough to become strong in your new habits) and you stop taking care of your inner child self for too long a time.

In childhood, you probably learned to escape overwhelming pain or responsibility by using substances, obsessing on a person or action, emotionally acting out, or compulsively doing self-destructive things. When you find yourself tempted to do these things again, and regard those behaviors as signals you can catch early, relapse will never be a problem, because you'll know how to reconnect to your inner child (use "Finding Your Trouble Spot" or other self-awareness exercises) and resume autonomous thinking long before your old behaviors become a problem.

Autonomous relating requires learning how to keep your grown-up aspect of yourself present and in charge. When danger signals are present, understand that your childlike mind feels abandoned and overwhelmed when you face circumstances without using your adult, rational thinking ability. When your partner exhibits these same signs, she or he is probably experiencing self-abandonment, too. It's as though you have surrendered your autonomy, you are out of control, and *no adult, competent person is in charge.* Each of us abandons the inner child from time to time; we get frustrated, tired, overloaded, careless, and upset, and forget to use our autonomous thinking. But if you know the steps to reactivating autonomous thinking, you can quite easily get back in charge.

When you notice signs of abandonment in yourself or your partner, it's time to take a break, calm down, and regain control of your thinking. Being autonomous, learning to be *present* in your own life, to be in charge, means not abandoning your inner child when the going gets rough. In other words, you retain your ability to think and figure out how to take care of yourself. Whether getting back in charge of yourself takes five minutes or 12 hours, it's worth doing, because it stops the destructive behavior, and gives you a chance to find solutions.

Techniques for Re-connecting after Abandonment

The following techniques will help you keep your grown-up rational and thinking mind present in the relationship. By using the techniques, you can overcome the tendency to repeat old, dysfunctional patterns. Regaining the ability to think clearly will put you in a *creative,* rather than a *reactive,* mode, and keep your autonomy intact.

These effective ideas (some of which are time-tested, and some new) will help you get back in charge. No matter who is feeling abandoned, hopeless, destructive, or upset, you or your partner, these three techniques will give you (alone or together) a chance to restore your own internal balance before facing each other again. Although you cannot force your partner to use them, you can certainly choose to use them yourself, no matter which of you is upset. Taking a break gives either or both of you time to regain your autonomy and thinking capacity once feelings have gotten out of hand.

"Taking Time Out" works no matter who is getting upset, because if one of you takes a break, the other is automatically given one, too. This break gives each of you a chance to get beyond your reactions and upset, and to think clearly. It's very helpful if the two of you discuss "Taking Time Out" before you need to use it, but even if you haven't discussed it in advance, it's a good thing to do. Taking a time-out is different from running away from an argument, because the technique includes coming back to discuss the issue. "Discharging Your Feelings" is for you to use when you're emotionally upset, whether you're the only one upset or not. "When Your Partner Shows Signs of Abandonment" is for you to use when your partner seems upset. You can use each of these techniques alone or in combination with each other.

Technique:
Taking Time Out

1. **Separate from the situation or person.**

   When either you or your partner is showing signs of abandonment, make the choice to separate yourself from the situation or person about which you feel hopeless or upset. Let your partner know that you're going to take time out, and that you will be back. Then, for five minutes to a half-hour, walk around the block, take a shower, visit or phone an understanding friend, or just go into another room—long enough to complete this exercise and then go back and deal rationally with the situation. If you're in public (at a party, at work, or at your in-laws' house, for instance) and you need a time-out, try going into the bathroom. (There is almost always a bathroom nearby, and people will not object if you excuse yourself to use it.)

2. **Talk to yourself.**

Once you have separated yourself from the source of upset, use your inner dialogue techniques to 1) make contact with your inner self or your child mind, who is feeling abandoned; 2) listen to how your child feels until you feel calmer; 3) internally discuss the problem and develop as many solutions and options as you can. For example, if you're at a party with your partner and you are having a bad time, your options might be to: go home early (by yourself if necessary), seek out a friend at the party to talk to, volunteer to wash dishes or refill the refreshments, take a walk or a drive (if it's safe) and then come back, or perhaps even dance.

3. **Make a choice.**

Once you have considered what your options are in this situation, make a choice about what to do, and then do it. You might decide to help with the dishes, and after a short time you'll be talking and laughing with others. Or if you've had an argument, knowing that there are several ways to solve it will make you feel much calmer. If you learn to take your time-out as early as possible, before you're too upset, this calmness will come to you rather quickly.

4. **Repeat to develop expertise.**

With enough repetition and practice of this exercise, you can recapture your calmness, get back in charge, and exercise the options you have in just a few minutes.

●

If one of you is so upset that "Taking Time Out" doesn't work, a period of emotional discharge may be necessary. This is easiest to do with someone who is not part of the problem, because anyone connected with the problem (such as a mate with whom you are upset) may not be able to listen to your *dumping* without taking it personally and reacting to it. Discharging *to someone other than your partner* allows you to express your feelings in a way that doesn't aggravate the problem. Once you acknowledge your feelings, you will be calmer and able to think clearly enough to solve the problem. With normal amounts of anxiety, aggravation, or other upset, talking to a friend can be very helpful. To make sure you are not dependent on others, also learn to discharge by yourself.

Be aware that in cases of rape, violence, child abuse, or other traumatic history, or where emotions have been pent-up for a long time, discharging is critically important, needs knowledgeable supervision, and can take some time to complete. In these cases, getting into group or individual therapy is essential.

Technique:
Discharging Your Feelings

1. Separate from the problem.

In order to discharge effectively, take a time-out, and *get away from the source of upset,* as in the previous technique. Find a secure place to be alone or with an uninvolved neutral person. Remember, discharging your feelings at the person you are upset with will just tend to make the problem worse.

2. Express your feelings.

Once you are in a secure place, discharge your feelings by *expressing them* in whatever way feels best to you—write, yell, talk, or cry. If you are alone, you can write or draw in your journal, talk or yell out loud, or discharge them physically: pound a pillow if you're angry, or cover your head with a blanket if you're scared. If you're with someone else—a friend, a sponsor, or a therapist—tell them how you feel.

3. **Wait for a release.**

The most important thing is to keep expressing your feelings until you feel a letting go or a release. This is the discharge, and you'll know when you get to it because you'll experience a feeling of relief. Along with the relief, you may also discover the "real" or central reason for the feelings, which often comes in the form of a new idea. It is often accompanied by a feeling of discovery (*Aha!*), or a feeling of relief (*Whew!*). As soon as you reach release, you'll find that your thinking capacity returns, and you can go on with problem-solving, either by yourself, or with the other person.

●

If your partner is the one acting helpless or very upset, or otherwise showing signs of an abandoned child, you cannot really fix it *for* him, because your partner's feelings are his own responsibility. The following technique can help you make sure you don't make the problem worse.

Technique:
When Your Partner Shows Signs of Abandonment

1. **Listen to the problem.**

Often, people get loud or upset, or quiet and helpless, because they believe their opinion, point of view, or feelings are not being heard. If you believe this may be the case, try giving your partner a chance to talk. Say, "You seem upset, will you tell me about how you feel?" or, "You're so quiet. Please tell me what you think." or just, "Please tell me about it," and then listen quietly. Listening is not the same as agreeing, and you might hear something useful in your partner's point of view. If you can listen without getting upset yourself, and remain calm, you may find that your partner will then become willing to hear your side of the story. However, if you cannot listen calmly right now, skip to Step 3. If listening works, but you still think your partner is not thinking rationally, move to Step 2.

2. Try to contact the adult, rational mind.

If your partner seems very helpless, or very upset, try asking some *calm,* rational questions. Questions about numbers, dates, details, and facts are most successful in engaging the rational, adult mind, because to think of the answers, your partner must be distracted from his or her subconscious feelings. For example, if your partner is yelling and accusing you of something, try asking calmly, "When did I do that?" Often the answer to such a question will be much calmer, and the yelling will stop. If your partner can access the rational part of his mind at all, he will suddenly find himself thinking again and may be relieved to find that you're interested. If that doesn't work, or your partner is still out of control, try Step 3.

3. Take a time-out.

If your partner is becoming very angry or violent, and your presence seems to be prolonging the problem or making it worse, or if you find you can't listen calmly, take a time-out. Even if you didn't start the argument, even if it's your house, or even if you believe *you're right*, you can be the one who disengages from the upset and takes care of yourself. Taking a break will give you both a chance to calm down and return to calmer, more rational thinking.

●

Active Speaking and Autonomous Communication

Many people today know active listening skills: We know to respond and rephrase what the other person is saying to show that we're attentive and understanding. What is not often taught is that you must pay attention to the other person when *you're* talking, too.

Intimacy and good communication require active *listening,* that is, being aware of what your partner is saying, and also active *speaking*—being aware of how your partner is *receiving* what you are saying. If you are not aware of your partner while you are speaking, you can be misunderstood, ignored, or confused by his or her reaction. When you know what to look for, your listener will give you many clues about whether he or she is understanding what you are saying, interested in it, and how he or she is reacting to it.

Active speaking will also help you correct bad speaking habits that make your communication less effective. By keeping the questions of the following exercise in mind, you can learn to practice active speaking, and pay more attention to the significant clues from your listener.

Exercise:
Active Speaking

1. **Do you have your listener's attention?**

    Is your listener looking at you, rather than somewhere over your shoulder, off into space? Does he or she seem to be alert and interested, rather than have glazed eyes or a vacant, bored expression? If the answer to these questions is yes, you're doing fine. If you've lost your listener's attention, your speech is in vain. If you suspect this is the case, try asking a question—it brings wandering attention back instantly. You can try: "What do you think?" or, "Has that ever happened to you?" or, "How does that feel to you?" If you lose your listener's attention frequently, pay attention to your speaking habits. You may want to make a recording of yourself in conversation, so you can check to see if you're speaking in a monotone voice, interrupting others, being unclear, or over-explaining your points.

2. **Does your partner's expression seem appropriate?**

    When you are talking to others, you probably have some expectations of how they're going to feel about what you're saying. If you say "I like you," you expect your caring to be returned, or at least appreciated. If your listener's expression seems to be the wrong reaction for what you are saying, try to find out what is happening. Is your partner thinking of something else? Did he or she misunderstand or misinterpret what you said? You can ask: "I thought I was giving you a compliment, but you don't look happy. Can you explain what you're feeling?" or, "You look like you don't understand. Do you have a question?" or, "I'm upset, and you're smiling. What does that mean?" or simply, "Does that make sense to you?" In this way, you can make sure you are communicating effectively, and that your listener understands what you are saying, and if there's confusion, you can clear up misunderstandings before they become problems.

Active communication shows you care about your listener and are interested in his or her responses. If you're vague, boring, or even upsetting your listener, you won't waste a lot of time before you find out. By paying attention to your partner's reactions, responses, and clues, and by staying present and aware, you can figure out on the spot how to create better communication, and therefore, better intimacy.

●

An additional benefit of learning autonomy is that it gives you skills that help you communicate. When you become proficient at internal intimacy, your deepened awareness of yourself and your sensitivity to your own feelings let you know how much better you feel. Whether you're talking to a friend, solving a problem with a lover, meeting someone new, or making love, by paying attention to how you feel on the *inside* about what's happening on the *outside,* you can learn to interact skillfully. You have the skills to:

- Slow down when you're going too fast.

- Keep things mutual by letting your partner make some of the moves.

- Recognize and respond to subtle invitations for more closeness.

- Keep a good balance between seriousness and fun.

- Avoid inappropriate interaction (don't become parental, childish, or struggle for control).

The next exercise is specially designed to help you develop this interaction skill. Following these steps will help you learn to use your awareness to achieve autonomous communication.

Exercise:
Autonomous Communication

1. Check in with yourself.

During communication, learn to check-in with your inner self and find out how you feel. Use the "Trouble Spot" or "Adult-Child Dialogue" exercises to check-in with your inner self as you talk to people. If you check in often, you'll become quite good at doing it on the spot. While you are in the presence of another person, your inner awareness will let you know how the conversation feels, whether you feel loved, appreciated, and comfortable, and whether the other person is indicating that it feels good or not. Keep this on-the-spot check-in simple, merely paying attention to how your inner self feels, whether you're comfortable, and if you feel you're putting out too much (or not enough) of the energy in the conversation.

2. Debrief prior conversations.

Develop a habit of reviewing your conversations with your partner and friends after you have them. Take some time after having a significant discussion and review it with your inner self, using the techniques you learned to find out how your inner self felt about the conversation and the person you spoke with. Ask your inner self questions like, "How did it feel when Ron said he wanted to slow the relationship down?" "Could I have responded more sympathetically when Amy said her feelings were hurt?" "What was going on when Billy was congratulating me that made me feel so uncomfortable about it?" Review your responses and decide what you would like to change about your communication.

3. Act on what you learn.

Whatever you learn about your inner reactions, pay attention to them and value them. Your intuition and inner emotional awareness are valuable clues about how comfortable and balanced (and, therefore, healthy and autonomous) your interactions are, and they will also help you be aware of which people feel best to talk with. If you feel that you're putting more energy into the conversation than your partner, learn to relax more—hold back, slow down, and give your companion a chance. If you're the one feeling overwhelmed by your partner, experiment with ways of balancing the energy. Speed up a little, or try to be a little more aggressive in speaking. If you consistently feel you can't get in a word, try talking about it with your partner.

If a conversation problem persists, remember that it could be an indication of other potential problems. If someone is unresponsive in a conversation, odds are they're going to be unresponsive emotionally and/or sexually, too. If in conversation your partner often feels hostile toward you, it may mean that he or she is angry most of the time. As you become more familiar with your internal, intuitive responses to people, and you learn to act on what you feel, you'll find you have more ability to create relationships that are more mutual, balanced, and successful.

●

The following exercise combines Magical Tool 3: Self-Love, with "Time Travel" to help you reassure your inner child self and enhance your friendship with yourself. Try it whenever you feel rejected, lonely, abandoned, or unloved. Loneliness is your emotional clue that you are feeling abandoned by *yourself*, and when that happens, you also feel abandoned by others. No one else can meet your internal needs for intimacy and love better than you can, because only you always know exactly what you want, and exactly how satisfying the different kinds of interaction are to you. With this exercise, you can autonomously experience and experiment with the giving and receiving of intimacy—how it feels to give love and how it feels to get exactly the kind of love you want.

By meeting your own needs for conversation, companionship, and attention, you free yourself from anxiety about being alone and simultaneously reduce your dependency on others. Without anxiety, when you have an opportunity to be with another person, you can be relaxed and open. Using internal intimacy to heal your abandonment also means you will be more free to choose who you spend time with, because when being alone feels good, you will only spend time with those who treat you as well as you treat yourself.

Exercise:
Healing Abandonment with Internal Companionship

1. **Find the source of your loneliness.**

   Whenever you find yourself feeling abandoned or lonely, or you long for someone else take care of you or "make it better," ask yourself what you would like them to do or say to you. Take some time with this, because it will give you clues about the source of your loneliness. Make a list. Do you want someone:

   - ☐ To make you laugh?
   - ☐ To tell you everything is okay?
   - ☐ To share an experience with you?
   - ☐ To protect you?
   - ☐ To reassure you?
   - ☐ To understand your feelings?
   - ☐ To be sympathetic and supportive?
   - ☐ To give you a hug?

   Once your list is made, put it aside for a moment, and go on to the next step.

2. Invoke the inner child.

Using "Time Travel," visualize yourself as a child, but instead of going back into your childhood, imagine bringing your child self into your present life. Picture your child with you wherever you are now—sitting with you in your apartment or house, or walking with you outdoors.

3. Choose an activity.

Using your list from Step 1 to help you, talk with your child self and figure out something you can do together. For example:

- ☐ Bike riding.
- ☐ Walking or hiking.
- ☐ Snuggling in bed.
- ☐ Eating while soaking in a bubble bath (especially good with messy food).
- ☐ Dancing to your favorite music.
- ☐ Doing a jigsaw puzzle.
- ☐ Going to the movies.
- ☐ Preparing a special dinner for one.
- ☐ Jumping rope.
- ☐ Going to a favorite restaurant.
- ☐ Taking a drive in the country.
- ☐ Going to a museum or gallery.
- ☐ Going to a play or concert.

4. Make a date and keep your commitment.

Once you find an activity that feels right, set a date and make plans with your child self just as you would with a friend. Plan to actually physically carry out this activity by being mentally in touch with your child self, as though you were doing the activity with an imaginary playmate or companion. When the time arrives, keep your commitment to your child self and carry out your plans. Prepare whatever you need for your date—"Time Travel" your child self here to be with you and do what you promised. For example, if you are going for a walk in the woods, you would go walking alone, but imagine your child self is with you and mentally talk to him or her throughout the walk.

5. **Treat yourself like a friend.**

Remember you and your child within are doing this together. Keep in touch, talk to each other (silently if you're in public), and *share* this experience. Be aware of the information from all five of your senses (Magic Tool 1): sight, hearing, touch, taste, and smell. *Be as attentive with yourself as you would be with a friend whom you love a lot.*

6. **Talk about your experience.**

By imagining talking to your child self, find out what he or she thinks about your time together. Laugh or cry together, share feelings. This may feel awkward at first, so give it a chance, take your time, build upon the internal dialogues you have done in previous exercises. Like Julie Ann in the following example, you will find that spending time with your child self is fun.

Julie Ann

Julie Ann, a 26-year-old from an alcoholic, abusive family, who had been in CoDA and ACA for several years before coming for therapy, rushed into my office one day, sparkling and excited. "I had such a great time this weekend! I can't wait to tell you. I decided to go roller skating at the beach—by myself. At first, I had a tough time. I was hot and sweaty, it was noisy, I was irritated at everyone and everything. Then I remembered little Julie, my little girl within. I decided to bring her along. All of a sudden, everything changed. Little Julie saw pretty colors, the beautiful light on the sea, the clouds in the sky. She laughed and joked with me about the people we passed. She enjoyed the air rushing by my face. We had a wonderful time, and we stopped to celebrate with frozen yogurt on the way home. I can't wait to go with little Julie again. It was more fun than I sometimes have with my friends!"

●

7. **Give yourself all the time you need.**

When you are learning to meet your own needs for love, give your-self plenty of time. Go slowly and give yourself a chance to over-come old shame, embarrassment, self-consciousness, and self-rejection left over from toxic childhood experiences. As a child, you may have thought you were unlovable, and that you didn't deserve attention from anyone, including yourself. If these feelings come up, they're just leftovers from early family experi-ences, and the legacy of a dependently oriented society. You can overcome them with love and caring, patience and practice. Ask yourself the following questions: How does it feel when I pay attention to myself? What do I like best about spending time with my child self? What would I like to do next time?

8. **Repeat to develop an ongoing relationship.**

Try this exercise several times with lots of different activities, until being *with yourself* becomes automatic (using Magical Tool 6: Repetition). Do this often, until it becomes easy and natural to spend time with and love yourself, and you no longer feel dependent on others for love.

●

With practice, these exercises and techniques (added to the magi-cal tools and autonomous thinking skills you have already learned) will make the intimate relationships in your life seem less mystifying and your relationship problems will seem much easier to solve. The more your use these tools and techniques, the more confident and effective you will become at building warm, loving, mutual, autono-mous relationships.

Chapter 8

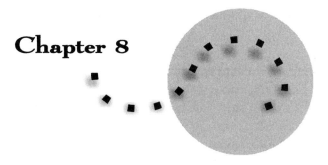

Autonomous Living:
The Promise and the Challenge

Original experience has not been interpreted for you, and so you've got to work out your life for yourself... The courage to face the trials and to bring a whole new body of possibilities into the field of interpreted experience for other people to experience—that's the hero's deed.

—Joseph Campbell

Once you accept responsibility for taking care of yourself and are no longer dependent upon other people, substances, or habits that fill your days and nights, life presents a new and unexpected challenge, one that is unlike anything you have ever experienced or imagined before. Life becomes much easier when you have mastered the skills of autonomy and the sense of self-confidence and self-reliance they bring.

In the beginning, this is a great relief, and you just relax and enjoy life with a minimal amount of chaos and difficulty for the first time. When your new skills of autonomy become natural and automatic, life is a lot more fun. Because you have learned to make effective choices and "play chess" to consider the short- and long-term consequences of your decisions, you no longer go from crisis to crisis. Because your life is much more predictable and calm, you have the energy to build healthier habits and thought patterns, experiment with new behaviors, and begin to enjoy life even more.

When you are no longer numbed out by addiction, exhausted by inner turmoil, or distracted by recurring problems, you experience a burst of enthusiasm and energy. Your inner self, now feeling safer and more confident, is free to be more playful, and you are willing to allow that playfulness to be expressed in your life. You can venture further into life and new situations, you can experiment, succeed, have victories, fail, and be disappointed, but because you feel more secure, you'll have the confidence that you can rely on yourself and adapt when things don't work out the way you planned.

As you begin to experience the childlike joy you didn't have in childhood, you begin to have more fun with friends, family, and co-workers. When your relationships are based on autonomous thinking and mutual respect, they are less chaotic and more positive and rewarding. Instead of struggling with people, you now work out problems with effective choice making and negotiation. Your experience is similar to that of the people whose histories have illustrated each part of this book:

Susan, the floral designer who overcame her compulsive overeating, said: "You told me this would happen, but I never understood how good it would feel! Life is so much easier, and now that I can handle my feelings directly, business problems no longer overwhelm me. Now, when I get angry, I just fix the problem, and the anger goes away! No eating, no depression—I never knew life could feel this good."

Warren, the ACA who had been abused as a child and then in his adult relationships, found he could now tell quite easily when he was being mistreated and break off relationships that felt abusive. He was now making new, healthier friends. He had a new feeling of calm inside, he was no longer having nightmares or flashbacks to his childhood, and he was now spending his weekends playing and relaxing with his child self and his new friends.

Suzanne, whose father had called her "selfish" when she took better care of herself, found that as she got more secure, her family treated her better, and so did others. "Even my boss treats me better now, and I can't believe I used to be so afraid of him! As soon as I stood up for myself, and refused to acknowledge him unless he spoke properly to me, he changed his attitude. All of my life is pleasant now, and I'm really enjoying having friends who treat me well."

Perry, who had been afraid of a new career change, said: "After I got over my old, childhood fear of being ridiculed, I found that my job search was actually enjoyable! I met a lot of new people in my field, and because I wasn't unemployed, I took my time and found the perfect job. My life is so much more enjoyable now. I feel good about my work and I have more personal time to enjoy myself, I'm now having fun looking for a new, autonomous romance."

Carla, the formerly battered woman whose children were now grown, said: "I never would have believed an old broad like me could have a new love, but I feel like a schoolgirl! He treats me well, and when we have a problem, we work it out together. And, I know that my relationship with me is the most important one, so that gives me the freedom to leave if this relationship ever gets abusive. Not that I think it will. Learning to take care of myself and negotiate with others has made all my relationships, even with my children, work better. I really like my life."

●

Like most of these people, you will probably have difficulty adjusting to this at first, after years of experiencing chaos and pain. It may take you a while to learn to trust your newfound calm and happiness, to believe it will last. In the early months, the calm and security of autonomous living seems fragile, as though you'll revert back to old behaviors at any moment. But, as you learn that you can correct any errors you make and sustain your new, healthy ways of living and relating, your feeling of competence and security in your new way of living will grow.

The relief of this new, uncomplicated, and straightforward style of living can last months or years, particularly if new dynamics such as a relationship, career, or lifestyle are being explored. For that period, it is enough just to have ended the chaos and be able to live functionally and effectively. But, after a while, as your new happiness becomes commonplace and feels natural, you will begin to notice something—a feeling of emptiness where all the struggle and chaos, followed by excitement and joy, has been. A sense of restlessness, as if there were something you ought to be doing, something missing from your life. This calm life has begun to be a little *too* calm, and you begin to wonder: "What else is there?" It may even feel as though your whole *being* is asking, "Now what?"

This phase worries most people who hit it, because they mistake their restlessness and need to challenge themselves with their old drive to addictive behavior. They fear it means they're looking for a relapse, to get back into crisis. However, you need not worry. Once autonomous thinking, effective choice, and functional internal and external relationships become easy and natural for you, any fear that you will revert to addictive behavior are groundless. Even if you try to go back to old behavior, you'll find that it feels too bad to continue doing it. You're a different person than when you were dependent, and your old habits don't work any more.

In your addictive, dependent period, all your time was taken up by struggling, avoiding, being overwhelmed by responsibility, and trying to get someone or something else to make it better. There was never any question of what to do with yourself or your time. And since then your life has been taken up with enjoying your new achievements of autonomy and your new ability to cope well with life. Now that the novelty has worn off, you are faced with a new situation, one you never had to face before: what to do with your time and energy.

Getting to this stage feels much like being healthy again after a long illness; for a while, it is enough just to feel well, to get up in the morning and sit in the sun. But soon, as your energy rises and your confidence in remaining healthy returns, you feel restless. You want to get back to your life, to your friends, to your accomplishments; just sitting and not feeling sick is no longer enough.

Finding Your Purpose in Life

When you begin to feel restless, as if there must be more to life (as many who learn to live autonomously eventually do), it is a signal that you need more challenge in your life. It tells you that just feeling good is no longer enough, that your individuality needs greater and more range to express itself more completely, and that you need a way to evaluate your ideas for creative expression before you act on your new energy and impulses. In short, you're looking for a new *purpose*, more meaning in your life.

Purpose is a very adult concept. Children have an automatic, built-in purpose: survival, and learning how to function in their world. Some adults never grow beyond this original purpose; the basic needs of survival (food, shelter, clothing, contact) occupy their entire lives. And indeed, in a chaotic, dependent, out-of-control life, just keeping the basics of survival together takes all your time and energy. But as you are now experiencing, people who learn autonomous living have a *surplus* of energy. People for whom the basics of life are already established need more: They need a sense of meaning and a higher purpose than just survival. When you know how to think clearly, and be effective, a life based on just survival is boring; a person with self-confidence and self-esteem needs a challenge to feel satisfied, a way to express her or his uniqueness and individuality to him- or herself, to friends, and to the world.

Each of us have special talents and abilities that begin to beg for expression when the issue of survival ceases to occupy all our time. In *The Power of Myth,* philosopher/teacher Joseph Campbell describes this "maturation of the individual, from dependency through adulthood, through maturity": "Some people are living on the level of the sex organs... Then you come to...the will to power... centered on obstructions and overcoming the obstructions. Then there comes giving oneself to others one way or another..." Finally, you begin "... to work out your life for yourself...to face...a whole new body of possibilities...."

When you learned autonomous thinking and effective choice, your life began to work better and you felt better about yourself, so your energy and enthusiasm rose. Because this success has enhanced your self-confidence, your capacity to meet and enjoy challenges is greater than it ever was. Your inner self is beginning to want to express itself to the world. But if your life's purpose is not evident to you already, how do you find out what it is? Where does a sense of purpose come from? Although finding a purpose that can encompass your whole life might seem impossible or overwhelmingly difficult and daunting at first—even for someone confident of their ability to rely on themselves to meet most challenges—you really don't have to look long or hard to find it. It is *your* purpose, remember. It comes from within you, and it is not imposed or chosen from outside. Bernie Siegel describes this sense of purpose as being within all living things "directing" them "from within." It is what "makes it possible for the fertilized egg to know who to grow up to be, physically, intellectually, psychologically, and spiritually."

In human beings, Siegel writes, our sense of purpose takes the form of "an inner message, an inner awareness, that says, 'This is your path, this is how you can be the best human being possible.' If you follow it, you will achieve your full growth and full potential." To find your purpose, you need not look any further than your own inner self: "...if you learn to listen, your inner voice will speak to you about your path, about... your... 'job on earth.'"

From this gradually grows a sense of purpose, what Dr. Siegel calls your "job on earth"—a sense of the significance of your life and the responsibility that goes with it. Your purpose may be your livelihood, or it may have nothing to do with how you make a living. Your purpose may be a simple one, like making a good, healthy life for yourself and your children, or it may be more dramatic and based on what you learned by healing your own childhood experience. Many people have experienced the power that inner purpose has to transform anxiety, anger, fear, and rage into powerful, life-affirming action:

Dr. Siegel knows about inner purpose because he experienced it himself: As a cancer specialist, he was so discouraged and frustrated about the lack of success of medicine against cancer, he had the courage to look at patients who had experienced "miracle cures" and "spontaneous remissions," which no physician had ever done. Although he was ridiculed by the medical establishment, he persevered in his autonomous thinking, and out of it came his ECaP (exceptional cancer patients) recovery groups, and his book, *Love, Medicine and Miracles.*

For Carla, finding purpose meant going back to college at age 55 to get the law degree she had wanted, before marriage and kids intervened.

Cleve Jones turned his rage, bitterness, and grief about AIDS into the Names Project Memorial Quilt, which has helped people throughout the world express, heal, and understand the grief resulting from this tragic epidemic.

For Marguerite, the young woman who was afraid to go out, it was volunteering to work with abused and abandoned children in a shelter.

Candy Lightner, after her 13-year-old daughter was killed by a drunk driver, used the power of her grief and rage to found Mothers Against Drunk Driving (MADD), to combat the problem and prevent the senseless deaths of other children.

For Warren, it was quitting his lucrative and successful career as a programmer to work part-time and become a gardening landscaper.

Sojourner Truth, an African-American and former slave, was instrumental in developing the Underground Railway to guide slaves to freedom before and during the American Civil War.

Ron Kovic, a soldier who was paralyzed from the waist down in what he felt was a senseless war, turned first to alcoholism, but then recovered and channeled his resentment and rage into anti-war protest. He later wrote the best-selling book and Oscar-winning movie script, *Born on the Fourth of July.*

●

A life purpose means you can control your destiny, no matter what the force of the hardships you have incurred through dependency and addictive behavior. You already have everything you need to find your purpose, and you can begin at once, through the exercise that follows later in this chapter. You have already mastered the earlier exercises designed to help you communicate and listen to your inner self, your subconscious mind, and it is through these techniques, by focusing them on your inner purpose, that you can find your answers. By now, you may already have many ideas but not trust them or take them seriously. Many therapy clients knew what their "job on earth," or life's purpose, was long before they got into recovery, but they were too distrustful of themselves, or too hopeless and helpless to believe it or act on it.

Your purpose may make itself clear to you in one instant flash, or gradually, as if you were supposed to follow clues. Whether you get it all at once or a piece at a time, it will still take work and experience to bring it about. With the help of your magical tools, your inner, subconscious, childlike mind can become a source of inner wisdom. This wisdom is not rational or practical in nature, but more intuitive and spiritual. It can provide a way to see the *big picture,* or a more *detached* and *objective viewpoint* of the issues and problems of life. Combined with autonomous, adult thinking, "Playing Chess" and choice making, inner wisdom gives you one more viewpoint from which to evaluate decisions and actions.

Access to inner wisdom, coupled with autonomous thinking, endows everything you experience with extra meaning. All the events, activities, and patterns of your life can be viewed from both perspectives. Using both viewpoints (intuitive wisdom and autonomous thinking) can even become the basis of your partnership with, instead of dependency on, the Higher Power spoken of in discussing the power of the Twelve Steps.

Many people have successfully changed their attitudes, livelihood, activities, and environment, they thought ahead, "played chess," and did not proceed blindly. Using both your subconscious, inner wisdom and adult, rational mind thinking builds a successful life.

The Need for Stimulus

Another reason you will be compelled to find your purpose in life is that human beings need stimulus: a challenge from yourself, another, or your environment, that causes you to think and react. Newborn babies die without enough stimulus. It keeps the mind alert and healthy. We all thrive on stimulus, and some of us crave more than others. In dysfunctional families, the need for stimulus that normally would lead us to take risks and seek to learn new things is often sidetracked into the drama of compulsion, addiction, and dependency, which supplies lots of action and excitement. It keeps us occupied, adrenalized, and stimulated while, because the family creates drama according to an established pattern, it still feels familiar, predictable, and therefore safe. As we grow up, this need for the old, familiar excitement and stimulus remains one of the most tempting and compelling aspects of dependency, as Joy Davidson expertly outlines in *The Agony of It All:*

> ...I began to see over and over again, a sometimes subtle, sometimes distinct straining toward the acting out of intense scenarios that were highly distressing and equally stimulating...*not* out of a hidden wish to suffer or a belief that they deserved pain, but out of a *restrained or severely misdirected, but essentially healthy, drive for heightened stimulation...* When we create our own exciting melodramas...we set up or build upon potentially dramatic or explosive situations so that they are exaggerated, sensationalized, and pushed to the limits. As these scenarios become more volatile, they also become more thrilling...we are frequently unconscious of making it happen.

Replacing that excitement is essential, for without sufficient stimulus, we cannot experience enough satisfaction. Health and sobriety, if we allow it to be dull and boring, cannot be sustained. Some people even fall off the wagon and revert to destructive behaviors, unhealthy relationships, and old addictions because they don't know what else to do to relieve their boredom.

Having a purpose supplies plenty of stimulus. The challenge of real fulfillment becomes as exciting as the old addiction, compulsion, obsession, and drama, but with positive, healthy results. The popular image of excitement is often destructive, violent, and frightening. There are few positive images of excitement: of healing and growth, of helping others grow and change, of fighting for human rights, of saving the Earth, or of the challenge and satisfaction of building a healthy, productive life.

Having a higher purpose provides plenty of stimulus, because it constantly challenges us with new ideas and the necessity to work out new solutions to new problems. Your life feels stimulating and rewarding and you feel enthusiastic about the next step toward your goal, because living according to a heartfelt purpose is motivating and energizing.

We are all used to thinking of excitement as nonproductive, but there is no need to manufacture melodrama as a source of stimulation, because life itself presents so many opportunities for excitement. As Carlos Castanada's Don Juan said: "In a world where Death is the hunter, my friend, there is no room for regret or doubt. There is only room for decision." Life itself is a challenge, and using our limited time on the planet for a purpose—to create something unique, special, and that feels good to us—is both exciting and satisfying. Joseph Campbell explains how stimulating and life-giving following your inner purpose can be:

> My general formula is "follow your bliss." Find where it is, and don't be afraid to follow it...in doing that, you save the world. The influence of a vital person vitalizes, there's no doubt about it. People have the notion of saving the world by shifting things around, changing the rules, and who's on top, and so forth. No, no! ...The thing to do is to bring life to it, and the only way to do that is to find in your own case where the life is and become alive yourself.

Marsha Sinetar, who studied people with the courage to live fulfilling lives, says there is a "predictable sequence" to the "life-enhancing choices" those people made. In *Elegant Choices, Healing Choices,* she outlines the steps of the experience of living autonomously:

- We choose in a wholesome direction *despite* feelings of fear or our need to cling to the familiar.

- Instead of avoiding those things we fear, we start proactively selecting those ways of being, thinking, and acting that most efficiently take us toward what we consciously want.

- Our self-acceptance for our truest, 'living self' increases; we move to present our real self to others, to live our real selves in our lives.

- Ultimately, our choices *flow* from this core-self, instead of being *forced*. We are faithfully courageous and loving toward ourselves and—eventually—toward others. Growing more closely attuned to our inner workings, we also grow more conscious and self-accepting.

- Soon we notice how our negative feelings can actually *help* us by providing information to us much as a mirror or photograph.

Danaan Parry, who worked with Vietnam War Veterans of *both sides* to heal the after-effects of the war, wrote of the "new warrior" (his term for those who turn violent, destructive energy into life-affirming, purposeful, and stimulating action), and the challenge of disagreeing with those who think that dependency is safe:

> The new warrior...says, "I am going to show... that there is no real [problem] out there. That darkness exists within each one of us, and I will demand that we have the courage to look at it." So...warriors have to have the courage to put up with some pretty heavy flak from their own people. We are asking our own people to grow and not to project.

Life with a purpose can be new, different, and challenging, but it contains the vitality and stimulus that give life meaning. Living with purpose is constantly a new ball game. Every situation you encounter is unique and requires clear thinking ability, and it must be constantly checked against your purpose to see what steps you need to take. Many of my former clients find that living life according to their inner purpose feels courageous and exploratory. Like Carla, they can now say, "I really like my life."

It *is* akin to living as a warrior, a new, exciting way to live that can satisfy the stimulus hunger that was once satiated by the drama of dependency. Your life no longer needs to be desperate to be exciting, because your purpose is stimulating enough. Look around you at the people who have the most fulfilling and rewarding lives. Then look at the ones who seem to have a definite purpose. You'll find both groups contain the same people.

Your Inner Purpose

Here's a guided fantasy (Magical Tool 3: Imagery) designed to help you communicate with your inner self and use clues contained in your personality characteristics, desires, and talents to find your "job on earth." It is not necessary to believe in a Higher Power to do this, but imagining what a Higher Power intended often gives you a broader, more detached, wiser, and kinder view of yourself and your life. The purpose of this exercise is to examine who you are from a different vantage point, as an all-knowing being might see it. For the purpose of the exercise, assume that an infinitely wise and creative being designed your own unique mix of traits to accomplish a specific goal. What could a benevolent Higher Power have possibly had in mind when you were created? Be careful, now, and don't insult or demean the special creation that you are. This is holy handiwork we're talking about.

Exercise
Finding Your Inner Purpose

Imagine your Higher Power's plan. If you were an intelligent, loving God, or your Higher Power, who designed the Earth with a plan, and designed you just the way you are to fit into that plan, what purpose would you have?

Look for clues to your purpose in your inherent talents and qualities. What might a Higher Power intend them to accomplish? If you have trouble focusing on your talents and qualities, the following questionnaire is designed to help you find them. It will give you an opportunity to discover or review the kind of person you are, and to identify the abilities that come naturally to you (even if they sometimes get you into trouble). Read it over, choose one or several answers in each category that fit you best, and use each list to stimulate your own ideas. Some people have an instant "aha" when doing this exercise. Others take longer to ponder it before it makes sense. The point is to "shake up" your perception of yourself and your talents, qualities, and circumstances, and give you a chance to view them differently.

Using the following lists as guides, write your personal qualities, talents, desires, and circumstances down on a separate sheet of paper.

Personal Qualities

Parents know that babies are born with different personality traits; one baby will be easygoing, the next more sensitive. Although these inherent qualities are further shaped (or sometimes distorted) by the growing-up experience, where they come from initially is a mystery. Approach this list as if you were made uniquely the way you are for a reason.

What Are Your Personal Qualities?

- ☐ Friendly, open, outgoing.
- ☐ Solitary, quiet, reserved.
- ☐ Communicative, verbal.
- ☐ A good listener, receptive.
- ☐ A dreamer, mental.
- ☐ A conscientious worker, productive.
- ☐ Physically active, outdoorsy.
- ☐ Relaxed, meditative.
- ☐ Practical, thrifty, cautious.
- ☐ Courageous, bold, experimental.
- ☐ Fun, enthusiastic.
- ☐ Imaginative, creative.

- ☐ Funny, witty.

- ☐ Original, innovative (sometimes called "weird").

- ☐ Do you work better or have more fun alone or with others?

- ☐ Do you prefer structure or openness?

- ☐ Is productivity or play more important to you?

List the personality traits you have that were not on this list.

Talent

All of us have special talents and abilities, but we may have been raised to discount them and may not even be consciously aware of them. After determining where you talents lie, add them to your list and try to imagine why a Higher Power might have given them to you in your particular combination.

What Are Your Talents?

- ☐ Music (playing, singing, composing, appreciating, critiquing).

- ☐ Communication (conversation, public speaking, writing, explaining).

- ☐ Artistic (visual arts, pottery, dance, acting, directing).

- ☐ Mental skill or play (mathematics, spatial relations, puzzles, computer games or programming, crosswords).

- ☐ Good with your hands (mechanical, crafts, carpentry, pottery, needlework, sculpture).

- ☐ Sports (playing individual or team sports, coaching, refereeing, big fan, commentator).

- ☐ Negotiation (seeing both sides of a question, helping people understand each other, interpretation, brainstorming options).

- [ ] Nurturing (caring for children, the sick, the elderly, friends).
- [ ] Getting things done (efficiency, dedication, follow-through, determination, job satisfaction).

List your talents that don't appear on this list.

Desire

Just as we are born with different qualities and talents, we are born with different wants. Why might a Higher Power have given you yours? There is a saying in mystical writings that "all wants lead to God." The belief behind it is that if you seek to understand your deepest desires and follow them, you will find your path through life. This is what Joseph Campbell calls "following your bliss."

What Are Your Desires?
- [ ] Clean up the environment.
- [ ] Make a political difference.
- [ ] Express yourself musically or artistically.
- [ ] Travel.
- [ ] Make a quilt.
- [ ] Do Shakespeare in the park.
- [ ] Make a film.
- [ ] Be powerful.
- [ ] Become a healer or healthcare worker.
- [ ] Grow a garden.
- [ ] To follow a spiritual path.
- [ ] Love and be loved.
- [ ] Fly an airplane.

- ☐ Save animals or human lives.

- ☐ Get a college degree.

- ☐ Write a book.

- ☐ Teach and/or write philosophy.

List your desires that don't appear on the above list.

Circumstances

Certain patterns seem to repeat in our lives, whether or not we want them to. Some are pleasant, some are not, but often the unpleasant, unwanted events turn out to be as valuable as the pleasant ones, because we may learn something new, or break through some resistance that held us back. What if these patterns are happening repeatedly for a reason? What might a Higher Power be trying to teach or show you?

Circumstances That Repeat in Your Life

- ☐ People tell you their life stories (whether or not you ask).

- ☐ You often wind up teaching, talking to, organizing or leading groups.

- ☐ You are exposed to people vastly different from you, of whom some people might be contemptuous or afraid.

- ☐ You're drawn to churches, museums, forests, bookstores, farms, schools, hospitals, theaters, and factories.

- ☐ You find yourself repeatedly working with computers, plants, paintbrushes, horses, babies, heavy machinery, and microscopes.

- ☐ Your career self-destructs, and you have to find something else.

☐ You keep thinking about helping AIDS babies or Mother Teresa, writing a play or novel, going to Brazil, having sex, organizing Eastern Europe, living in the woods.

☐ You keep feeling that there's something you're supposed to be doing, but you don't know what it is.

List the circumstances you repeatedly encounter that don't appear on this list.

Putting It All Together

Fill in the blanks below with the appropriate words. You may have several words for each blank in the sentence. If you have lots of choices for each blank, you may want to write out the sentence several times with numerous variations. When you've done this, your sentence may make perfect sense to you, or the result may be gibberish or sound silly. Experiment with it for a while. Allow your intuition to help out here. Make wild guesses and play with the concept. Taking your list of traits, talents, wants, and events that seem characteristic of you, put them in sentence form like this:

I (your Higher Power) designed _____
(your name) to be a _____
(quality) person who can _____
(talent) and I put (him, her) in _____
(circumstance) often, because I want_____
(your name) to help me out by_____
(your desire).

●

Once your unconscious inner self gets the idea that you're considering your "job on earth," mysterious things will begin to happen. You'll notice qualities and talents in you that you never noticed before, or you'll view traits positively that used to feel negative. You'll view the circumstances of your life differently, as though they have more than just the obvious meaning, and you'll consider your desires more carefully, rather than just discounting them. Assume that both your character traits and the events of your life, if used appropriately, are positive and purposeful. After a while, a pattern will emerge; you'll begin to understand your "job on earth," and it might even surprise you.

If you do this exercise conscientiously, it will begin to create change in your life. Marsha Sinetar says that by "growing more closely attuned to our inner workings, we also grow more conscious and self-accepting." Your acceptance of personal characteristics that may have been downgraded or ridiculed in your past and a new open-mindedness about the meaning of events in your life will give you more options from which to choose.

As your awareness of your purpose grows, don't just surrender your autonomy and depend only on your inner voice; apply autonomous thinking as in other matters, evaluate what you inner voice says, and exercise choice making before you make drastic changes. If you follow this advice, you will be able to work with the information you get from deep within, adjusting it to your outer reality and using your adult rational mind to make sure you're successful.

Jason

Jason, a 33-year-old lawyer in recovery who did this exercise, realized he wanted to be a playwright, but he was afraid to quit his job and take the time he needed to write. Once he saw writing plays as his "job on earth," he was able to quit the law firm he hated, work part-time and write. He has since won several awards and had plays produced in small theaters. He says, "I'm poorer in money, but I'm so much richer in happiness and satisfaction. This is the me I always wanted to be."

●

Endowing your life with a specific purpose makes a profound difference in everything you do because you can compare all your actions and decisions against a new criterion: Will this move you closer to or farther away from your purpose?

Finding your purpose in life is much like choosing your destination for a journey. As soon as you determine where you are going, many decisions are already made for you; what to spend your money on, what to learn for the journey, and which direction to go in. Each fork in the road you encounter is evaluated and chosen according to whether or not it takes you toward your destination.

Jason, the lawyer turned playwright, once said: "Ever since I was a small boy I knew my dad wanted me to be a lawyer. When someone asked me what I was going to be when I grew up, I *always* said 'a lawyer,' and I liked it that people were impressed. But I never thought about what a lawyer *was*. I don't like the work; it's too technical and not creative, I'm not interested, and I don't really care. I drag myself to work every day."

Like Jason, you may be living many parts of your life the way *others* think you should. Or, you may be living in rebellion, according to what *upsets* certain people. Either way, you haven't made your own decision; you're living because of others, not for yourself. For as long as you do it that way, you will feel dissatisfied. Jason says, "Some days it's really hard, and it's scary, sometimes, but I'm so much *happier* this way. *I know I'm doing what I was born to do.*"

The challenge of living your life toward a specific purpose is exciting enough that you will not be tempted to fall back into old, addictive/compulsive forms of stimulation. It's the autonomous, heroic way of challenging yourself—the rewards are a sense of satisfaction that comes from knowing you're doing what you were "born to do."

Evaluating Autonomous Living

Sooner or later, you will probably reach a point where you're wondering: "Okay, I've taken the Real Thirteenth Step. I have now decided what I think is my purpose. So how do I know my purpose is correct? I can evaluate my individual choices and decisions, but how do I evaluate my life? If I don't live by other's ideas of who I am and what I should do, then what are the guidelines I do live by?"

There are three criteria against which your choice of a higher purpose can safely be checked: results, experience, and ethics. Let's take a look at these checkpoints, and see how they are developed.

Results

Although the initial inspiration comes from within, there are also concrete, external clues by which you can evaluate whether you have chosen your purpose wisely. By paying attention to the results, the way a scientist doing a lab experiment would, you can know if you're on the right track in your life. Life is your laboratory, because all your actions have results.

By paying attention to whether the circumstances are working in your favor, you can tell how well you are doing. These circumstances include your stress level, your finances, your relationships, the time spent at leisure and work, and whether the steps you need to follow to achieve your life purpose are going smoothly or with difficulty.

For example, Jason is aware that his finances are not as abundant as they were when he was a lawyer, but he does make sufficient money to live comfortably, if simply, his stress level is less; he has more free time, more self-expression; and he is more relaxed and pleasant in his relationships. These results, for Jason, mean that his life works better *in the ways that are important to him* than it did as a lawyer, when his stress level (resulting from frustration with his job, commuting, and pressure to perform) was extremely high, he had little free time, and consequently, he had less patience and energy for his relationships.

Sometimes things in your experiment with purposeful living will go wrong, even when your purpose is good, and your attempts are honest. Or your results may be mixed and inconclusive. When you get a negative result, to analyze whether you need to reevaluate your purpose, you can ask yourself two questions:

1. ***Is this an important result?*** One negative, amid a lot of positives, may not be important. Also, in some circumstances, a certain number of negative results are to be expected. All successful people have many stories of failure and rejection, but they never gave up and scrapped their work because of failure. They just reevaluated, corrected errors, and tried again. In your case, you can learn from some negative results and improve your work; others you'll consider, find that you don't agree, and you'll ignore them and persevere.

2. ***How does this affect my original idea?*** Is the result so different from what you expected that you want to reevaluate what you are doing in life, or could it just give you some new ideas about how to do it more effectively, if you approach the situation more creatively?

Marsha Sinetar discovered that people with purpose often learn how to use negative results in a positive way: "Soon we notice how our negative feelings can actually *help* us, provide information to us much as a mirror or photograph."

In addition to the concrete, observable results, there are other internal results that help you decide whether your purpose and your autonomous living are going well. Your disappointment, dissatisfaction, anger, grief, frustration, and fear, if you pay attention to them and learn from them, are all *clues* about whether or not your life is satisfying and healthy for you. So are your positive emotions, such as happiness, fulfillment, satisfaction, contentment, and excitement.

Carla, for example, who enrolled in law school at age 55, is experiencing a lot of stress, and has less free time than ever, but she feels a very high degree of inner satisfaction, which tells her that what she's doing is good for her, and worth the stress and hard work she has to go through to achieve her purpose.

Carla is sure that she has found the right purpose because of her feeling of deep inner satisfaction, which according to the dictionary is "a state of well-being consequent upon having achieved a goal, or gratified an appetite or motive." Knowing you can cope with the world on your own terms, focusing on your life purpose, and achieving goals on the way to making your purpose a reality produces a high degree of satisfaction. It gives you a specific goal or goals you can strive for, and a way to know when you've achieved each goal.

Many frightened, dependent people *never* feel satisfied or content. Their feeling of dissatisfaction, of emptiness, comes from not having a purpose, because without a purpose to compare to, they cannot know when they reach goals. It's like never knowing when your journey is finished because you never decided on a destination, or never getting the satisfaction of graduation because you never chose a major subject in which the university could say you had completed the requirements. Addiction, obsession, and compulsion are often ineffective attempts to quench your longing for satisfaction, for completion of some goals. In contrast, having goals you can reach and living in quest of your higher purpose means you are guided by internal wisdom and have criteria for evaluating your choices.

Fulfillment from Results

Another result or positive sign that you have chosen your purpose well is fulfillment. Fulfillment is the difference between feeling that life is empty, meaningless, and out of your control, and feeling that it is significant, rewarding, deeply nourishing, and sustaining, and you are getting what you want out of it. Fulfillment and satisfaction produce a feeling of internal warmth, much like the feeling that arises from autonomous loving. When you have a sense of purpose, and you are working to bring that purpose into reality, each step or small achievement along the way makes you feel better about yourself. You can judge the appropriateness of your purpose and the way you are carrying it out by your inner sense of pride in yourself, feeling worthwhile and valuable as a person, and your level of enjoyment or happiness. Because your sense of purpose has meaning for you in terms of your own personal value system, to work toward achieving that purpose helps you feel worthwhile as a person and gives you a life of which you can feel proud, not because it pleases others, but because you feel it has intrinsic value. That is, whether anyone knows you're doing it or not, it feels worth doing. Joseph Campbell writes when you follow your bliss you have a feeling that "the life that you ought to be living is the one you are living" and a sense that "... no matter what happens, this is the validation of [your] life."

Experience

The second criterion for evaluating your higher purpose is experience. As you experience bringing your idea or fantasy of your purpose toward the reality of fulfillment, both the original idea and the final expression of it will change. In the beginning, your purpose is a dream, a fantasy. It is real only in your mind, and until you *experience* it, you can only *imagine* it. Anything that exists only in your imagination is bound to need some adjustment as you begin to make it a reality.

For example, Carla's dream of being a lawyer is *only* a dream as long as she's in law school. But, the more she learns in school, the clearer her idea of what a lawyer does and all the ways you can be a lawyer will change. By the time she graduates, works in some law offices as a legal clerk, and passes the bar, she'll have a much better idea of what she wants. Instead of thinking she wants to be "a lawyer," she'll know whether she wants to be in corporate, insurance, civil, or criminal law, and she may have an idea that she'd like to be in private practice rather than in a big firm. Even if she starts out dreaming about lots of money and a lovely office with antique furnishings and a great secretary, she may find herself, years later, in a plain little office, making modest money, because she gets the most satisfaction out of helping battered women and children, which is not the most prestigious or lucrative work. This may be far from Carla's original dream, but, because she made the choices according to her inner sense of what was most important, she'll still be certain that it's the right thing for her to do. Her inner satisfaction is more important to her than external evidence of success. Watching her vision change as she brought it into reality, and her reality change as her vision affected her decisions, affirmed for her that she was on the right path.

No matter what your life purpose turns out to be, the reality of it will change as, in the experience of making your dream come true, you learn more about how it works. This evolution of experience happens not only with your main purpose, but with every little goal you strive for. Knowing that you can *adapt* your goals as you learn more means that your autonomous thinking will remain based on reality, even as your reality changes. Only if your idea of your original goal is so rigid that you cannot accept the need to adapt it, and make it more realistic or more possible for you to accomplish, do you need to reevaluate it as your life purpose.

Ethics

Taking care of yourself and being responsible for yourself means creating your own standards for ways of treating yourself and others that are healthy. Both your inner, subconscious self and your outer, rational self need to feel good. When you are aware of and intimate with your inner self, treating yourself or others badly is too uncomfortable. People with healthy internal intimacy do not need outside rules to tell them how to behave. Once your internal intimacy is in place, your inner standards of behavior will cause you to stay well inside of the law, as long as the law is sensible and just, and cause you to behave in a highly conscious manner. Lying, stealing, and coercing or using others just feels too bad to do. Inner intimacy and self-reliance develops a set of inner values that will guide you well.

Anyone who regularly considers effective choices, "plays chess," values the warmth in relationships, and compares their internal and external relationships continuously, will live by a far higher standard of ethical behavior than anyone could impose via "rules to live by" from outside. Standards imposed or accepted from without can never be completely right for you or fully match your personal criteria. Inherent in your life purpose is a set of values and standards; comparing your life frequently to these standards, and living by your internal values, is living ethically. Most dependent people operate (by either complying or rebelling) on a moral basis.

For this discussion, morality can be defined as rules for conduct that originate outside oneself: for example, the law codes, the Ten Commandments, and "what Mom and Dad say is right." Morality is dependent and reactive.

Because the pre-set, rigid rules of morality cannot apply to every situation, people who blindly and dependently follow an outside morality eventually reach a crisis of conscience when they encounter a situation for which their "rules to live by" are inadequate. Sooner or later, there is a situation that can't be covered by the rules in advance. For example, the Ten Commandments' order to "honor thy father and thy mother" can precipitate a moral crisis for someone who suddenly remembers being abused by his or her own parents, and "to keep coming back," although appropriate for newly recovered people, doesn't work for every member forever.

There is no substitute for the ability to think for yourself, and there is no one who can make your decisions better than you can. In using your ability to make effective choices and create your own personal inner values, awareness, and purpose, you develop an ethical evaluation ability that will not fail you in time of crisis. With this ability, you can evaluate each situation as it arises and make effective choices based on your inner values to come up with a response that suits the situation. Nathaniel Brandon, a pioneer in self-esteem studies, describes autonomous ethical self-evaluation in *Honoring the Self:* "Living by one's own mind....we do not attempt to live by unthinking conformity and the suspension of independent critical judgment. We take responsibility for the ideas we accept and the values by which we guide our actions."

Though you may not realize it, you have begun the work of formulating your own ethics. As you read and learn about people you admire, *if you evaluate what you are learning and choose what parts to adopt as your own,* you can develop your personal ethics further. When you study the lives of people who live ethically, you are using Magical Tool 5: Environment to influence and develop your own ethics.

Once your ethics are developed, they form the criteria against which you can evaluate your life purpose, as well as all your other behavior. Ethics are what you as an individual feel you must do to make your life worth living and to maintain your self-esteem. Ethics are autonomous and creative. While morality is obeying someone else's rules, being ethical requires evaluating your own life and actions, and it requires thinking rather than blind obedience. It is a sense of personal ethics that prompts people to confront behavior they find unacceptable, even though everyone else does it, as when someone speaks out against war when the whole country is excited about it. Once you become aware of and develop your personal ethics, you become your own guide and teacher. You are free to ask others' opinions of your actions, thoughts, and behavior, but the final judgment of rightness of your actions and your life purpose belongs to you as an autonomous person.

Living by ethics requires a solid sense of self-esteem and self-worth, plus judgmental ability and the capacity for making decisions on the spot. To live ethically, you must *think* about the implications of your actions. A beginning attempt at personal ethics is made in twelve-step programs in the experience of taking "personal inventory." Twelve-step programs, because they are reluctant to tell people what to do but still offer the Steps as guidelines for living, straddle the fence between morality and ethics. They teach you a little about setting criteria for yourself, but they don't complete the experience. Only autonomous thinking does that.

Morality developed as humankind became social and needed to learn to live together without constant struggle between individuals. The earliest, most primitive societies developed rules each person must live by or suffer punishment. People were expected, and if necessary coerced by force, to accept and adapt to these rules in order to reduce crime, conflict, and exploitation. We still operate by that system today on a social level.

But living solely by such rules and following them blindly is dependent, because it leaves the vital question of what behavior is acceptable up to others. It means you don't trust yourself to make your own decisions. For people who cannot control their behavior, laws and rules are essential, both to keep them from damaging themselves and to protect society from them. However, we have seen in our society how these rules can be ignored, abused, and misused.

These laws of society are far below the level of life on which autonomous people live. They are sensitive both to their own needs and feelings and to the well-being (as opposed to the demands or wishes) of others. As an autonomous person, you are already monitoring your own behavior to the point where you would not intentionally injure yourself or another, and you've reduced your level of mistakes and unconscious behavior considerably by practicing effective choice and maintaining your internal intimacy. You are ready for more than just obeying the rules of others. Instead of just following the minimum acceptable standard, you can now begin to live according to your own internal values and contribute to a better world (another way to take care of yourself) through your behavior and actions.

Using these three criteria—results, experience, and ethics—will help you evaluate the effectiveness and suitability of your inner purpose. In addition, because you now know how to build successful, autonomous, supportive relationships with people who will tell you the truth, the responses of those friends you know to be supportive of you can give you another viewpoint from which to evaluate your goals and your purpose. This is not to say that you allow friends to tell you what to do; rather, you consider the opinions of selected friends along with the other criteria you use for evaluating the success, appropriateness, and effectiveness of your goals and overall purpose.

The Rewards of Autonomous Living

A distinguishing feature stands out in the lives of autonomous people: Although there are struggles and disappointments, there is also an experience of joy. As an autonomous person, you experience what noted humanistic psychologist Abraham Maslow called "self-actualization." That is, because you are in charge of your own life, you have the ability to exercise your potential and be the best person you can be, by your own definition.

According to Maslow, when our needs for survival are met, and we experience safety, security, and successful intimacy with others (in short, when we are successfully autonomous), we can become self-actualized, which allows us to have "peak experiences"—what most of us would call joy. University of Chicago's professor Mihaly Czinksentmihaly calls it "Flow" in his book of the same name. Joy occurs when we are comfortable with who we are, and feeling in the right place and time within life.

Many people who said they wanted autonomy find that they are frightened of joy. Because the kind of joy that wells up from deep inside feels unfamiliar to people who grew up in dysfunctional families where they were discouraged from intimacy with themselves, many of them long for, yet fear, true happiness. Years of pain, failure, and feeling unable to cope with life convinced them that being happy always led to disappointment or suffering.

To be able to experience joy, you must understand that happiness, like sadness, anger or fear, doesn't last. Healthy emotions are changeable, like mental weather conditions. When emotions are felt, rather than repressed, they evolve and flow. Happiness will give way to thoughtfulness, sadness to nostalgia, anger to determination. Emotions are momentary reactions to events, interactions, and circumstances.

However, there's no need to fear losing your happiness. Once you learn what makes you happy, you can create happiness often. Sadness, anger, and fear are not the only feelings that you can feel in response to life. You can be surprised by spontaneous good feelings, too. When you live autonomously and are no longer in chaos and you make effective choices that minimizes your disappointment; when you have autonomous relationships that surround you, inside and out, with warmth; and you are living life with purpose, which gives you satisfaction, then happiness comes back to you, over and over again.

This recurring happiness and inner joy can only be achieved by meeting your own needs completely enough to create sufficient self-confidence and satisfaction to allow you to develop fully your potential as a person. It is the lifelong experience of recurring joy and satisfaction that allows you, at the end of life to say, like Edith Piaf, "Je ne regrette rien" ("I regret nothing").

You now have a choice: You can be the autonomous hero of your life, or your can be the dependent, helpless victim of your past and your circumstances. Your reward and motivation to choose this journey is joy. My wish for you is that you will be the most you can be and claim your full share of joy.

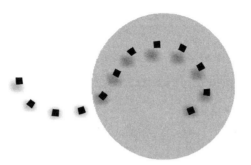

Further Study

Once they've become accustomed to the thirteenth step, most of my clients are committed to lifelong learning and growth. This is no surprise; I have found that following your "job on earth" (or inner wisdom) leads to lifelong learning of psychology, spirituality, and philosophy. I find all three to be compatible, essentially leading further beyond the thirteenth step. The following book list offers some of the paths my clients took, and these books in turn lead to others. Many of the quotes in this book are taken from these sources; some are classics in the recovery field. Warriors of the mind whom I know are constantly sharing new discoveries of books and ideas; we enthusiastically welcome all new thought, because it both exercises our judgment; and stimulates our own creativity. Please share the following book list in that spirit. I hope it helps you to have growth, satisfaction, and joy in your continuing life adventure.

In addition to the books that follow, try reading some current events and alternative publications. *The Utne Reader,* a magazine digest of the alternative press, gives a broad sampling of non-majority views in print. Popular educational magazines, such as *Psychology Today* or *Bottom Line Personal* are entertaining, easy to read, and give a light overview of new research and ideas.

Book List for Further Reading

Alcoholics Anonymous. *Alcoholics Anonymous.* N.Y.: A.A. World Services, 1976.

———. *Twelve Steps and Twelve Traditions.* N.Y.: A.A. World Services, 1982.

Altea, Rosemary. *You Own The Power.* N.Y.: William Morrow, 2000.

Alter, Robert and Jane Alter. *The Transformative Power of Crisis.* N.Y.: HarperCollins, 2000.

Bass, Ellen and Laura Davis. *The Courage to Heal: A Guide for Women Survivors of Sexual Abuse.* N.Y.: Perennial Library, 1988.

Beattie, Melody. *Beyond Codependency (And Getting Better all the Time).* San Francisco, Calif.: Harper & Row, 1989.

Black, Claudia. *It Will Never Happen To Me.* Denver, Colo.: M.A.C., 1982.

Bradshaw, John. *Bradshaw on the Family.* Deerfield Beach, Fla.: Health Communications 1988.

———. *Coming Home: Reclaiming and Championing Your Inner Child.* N.Y.: Bantam, 1990.

———. *Healing the Shame that Binds You.* Deerfield Beach, Fla.: Health Communications 1988.

Brandon, Nathaniel. *Honoring the Self: Personal Integrity and the Heroic Potentials of Human Nature.* Los Angeles, Calif.: Tarcher, 1983.

Cameron, Julia and Mark Bryan. *The Artist's Way.* Los Angeles, Calif.: Tarcher, 1995.

Campbell, Joseph, with Bill Moyers. *The Power of Myth.* N.Y.: Doubleday, 1988.

Cappacchione, Lucia. *The Creative Journal, Second Edition.* Franklin Lakes, N.J.: New Page Books, 2001.

———. *The Picture of Health.* Santa Monica, Calif.: Hay House, 1990.

———. *The Power of Your Other Hand,* N. Hollywood, Calif.: Newcastle, 1988.

Carlson, R. and B. Shield, eds. *Healers on Healing.* Los Angeles, Calif.: J.P. Tarcher, 1989.

Cermak, Timmon. *A Time to Heal (The Road to Recovery for Adult Children of Alcoholics).* Los Angeles, Calif.: Tarcher, 1988.

Chandler, Mitzi. *Gentle Reminders: Daily Affirmations for CoDependents.* Deerfield Beach, Fla.: Health Communications, 1989.

Csikszentmihalyi, Mihaly. *Flow: The Psychology of Optimal Experience.* N.Y.: HarperCollins, 1990.

——————————. *Creativitiy: Flow and the Psychology of Discovery and Invention.* N.Y.: Harper Collins, 1996.

——————————. *The Evolving Self: a Psychology for the Third Millennium.* N.Y.: HarperCollins,1993.

Covington, Stephanie and Liana Beckett. *Leaving the Enchanted Forest: The Path From Relationship Addiction to Intimacy.* N.Y.: Harper & Row, 1988.

Crawford, Christina. *Survivor.* N.Y.: Donald I Fine, 1988.

Davidson, Joy. *The Agony of It All.* Los Angeles, Calif.: Tarcher, 1988.

Davis, Bruce and Genny Davis. *The Magical Child Within You.* Berkeley, Calif.: Celestial Arts, 1982.

Elgin, Duane. *Voluntary Simplicity.* N.Y.: Morrow, 1981.

Ellis, Albert. *Humanistic Psychotherapy.* N.Y.: Julian Press, 1973.

Engel, Lewis and Tom Ferguson. *Imaginary Crimes.* Boston, Mass.: Houghton Mifflin, 1990.

Feinstein, David and Stanley Krippner. *Personal Mythology: The Psychology of Your Evolving Self.* Los Angeles, Calif.: Tarcher, 1988.

Forward, Susan. *Toxic Parents: Overcoming Their Hurtful Legacy and Reclaiming Your Life.* N.Y.: Bantam, 1989.

Friedman, Sonya. *Men Are Just Desserts.* N.Y.: Warner Books, 1983.

Fromm, Eric. *The Art of Loving.* N.Y.: Harper & Row, 1956.

Gershon, David and Gail Straub. *Empowerment: The Art Of Creating Your Life As You Want It.* N.Y.: Delta, 1991.

Gawain, Shakti. *Living in the Light.* Mill Valley, Calif.: Whatever Publishing, 1986.

Golden, Pamela. *Choose the Happiness Habit.* N.Y.: Roedway Press, 1998.

Hay, Louise. *You Can Heal Your Life*. Santa Monica, Calif.: Hay House, 1984.

Hayes, Jody. *Smart Love: A Codependence Recovery Program Based on A Relationship Addiction Support Group*. Los Angeles, Calif.: Tarcher, 1989.

Helfer, Ray E. *Childhood Comes First: A Crash Course in Childhood for Adults*. Ray Helfer, East Lansing, Mich., 1984.

Hillman, James. *The Soul's Code: In Search of Character and Calling*. N.Y.: Random House, 1996.

Hoff, Benjamin. *The Tao of Pooh*. N.Y.: Viking, 1983.

Isaacs, Florence. *Toxic Friends, True Friends*. N.Y.: Morrow, 1999.

Keyes, Ken. *A Conscious Person's Guide To Relationships.* Coos Bay, Ore.: Living Love Publications, 1979

Langer, Ellen. *Mindfulness.* N.Y.: Addison-Wesley, 1989.

Leder, Drew. *Spiritual Passages: Embracing Life's Sacred Journey*. N.Y.: Tarcher/Putnam, 1997.

Lerner, Harriet. *The Dance of Intimacy: A Woman's Guide to Courageous Acts of Courage in Key Relationships*. San Francisco, CA. Harper & Row, 1989.

London, Peter. *No More Secondhand Art: Awakening the Artist Within*. Boston, Mass.. Shambhala, 1989.

Miller, Alice. *For Your Own Good: Hidden Cruelty in Child-Rearing and the Roots of Violence.* Farrar-Strauss. N.Y.: Giroux, 1980.

Moore, Thomas. *Care of the Soul.* N.Y.: HarperCollins, 1998.

Ornish, Dean. *Love and Survival: The Scientific Basis for the Healing Power of Intimacy.* N.Y.: HarperCollins, 1998.

Peck, M. Scott. *The Road Less Traveled*. NY: Simon and Schuster, 1985.
_____. *Further Along The Road Less Traveled.* N.Y.: Simon and Schuster, 1993.

Perry, Susan K. *Writing in Flow: Keys to Enhanced Creativity.* Cincinnati, Ohio: Writer's Digest Books, 1999.

Peele, Stanton. *The Diseasing of America.* Boston, Mass.: Lexington Books, 1989.

Pollard, John K. *Self Parenting.* Malibu, Calif.: Generic Human Studies Publishing, 1989.

Roberts, Denton. *Able & Equal.* Culver City, Calif.: Human Esteem Publishing, 1984.

_____. *Find Purpose, Find Power.* Culver City, Calif.: Human Esteem Publishing, 1997.

Roche, Lorin. *Meditation Made Easy.* San Francisco, Calif.: Harper San Francisco, 1998.

Rossman, Martin L. *Healing Yourself: A Step-by Step Program for Better Health Through Imagery.* N.Y.: Walker and Company, 1987.

Schaef, Anne Wilson. *When Society Becomes an Addict.* San Francisco, Calif.: Harper & Row, 1987.

Seligman, Martin E.P. *Learned Optimism.* N.Y.: Knopf, 1991.

Siegel, Bernie, M.D. *Peace, Love and Healing.* N.Y.: Harper & Row, 1989.

Siegel, Ronald K. *Intoxication: Life in Pursuit of Artificial Paradise.* N.Y.: Dutton, 1989.

Sinetar, Marsha. *Elegant Choices, Healing Choices: Finding Grace and Wholeness in Everything We Choose.* Mahwah, N.J.: Paulist Press, 1989.

_____. *Ordinary People as Monks and Mystics.* Mahwah, N.J.: Paulist Press, 1986.

Smith, Riley K. and Tina B. Tessina, *How To Be a Couple and Still Be Free, Revised Edition.* Franklin Lakes, N.J.: New Page Books, 2001.

Szasz, Thomas. *Heresies.* N.Y.: Anchor, 1976.

Wegner, Daniel M. *White Bears and Other Unwanted Thoughts: Suppression, Obsession and the Psychology of Mental Control.* N.Y.: Viking Penguin, 1989.

Weil, Andrew and Winifred Rosen. *From Chocolate to Morphine: Everything You Need to Know About Mind-Altering Drugs.* N.Y.: Houghton Mifflin, 1993.

_____. *Spontaneous Healing.* N.Y.: .Knopf, 1995.

Whitfield, Charles L. *Healing the Child Within.* Pompano Beach, Fla.: Health Communications, 1987.

Wilbur, Ken. *A Brief History of Everything.* Boston, Mass.: Shambhala, 1996.

_____. Integral Psychology: Consciousness, Spirit, Psychology, Therapy. Boston, Mass.: Shambala, 2000.

Williamson, Maryanne. *Illuminata.* N.Y.: Random House, 1994.

_____. *A Return to Love.* N.Y.: HarperCollins, 1992.

Zweig, Connie, Ed. *To Be A Woman: The Birth of the Conscious Feminine.* Los Angeles, Calif.: Tarcher, 1990.

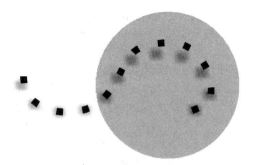

Index

M

Magical mind, 111
Magical thinking, 101-103, 104, 105, 112, 114
Magical tools, 112, 184
  for reaching the child mind, 113-144
Maintaining autonomy with unaware people, 256-258
Maslow, Abraham, 301
Memorization and the power to effect beliefs, 140-144
Mental attitudes that perpetuate dependency, 32-33
Miller, Alice, 48, 81
Mindlessness, 32, 99
Model for the autonomous relationship, a, 248-250
Models for healthy relationships, 78-79

N

Narcotics Anonymous, 12
National Association of Children of Alcoholics, the, 33
Need for stimulus, 282-286
Negotiating Table exercise, 166-169, 204
New seeds of consciousness, 142-144

O

Overcoming resistance, 150-153
Overeaters Anonymous(OA), 13, 19

P

Parry, Danaan, 131, 285
Passive personalities, 257-258

Paying attention, 199-200
Peck, M. Scott, 148-149
Peele, Dr. Stanton, 12, 60
"Playing Chess," 220
  exercise, 221-223
Problems underlying addiction, 31-37
Problem-solving, 94-95
  and intimacy, 235-236
Psychotherapy, 9

R

Rational Recovery, 23
Real Thirteenth Step, The, 241, 293
  understanding of, 25
Reality/Fantasy Dialogue, 218-221
Re-connecting techniques for after abandonment, 260-265
Relapse, causes of, 38-42
Related attitudes to
  Autonomy, 35-36
  Recovery, 35-36
"Relationship addiction," 11
Relationships,
  awareness and, 236-237
  commitment and, 251-252
  forgiveness and, 237-238
  humor and, 246-247
  learning and, 237
  truthfulness and, 252
  warmth and, 244-246
Religious conversion, 23
Repetition and the power to effect beliefs, 140-144
Replacement habits, 75-77
Resistance
  against autonomy, 147-153
  to inner change, 208-210

W

Y

Z

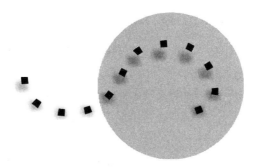

About the Author

Tina B. Tessina, Ph.D., LMFT, has 25 years of experience as a licensed marriage, family therapist. She has worked extensively with people in recovery and their sponsors for more than 20 years. She is the author of 10 books, including *The Ten Smartest Decisions a Woman Can Make After Forty* (Renaissance, 2001); *The Unofficial Guide to Dating Again* (IDG,1999); *The 10 Smartest Decisions A Woman Can Make Before 40* (HCI, 1998) (in Spanish, Pearson Educacion, 1999); *Gay Relationships: How To Find Them, How To Improve Them, How To Make Them Last* (Tarcher, 1989 soft-cover 1990); and *Lovestyles: How To Celebrate Your Differences* (Newcastle, 1987).

She co-authored (with Riley K. Smith): *How To Be a Couple and Still Be Free* (revised edition, New Page Books, 2001); *True Partners: A Workbook for Developing Lasting Intimacy* (J.P. Tarcher, 1992) (in Spanish, Pearson Educacion, 2001); and *Equal Partners* (Hodder and Stoughton, London, 1994).

Dr. Tessina lectures and conducts workshops nationwide on all of her books, and has appeared on major television and radio shows, including *Donohue*, *Oprah*, *Geraldo*, and *Larry King Live* . She lives in Long Beach, California, with her husband, Richard Sharrard.

To reach Dr. Tessina for questions, lectures, workshops, and individual and couple therapy:

Tina B. Tessina, PhD, LMFT
License MX 13629
P.O. Box 4883
Long Beach, CA 90804
562-438-8077

Other Books by the author:

The Ten Smartest Decisions a Woman Can Make After Forty (Renaissance, 2001)

The Unofficial Guide to Dating Again (Macmillan/IDG, NY 1999)

Gay Relationships: How To Find Them, How To Improve Them, How To Make Them Last (Tarcher, 1989)

Lovestyles: How To Celebrate Your Differences (Newcastle, 1987)

With Riley K. Smith
How To Be a Couple and Still Be Free (revised edition, New Page Books, 2001)

With Elizabeth Friar Williams
The 10 Smartest Decisions A Woman Can Make Before 40 (HCI, Deerfield Beach, 1998)